THE JAM AND JELLY NOOK

AN AMISH MARKETPLACE NOVEL

D0169730

Amy Clipston

ZONDERVAN

The Jam and Jelly Nook

Copyright © 2021 by Amy Clipston

Requests for information should be addressed to:
Zondervan, *3900 Sparks Dr. SE, Grand Rapids, Michigan 49546*

ISBN 978-0-310-35654-7 (trade paper)
ISBN 978-0-310-35653-0 (e-book)
ISBN 978-0-310-35655-4 (audio download)
ISBN 978-0-310-36094-0 (library edition)
ISBN 978-0-8407-0694-2 (mass market)

Library of Congress Cataloging-in-Publication Data
CIP data is available upon request.

Zondervan titles may be purchased in bulk for educational, business, fundraising, or sales promotional use. For information, please email SpecialMarkets@Zondervan.com.

Printed in the United States of America

22 23 24 25 26 CWM 10 9 8 7 6 5 4 3 2 1

For my mother, Lola Goebelbecker, with
love, appreciation, and admiration.
You're my partner in crime, my movie buddy,
my binge-watching pal, my cheerleader,
my company while I write, my rock, and my best friend.
Thank you for all you do for our family.

Glossary

ach: oh
aenti: aunt
appeditlich: delicious
bedauerlich: sad
boppli: baby
bopplin: babies
brot: bread
bruder: brother
bruderskind: niece/nephew
bruderskinner: nieces/nephews
bu: boy
buwe: boys
daadi: granddad
daadihaus: small house provided for retired parents
daed: father
danki: thank you
dat: dad
Dietsch: Pennsylvania Dutch, the Amish language (a German
    dialect)
dochder: daughter
dochdern: daughters
dummkopp: moron
Englisher: a non-Amish person
faul: lazy
fraa: wife

freind: friend
freinden: friends
froh: happy
gegisch: silly
gern gschehne: you're welcome
grossdaadi: grandfather
grossdochder: granddaughter
grossdochdern: granddaughters
grossmammi: grandmother
gross-sohn: grandson
Gude mariye: Good morning
gut: good
Gut nacht: Good night
haus: house
Ich liebe dich: I love you
kaffi: coffee
kapp: prayer covering or cap
kichli: cookie
kichlin: cookies
kind: child
kinner: children
kuche: cake
liewe: love, a term of endearment
maed: young women, girls
maedel: young woman
mamm: mom
mammi: grandma
mei: my
naerfich: nervous
narrisch: crazy
onkel: uncle

schee: pretty

schmaert: smart

schtupp: family room

schweschder: sister

schweschdere: sisters

sohn: son

Was iss letz?: What's wrong?

Wie geht's: How do you do? or Good day!

wunderbaar: wonderful

ya: yes

The Amish Marketplace
Series Family Trees

Grandparents
Erma m. Sylvan Gingerich
|
Lynn m. Freeman Kurtz
Mary m. Lamar Petersheim
Walter m. Rachelle
Harvey m. Darlene

SECOND GENERATION PARENTS AND CHILDREN
Lynn m. Freeman Kurtz
Christiana m. __|__ Phoebe
Jeffrey Stoltzfus

Mary m. Lamar Petersheim
Cornelius (Neil) m. __|__ Salina m.
Ellen   William Zimmerman

Ellen m. Cornelius (Neil) Petersheim
Betsy Kay __|__ Jayne

Darlene m. Harvey Gingerich
Bethany m. __|__ Anthony
Micah Zook

Rachelle m. Walter Gingerich
|
Leanna m. Marlin (deceased) Wengerd

Leanna m. Marlin (deceased) Wengerd
|
Chester

Christiana m. Jeffrey Stolzfus
Kaylin ——|—— Angelie

Salina m. William Zimmerman
|
Karrie

Viola m. Clemens Speicher
Emory ——|—— Justin

Emory Speicher
|
Maggie (mother: Sheryl, deceased)

Natalie m. Justin Speicher
|
Lee

Note to the Reader

While this novel is set against the real backdrop of Lancaster County, Pennsylvania, the characters are fictional. There is no intended resemblance between the characters in this book and any real members of the Amish and Mennonite communities. As with any work of fiction, I've taken license in some areas of research as a means of creating the necessary circumstances for my characters. My research was thorough; however, it would be impossible to be completely accurate in details and description, since each and every community differs. Therefore, any inaccuracies in the Amish and Mennonite lifestyles portrayed in this book are completely due to fictional license.

CHAPTER 1

Leanna Wengerd awoke with a start. She scanned her bedroom, which was cloaked with darkness. The early July humidity hung in the air and stuck to her like a second skin. She turned toward the bright green numbers on the battery-operated alarm clock that sat on her nightstand, then blinked and squinted as her brain worked to comprehend the time: 12:10 in the morning.

Sitting up, she took a deep breath. It was after midnight, but she hadn't yet heard her sixteen-year-old son arrive home. Normally on Sunday nights around ten o'clock she could count on the sound of his heavy footsteps echoing up the stairs and down the hallway to his bedroom, which was located across from hers.

What if he hadn't gotten home yet?

Has he been in an accident?

With a heaving breath, Leanna reached for her flashlight, jumped out of bed, and dashed across the hallway to Chester's room. She pushed his door open and pointed the flashlight toward the worn linoleum floor.

"Chester?" she whispered. "Are you asleep?"

Silence surrounded her. She lifted the flashlight and shined it around his room. Her heartbeat spiked when she found his double bed empty, the blue Lone Star quilt her grandmother had made him lying perfectly straight.

"*Ach*, no," she said before rushing back to her room, pushing her bare feet into a pair of slippers, and tying a scarf over her waist-length hair. Then, with her heart pounding in her ears, she rushed down the stairs, through the kitchen and mudroom, and out the back door.

The cicadas sang their nightly chorus as Leanna hurried down the porch steps. Her father's vast pasture was shrouded in darkness, and the nearby *daadihaus* where her grandparents lived was also quiet and still, the green shades drawn for the night.

Leanna hustled through the humid night air toward the barn, where of late she'd find Chester doing woodworking when he wasn't at his job at the local hardware store or helping his grandfather with chores on the farm.

"Please be in here, Chester. Please be in here," she whispered as she wrenched open the barn door. The heavy scent of animals and hay wafted over her as she moved past the cows and headed back to his workshop.

"Chester?" Her voice boomed in the darkness of the barn. "Chester? Are you here?"

She stepped into his wood shop and was greeted by the scent of wood and stain. Also the sound of silence.

She spun in a circle, worry engulfing the air around her as her breath came out in short bursts. She scurried out of the wood shop to the stable. Perhaps Chester had just arrived home and was stowing his horse. Maybe she'd missed him when she walked out to the workshop.

Holding on to that glimmer of hope, she stepped into the stable, and her heart sank when she found his horse's stall was empty.

Oh no. Chester, what has happened to you?

The sudden ringing of the phone pierced through the silent, heavy air and caused icy fear to slither down her spine. Unbidden, terrifying thoughts crashed into her mind.

"No, no, no," she whispered, her voice raspy as memories of the night her husband died flooded her mind. "Please, God, no. No, no, no!"

She stood frozen for a moment as the phone continued to ring. Then she pushed her feet into motion, praying as she made her way to it.

"Please, God," she whispered. "Don't take Chester. He's all I have left. Please, God, protect him. Please!"

Her hands trembling, Leanna picked up the phone and held it to her ear. "Hello?" Her voice quavered, and her eyes stung with tears.

"Mamm?"

She blew out a deep breath as she dropped onto the chair next to the phone. "Chester! Where are you?"

"I'm at the police station. I need you to come here to get me."

"What happened? Are you hurt?"

"Mamm," he spoke slowly, "I'm okay. I'm not hurt, but I need you to pick me up. I got caught trespassing, and the police came. They won't let me go unless you come."

"Oh." Leanna's fear snapped to irritation in a flash. "Why were you trespassing? Did you get arrested?"

"Mamm, can you please just come now?" His voice was heavy with impatience.

Leanna's body began to vibrate with frustration as she nodded. *At least he's safe!* "Ya. I'll be right there."

After hanging up the phone, Leanna jogged back to the house and made her way to her parents' bedroom, which was located on the first floor. She lifted her trembling hand to knock and then closed her eyes. While she regretted having to wake her parents, she also needed her father's emotional support to help her deal with Chester.

Lord, give me strength!

She rapped on the door and then waited a moment before pushing it open. She kept the flashlight pointed at the floor as she looked over at her parents, sleeping soundly in their double bed.

"*Dat?*" she whispered as she padded over to his side of the bed. "*Dat?* Are you awake?"

Dat snorted and sniffed before sitting up. "Huh?"

Mamm sat up next. "Leanna? What time is it?"

"It's late. I'm sorry for waking you, but I need your help," Leanna said, working to slow her galloping pulse.

"*Was iss letz?*" *Dat*'s voice was clear, as if he were suddenly fully awake.

"Chester just called. He's at the police station."

"The police station?" *Mamm* gasped. "What happened?"

"He said he was picked up for trespassing, but he didn't give me any details." Leanna looked at her father. "Will you go with me to get him?"

"*Ya*, of course." *Dat* pushed himself up out of bed. "I'll get dressed."

"I will too." Leanna hustled out of the room and zipped back up the stairs to her bedroom, where she quickly pulled on a blue dress, black apron, and shoes before pulling her hair into a tight bun and covering it with her prayer *kapp*.

Then she hurried back downstairs and found her mother standing in the middle of the kitchen, hugging her arms against her white nightgown, a baby-blue scarf covering her graying dark brown hair. A lantern sat on the counter, casting a warm yellow light in the large, dark kitchen.

When she was a teenager, Leanna's cousin Salina had once commented that Leanna and her mother could be mistaken for sisters with their matching hair, brown eyes, and petite stature. Although her mother was now sixty-three and wrinkles had taken up residence around her eyes and laugh lines around her mouth, Leanna still saw the resemblance between her mother and herself.

"Everything will be okay, *mei liewe*," *Mamm* said softly as she walked over to Leanna and touched her hand. "Go easy on him. Chester just seems to be going through a difficult time lately."

Leanna's lip trembled as she shook her head. "I don't understand why he's suddenly become so sullen and defiant." *What am I doing wrong?*

Mamm touched her cheek. "We'll get through this with God's help. Have faith."

"Leanna?"

Dat stood in the doorway leading to the mudroom clad in dark trousers, a blue shirt, suspenders, and a straw hat covering his dark brown hair. Several inches taller than *Mamm* and Leanna, *Dat* was still in good shape for his age due to working on the dairy farm beside the helpers he had hired. His dark brown beard matched his hair, which had become peppered with gray during the past few years. While Leanna had inherited her mother's dark eyes, *Dat* had warm blue eyes he'd received from his mother.

"The horse and buggy are hitched. Let's go." He turned toward *Mamm*. "We'll be back soon, Rachelle."

"Be careful, Walter," *Mamm* responded before turning back to Leanna. "Remember—be patient with him."

Leanna nodded, but her frustration continued to plague her as she followed her father outside and climbed into his buggy.

The short ride to the police station was silent as both Leanna and her father looked out the window at the dark rolling fields dotted with quiet farmhouses. Leanna imagined the families sleeping soundly in their cozy homes—not worrying about what their teenaged sons were doing or what kind of trouble they'd gotten themselves into.

She swallowed a sigh and rubbed her forehead where a headache was brewing. How had Leanna failed as a mother? She'd done the best she could since Marlin had passed away, and she'd assumed her parents would rise up where she'd fallen short.

Even so, Chester had changed since he'd turned fifteen last year. It was almost an overnight transformation. Suddenly her sweet, helpful son was gone and replaced by a rebellious, defiant, unhappy young man. At times she barely recognized him.

She closed her eyes and took deep breaths, working to calm her frayed nerves and keep her tears at bay.

When the police station came into view, she gripped the buggy door and sent up a silent prayer.

Lord, keep me calm. Give me guidance when dealing with Chester. Help me figure out how to get through to him. I can't do this alone.

Dat halted the horse, climbed out of the buggy, and tied the horse to a fence before he and Leanna walked across the parking lot and into the police station. Once through the doors they were met with a wall of cold air and the humming of air-conditioning.

Leanna's heart began to pound so hard she worried her father could hear it as they walked toward the front desk, where a middle-aged man in a police uniform with thick, horn-rimmed glasses and a bushy brown mustache sat staring at a computer screen. Leanna stood beside her father as he leaned on the counter.

"Excuse me," *Dat* began. "I'm here for my grandson."

The man looked up and cleared his throat. "What's his name?"

"Chester Wengerd," *Dat* said.

The man nodded toward a row of chairs across from the desk. "Have a seat. Someone will be with you shortly."

"Thank you," *Dat* said.

The fluorescent lights above them buzzed while Leanna sat beside her father in one of the hard chairs. She looked across the room and spotted a young man dressed in all black with black spiked hair, a nose ring, and tattoos on his face. He peered back at her, his dark eyes cold and angry. She shifted under the weight of his glare as her throat dried.

If she didn't get ahold of Chester's attitude, would he wind up like this angry *Englisher*? More worry ripped through her like a bullet.

Help me, God!

A uniformed police officer who looked to be in his mid-forties stepped out into the waiting area and walked over to Leanna and her father. His hair was cut short, and his blue eyes were kind despite the holster and handcuffs hanging from his belt.

"Are you the family of Chester Wengerd?" he asked.

"We are." *Dat* stood and shook his hand. "I'm Walter Gingerich, and this is my daughter, Leanna Wengerd."

"Nice to meet you. I'm Officer Rhodes." He gestured toward the doorway behind him. "Please come with me."

Leanna clasped her hands together and worked to slow her breathing as they walked down a hallway and into a small room. There Chester sat at a table across from a pretty Amish girl who looked to be around his age.

Chester was slumped in his chair, arms crossed over his chest. He met Leanna's stare and then pressed his lips together before looking down at the floor.

The girl glanced at Leanna and then gasped, her light blue eyes glinting with tears before she sniffed. Panic welled up in Leanna. What had happened to her?

Officer Rhodes sat down in front of a stack of paperwork at the table, then pointed to two seats across from him. "Why don't you have a seat, Mr. Gingerich and Mrs. Wengerd."

Leanna sat down and looked over at the girl, who took a tissue from the box on the table and wiped her eyes and nose. "Are you hurt?" Leanna asked.

"No." Her voice was soft and shaky.

"What's your name?"

The girl sniffed. "Maggie Speicher."

"I'm Leanna," she said. Then she pointed to her father. "This is *mei dat*, Walter Gingerich."

Maggie nodded and then sniffed again.

Leanna looked over at Chester, who continued to scowl while his chocolate-brown eyes focused on the floor. "What happened?"

"They were caught on private property," the officer said as he examined his paperwork.

Leanna noticed that Chester's hair, which was normally a lighter shade of brown, almost blond like his late father's, looked darker. She gasped when she realized his hair was wet, along with his dark blue shirt and his trousers.

Maggie, however, wore a gray dress and black apron that were dry. Dark brown hair peeked out from under her prayer covering.

"Why are you soaking wet, Chester?" Leanna asked slowly.

Chester peeked up at her and didn't answer, which caused Leanna's fury to boil under her skin. Why was he so disrespectful and rude? Where had she gone wrong with this young man?

"They were swimming," the officer said.

"Alone?" *Dat*'s expression seemed worried.

Chester shook his head, and his eyes narrowed. "No, but we were the ones who got caught."

Dat looked at the officer. "Does the landowner want to press charges?"

"No," Officer Rhodes said. "He said he just wants them to be warned not to do it again. It's dangerous swimming at night."

Leanna opened her mouth to say something, but the door of the room opened, and an Amish man burst in.

"Maggie!" the man said as he rushed over to the girl. "Are you all right?"

"*Ya*," she whispered before her gray-blue eyes filled with tears and then spilled over. She covered her face with a tissue as she cried.

The man pulled a chair over and sat beside her, pulling her little body into his muscular arms. He rubbed her back as he consoled her.

"I'm so sorry, *Dat*," she said between hiccups. "I didn't mean to cause any problems. I should have been home sooner. I'm sorry to make you worry."

He sighed and shook his head. "It's all right."

"I assume you are Emory Speicher?" the police officer asked.

"*Ya*," the man said. He took in the rest of the room and then looked toward Leanna.

His azure eyes were a striking complement to his dark brown hair and matching beard, both flecked with gray. She surmised he was in his early to midforties. He nodded a greeting at her and then divided a look between *Dat* and Chester.

Maggie stopped crying and hiccupped as she wiped her eyes.

"What happened?" Emory asked.

"Some teens were trespassing on Bob Janitz's farm. A few of them were swimming," the officer explained. "We were only able to pick up Maggie and Chester. Good news for you is Mr. Janitz doesn't want to file any charges as long as they agree to stay off the property."

Leanna gave Chester a pointed look.

"I'm not planning to go back there," Chester said, his expression seeming less angry and more exhausted.

The officer stood. "Excuse me for a moment. I need to go get some paperwork I printed out earlier. I'll be right back." He left the room, the door clicking shut behind him.

"What were you doing on that man's property?" Emory asked Maggie.

Maggie's lip vibrated as she looked up at him. "Alea wanted to go. I didn't want to, but she insisted." She held her hands up. "I didn't swim. I was just waiting when the police arrived. I jumped into Chester's buggy because it was the closest." She pointed at Chester.

Leanna pursed her lips and frowned as she looked over at Chester, who had returned to staring at the floor while rubbing the back of his neck. Why had Chester gotten this seemingly sweet girl into trouble? When was he going to grow up?

The officer returned with a stack of paperwork and then set a piece of paper in front of Leanna and then Emory, along with a pen.

"If you would please sign this. It just says that you understand this is a warning."

Leanna read the notice and then signed it. She glanced over as Emory did the same.

"That's about it," Officer Rhodes said. "You're free to go."

"Thank you, Officer," *Dat* said as he stood.

The officer stood and looked at Emory. "Do you happen to own Gordonville Sheds?"

"I'm part owner actually." Emory's expression was warm and pleasant. "My father, brother, and I own it."

"I thought you looked familiar. I bought a shed there, and it was great quality."

"I'm so glad you're happy with it." Emory shook the officer's hand. "Thank you for your help tonight. I'm sure *mei dochder* won't trespass again. Isn't that right, Maggie?" He smiled down at his daughter, who nodded her head as her cheeks blushed bright pink.

Leanna watched the tender expression Emory shared with his daughter. He seemed relaxed despite this serious situation. Was he always this easygoing and nonchalant under duress?

"Great. Let me make copies of these forms, and I'll walk you out." The officer gathered up the papers they had signed and left the room again.

Leanna turned toward Chester. "What were you thinking? Have you made a habit of trespassing on other people's property?"

"Not now, okay, *Mamm*?" Chester sighed and rubbed his eyes. "I'm tired. We can talk about this tomorrow. I just need some sleep."

Heat infused Leanna's cheeks. She couldn't even imagine what Emory thought of her and her son since it was obvious she had no control over him.

Officer Rhodes returned and handed them their forms. "Here you go." He divided a look between Maggie and Chester. "Next time swim in the daylight in a public place or on your own property, okay?"

"*Ya*." Maggie nodded with such vigor that the ties to her prayer covering bounced off her shoulders.

"I understand," Chester muttered as he stood. Not only had he inherited his father's light hair, but he also had his father's height. He had towered over Leanna for nearly three years now.

The officer led Leanna, *Dat*, Chester, Emory, and Maggie out to the waiting area, where the young man with the tattoos still sat, looking more bored than annoyed.

"Well, it was nice meeting you all, but hopefully we won't see each other again anytime soon." Officer Rhodes smiled as he shook *Dat*'s hand and then Emory's. "Be safe going home."

"We will," *Dat* said.

CHAPTER 2

Leanna pushed open the door of the police station into the sticky, humid night air, which clung to her skin once again. Above her, the stars sparkling in the clear sky seemed to mock her grim mood.

She peered across the parking lot and spotted Chester's horse and buggy waiting in the corner. She must have been so stressed when she arrived that she had missed it. An officer must have driven it to the station.

Chester slipped past her and started toward the horse and buggy.

"Wait," she called after him. "I'm riding with you."

He kept walking as if he hadn't heard her, and once again, her anger flared. What had she done to cause her son to act as if he despised her?

Lord, guide my words and my heart!

"We haven't formally been introduced," Emory said.

Leanna pivoted to face him as he stood by the door with Maggie at his side. Emory was taller than she was, just like most everyone else she knew, but he was even taller than her father. She guessed he stood close to her late husband's six-foot height.

"I'm Emory Speicher, and this is *mei dochder*, Maggie." Emory shook *Dat*'s hand.

Dat smiled. "Nice to meet you, Emory. I'm Walter Gingerich.

This is *mei dochder*, Leanna, and that antisocial young man over there is my grandson, Chester."

Emory gave a little laugh as he waved over at Chester, who stood brooding by his buggy. He lifted his hand at Emory.

Then Emory turned to Leanna and held out his hand. "I'm sorry we had to meet under these circumstances."

"No, I'm the one who is sorry." Leanna shook his hand.

Emory held on to her hand for a moment longer than necessary. "Fortunately, no one got hurt. The kids have learned their lesson, I hope, so everything is going to be just fine." Then, still smiling, he released her hand.

Leanna nodded at him and turned to face Maggie, who gave her a hesitant expression. "It's nice to meet you, Maggie."

Maggie nodded. "You too."

"Well, we better get home," *Dat* said. "Work comes early in the morning."

"Take care," Emory told Leanna before he steered Maggie toward his horse and buggy.

Leanna looked at *Dat*. "I'm going to ride with Chester and have a talk with him."

"All right," *Dat* said. "See you at home."

Leanna stalked across the parking lot and climbed into Chester's buggy. As she settled into her seat, a pungent odor overcame her.

"Is that smoke I smell?" she asked Chester as he sat in the driver's seat and turned on a small flashlight that illuminated the inside of the buggy.

"It wasn't me." Chester guided the horse out of the parking lot, looking straight ahead.

"You let someone else smoke in your buggy?"

He shrugged while keeping his eyes focused on the road. "It's no big deal."

She studied his expression with suspicion. She could always tell when her son lied to her because he wouldn't make eye contact. Now, as he stared out the windshield, she was certain he was lying, and the realization broke her heart.

Where had her sweet, helpful son gone?

"Whose idea was it to go onto that farm?" she asked him.

"Danny's. He wanted to go swimming."

"And how did you meet Maggie?"

"She was with this *maedel* named Alea that Danny knows. They both live in Gordonville."

"Oh." Leanna considered what she'd seen of Maggie. The girl seemed quiet and sweet—as if she didn't belong with Chester and Danny, trespassing on that farm.

A thick, heavy silence settled over the buggy for the remainder of the ride. When they reached Leanna's father's farm, Chester guided the horse up the driveway, and Leanna heard a hum and saw a light shining off the buggy floor.

"What is that?" She reached down and fumbled around the floorboard until her hand grasped a cell phone. Irritation now buzzed through her like a hive of hornets. "Chester, why do you have a cell phone?"

"*Mamm.*" He sighed with impatience. "It's just a phone. It's no big deal."

"It *is* a big deal, Chester." Her voice rose. "You don't need a phone. You don't have a job that requires one, so you have no reason to have one."

He halted the horse and then angled his body toward her, his expression exasperated. "I'm tired, and I have to get up early tomorrow for work. We can talk about this another time." He narrowed his eyes. "Why don't you get off my back?"

She blew out a puff of air and sniffed as furious tears stung her eyes. "Everything is an argument with you lately. Where did my sweet little *bu* go?"

He gave her a sardonic smile. "I guess I grew up."

Before she could respond, he took the phone from her hand and pocketed it, then pushed the buggy door open. "Go to bed, *Mamm*. I need to take care of the horse."

Leanna climbed out of the buggy and then made her way up the rock path to the house. She was grateful to find her parents talking in the kitchen.

"I don't know what to do with him," Leanna announced as she set her flashlight on the table. "He's disrespectful to me, and I know he's lying to me. Plus, he has a cell phone, and I think he's smoking!"

"Calm down." *Mamm* patted her shoulder. "It's late, Leanna, and we all have to get up early in the morning."

Leanna looked at her father. *"Dat?"*

"Your *mamm* is right. Get some sleep, and we'll talk about this tomorrow morning."

"Fine." Leanna swallowed back her annoyance. *"Danki* for going with me, *Dat. Gut nacht."*

Her posture sagged as she headed up the steep steps to her childhood bedroom that had become her room once again after Marlin died seven years ago and she and Chester moved in with her parents.

Leanna's thoughts spun as she changed back into her nightgown, removed her prayer covering, and released her hair from the tight bun. Then she turned off her lantern and crawled back into bed.

She looked up at the dark ceiling as a vision of Marlin's handsome face filled her mind. With tears streaming down her face, she whispered, "I miss you, Marlin. Your *sohn* and I need you."

Leanna closed her eyes as memories filled her mind. She recalled how Marlin would hold her, his strong, muscular arms wrapped around her when she was upset and needed a good cry. She could almost feel him now, his strength encircling her as he shielded her from the sadness and grief that nearly swallowed her whole. He had been her rock when she felt her weakest. He'd held her up when she was certain she'd fall down and dissolve into a puddle.

But he was gone now. He'd been gone for seven years.

She needed to figure this out on her own.

She rolled over onto her side, but sleep would not come. How could she get through to Chester? Her mind kept recalling an image of sweet Maggie crying in the police station. It was obvious this whole ordeal had deeply affected her while Chester acted as if it was all an inconvenience. The stark contrast between Maggie and her son was overwhelming. Oh, how she longed to teach Chester a lesson and change his disrespectful attitude!

And then excitement filled her when an idea popped into her mind. She reached toward her clock and reset her alarm for earlier than she normally got up on a weekday, then snuggled back down in her bed and waited for sleep to find her.

. . .

"So, what exactly happened tonight?" Emory asked Maggie as he guided the horse down the road toward their house.

He was careful to keep his voice even in an effort not to

upset his *dochder* once again. Seeing her cry at the police station had nearly torn his heart in two. Lately, she seemed even more emotional than usual, and it worried him.

"Alea had heard about a combined event with a couple of youth groups in Bird-in-Hand." Maggie's voice was soft, barely audible over the clip-clop of the horse and the whir of buggy wheels. "We all met up at someone's farm, and then the group broke apart. Alea wanted to go swimming with Danny and his friend Chester."

She turned toward him, and once again, he saw tears spilling from her blue-gray eyes. "I didn't want to go, but Alea insisted. I didn't know we were trespassing. I didn't even want to go swimming with those two *buwe* I hadn't met before. Plus, it was so late, and it's dangerous to swim in the dark. So I just went and sat in Chester's buggy because it was the closest one. I was actually starting to fall asleep when the police officer arrived."

Maggie sniffed and wiped her nose with a tissue. "I'm sorry for having to wake you up. I know you're probably so disappointed in me, and I deserve any punishment you see fit."

Emory sighed. He couldn't think of one time he'd ever had to punish Maggie, since she'd never given him or his late wife a moment's trouble. Emory, however, couldn't even manage to count how many times he and his brother had gotten into trouble with their rowdy friends when they were teenagers.

That was part of the problem with Maggie. She rarely wanted to go out or be with her friends, so he'd been grateful she'd agreed to go to youth group with Alea. He was convinced Maggie had finally felt like a part of her youth group and would start to spend time with friends her age before deciding to get baptized, join the church, and then possibly start dating.

Emory couldn't wait to hear how her time had gone with the youth group. In fact, he had tried to wait up for her but had fallen asleep reading on the sofa.

When he awoke around midnight and realized Maggie hadn't returned, he became frantic, searching the house for her and then outside. Then the phone rang, and his fear had spiked, assuming the worst—that Maggie and her friends had been in an accident.

When he answered the phone, he heard her little voice on the phone, crying as she asked him to come to the police station, and all of his excitement about her attending a youth gathering had evaporated. Instead of Maggie coming home eager to go to another youth gathering, the night had ended in disaster. He was grateful she was alive, but still, he assumed the worst.

"Maggie, it's okay, *mei liewe*." Emory reached over and patted her slight shoulder. "Like I told Leanna and Walter, no one got hurt, and that's what matters."

"But what would *Mamm* say?" she blubbered as more tears fell from her pretty eyes.

Emory pressed his lips together. "Your *mamm* and I met at a youth gathering. She'd want you to make *freinden* and enjoy being young."

"No." Maggie shook her head. "No, *Mamm* would want me to take care of you."

Emory felt his brow furrow as he stared out the windshield, and the familiar grief and frustration that had been his constant companion for the past six years twined in his gut.

He'd struggled to be a good father and also mother ever since Sheryl had died six years ago, but he was aware of how much he lacked every time he heard Maggie tell him it was her job to care for him. But it wasn't her job to care for him. Instead, it was her job to do her chores and then enjoy being a teenager in her community—to make friends and have fun before the burdens of adulthood overtook her life.

But no matter how often he told her to enjoy being young, she told him that she had to care for him. He felt as if he were talking to a brick wall at times.

"Maggie, I'm the *dat* here. You know it's not your job to take care of me."

"*Ya*, it *is* my job. I still remember Great-*Aenti* Trudy saying it was my job to take care of you after *Mamm* died, and she was right." She turned toward him, her face clouded with a frown. "And if I don't take care of you, then who will?"

Emory closed his eyes for a moment and then opened them. He was too tired to have this argument right now. Instead, he would change the subject. "What do you know about Chester Wengerd?"

"Not much. He's kind of wild like his *freind* Danny. He smokes and has a cell phone."

Emory shook his head, recalling how the wild bunch in his youth group frequently got into trouble for drinking. He'd gotten into trouble for racing buggies and staying out too late, but he never was into drinking or illegal drugs. "In that case, you should stay away from him."

"Oh, don't worry. I'm not going back to youth group."

Great. We're right back where we started. "That's not what I meant. I only meant to stay with your *freinden* and not get involved with the wild ones."

"No, I don't want to go back." Her voice sounded gravelly. "I only went today to make you *froh*, and I had a terrible time. Please don't make me go back."

"You need to be around young people your age."

"No, I'm happy with you!" She sniffed.

Emory gripped the reins tighter. *Lord, help me get through to her!*

He would fight this battle another day.

They spent the remainder of the ride in silence. When they arrived at their home in Gordonville, Emory guided the horse up the long driveway that led to the two-story brick home he had built for Sheryl shortly after they were married.

His heart squeezed as he recalled the day he and Sheryl had moved in. They were newlyweds and so in love. He had been twenty-five, and she was twenty-three. They had dreamt of filling the large house with children and love. Maggie had arrived two years later, and then Sheryl died in childbirth when Maggie was ten, and the baby boy had died as well. He had never imagined he'd become a widower at the age of thirty-seven.

Their marriage had been too short. And now Emory struggled to be the parent that Maggie needed without the love of his life by his side.

Shaking away the memories, Emory halted the horse by the barn and then pushed the buggy door open. He set his brightest lantern down on the ground and then began to unhitch the horse.

Maggie grabbed her flashlight and walked around to him. *"Gut nacht, Dat."*

"Gut nacht," he said.

Then she ran toward the house as if someone were chasing her.

Emory bit back another sigh as he looked up at the stars glittering above him in the dark sky. "Lord, please help me be a better *daed* to Maggie. I feel like I'm failing, and I don't know how to fix it. I miss Sheryl so much, and I want our *dochder* to have a *gut* life. Please lead me in the way I should go."

Then he stowed the horse in the stable and walked into the dark, quiet house. Tomorrow he'd try to figure out how to get through to Maggie. But until then, he'd try to sleep.

CHAPTER 3

Leanna popped up out of bed when her alarm buzzed the next morning. After dressing, she crossed the hallway and knocked on Chester's bedroom door. She waited a few moments and then knocked again.

Chester groaned from the other side of the door. "It's too early. I have another hour."

"No, you don't." Leanna pushed the door open. "Get up now."

"Why?" His voice was gravelly from underneath his sheet.

"Because you're going to run an errand on the way to work. Time to get moving." She started toward the doorway.

"What errand?"

Leanna turned to face him and found him sitting up in bed, rubbing his eyes. His light brown hair was a mess, standing up at odd angles on his head. "You're going to Gordonville Sheds and apologizing to Emory on your way to work, and I'm going to follow you in *Daadi*'s buggy."

"What?" Chester's voice was flinty and sharp, his face twisted in a dark frown. "Why would I do that? He already said everything was fine since no one was hurt."

Her pulse began to pound. She took a deep breath and worked to keep her voice even. "It was obvious Maggie was upset last night, and I can't get her humiliated face out of my mind. That's why you are going to go and apologize to Emory. It's the right thing to do." She pointed her finger at him. "Now, get up and get dressed. We're leaving shortly."

She ignored his dramatic sigh as she marched out of his room and downstairs. She found her parents in the kitchen, both eating breakfast.

"Leanna!" *Mamm* announced as she jumped up from the table and headed toward the counter. "You're up earlier than usual." She gathered a plate and utensils.

"*Ya*, I am. I can get that, *Mamm. Danki*." Leanna joined her mother at the counter and picked up a mug. "I also just told Chester to get up."

"Why?" *Dat* asked.

Leanna took a seat at the table. "I can't stop thinking about last night and how upset the girl, Maggie, appeared to be. Meanwhile, Chester just looked annoyed by the whole thing." She shook her head and explained how she'd told Chester he needed to stop by Emory's shed business to apologize to him. Leanna turned to her father. "I want to go with him and make sure he does it. Is it okay if I use your horse and buggy?"

"Of course." *Dat*'s smile was warm.

"*Danki*. I'd like to go see my cousins after we talk to Emory."

"Leanna, you might be worrying too much about Chester. He's just going through a phase."

Mamm patted her hand. "*Ya*, your *dat* is right."

Leanna plastered a smile on her face as her spirit sank. Why couldn't her parents see that Chester wasn't going to be fine unless they found a way to show him that his behavior was unacceptable?

• • •

In the parking lot at Gordonville Sheds, Leanna tied her horse beside Chester's on a hitching post. Then she and Chester walked side by side toward the front door. Chester had been silent during breakfast, eating with his head down and only giving one-word answers to any questions her parents asked to try to draw him into a conversation.

She glanced around the building's exterior and spotted sheds of various sizes and designs, which she assumed were examples of the types for sale. At the back of the parking lot, she saw a small stable and assumed that Emory, his brother, and his father kept their horses in there during the day.

Chester held the door open for Leanna, and a bell above them rang as she stepped into a small room with a counter covered with catalogs and a phone.

A young Amish man who looked to be about Chester's age walked over to the counter and smiled. He was tall like Chester, and he had dark hair and blue eyes that reminded Leanna of Emory's and Maggie's. She wondered if he was Emory's son.

"*Gude mariye*," he said. "How may I help you?"

"Hi," Leanna said. "We were hoping to talk to Emory. Is he here?"

"*Ya*, just a minute."

When the young man disappeared, Leanna turned to Chester and lowered her voice. "You will apologize and say you never meant to upset Maggie."

Chester sighed. "I know. I will."

A few moments later, Emory appeared at the counter, his expression bright and his smile wide. His blue eyes seemed to dance in the sun spilling in through the skylights above them. "Leanna. Chester. What a surprise. How may I help you?"

Leanna turned to her son. "Chester has something he wants to say to you."

Chester's shoulders seemed to droop. "I'm sorry for getting Maggie into trouble last night."

Emory blinked and tilted his head as he continued to smile. "It's okay. No harm was done." He looked over at Leanna and then back at Chester. "I appreciate your apology."

"I didn't mean to be disrespectful in any way to you or to Maggie," Chester continued.

Leanna stood up a little taller, proud of her son's words. Maybe Chester did understand how his behavior had impacted everyone involved.

Emory reached out and shook Chester's hand. "It's all forgiven and forgotten. *Danki* for coming here today."

Chester nodded and cleared his throat. "I need to get to work." He looked over at Leanna as if waiting for her to excuse him.

"Be safe. I'll see you at suppertime." She looked at Emory. "Have a *gut* day." Then she turned to go, embarrassment weighing down her steps as she turned to follow her son to the door.

"Leanna?"

She turned back toward the counter and found Emory walking toward her. "*Ya?*"

"Are you okay?" His warm blue eyes were filled with concern.

Leanna watched him for a moment, stunned by his earnestness.

"I'm sorry." He held his hands up. "You don't know me, and this is none of my business."

"No, it's kind of you to ask." Her tight muscles began to relax slightly. "And no, actually, I'm not okay."

He nodded. "Do you want to talk about it?"

Yes, yes, she did want to talk about it! But Emory was a stranger. She gazed toward the door and found that Chester was gone.

Then she looked at Emory and felt something inside of her break apart as the truth spilled out. "To be completely honest with you, I feel like I'm coming apart at the seams. I'm doing the best I can with Chester, but everything I do seems to be wrong. My parents keep telling me Chester will be okay, but I'm not sure he will. I pray and pray for guidance with him, but I feel like I'm a terrible *mamm*."

She blew out a breath and her cheeks began to burn as she realized she'd said too much. She'd just bared her soul to a complete stranger. Surely he thought she had lost her mind!

Emory's azure eyes studied her. "I understand how you feel. I'm trying my best with my Maggie, too, but I feel like I'm always giving her the wrong advice or not getting through to her."

When the pieces came together in Leanna's mind, she sucked in a breath. "You lost your *fraa*?"

"*Ya*. And you lost your husband?"

"*Ya*, seven years ago."

"Six for me."

Something warm filled Leanna's chest as she felt a sudden camaraderie with this man she didn't even know.

"*Onkel* Emory?" The young man appeared at the counter again. "*Mei dat* says he needs your help." Then he smiled at Leanna. "Excuse me for interrupting."

Emory turned toward him. "Okay, Lee. Please tell him I'll be right there." Then he looked at Leanna. "I have to go, but I'd like to talk to you some other time. We're busy right now, but can you possibly meet for *kaffi* to chat Thursday or Friday?"

"*Ya*, that would be perfect. I run the Jam and Jelly Nook at the Bird-in-Hand marketplace across from Zimmerman's Family Restaurant. We could have *kaffi* there at the Coffee Corner."

"Great. Thursday morning works for me."

"Perfect," she said, and they agreed on a time.

"I'll see you then."

Leanna's grin was wide as she headed back out to the horse and buggy. Nothing about the morning had been usual, but somehow she had made a new friend.

. . .

Emory watched Leanna walk out the door, his mind spinning with what had just happened. He'd just met someone who understood how he felt. Was he dreaming?

"Who was that?"

Emory turned toward his younger brother standing at the counter, watching him with curiosity. "Her name is Leanna Wengerd."

Three years younger than Emory, Justin was forty and had the same dark hair, blue eyes, and tall stature that Emory had inherited from their father. "How do you know her?"

"Funny you should ask." Emory walked over to the counter and rested his elbows on it. "I met her late last night at the police station."

Justin's eyes rounded. "At the *police station*?"

Emory explained the mess Maggie had gotten herself into, and Justin listened with mouth agape and eyes wide.

"Maggie snuck onto private property and swam with two *buwe* and a *maedel*?"

"Well, you know how timid Maggie is." Emory shook his head. "She was *with* them, but she waited in Chester's buggy while they swam. She was mortified over the whole thing."

"Wow." Justin peeked over his shoulder, as if looking for his son. "I can't see Lee ever doing anything that daring." He snickered. "He's nothing like we were." Then his smile faded. "Maggie is okay, right?"

"*Ya*, and the property owner didn't want to press charges. Leanna just brought her *sohn* here to apologize to me." Emory smiled as he recalled their conversation. "She's a struggling widow raising a teenager. I told her I'm dealing with the same issues, so I asked her if I can meet her for *kaffi* and talk sometime soon."

Justin's grin was wide. "Maybe she's your future *fraa*."

Emory groaned and rolled his eyes. "You sound just like your *fraa*."

"And what's wrong with that? You need a *mamm* for Maggie. That's what's lacking in Maggie's life. You're doing a *gut* job, Emory, but you're not a woman."

"I'm not looking for a *fraa*, but I could use a *freind*." *And I think maybe Leanna could be that* freind.

Something in Leanna's chocolate-brown eyes drew him in. He couldn't put his finger on what it was. Maybe he was imagining it, but a tickle of curiosity stirred at the back of his mind.

All he knew for sure was that he couldn't wait to see her again.

CHAPTER 4

Leanna walked up the porch steps to her cousin Christiana's house and knocked. The bright July morning sun warmed her neck and back as she breathed in the refreshing scent of moist earth. She glanced across at Christiana's husband's dairy farm and took in the green, lush fields, and then she felt herself relax as she imagined talking with her three favorite cousins— Christiana Stoltzfus, Salina Zimmerman, and Bethany Zook.

While Leanna was thirty-eight and her cousins were still in their twenties, the age difference didn't get in the way since they were her best friends. Actually, they were more like her sisters since Leanna was an only child. All three of them had been a tremendous support to her when she'd lost Marlin, and she had been a help to them during their difficult times. Leanna was certain her cousins would help her deal with her constant anxiety caused by Chester's behavior and attitude.

She missed the time when she and her three cousins all ran booths at the Bird-in-Hand market. However, since Christiana and Salina had both married and started families, Christiana had closed her Bake Shop, and Salina had to stop running her Farm Stand.

Leanna was grateful that Bethany still had her Coffee Corner, where she sold flavored coffee and donuts when the market was open on Thursdays, Fridays, and Saturdays. This gave Leanna and Bethany the opportunity to see each other three days per week.

"Leanna!" Christiana pushed the screen door open with one arm while balancing her two-year-old daughter, Kaylin, on her hip. *"Wie geht's?"* Christiana was twenty-nine, and Leanna had always considered her to be beautiful. Now Kaylin shared her mother's striking green eyes and bright red hair.

"Good morning." Leanna kissed Kaylin's head. "How are you doing this morning?"

Christiana turned loving eyes toward her daughter. "We're great, right, Kaylin?"

"Ya!" Kaylin threw her arms up in the air, and the cousins laughed.

"Come in," Christiana said. "Salina and Bethany are already here."

Leanna followed Christiana and Kaylin into the kitchen where Salina and Bethany sat at the table. Salina held her eighteen-month-old daughter, Karrie, while Angelie, Christiana's ten-month-old, sat on Bethany's lap.

The delicious aroma of Bethany's donuts and her bananas foster–flavored coffee filled Leanna's senses.

"Hi, Leanna," Salina grinned as she handed Karrie a cinnamon donut. At twenty-nine, Salina had the same dark brown hair as Leanna, but she had been blessed with gorgeous blue eyes instead of Leanna's brown eyes. She looked down at Karrie and pushed her dark hair back from her face. "Karrie and I were just discussing how we couldn't wait to see you."

"Hi, Karrie, *mei liewe.*" Leanna's eyes immediately moved to Salina's belly and she smiled. She was now seven months pregnant with her second child, and Leanna was thrilled for Salina and her husband, Will.

"How are you today, Leanna?" Bethany handed Angelie a piece of cinnamon donut, and the ten-month-old squealed.

Although Angelie was Christiana's daughter, she had Bethany's blond hair and blue eyes. Leanna imagined that Bethany's future daughter might look just like Angelie, and she wondered when Bethany and her husband, Micah, might be blessed with children. Bethany was twenty-six, and she was known for always being upbeat with her smile that reminded Leanna of sunshine.

"I'm great now because I smell your *appeditlich kaffi* and donuts." Leanna picked up a mug from the counter and poured some coffee from the carafe in the middle of the table. She added some creamer and then chose a chocolate-covered donut from the box in the center of the table before sitting across from Bethany. "*Danki* for bringing these." After a silent prayer, Leanna took a bite of the donut.

"You know I don't mind." Bethany pushed Angelie's blond hair back. "I miss seeing all of you at the market."

"*Ya*," Salina sighed. "I do too."

"That's why we have these special days together." Christiana sat Kaylin in a booster seat beside her and handed her a donut. "I cherish these times." She looked over at Bethany. "I'm sure pretty soon you and Micah will welcome a *boppli*, and you'll have to close down your Coffee Corner."

"Maybe so." Bethany's ever-present smile faded, and longing seemed to fill her eyes, making Leanna's heart squeeze for her.

"How are you feeling, Salina?" Leanna asked before sipping her coffee.

Salina reached for a napkin and began wiping Karrie's face. "I'm tired, but I'm doing fine. Will is working long hours at the restaurant, but he helps when he gets home. How are you really doing, Leanna?"

Leanna swallowed and considered her answer. While she trusted her cousins with all of her secrets, the thought of admitting she'd spent time at the police department last night was humiliating. She felt her face twist up with a frown.

Salina reached over and touched her arm. "Leanna? Are you okay?"

Leanna took a deep breath. "Not really. I wound up at the police station last night."

"What?" Bethany gasped.

Leanna shared every detail about the night before with her cousins. "The *gut* news is the property owner didn't press charges, but the bad news is I still can't figure out what I'm doing wrong with Chester."

Christiana shook her head. "What you're doing wrong? You're a great *mamm*."

"Absolutely," Bethany agreed.

"I appreciate the compliments, but I'm not doing a *gut* job if all he does is talk back and disrespect me." Leanna rested her elbow on the table and her chin in her palm. "I also found out he has a cell phone and he's smoking."

Salina waved off her worry. "It's a phase. *Mei bruder* went through it, too, and now he's the deacon and as strict as *mei dat*. You all remember how he disapproved of Will when we first met."

"That's what my parents keep saying, but I feel like it's more than that." Leanna worked to keep her emotions in check as her throat began to thicken. "I can't shake this guilt that seems to follow me everywhere. No matter what I do or say, Chester either disagrees with me or tells me I'm overreacting. Then this morning I spoke to Emory, and he said he feels the same way about trying to raise his *dochder* alone."

Bethany's smile was back as she leaned across the table toward Leanna. "Who's Emory?"

"He's Maggie's *dat*."

"The same Maggie who was at the police station last night?"

"*Ya*. Maggie seemed so upset and humiliated by the whole incident that I made Chester go see Emory this morning to apologize. After Chester left, I spoke to Emory for a few minutes and found out he lost his *fraa* six years ago. We're going to meet for *kaffi* at your booth Thursday morning."

Bethany and Salina shared a grin.

"Tell us more," Christiana said.

"*Ya*," Salina said. "Is he handsome?"

"Is he tall? Oh, right. *Everyone* is taller than you," Bethany joked, and Salina and Christiana laughed in return.

Leanna rolled her eyes. "Stop. He seems very nice, and we're just having *kaffi*."

Christiana wagged a finger at her. "That's how the best relationships start."

"Relationship?" Leanna held her hands up. "It's not like that. We just want to compare notes about how hard it is to raise our kids alone."

"And you have a lot in common," Bethany sang.

Leanna gripped her mug. "Knock it off. I'm almost forty, and I'm used to being alone."

"But you shouldn't be," Salina said. "You're young, and you'll find love again."

Bethany's grin widened. "And maybe you'll find that with Emory. So, is he handsome? You avoided that question."

"Just stop." Leanna waved them off, but she found herself

thinking about his deep voice and sky-blue eyes. They seemed almost too blue to be real.

Then she pushed the thought away. Marlin had been the love of her life, and she'd never find another man like him. She'd never love a man as much as she loved Marlin, and no one would love her as much as Marlin had.

Surely love like theirs happened only once in a lifetime.

. . .

On Thursday morning, Emory tied his horse to the hitching post outside the Bird-in-Hand marketplace. Birds sang in nearby trees and colorful potted flowers smiled up at him as he walked toward the entrance.

He stepped through the large glass doors into the marketplace and was greeted by a blast of cool air-conditioning, loud voices chatting, and the succulent smells of candy, chocolate, baked goods, and coffee.

He smiled and nodded as he passed *English* and Amish customers moving in and out of the booths. He stepped aside as a young Amish woman pushed past him with a stroller carrying identical toddler girls. Then he was swept along in the sea of people.

As he rounded the corner at the Quilt Shop, he noticed colorful quilts draped around the booth, while a table at the front contained smaller quilted gifts, including potholders, oven mitts, dolls, tote bags, coasters, and other homemade crafts.

A young Amish woman with dark hair stood at the back of the booth, folding a large quilt with a blue and gray block pattern. She nodded a greeting, and he returned the gesture.

She looked familiar. And then it struck Emory—her name was Sara Ann King, and she used to quilt with Sheryl. He hadn't seen her in nearly a decade.

As he rounded another corner, the scent of coffee enveloped him. He was almost certain he also smelled chocolate as he came upon the Jam and Jelly Nook, which was across from the Coffee Corner.

He stopped in front of Leanna's booth and spotted her stocking shelves with jars of different jams and jellies while a few customers milled about, picking up jars and examining them.

Emory stepped into the booth as Leanna continued to pull jars out of a box and set them on the shelf. With Leanna's petite stature and dark hair, she seemed to be the exact opposite of Sheryl, his late wife, who was golden-haired and only a few inches shorter than his six-foot height. The only feature the women had in common was their chocolate-brown eyes.

His eyes scanned the shelves, taking in the different flavors—apple, peach, strawberry, grape, raspberry, apricot, blackberry, and blueberry—and he silently admired how the shelves were arranged with care, evidence that Leanna not only loved her jams and jellies but took pride in them.

Leanna set another jar on the shelf and then turned toward him, a pretty smile overtaking her pink lips. "Emory! *Wie geht's?*"

"I'm doing great. You?" He felt something rub his leg and then he stilled. Glancing down toward his work boots, he found two cats looking up at him. Both tabby cats, one was rotund and gray while the other was a sleek brown. Each of them meowed up at him as he chuckled. "Who are these two?"

"These are our marketplace cats. All of the vendors give

them treats and water. The gray tabby is Daisy, and the brown tabby is her *dochder*, Lily." She bent down and rubbed Daisy's ear as the cat purred with delight.

Squatting down, he rubbed Lily's chin and then touched Daisy's nose. "So nice to meet you."

When the cats scrambled out of the booth toward the Coffee Corner, Leanna grinned. "They're probably going to see my cousin Bethany. She feeds them treats every morning she's here. I imagine she would try to take them home if her husband allowed it."

"Your cousin runs the Coffee Corner?"

"*Ya*. Two of my other cousins used to run booths here, too, but they closed them down after they were married and started having *kinner*."

"Really?"

"*Ya*. Salina ran the Farm Stand. She had the best produce around. Christiana had the Bake Shop, and she sold the most *appeditlich* treats." She leaned toward him and lowered her voice. "The new bakery stand isn't as *gut* as Christiana's."

He grinned at her conspiratorial tone. "I'll keep that in mind."

She laughed. "Christiana's husband also used to have a booth here called Unique Leather and Wood Gifts, where he sold personalized bracelets, key chains, and belts, along with wooden signs, blocks, and letters. He closed it down after their first *boppli* was born. They met because her booth was next to his."

He gestured around the nook. "Well, your booth is quite impressive. Tell me how it came about."

"After Marlin died, Chester and I moved in with my parents, and they insisted on supporting us." She folded her arms over her black apron, which covered her dark blue dress. "*Mei mammi* had taught me how to make jams and jellies when I was a teenager, and I used to make them occasionally for my family. After I lost Marlin, I thought I'd give it a try as a way to help my parents. I started selling them to *freinden* and neighbors. One day *mei mamm* and I visited the market and I saw the open booth. I immediately wondered if I could make my jams and jellies into a real business. I spoke to the market manager, and then the Jam and Jelly Nook was born. At first I thought it wasn't going to be profitable enough, but I was able to help pay for Chester's horse and buggy and some other expenses."

"That's fantastic." Emory picked up a jar of strawberry jam and then turned it over in his hand. When he read "Marlin's Strawberry Jam" on the back, he looked up and found her watching him. "This was Marlin's favorite?"

"*Ya*, I named my family's favorites after them." She fetched a jar of grape jelly. "And this is Chester's." She pointed to a shelf of orange marmalade. "That's *mei mamm*'s." And then she pointed to another and said, "And *mei dat*'s favorite is blackberry jam."

She turned toward him, and a hint of a smile played on her lips. "What's your favorite?"

"Apple cranberry." He set the strawberry jam back on the shelf as she crossed the booth.

She returned with a jar and handed it to him. "Here you go."

"Oh." He pulled his wallet from the back pocket of his trousers. "How much?"

"Oh no, this is on the *haus*."

He shook his head. "No, I can't possibly take it for free." He looked at the price and then began pulling out bills.

She reached for his hand and then stilled. "I insist. It's for your trouble."

"What trouble?"

Leanna sighed as her cheeks turned bright pink. "I could see how upset Maggie was Sunday night, and it really broke my heart. I feel like I need to make it up to you somehow. So, please. It's the least I can do."

He slipped the bills back into his wallet and shook his head. "I promise you Maggie is fine. She seems to be going through a really emotional stage right now."

Leanna seemed satisfied with that, but her expression was hesitant.

Emory looked around the booth and found a few customers browsing. "Are you still able to have *kaffi*?"

"*Ya.*" She pointed toward the customers. "I just need to help them, and then I'll put up a closed sign."

Emory couldn't help but grin as he watched Leanna take care of her customers. Women like her didn't cross his path every day, and he couldn't wait to get to know her better.

CHAPTER 5

Emory followed Leanna into the Coffee Corner, where customers sat at high-top tables and enjoyed their morning treats. The delicious aroma of coffee mixed with something else—maybe chocolate or banana?—drifted over him as he took in the array of donuts on shelves behind the counter where a young woman with blonde hair and blue eyes stood talking to customers.

Emory looked at Leanna. "This place is incredible."

"I know. I think it's the most popular booth in the market." She pointed to the blackboard behind the counter. "Bethany offers a special of the day, and she always likes to mix up the flavors. You never know what she'll come up with. She even has eggnog-flavored *kaffi* at Christmastime."

Emory chuckled as he took in the specials—coconut almond, bananas foster, butter pecan, regular, and decaf. "Oh my. I don't know what to pick." He looked at Leanna again. "What do you recommend?"

"Hmm." Leanna rubbed her chin. "It's a tough choice. They all taste *appeditlich*, but I think my favorite is butter pecan."

"You've sold me." He retrieved his wallet as he took in the variety of donuts—cinnamon sugar, chocolate, strawberry iced, chocolate iced with sprinkles, vanilla iced with sprinkles, and plain glazed. There were too many choices!

"I like the vanilla iced with sprinkles best."

He grinned over at Leanna. "Are you reading my thoughts?"

"Maybe." She shrugged and then laughed.

When the customers in front of them left the counter with their coffee and donuts, Emory and Leanna approached the blonde. Her already bright smile seemed to tick up a few notches, reminding him of the afternoon sun.

"Gude mariye!" Bethany's enthusiasm came off of her in waves as she stuck her hand out to Emory. "I'm Bethany Zook. You must be Emory."

"Nice to meet you." Emory shook her hand.

Bethany peered at Leanna, and a look seemed to pass between the cousins. He was almost certain Leanna shot her a warning before Bethany looked away.

"We'd like two cups of your butter pecan *kaffi* and two vanilla donuts with sprinkles, please." Emory retrieved his wallet.

"Great choice," Bethany declared. "Coming right up."

Leanna held up her hand. "I can pay for my own."

"Nonsense. This was my idea, so I'm *froh* to pay."

Leanna pressed her lips together. It seemed she was used to paying her own way.

"How about this," he offered. "You can pay next time."

Leanna seemed satisfied with his solution. "That sounds *gut.*"

"Great." He would never let her pay, but he wasn't going to admit that to her.

Bethany returned with their coffee and donuts and then took his payment. "You two enjoy," she sang as she handed him his change.

Emory followed Leanna to a table at the far end of the

booth, where Bethany stocked the creamer, stirrers, powdered flavorings, and sweeteners. They each prepared their drinks to their liking, then made their way to the only empty table in the corner.

Emory hopped up on a stool across from Leanna before taking a sip. "Oh my goodness. This is fantastic."

"I told you it's the best!"

Emory took another sip and then bit into the donut, which was still warm. "Your cousin is truly talented."

Leanna laughed. "I agree."

They drank and ate in silence for a few moments as conversations swirled around them. A line began to form in front of Bethany's counter, and Emory silently marveled at her booth's success. He met Leanna's gaze, and she gave him a shy smile.

"Tell me about Marlin," he said, hoping the question wasn't too personal.

Leanna set her donut on the piece of wax paper Bethany had provided. "Well, we knew each other our whole lives." She smiled and fiddled with a paper napkin. "I had a crush on him from when I was thirteen. He was handsome, kind, funny, outgoing, and sweet. After we were baptized, he took a while to ask me out because he thought I liked someone else."

She laughed. "I only had eyes for him, but he said he was *naerfich* I would reject him."

Emory smiled and sipped his coffee.

"We married young. We were only twenty, but we were convinced that God had intended us to be together. And then Chester came along two years later. I had dreamt of having more *kinner*, but God had other plans for us."

Emory nodded. "I can relate. Sheryl and I wanted more

kinner too." He spun the warm cup around in his hands. "What did Marlin do for a living?"

"He was in construction. He built fences, and he dreamt of starting his own business." She took a bite of her donut and swallowed. "We rented a little *haus* over in Gordonville, but he wanted to build us our own *haus* someday." Her smile turned melancholy. "But we're not supposed to question God's will, right?"

"May I ask what happened to Marlin?" Emory was careful to keep his tone gentle.

Leanna blew out a breath. "He was riding in the company's work truck on his way home from a job in Lancaster late one night, and he was hit by a drunk man driving on the wrong side of the road. That was seven years ago."

Emory grimaced. "I'm so sorry."

She gave him a sad smile. "My parents insisted I move in with them and stop renting the *haus* Marlin and I had in Gordonville. I had no choice since I had no income once Marlin was gone. In a way, it was a blessing to be back in my family's church district, and I became closer to my three cousins than I had ever been. I found my way with the help of prayer and my family." She tilted her head. "Would you tell me about Sheryl?"

Emory shifted on the stool. "Well, sounds like Sheryl was a lot like Marlin. She was outgoing and funny. She never met a stranger." He smiled as memories filled his mind. "We met through *freinden*." He ran his fingers along the edge of the wooden tabletop. "I thought she was too *schee* to pay attention to me."

"Aww. Don't say that."

He chuckled. "Well, she did notice me, and she came into

my life like a tornado. We quickly fell in love and were married a couple of years later. I was twenty-five and already thinking about building my own *haus* since I was making a *gut* living working with *mei dat* and *bruder* at our shed business. Sheryl was twenty-three when we married. I built her a *haus*, and a couple years later Maggie came along. And then I lost her when Maggie was ten. That was six years ago now."

He looked down at his half-eaten donut as the details of that day came into focus in his mind. "I lost Sheryl in childbirth. We were so surprised when we found out she was expecting since we thought we wouldn't be blessed with more children. She insisted upon giving birth at home since she had a fairly easy time with Maggie. But something went wrong, and by the time the rescue squad got to our *haus*, it was too late. We lost Sheryl and the *boppli*. A *bu*."

Leanna's chocolate eyes seemed to glitter with unshed tears. "How terrible, Emory."

He sat up straighter, trying to shake off his lingering grief. "I feel like I'll always carry some guilt with me because I wanted her to go to the hospital. She said something felt wrong, and I wanted to call nine-one-one. But Sheryl was strong, and she and the midwife insisted upon staying put. I can't explain it, but that morning I had woken up with this bad feeling." He touched his chest. "Sometimes I wonder if I had called for help sooner, or if we had gone straight to the hospital when her contractions started, maybe they would have been okay."

"I understand. I deal with guilt every day with Chester."

"I know what you mean. *Mei mamm* has been a tremendous help with Maggie, but I still feel like I'm not the parent she needs. I never seem to do or say the right things."

She threw her hands up. "Exactly! Chester and I don't speak the same language sometimes. No matter what I say, he over-reacts or gets upset."

"Maggie seems to think she has to live up to a standard that Sheryl set for her—that she has to be the perfect *dochder* and take care of me. I mean, Sheryl wasn't perfect either." He chuckled as fond memories flooded his heart. "I remember plenty of times when she burned dinner. Or when she forgot we had company coming, and the *haus* was a mess when they arrived. Neither of us was ever perfect. Every so often I'd do something thoughtless, and we would argue and argue, just like most married couples do. But somehow Maggie has this idea that her *mamm* never made mistakes, and she's afraid she'll hurt Sheryl's memory by not being perfect too."

He rubbed his hand down his beard. "The reason she was so upset Sunday night is because she was worried that she would have disappointed her *mamm* because she was caught tres-passing. I can't ever get her to leave the *haus* to go to youth group. I finally convinced her to go with her *freind* Alea, and they wound up in trouble." He groaned. "Now I'm worried she'll never go again."

"I'm so sorry." Leanna looked pained. "That was Chester's fault."

"No, no, no. That's not what I meant at all. It's not Chester's fault that *mei dochder* thinks she's supposed to stay home and make sure the *haus* is perfect and my meals are made. After Sheryl died, *mei aenti* Trudy told Maggie at the funeral that she had to take care of me. She didn't mean anything by it, but I wish *mei aenti* had never said that. It's not a *dochder*'s job to take care of her *dat*. I want her to enjoy being young."

Leanna broke off a piece of donut and then studied it. "Well,

I think my Chester enjoys being young a little too much. He used to be sweet and helpful, but now he's bitter and sullen all the time. My parents keep telling me he's going through a rebellious phase and will be fine, but I worry about him all the time. I'm so afraid of losing him."

She met his gaze, and her expression was serious. "I feel so inadequate, and I find myself talking to Marlin all the time, telling him that we need him and miss him." Her eyes rounded and then her cheeks were pink again. "Have I lost my mind? I can't believe I just admitted that out loud." She pressed her fingertips to her forehead.

"Don't worry about it. I talk to Sheryl too. Maybe we've both lost our minds?"

They both laughed, and once again he felt a deep connection to this woman he hardly knew. Here he was pouring out his heart to a stranger, and it felt good—so good! He'd finally met someone who understood how he felt. What a blessing!

"Have you dated since Marlin passed away?" he asked before finishing his donut and wiping his fingers on the napkin.

"No, but I've had offers." She shook her head and shrugged. "I don't think I could find someone to love the way I loved Marlin or who would love me the same way. What about you?"

"I haven't dated, but my family is always trying to set me up with someone. *Mei bruder*'s *fraa* is the worst."

Her pretty face seemed to fill with curiosity. "Is she?"

He nodded. "She always has someone in mind for me. I'm just not ready."

"Do you think you'll ever be ready?"

"I don't know. Do you?"

"I don't know either."

They smiled at each other, then she peeked past him, her smile fading. "Oh no. It looks like I have a line at my booth."

Emory turned to see a group of older *English* ladies peering at her jams and jellies. Disappointment threaded through him. He longed for another hour to talk to Leanna.

He turned back toward her. "You need to get back over there before they leave. I should get to work too."

"*Ya.*" She seemed as disappointed as he was. "This was a nice visit."

"It was. Let's do this again soon."

"I'd like that." Then she grinned. "But I'll pay for the *kaffi* and donuts next time."

"No, you probably won't."

She laughed, and he enjoyed the sound. "We'll see about that. Have a *gut* day, Emory."

"You too." Emory tossed his empty cup, wax paper, and napkin into the trash can on his way to the door. As he stepped out of the booth, his cheeks warmed at the thought of seeing Leanna again soon.

. . .

After Emory had left the Coffee Corner, Leanna hopped down from her stool and almost rammed right into Bethany.

"Oh my goodness, Leanna," Bethany gushed. "He is *so* handsome, and it looked like you two were getting along great."

"He's very nice, but we're only acquaintances." Leanna dropped her trash into the can in order to avoid Bethany's wide grin.

The truth was that Leanna was struck by how comfortable

she felt with Emory. She had poured her heart out to him, and he had listened intently, seeming to understand and relate to her. The strong connection between them both shocked and scared her. Did he feel it, too, or was she only imagining it?

"Are you going to see him again?" Bethany asked.

"Maybe." Leanna pointed toward where a line had formed outside of her booth. "Can we chat later? Looks like I need to get back to work."

"Of course!"

Leanna hurried over to her booth and smiled at her customers, trying to direct her thoughts away from her conversation with Emory. "Good morning. I'm Leanna. Welcome to the Jam and Jelly Nook. Thank you for your patience. I'm open now. Please let me know if you have any questions."

"Do you have any orange marmalade?" a woman with bright red hair and thick glasses asked.

"I do. Please follow me." Leanna helped six customers find their items and moved to the counter, where they paid and she packaged up their jars.

After the last customer left, Sara Ann King, who ran the Quilt Shop, sashayed into the booth with a wide smile.

Leanna forced her lips into a smile as Sara Ann approached. Leanna and her three cousins called her Simply Sara Ann behind her back, because when she introduced herself, she coyly said, "I'm Sara Ann King, but you can call me simply Sara Ann." Although Leanna and her cousins had known Sara Ann for years, they always tried to avoid too much conversation with her. None of them were thrilled with Sara Ann's habit of playing the marketplace gossip.

"*Gude mariye,*" Sara Ann sang, her gray eyes sparkling in the fluorescent lights buzzing above them.

"Hi, Sara Ann." Leanna busied herself with straightening her countertop.

"So." Sara Ann leaned an elbow on the countertop. "I stopped into the Coffee Corner earlier, and I saw you sharing a cup of *kaffi* with someone who looked familiar to me." She snapped her fingers. "And then I realized it was Emory Speicher! I thought, 'Well, I remember Emory and his *fraa*, Sheryl.'"

Oh no! Leanna's stomach twisted as she felt her jaw go rigid. "Really?"

"Oh *ya*. I used to quilt with Sheryl." Sara Ann gave a dramatic frown. "So *bedauerlich* what happened to her and her *boppli*."

Leanna resisted the urge to ask Sara Ann about Sheryl. What did she look like? Did she and Emory get along well?

But asking Sara Ann anything would result in disaster. After all, she interfered in all three of her cousins' relationships, and Leanna didn't want to risk Sara Ann repeating anything she said to Emory.

"How do you know each other?" Sara Ann leaned forward as if to make sure she didn't miss a detail.

"We just met." Leanna did her best to give a casual shrug. "I really don't know him well."

"Interesting." Sara pointed at Leanna. "You both have lost your spouses, so you would be a perfect match, *ya*?"

"Oh, I don't know about that." Leanna shook her head and fiddled with a pen. "I'm not looking for someone to date. I'm perfectly *froh* here with my booth, and I'm busy with chores and with Chester."

"Oh, come on now. No one wants to be alone, right? Everyone wants to find a spouse." Sara Ann grinned again. "Emory is such a nice man, and he's handsome too. I'm surprised he's stayed single for so long. I think he's in his early forties. It's about time he settled down again."

Leanna glanced toward her booth entrance, relieved to find a group of middle-aged *English* women walking in wearing matching pink shirts featuring a horse and buggy on the front. "Oh, look. I have customers." She gave Sara Ann her best sugary smile. "I better get back to work. You go sell lots of quilts."

Sara Ann peered over her shoulder at the women and then turned to Leanna. "I'll talk to you soon."

I hope not! "Have a *gut* day, Sara Ann," Leanna said as Sara Ann walked toward the booth exit.

As Leanna turned her attention toward her customers, she tried to evict thoughts of Emory from her mind, but his smile lingered there, taunting her.

For the first time in a long time, someone seemed to understand her. She peered over at the Coffee Corner and imagined sitting at a high-top table with him again soon. Perhaps God had meant for them to cross paths. Maybe Emory was the friend she needed.

CHAPTER 6

Later that evening, Emory stepped into the kitchen and inhaled the delicious smells of his favorite supper—steak and potatoes. The table was set for two in their spacious kitchen, and Maggie carried a pitcher of water to the table.

"Hi, *Dat*. I made your favorite." Maggie gestured around the table.

"I see that. *Danki*." Emory crossed to the kitchen sink and began scrubbing his hands. "How was your day?"

She filled two glasses with water as she spoke. "It was *gut*. I did the laundry, mended a few of your shirts and pairs of trousers, dusted, cleaned the bathrooms, and weeded in the garden."

"Wow." Emory shook his head. "You make me feel *faul*."

"Don't be *gegisch*. You work harder than I do."

"I'm not so sure about that." He pulled the jar of jelly out of his pocket and set it on the counter. "I brought home a special treat."

She picked up the jar and examined it. "Oh, what's this? Apple cranberry jelly?" Her pretty brow furrowed as she looked up at him. "Where did you get this?"

"I went to see Leanna Wengerd today. She has a booth at the Bird-in-Hand marketplace called the Jam and Jelly Nook."

He pointed to the jar. "She gave me a jar of my favorite flavor of jelly."

"Why did you go to see Leanna?"

"She and Chester had come to see me on Monday so that Chester could apologize for getting you in trouble. After Chester left, I spoke to Leanna for a few minutes, and I went to see her today so that we could talk a little longer."

Maggie's expression twisted as she eyed him with something that looked like suspicion or possibly even panic. "Do you like her?"

"We're *freinden* who have a lot in common. You don't have anything to worry about." He took the jar of jelly from her and set it on the counter. "We both lost our spouses, and we're both raising teenagers alone."

"Chester lost his *dat*?"

"*Ya*, seven years ago." Emory pointed to the platter of steaks. "But enough about that. Why don't we sit down and enjoy this *appeditlich* meal?"

He took his usual seat across from Maggie. After a silent prayer, they began to fill their plates with steak, potatoes, green beans, and rolls.

"When did you go to see Leanna?" Maggie asked as she buttered her roll.

He sliced his baked potato and then began to smother it in butter and sour cream. "This morning. We went to her cousin's booth called the Coffee Corner, and we had flavored coffee and a donut while we talked. I'll have to take you there. Bethany's *kaffi* is amazing. Leanna and I had butter pecan *kaffi*."

"What did you and Leanna talk about?" Maggie's expression was unreadable as she looked over at him.

"We talked about a lot. Mostly our lives since we lost our spouses."

She nodded slowly, her expression hesitant. "Are you going to see her again?"

"Maybe." *Hopefully!* He took a bite of steak and groaned. "Maggie, you're the best cook I know."

She laughed. *"Danki."*

"So, tell me. Are you going to go to the youth gathering after church on Sunday?" He took another bite of steak.

"Oh, I don't . . ." The familiar wide-eyed panic filled her pretty face again. "I don't want to go back."

Emory took a deep breath and racked his brain for something encouraging to say. "You can't give up, Maggie. You need to be around other people your own age instead of staying here all day. You have to admit that at least a few of your *freinden* are more interesting than me."

Instead of laughing at his joke, Maggie looked down at her plate.

"Hey, Maggie." Emory leaned forward on the table, and she looked up at him, her blue eyes shimmering in the sunlight streaming in through the kitchen windows. *Please don't cry! Please don't cry!* "I only want what's best for you, and I want you to be *froh*. You can't be happy being cooped up in this *haus* all day doing chores."

"But I am *froh*." She sat up straighter, her expression suddenly bright. "In fact, I want to go to the craft store and get more supplies for the dolls and quilts I'm working on for the auction. I've made several dolls already, and I have designs ready for more. I also want to make some tote bags, purses, and wall hangings."

As she talked on about her projects, Emory released a sigh.

If he could figure out a way to bring his sweet daughter out of her shell, then she would have a chance at a happy life full of wonderful experiences and memories—things he wanted for her more than anything else in the world.

. . .

Later that evening, after taking care of the animals, Emory stepped out of the barn. He looked up as the sunset exploded across the sky in brilliant hues of yellow and orange. He leaned forward on his split rail fence and breathed in the fresh, warm evening air as he recalled his conversation with Leanna from earlier in the day.

He smiled, remembering how they'd laughed together and spoken so freely about their spouses. It felt wonderful to meet someone who understood his grief and what it was like to struggle without someone by his side to help. He rubbed his hand down his face and thought of Sheryl and suddenly felt the urge to talk to her.

"Sheryl," he said quietly, "I made a new *freind*. Her name is Leanna, and I met her for *kaffi* today. She's great. I think you'd really like her. We have so much in common." He looked out over his lush, green pasture and heard a dog bark in the distance as a car horn sounded somewhere out toward Old Philadelphia Pike.

He suddenly felt silly for standing by his pasture, talking to his dead wife, but he shook off the embarrassment and sighed. "I miss you, Sheryl. If only you were here to help me raise Maggie. I have no idea what I'm doing, but you would know what to do."

Pushing off the fence, he carried his lantern toward the

house, his work boots crunching on the rock path. He stepped into the mudroom and hung his straw hat on a hook and kicked off his boots before walking into the kitchen.

As usual, the table and counters were spotless and all of the dishes were stowed away. Above him, the sewing machine chattered, indicating that Maggie was working in her favorite place.

Emory's footfalls echoed in the stairwell as he made his way to the second floor where Maggie's bedroom, sewing room, another spare room, and the second bathroom were located.

He walked to the sewing room and pushed open the door. A warm breeze filtered in through the two open windows as three lanterns placed around the room offered soft yellow light. He smiled as he scanned the four folding tables piled with colorful dolls, quilts, potholders, purses, tote bags, wall hangings, and pillows she had created. His heart warmed with pride and happiness as he admired her talent.

Maggie looked up from the sewing machine. "Oh hi, *Dat*. How long have you been standing there?"

"I just got here." He crossed to her worktable and pointed to the purple material dotted with flowers that she had been sewing. "What will that be?"

"A pillow." She pointed to the stack of pillows on the table behind her.

"Wow. It's *schee*." He leaned against the worktable. "Your *mamm* would be so proud of you."

"I hope so," she whispered, her voice hoarse as tears sparkled in her eyes.

Emory swallowed back his own emotion as he leaned down and hugged her. "I'm going downstairs for a snack. Do you need anything?"

Her smile returned. "No, *danki*."

"Okay." He descended the stairs and entered the kitchen, where he set his lantern on the table beside the jar of jelly. He picked up the jar and read the label once again, taking in the words "Jam and Jelly Nook."

After locating one of the leftover rolls, he cut it open and spread a generous amount of apple cranberry jelly on it. Then he bit in and groaned as the sweet and delicious flavors played over his taste buds. It was the best jelly he'd ever had.

He smiled as he took another bite. Soon the roll was gone, and he closed the jar before setting it on the top shelf of his propane-powered refrigerator.

In the quiet of the kitchen, an idea gripped his mind. What if Leanna could offer him advice on how to get Maggie out of her shell? Leanna was sweet, outgoing, and thoughtful. Maybe she could give him the words to encourage Maggie to spend time with her youth group and make more friends.

Perhaps God had led Emory to Leanna as a way to help Maggie! The thought filled him with excitement and gratitude.

He picked up the lantern and started toward his bedroom. Now he needed to find a way to see Leanna again soon.

• • •

That same evening, Leanna knocked on the door to Chester's workshop. When the knock went unanswered, she knocked again.

"Chester? Are you in there?"

"*Ya.* Come in." His voice was muffled behind the door.

Leanna was met by the smell of wood and stain and a tiny hint of cigarettes as she walked into the shop and found Chester sitting at a large worktable covered in birdhouses. She hadn't noticed the birdhouses Sunday night when she'd been in there, panicked and anxious to find him.

Chester looked up at her, a piece of wood and a hammer in his hands. His expression was hesitant, as if he were waiting for her to criticize him or start an argument.

Guilt pressed down on her shoulders. Had she argued with him so much that now he only expected the worst from her? *God, help me become a better mother!*

"When did you start making birdhouses?" She ran her fingers over one—a rectangular box with a sloping roof. It had been stained dark red oak.

"About a month ago."

"They're lovely." She touched another one that was a larger rectangle with two openings for birds. "Did something inspire you?"

He turned his attention back to the birdhouse he had been working on. "I wanted to build something, and I found the birdhouse I'd made with *Dat* right before he died."

Leanna's heart twisted as grief washed over her, threatening to pull her under. "Where's the birdhouse you made with your *dat*?"

Chester pointed to the workbench behind him where a lone birdhouse sat.

Leanna walked over to it and picked it up, the sweet aroma of cedar filling her nose. She ran her finger over the simple design, taking in the angles of the roof, the little hole for the bird to go in, and the small piece of wood jutting out from the base for a bird to sit on.

She touched each piece of the birdhouse as she imagined Marlin patiently standing at the workbench with his nine-

year-old son while they assembled the little birdhouse together. Her eyes grew damp with tears at the image she had
summoned.

Taking a deep breath, Leanna pasted a smile on her face and
turned toward her son. "I had no idea that you and your *dat*
built a birdhouse. We should hang this in my garden so the
whole family can enjoy it."

"No." He shook his head while he sanded a piece of wood.
"I'd rather keep it in here."

"So you can look at it?"

He nodded, keeping his eyes focused on the wood.

She set the birdhouse back on the workbench and then
walked over to Chester. "You're doing a great job." She pointed
to the line of birdhouses sitting on the workbench across from
him and surmised that there had to be at least two dozen. "I
didn't know you liked working with wood."

"It makes me feel better."

Glancing around the workshop, she searched her mind for
something to say that might pull him into a conversation with
her. "Has your *daadi* seen these?"

He nodded. "He said they're nice."

"They are. You're very talented, and it's a shame to let these
schee birdhouses sit in this workshop. Have you thought about
selling them?"

"Not really."

"Why not?"

"I don't want to."

"Why would you make these amazing birdhouses and leave
them in the shop for no one to enjoy?"

When Chester met her gaze, his deep brown eyes glistened
with unshed tears. "Because it makes me feel closer to *Dat.*"

Leanna tried to smile, but the grief in her son's eyes nearly tore her in two. "Your *dat* would be so proud of you."

Chester pursed his lips and then returned to sanding.

Leanna stood by him for a few moments, watching him work. Persuading him to talk to her felt like pulling teeth.

When the silence continued to stretch between them, her heart sank. Did all mothers have trouble speaking to their sons? Or was Leanna the only mother in the world who had no idea how to relate to her own child?

She pointed toward the door. "Well then, I'm going back inside. Did you want me to bring you a drink or a snack?"

"No, *danki*."

She lingered at the workbench, hoping he'd speak to her, but he remained reticent. "You need to get up early for work tomorrow, so don't stay out here too late."

"I won't."

Leanna grabbed her flashlight and made her way through the dark toward the house. When she reached the porch, she looked up toward the stars glittering in the sky above her. "Lord, help me reach *mei sohn*. Help close this chasm between us."

Then she headed into the kitchen, where her mother stood at the sink drinking a glass of water. A lantern sat on the counter, illuminating the room. "Did you know Chester builds birdhouses in the workshop so that he can feel closer to Marlin?"

Mamm turned toward her and smiled. "Your *dat* mentioned it to me. I think it's sweet."

"I feel like I need to do more for him." Leanna switched off her flashlight and leaned against the counter beside her mother. "I just don't know what to do. I feel so inadequate.

Chester needs his *daed*. If Marlin were here, he could build the birdhouses with him, and they would have time to talk."

"You're doing your very best." *Mamm* patted her shoulder. "Chester will find his way with God's help."

Leanna rubbed her temple. If only her parents would listen to her!

"I'm heading to bed. You should get some rest too."

"*Gut nacht*," Leanna said as her mother picked up the lantern and headed toward their downstairs bedroom.

After grabbing her flashlight, she padded up the stairs to her bedroom, her heart heavy. She sat on the corner of her bed as memories of Marlin and their life together swamped her.

She scanned her childhood bedroom as tears pooled in her eyes. She missed their little house and their plans for the future. She missed Marlin's handsome face, his smile, his quick wit.

Leanna's heart twisted as she recalled how Marlin had held her close at night. Oh, how she missed feeling so protected, so cherished, so loved! She tried to recall his smell—soap, wood, and the musky scent of his deodorant—and the sound of his deep, rich voice, his contagious laugh. She'd planned to spend the rest of her life with him, but that wasn't what God had chosen for them.

Now she was all alone.

"Why did you leave us, Marlin?" she whispered. "I know God chose your time, but we miss you. I despise being a burden to my parents. I miss our life together."

Then she flopped onto her bed and let her tears flow.

CHAPTER 7

Leanna stood in her *aenti* Mary's kitchen surrounded by her three favorite cousins before the Sunday morning service. Today the community was assembling at her *onkel* Lamar's house. *Onkel* Lamar was Salina's father, but he was also the bishop of their church district.

"How was the rest of your week?" Salina asked, placing her hand on her belly. She looked down at Karrie, who sat in a stroller and ate Cheerios from a plastic container.

"I got some sewing done and little bit of baking," Christiana said. She shifted Angelie on her hip as Kaylin walked over to Christiana's mom, *Aenti* Lynn. "I was hoping to get a new bake stand going at the end of our road, but that will be impossible now. I have to wait for this one to get a little older." She touched Angelie's nose, and her daughter snuggled her face into Christiana's neck.

Bethany smiled brightly. "My week was very *gut*. I sold a lot of *kaffi* and donuts at the market." Then she winked at Leanna. "In fact, I sold two cups of *kaffi* and two donuts to Leanna's new *freind*, Emory."

Salina straightened. "Oh my goodness! I completely forgot you were meeting Emory for *kaffi*!"

"How did that go?" Christiana asked.

Bethany lifted her chin and wagged her finger at Leanna.

"From what I saw, it went really well, but Leanna is down-playing it."

Leanna rolled her eyes and laughed. "Bethany is making a much bigger deal out of it than it truly was. Emory and I had a nice talk. We have a lot in common since we've both lost our spouses and are both trying to raise teenagers."

"Hmm." Christiana's green eyes gleamed. "It sounds to me like you should date each other!"

Leanna shook her head. "No, no, no. We're just *freinden*."

"I want details," Salina said, and Christiana nodded in agreement. "What exactly did you talk about?"

Leanna scanned the kitchen, making sure no one was listening. "I told you. We talked about our *kinner* and being single parents. That's it."

"Does he want to see you again?" Christiana asked.

Leanna hesitated, considering telling her cousins that he didn't, just so they would drop the subject. But she was standing in the bishop's kitchen preparing to go into his barn for the church service. Telling a lie, no matter how small, was a sin, and she couldn't bring herself to do it.

"Well?" Salina gave her a palms-up.

"*Ya*, he does."

Bethany looped her arm around Leanna's shoulders. "He seems perfect for you."

Leanna opened her mouth to respond and was grateful when the clock on the wall began to chime nine. She then followed her cousins into the barn, where they joined the other married women. She sat between Salina and Bethany as they waited for the rest of the congregation to file in and sit in their designated areas.

When the young, unmarried men entered the barn, Leanna

watched Chester sit down beside Danny in their section. Chester's expression was somber as he studied the cover of his hymnal. She recalled their conversation in the workshop Thursday night and her heart grew heavy. Oh, how she wished he would confide in her.

The remainder of the congregation made their way into their sections, and a young man sitting across the barn served as the song leader. He began the first syllable of each line, and then the rest of the congregation joined in to finish the verse.

Leanna tried to focus on the service and praising the Lord, but her mind wandered to Emory and Maggie. She tried to imagine Emory sitting with the married men in his congregation as they began their opening hymn. Was he at church today, or was it an off-Sunday without a service for his congregation?

She tried to take control of her thoughts and concentrate on the holy words of the hymn. But her heart wouldn't stop wondering when she would have the opportunity to see him again.

. . .

Chester hustled over to where Leanna stood with her cousins after the noon meal was over. He acknowledged the women with a nod, then turned to Leanna. "*Mamm*, I'm going out with *mei freinden*."

Leanna's chest constricted. "Where are you going?"

"To play games at Danny's *haus*." He jammed his thumb toward where a group of his friends headed to their buggies. "We're leaving now."

"Please make *gut* choices. Be safe and be home by ten."

"I know. I will." He waved back at her as he hurried off toward his friends.

"You okay?"

Leanna turned and found Bethany standing closest to her.

"*Ya.*" Leanna blew out a sigh.

Bethany raised a blond eyebrow. "That wasn't very convincing. You're still worried about him."

"I am." Leanna almost opened her mouth to tell Bethany about the birdhouses in the workshop, then decided to keep that conversation close to her heart. It was too personal, and she feared she might get emotional if she started talking about Chester's grief. "I just hope he stays safe and doesn't decide to trespass again."

Bethany grinned. "I have a feeling he learned his lesson."

"I hope so." Leanna gazed out toward the rock driveway as Chester and his friends guided their buggies to Danny's house, silently praying words of comfort and safety over them all.

. . .

Emory sipped a cup of coffee as he sat at his parents' kitchen table with his brother, sister-in-law, and father Sunday afternoon after church. He looked down at the cup, comparing it to Bethany's flavorful coffee. Then he smiled to himself as he recalled his conversation with Leanna.

He gazed across the room as Maggie and his mother chattered about quilting projects. He felt his smile slip a fraction of an inch. He'd tried again after church to convince Maggie to spend time with her friends, but she insisted upon coming with him to see her grandmother. What was he going to do with her?

His mother's and Maggie's footsteps echoed in the stairwell as they headed upstairs toward the sewing room, which had been Emory's bedroom when he was a child.

"I think it's time we discussed hiring someone else to help us with the sheds," *Dat* said, and Emory's gaze snapped to his.

Mamm had always said that *Dat* couldn't deny his sons, and it was true. While *Mamm* was petite with graying light brown hair and green eyes, *Dat* was tall and lean and had the same dark brown hair and light blue eyes that he'd given to Emory and Justin. The only difference was that *Dat* now had wrinkles around his eyes, laugh lines around his mouth, and gray threaded through his receding hairline and long beard.

"You think so?" Emory asked as his father and Justin nodded in unison.

"Absolutely," *Dat* said. "I'm having a tough time keeping up with the books and trying to help you two with my limited schedule at the shop. Having another full-time man to help build the sheds would take the pressure off of you two and Lee. Then I could concentrate solely on the orders from both the customers and the companies we supply. Besides, I'm almost seventy and I want to retire at some point."

"You'll never retire, *Dat*. You want to keep working with us to make sure we're behaving." Justin grinned, and his wife, Natalie, laughed.

"That's true," she said. With her light brown hair, hazel eyes, and outgoing personality, Natalie had been the love of Justin's life since they'd met at a youth gathering when they were eighteen.

Dat laughed and shook his head. "I really am ready to retire. I'll handle the books for another month or two, but then I'm done. You two are more than ready to take over the business."

"You sure we can afford to pay someone else?" Emory asked.

Dat chose a homemade chocolate chip cookie from the

plate in the center of the table. "*Sohn*, I wouldn't have suggested it if we couldn't afford it."

"Then I'll ask around." Emory picked up a cookie and took a bite. Oh, his mother made the best chocolate chip cookies!

"How is Maggie doing after the incident last Sunday?" *Dat* asked.

Emory looked at Justin, who averted his eyes by staring down at his cup of coffee. He hadn't wanted to tell his parents about Maggie and cause them any undue worry. But apparently Justin had taken it upon himself to share the news.

"*Ya*, your *bruder* told your *mamm* and me," *Dat* said. "And I don't see why you couldn't tell us."

Emory settled back in his seat. "There's nothing to tell. No one was hurt, and no charges were filed."

"Which is good news." *Dat*'s expression warmed. "But how is Maggie? You've mentioned how you've encouraged her to spend time with her *freinden*, but she seems to stay close to home."

Emory took a sip of coffee and considered his response.

"She wouldn't go to youth group today," Justin said. "Lee even invited her to ride with him."

"She needs a *mamm*, Emory." Natalie pointed at him. "That's what she needs."

Emory blew out a puff of air and tried to mentally prepare himself for his sister-in-law's favorite lecture.

Natalie gave him a sad smile. "You're a *wunderbaar dat*, and you're doing the best you can alone. It's time for you to settle down again. I know you miss Sheryl. We all do, but you should move on for your sake and for Maggie's."

Emory took another drink of coffee as his jaw tightened.

"I know a sweet woman who is thirty-five and has never been married. Still, she's very maternal. She helped raise her young siblings, and she'd be perfect for you. I'm certain she and Maggie would hit it off too. She's just what you both need."

Emory tried not to roll his eyes. Why had Natalie decided it was her job to play matchmaker for him?

"*Danki*, Natalie, but I'm fine. Maggie is fine too. We're just doing our best like everyone else."

"What about Leanna?" Justin said. "You said you had a nice *kaffi* date with her on Thursday."

Natalie's eyes widened as she divided a look between Emory and Justin. "Who's Leanna?"

Emory shot Justin a look. *Thanks, Justin.* "She's the mother of the *bu* who was with Maggie Sunday night."

"Tell me more." Natalie grinned.

"She has a booth at the Bird-in-Hand marketplace called the Jam and Jelly Nook." Emory picked up the carafe from the middle of the table and poured more coffee into his mug. He suddenly felt a strange protectiveness over his new friend and didn't want to share too much information about her.

"And . . . ?" Natalie asked.

"And that's about it. We had a cup of *kaffi* and a donut together."

"And she's a widow," Justin added.

Natalie nodded. "Sounds like she's the perfect match for you. You both lost your spouses, and you both are raising teenagers."

"We're just *freinden*." Emory shook his head.

Natalie perked up again. "Well, then, if you're not interested in Leanna, you need to meet *mei freind*. She likes to sew, so she'd be *wunderbaar* with Maggie. They could make crafts together. It would be the perfect way to bond!"

"Who likes to make crafts and would want to bond with me?" Maggie asked, surprising everyone with her presence as she stepped into the kitchen.

"I have this *freind* I want your *dat* to meet. She loves to sew, and she's great with *kinner*." Natalie beamed at Emory. "And she'd be a perfect match for your *dat*. I'm sure you both would love her."

Emory sucked in a breath as Maggie's smile melted and panic clouded her pretty face.

"*Mei dat* doesn't need a *fraa*," Maggie said, her words wobbling. "I take *gut* care of him."

Mamm appeared behind her and rubbed her shoulder. "It's okay, Maggie. Even if your *dat* falls in love again, you'll still be an important part of his life."

"That's right, dear," Natalie said. "Your *dat* will move on, just like you will. You'll meet someone, marry, and leave your *dat* when you start your own life. It's natural for you to move on, and your *dat* deserves to have someone too."

"No, we're fine on our own," Maggie blurted before turning and rushing upstairs.

Emory's nostrils flared as he stood. Why couldn't Natalie mind her own business?

"I'll handle it," *Mamm* said before heading toward the stairs. Then Natalie stood and followed her.

With a heavy sigh, Emory carried his mug to the counter and began scrubbing it, but the motion did little to release the frustration coiling in his muscles.

"Is she always like that when the subject of your dating comes up?" *Dat* asked.

"*Ya*, she is." Emory rinsed the mug, set it on the drying rack, and faced his father and brother as he leaned back against the counter.

"Do you know why she reacts that way?" Justin asked.

"It's hard to say. Maybe she thinks she has to live up to some unrealistic expectation to honor Sheryl's memory." Emory rubbed at the tightness in his neck. "I keep telling her it's not her job to take care of me, but she acts like she doesn't believe me."

Dat's blue eyes seemed to study him. "Do you want to move on?"

Emory shrugged. "I guess so, if God leads me to the right person for Maggie and me."

Dat smiled. "Just make sure you're listening if God is trying to tell you something."

"I'll do my best."

. . .

"Do you want to meet *Aenti* Natalie's *freind*?" Maggie asked as she sat beside Emory in the buggy on the way home later that evening.

Emory gripped the reins and shook his head. "I'm not really interested." Then he gave her a sideways glance, taking in her hesitant expression. "But Maggie, what if I did meet her *freind*? Why would that upset you?"

She bit her lower lip.

"What are you afraid of, *mei liewe*?" he asked gently.

She hesitated for a beat and then swallowed. "I don't want anything to change. I don't want to lose you too."

Her words were like a knife to his heart. "Maggie, things

will change because they *always* do. But I promise you that you'll always have me. That will *never* change."

Reaching over, he touched her hand and then looked up at the sky as he once again asked God for the right words to convince his daughter that no matter what, she would be okay.

CHAPTER 8

The following Wednesday afternoon, Emory stepped into Gordonville Hardware and chose a shopping cart before pulling out his list and heading to the gardening aisle.

Since he'd promised Maggie he would bring home string for her edger, a new trowel, and some fencing for her garden, he'd decided to use his afternoon break to complete the errand. He found Maggie's supplies and then moved over to the nails and screws aisle to get a few things he needed.

After filling his cart, he headed to the cashier. At the counter, he was surprised to find Chester standing behind the cash register. "Chester. *Wie geht's?*"

Chester looked up and smiled. "Hi, Emory." He then began to ring up Emory's items.

"How are you doing?"

Chester tapped on the register keys. "Fine. Looks like Maggie is working in her garden?"

"She is. She gave me a list." Emory gestured around the store. "I didn't realize you worked here. Has it been for long?"

"Almost a year."

"Do you like it?"

Chester shrugged. "It's all right. *Mei daadi* hired a few

farmhands and told me I could get a job somewhere else if I wanted to since farming isn't really my interest."

"And you're not thrilled with retail either?"

Chester looked around as if making sure his boss wasn't within earshot and then shook his head. "Not really."

"What would you like to do?"

Chester looked down at the box of nails and rang it up. "I'm not sure."

From the way Chester avoided Emory's gaze, Emory guessed Chester knew exactly what he wanted to do—but he didn't want to share. And this realization intrigued Emory.

As Chester read out the total, Emory pulled out his wallet.

"How's your *mamm* doing?" Emory asked, handing over a few bills.

Chester looked up at Emory and hesitated for a moment. "She's fine."

"Please tell her I said hello." Emory took his change and slipped it back into his wallet. "And you take care, Chester."

"You too, Emory."

Emory loaded his bags into the back of his buggy, and his mind swirled with reasons to go see Leanna. As he climbed into the buggy, he recalled the delicious jelly he had enjoyed at breakfast for the past two weeks. Perhaps it was time to go to her booth and buy more.

He smiled as he guided the horse toward the parking lot exit. Yes, that might just be the perfect excuse!

. . .

Leanna set a dish on the table and looked up as Chester walked into the kitchen. "How was your day?"

"*Gut.*" He crossed to the sink and washed his hands.

"Was the store busy?"

He nodded.

"That's *gut.*" Leanna tried to swallow back her disappointment at always having to pull information out of her son. She looked toward her mother, standing by the counter, and raised her eyebrows, hoping her mother would compel him to talk.

"Did you see anyone interesting at the store today?" *Mamm* asked.

"*Ya.*" Chester craned his neck over his shoulder to look at Leanna. "Emory came in to shop."

Leanna set down the last plate and faced him. "What was he doing there?"

Chester looked at her as if she were crazy. "Buying hardware supplies, of course." When he smiled, warmth swirled in her chest. "He needed some gardening supplies for Maggie and then some screws, nails, and a hammer."

She bit her lip, hoping for more information. "Is he doing well?"

"*Ya.* He asked about you." He looked back at the sink.

Leanna's heart did a funny little dance as she walked over to him. "What did he say?" She hoped her tone didn't betray her. Surely she didn't want to give her mother and Chester the wrong idea.

He looked over at her. "He just asked how you are. And he told me to tell you hello."

"Oh." Leanna gathered up utensils and turned back to the table. She was almost certain she felt Chester watching her, but she kept her attention on the table.

"Chester, would you please call your *daadi* in for supper? He's reading in the *schtupp.*"

"Sure," Chester said, heading into the family room. Then Leanna released a breath she didn't realize she'd been holding.

. . .

After supper, Leanna scrubbed the dishes while *Mamm* wiped down the table.

"I thought we'd have leftover pork chops, but the men were hungry tonight," *Mamm* said. "What should we have tomorrow night?"

"I don't know." Leanna glanced over at her. "I'll be coming home from the market tomorrow night, so I won't be here to help. What's easiest for you? Maybe a casserole?"

"*Ya*, that's a *gut* idea."

"I'll mix it up for you tonight and put it in the refrigerator."

"*Danki.*"

Leanna finished washing and stowing the dishes and then retrieved her favorite cookbook. She found the chicken bacon ranch casserole recipe she enjoyed, then pulled a large baking dish out of the cabinet. Leanna didn't want her mother to feel like she had to handle all of the chores on marketplace days, so she began gathering enough ingredients to make at least two meals' worth of casserole.

After the casserole was mixed and stowed in the refrigerator, and the counter cleaned, she walked out to the barn and found Chester in his workshop sanding one of his birdhouses. She breathed in the familiar scents of wood and stain.

When she also detected the hint of cigarette smoke, she felt her lips pull down into a frown. She tried to shove away her irritation in hopes of not starting an argument with him when their relationship felt so tenuous.

She hopped up on a nearby stool and took in his work—a birdhouse with a rectangular roof and a hole through which the bird would enter. It was simple, but it was also beautiful. Her chest swelled with pride. "That's lovely."

He snorted as he looked up at her. "It's really basic."

"Well, I think it's great." An idea struck her, and she tapped the workbench. "You could sell them at my booth. I'll set up a section for you and give you the money. Would you like that?"

"Not really. You'd be wasting the space in your booth. They aren't *gut* enough to sell."

"*Ya*, they are. Not only are they *gut*, but the *Englishers* love buying things that are Amish made. You could take the money and put it into your savings account." She gestured around the workshop. "Or you could use it to buy more tools and supplies for your other projects."

"No, but *danki*."

Why was Chester so hard on himself? Had she not given him enough compliments when he was younger? Had she not told him enough that she loved him? Leanna felt her shoulders sag with the weight of her constant guilt.

Silence fell between them and she tried to think of something to say as the sound of his sanding filled the little workshop.

Chester suddenly stopped sanding and looked up at her. "Do you have feelings for Emory?"

She blinked at him and shook her head. She was surprised not only by the question but also by the resentment she detected in his voice and in his brown eyes. "I don't even really know him. I've only spoken to him a few times."

He watched her for a beat and then looked down at the birdhouse again.

Curiosity nipped at her. "How would you feel if I were to start dating?"

Alarm flickered over his face as he looked up again. "Are you planning to date Emory?"

"No." She gave a little laugh. "I'm asking in general. How would you feel if I were to meet someone I wanted to date?"

His lips twisted as he frowned. "I like things the way they are."

"But wouldn't you like to have a *dat*?"

"I do have one. I have *Daadi*."

"Right." Leanna nodded as a thought filled her mind. Perhaps if she had remarried when he was younger, Chester wouldn't have been so lost and unhappy.

. . .

Emory's heartbeat sped up as he stepped into the marketplace the following morning and breathed in the delicious scents of coffee and candy. He'd spent the evening trying to come up with an excuse to visit Leanna today, but then he realized the most obvious one of all—to get coffee for Justin, Lee, and himself.

He'd headed straight to the market on the way to work. He just hoped Leanna had a few minutes to talk to him since her booth had seemed so busy the last time he'd visited.

Emory weaved through the knot of customers standing outside of the candy booth and the used bookstore booth before he rounded the corner past the Quilt Shop. Sara Ann looked over at him and smiled, and he nodded before continuing toward the Jam and Jelly Nook.

Emory's smile widened when he spotted Leanna talking to

a young *English* couple. He took in her pretty face and admired how her red dress complemented her dark hair and eyes.

She must have felt him watching her, because she met his gaze and blessed him with a sweet smile before continuing her conversation. Then the couple followed her toward the counter, where she rang up the four jars of jelly they had chosen.

Emory busied himself by perusing the shelves. He picked up a shopping basket and placed a jar of strawberry jam and apple cranberry jelly in it. Then he moved to another section and began looking at more flavors.

"Have you run out of jelly already?"

Emory turned and grinned at Leanna. "Would you believe the jar is almost empty?"

She laughed. "I'm so *froh* to hear that." She gestured around the booth. "What brings you here this morning?"

"I thought I'd stop in and pick up some *kaffi* for Justin, Lee, and me."

But I really wanted to see you.

"Ahh." She wagged a finger at him. "I warned you that Bethany's *kaffi* was addicting."

"You were so right." He nodded toward another group of customers, this time four middle-aged Amish women. "I see you're staying busy."

"*Ya*, I usually do. How is work for you?"

"The same." He set the basket on the floor at his feet. "I ran into Chester at the hardware store yesterday."

"He told me. What a nice surprise."

"I get the impression he doesn't like his job."

Her smile faded slightly. "That's true." She folded her arms over her black apron. "He seems so unhappy lately, but I can't seem to put my finger on the reason."

Her gaze moved to something behind him, and her smiled completely flattened. When he turned, he found the customers lined up at the counter, and disappointment filled him too.

"Go on and help them," he said, and she nodded. He held up the two jars of jelly. "How much for these?"

"Take them."

He shook his head. "I couldn't."

"*Ya*, you can." She touched his hand, and a shock of heat ran up his arm.

What was that?

"No, I insist."

She sighed and told him the price. He pulled the money out of his wallet and handed it to her.

"*Danki.* Let me get you a bag." She slipped over to the counter and told the customers she'd be right with them. Then she returned to Emory with a bag and set the jars inside. "Enjoy."

"I will." He took the bag from her, then pointed to the Coffee Corner. "Have a *gut* day, Leanna." He started toward the booth exit.

"Wait," she called, and he spun to face her. "Why don't you and Maggie come for supper tonight? We're having my favorite casserole—chicken bacon ranch. I mixed up a large pan of it last night. Would you and Maggie like that?"

"*Ya*, that sounds amazing. What time?"

"How about six?"

"Perfect. I can't wait."

"Hand me your bag for a moment?"

He gave her the bag and she pulled a pen from her apron, wrote something on it, and then handed it back to him.

"There. Now you have my address." She smiled, and his heart thudded in his chest.

What was wrong with him?

"See you soon," she said before returning to the counter and smiling at her customers.

Emory's pulse took on wings as he walked into the Coffee Corner. He made his way to the counter, where Bethany greeted him with a wide smile.

"*Gude mariye*, Emory. *Wie geht's?*"

"I'm great. You?"

"Fantastic." She peeked behind him. "Where's Leanna?"

"She's busy at her shop, but I'm here for *kaffi* for *mei bruder* and *bruderskind*."

"That's a shame." She pointed to the blackboard, where the specials were listed. "What can I get you?"

"How about three cups of coconut almond *kaffi*?"

"Great choice. Coming right up." She poured the cups of coffee and then set them in a cardboard carrier.

He paid her and then picked up the drinks. *"Danki."*

"You have a great day."

"You too." Emory nodded at a young Amish man standing in line behind him, then stopped at the condiment table to collect creamer and sweetener before making his way out of the booth.

As he passed the Jam and Jelly Nook, he looked in to where Leanna spoke to more customers. He let out a big sigh and prayed the day would fly by. Tonight he would share a meal with his new friend—and he could barely contain his excitement.

CHAPTER 9

Busy day?" Leanna asked Bethany as she sat down at one of the high-top tables and pulled out her turkey sandwich. She had put up a sign stating the nook was closed for lunch, then took a seat in the Coffee Corner where she could keep an eye on her booth.

"It's going well." Bethany pulled open a bag of chips and then winked. "But I think yours is going better."

"What do you mean?" Leanna took a bite of her sandwich.

Bethany laughed. "Emory stopped in for *kaffi* this morning. He seemed *froh* to be here. Did you two have a nice talk?"

"*Ya*, he said he'd come by for *kaffi* on his way to work. We talked for a few minutes, and he bought two jars of jelly. Then I had to get back to my customers." She shrugged. "No big deal."

Bethany snorted. "Sure. No big deal. He probably came back to see you, Leanna. *Kaffi* was just an excuse."

"No, Bethany. He's addicted to your *kaffi*." Leanna pointed toward the counter. "He was here for *kaffi* and more jelly."

Bethany rolled her eyes. "Sure. Keep telling yourself that."

"I invited him and Maggie to join us for supper. I used the phone in the office earlier to let *mei mamm* know to expect guests."

Bethany's eyes brightened. "That's *wunderbaar*! What is your *mamm* going to make?"

"Last night I put together a chicken bacon ranch casserole, and I asked *mei mamm* to make a salad and some *brot*."

"That's a perfect meal." Leanna picked up a chip. "Your parents will enjoy meeting him."

Leanna felt a strange clutching in her chest at the idea of introducing Emory to her parents. She hoped they wouldn't get the wrong idea. After all, she and Emory were only acquaintances.

"I have a feeling you'll be dating him soon," Bethany said, then took a bite from her peanut butter sandwich.

"I doubt that. I'd just like to discuss Chester with him. We're both struggling with being single parents, so I think we can help each other."

Bethany grinned, and Leanna knew it was time to change the subject.

"So, tell me what's going on with you."

To her surprise, Bethany's signature smile dimmed, and she rested her elbow on the table before dropping her chin into her palm.

Alarm shot through Leanna. "*Was iss letz?*" She leaned forward on the table. "Are you and Micah having problems?" While she never imagined that Bethany and her husband would ever struggle, she could remember times when she and Marlin had argued.

"Sort of." Bethany stared down at her half-eaten sandwich and began to fiddle with her paper napkin. "I thought for sure I'd have *gut* news to share with him this month, but I was wrong."

Leanna blinked, and the pieces came together in her mind.

She recalled the longing she'd seen in Bethany's eyes while she held Angelie in her lap at Christiana's house. Then Leanna hopped down from the bench and scooted around the table to sit beside her cousin. She looped her arm over her shoulders. "*Ach, mei liewe.* I'm so sorry."

Bethany looked up, her eyes glistening. "I just didn't think it could be this difficult. It happened so quickly for Salina and Christiana, so I had no idea how some women struggled until it happened to me."

Leanna gave her shoulder a gentle squeeze. "Only God's timing is perfect."

"I know." Bethany sniffed and wiped at her eyes. "But I can't help feeling like I'm letting Micah down. He wants a family so badly, and I do too." She seemed to study Leanna's eyes. "Could it be my fault?"

"No, no, no." Leanna shook her head. "Sometimes it just takes a while. To be honest with you, Marlin and I wanted more *kinner*, and it didn't happen for us. We never knew why."

"I just hope I can give him at least one *boppli*." Bethany picked up her cup of mocha coffee and took a sip. "I'm so *froh* for Salina and Christiana, but deep down . . ."

"I felt the same way when we were trying for Chester. When we were first married, it seemed like all of the couples our age were having *bopplin*, and I wondered if something was wrong with me." Leanna offered her a smile. "But it wasn't my fault. It just wasn't our time. And when they all had their second and third *kind*, we still only had Chester. Everyone is different. God has a different plan for every family, and I'm certain you and Micah will have your time too."

Bethany nodded. "I'm sure you're right."

"I'll keep you and Micah in my prayers."

"*Danki.*" Bethany reached over and offered her a warm hug.

Leanna closed her eyes and smiled. She was so grateful for her tenderhearted cousin!

. . .

Later that evening, Emory guided his horse down his driveway toward the main road. Maggie sat beside him holding a coconut cream pie she had prepared earlier in the afternoon.

When Emory had arrived at the shop after leaving the marketplace, he had called Maggie at home to tell her they were invited for supper at Leanna's. Maggie hesitated at first, which made Emory worry she'd refuse to go, but when she offered to make a pie for dessert, he was relieved.

When he halted his horse at a stop sign, he turned toward Maggie and found her gripping her pie pan as if her life depended on it. "You okay?"

She nodded, but her expression seemed a bit anxious. "I'm just surprised we're going to Leanna and Chester's *haus.*"

He focused back on the road and guided the horse out into the intersection. "I thought it would be nice to get to know them a little better."

"Do you like her?"

"*Ya*, as a *freind.*" He gave Maggie a sideways glance and found her biting her lip.

"Are you going to date her?"

He chuckled. "No. It's possible for a man and a woman to just be *freinden.*"

Her expression relaxed, and he released the breath he'd been holding. Then he prayed Maggie would let down her guard and enjoy herself tonight.

. . .

Leanna scampered around the kitchen, setting the table as her mother pulled the glass dish from the oven. The delicious smells of chicken bacon ranch casserole and freshly baked bread filled her senses.

She had left the marketplace early to give herself time to prepare for supper. After changing into a fresh green dress and black apron, she had checked her hair and then hurried downstairs to work in the kitchen. She wanted everything to be perfect for Emory and Maggie.

After the dishes and utensils were placed on the table, she moved to the cabinet to find their best glasses. She groaned when she picked up one that looked cloudy.

"I'll have to rewash this one," she muttered as she moved to the sink and began scrubbing the glass.

Mamm sidled up next to her. "You're making an awfully big fuss over this Emory and his *dochder*. You certainly must like him a lot."

"I've told you, *Mamm*. We're just *freinden*."

"Right." *Mamm* laughed, and Leanna waved her off.

Mamm took the clean glass from her, dried it, and set it on the table while Leanna prepared a pitcher of water. She brought it to the table as *Mamm* set down the bowl of salad, two bottles of dressing, and a package of croutons.

The back door opened and clicked shut before Chester stepped into the kitchen through the mudroom.

"How was your day?" Leanna asked.

"Fine." Chester eyed the table and then looked up at Leanna. "Why is the table set for six?"

Mamm placed the bread in the center of the table, along

with a dish of butter. "We're having company. Your *mamm* invited Emory and Maggie to join us for supper."

Chester gazed at Leanna with suspicion. "Why?"

"Emory stopped by the market today, and we didn't have much time to talk. I thought it would be nice to have them over." Leanna waved toward the sink. "Please wash up and then find your *daadi*."

Then Leanna eyed the table and tapped her chin. What was missing? She snapped her fingers. Napkins! Leanna pulled some gingham napkins from a drawer and folded one under each fork.

Leanna crossed back toward the sink, where Chester gave her another skeptical expression before disappearing into the family room.

"I think we're ready," Leanna said. "*Danki* for your help, *Mamm*."

"*Gern gschehne*." *Mamm* walked over toward her and lowered her voice. "I'm thrilled to see you finally dating. It's about time."

Leanna gritted her teeth. "Stop, *Mamm*. We're not dating."

"Uh-huh." *Mamm* walked over to the window and grinned. "Looks like they're here." She walked over to the doorway leading to the family room. "Walter! Chester! Our company is here."

Leanna brushed her hands down her apron and dress and then hurried through the mudroom to the back door as Emory and Maggie walked up the porch steps. Emory met her gaze, and his face broke out with a wide smile.

He wore a blue shirt, which made his eyes seem somehow bluer, and she saw in that instant just how handsome he was. A faint, familiar stirring reawakened her heart. The realization made her nervous, and she tried to ignore it.

He is my friend and nothing more!

"Hi," Leanna said, opening the back door wide. "I hope you didn't have any trouble finding the farm."

"I didn't." Emory turned toward Maggie and gestured for her to walk in first.

Maggie handed her a pie plate. "Hi, Leanna. I made a coconut cream pie."

"Oh my goodness. *Danki!* I haven't had coconut cream in a long time." She breathed in the aroma. "It smells amazing, and I bet it tastes even better."

Maggie gave her a shy smile.

"Please come in." She led them into the kitchen, where her parents and Chester stood. "Emory and Maggie, please meet my parents, Rachelle and Walter. And you already know Chester."

"So nice to meet you." *Mamm* shook Emory's hand and then smiled at Maggie. "I've heard a lot about you both."

Oh no! Leanna cringed and hoped Emory wouldn't notice her flaming cheeks.

"We're excited to be here," Emory said as he shook *Dat*'s hand.

"We're excited you're here too." *Dat* pointed to the table. "I'm anxious to try Leanna's casserole. It's been a while since she's made chicken bacon ranch."

Leanna held up the pie. "And Maggie made a coconut cream pie."

"Oh, this is fantastic. All of my favorite foods." *Dat* touched his chest.

After Maggie and Emory washed their hands, they all sat down at the table. Emory took a seat across from Leanna and beside Chester. When he looked at Leanna, his eyes seemed to twinkle.

After a silent prayer, they began to fill their bowls with salad and their plates with the casserole and slices of bread.

"So, Emory, I hear you own a shed company with your *dat* and *bruder*," *Dat* began while buttering a piece of bread.

Emory passed the bowl of salad to Chester. "*Ya*, I do. *Mei dat* only works part-time now, and he's talking about retiring. He'll be seventy soon."

"Seventy is a great age to retire," *Dat* agreed.

While *Dat* and Emory talked on about Emory's work, Leanna turned to Maggie beside her. Maggie dropped a pile of casserole onto her plate and then handed the warm dish to Leanna.

"*Danki.*" Leanna took some casserole and then passed it to *Dat*, trying to think of something to say to Maggie. "Do you have any hobbies, Maggie?"

Nodding, Maggie gave her a shy look. "I like to make quilts. I also like to make other crafts, like pillows, tote bags, purses, and dolls."

"Really?" Leanna gazed over at her mother, who sat at the end of the table beside Maggie and looked equally impressed. "*Mei mamm* used to quilt."

"That's right," *Mamm* chimed in. "What's your favorite pattern?"

Maggie took a bite of casserole and hesitated. "Probably the Lone Star."

"Mine too. Tell me about your pillows and dolls," *Mamm* said.

Soon Maggie was talking about her crafts, her voice barely above a whisper. When Leanna stole a glance at Emory, she found him grinning. She met his gaze, and he gave her a nod before looking at Chester, who studied his plate with a sour expression on his face.

Leanna swallowed back her embarrassment and disappointment. *Please, Chester! Try to be friendly to our company!*

"Did you work at the hardware store today, Chester?" Emory asked.

"Ya." Chester spooned casserole into his mouth.

"Was it busy?"

Chester nodded while he chewed.

"Chester, I'm sure Emory would love to see your wood shop," Leanna said.

Chester shrugged, and Leanna felt her cheeks flame. Couldn't her son at least try to be more social?

Emory locked eyes with Leanna and winked as if telling her it was okay. She felt that same fluttering she'd experienced when he arrived. What was wrong with her?

After their plates were clean, Leanna and *Mamm* brought coffee and Maggie's coconut cream pie to the table. They enjoyed the dessert while *Dat* and Emory continued their conversation about work, and Leanna listened to *Mamm* and Maggie talk quilting techniques and fabrics. Soon the pie was gone, and the women began to clean up the kitchen.

"Chester," Leanna said. "Why don't you and *Dat* give Emory a tour of the farm."

Chester nodded.

"I really would love to see your workshop," Emory said.

"Okay." Chester started toward the mudroom.

Leanna met Emory's gaze and mouthed, *"Danki."*

Emory nodded, then followed her father and Chester out the back door.

Relief flooded Leanna. Somehow she knew that Emory would find a way to get through the wall Chester had built around himself.

CHAPTER 10

Emory followed Walter and Chester as they walked over toward the lush green pasture dotted with cows. "Your farm is *schee*. Has it been in your family for generations?"

"It has." Walter pointed toward the small house next door. "My parents live there. I have two older *schweschdere*. And since my younger *bruder*, Harvey, decided to become a carpenter, I wound up inheriting the farm since I was the only one interested. I hired a few farmhands to work it a few years ago because I wanted to retire. I suppose I'll sell it one day since Chester's not interested in it."

Chester looked out across the pasture as if avoiding their gazes.

"What does your younger *bruder* do?" Emory asked.

"He builds gazebos with his *sohn*. His son-in-law joined their company a few years ago, and they sell patio furniture now too."

"Really?" Emory tilted his head. "What's the name of their company?"

"Bird-in-Hand Custom Gazebos and Patio Furniture," Chester offered, looking over his shoulder at Emory.

Emory turned toward him and smiled. It was the most Chester had spoken since he and Maggie had arrived. "I've heard they do *gut* work."

"The best." Walter's expression was full of pride for his brother. He pointed toward the barns. "Why don't we show you the rest of the farm?"

"I'd like that."

Emory followed Walter through the barns, taking in the dairy barn where he milked the cows, the diesel-powered milkers, and their horses and donkey. Chester shuffled along behind the men, looking bored.

When they stepped out of the barns, Emory turned toward Chester. "So, where's this workshop your *mamm* mentioned?"

Chester pointed to one of the two smaller barns beside the dairy barn. "In there."

"Can we see it?"

Chester nodded and led the way. Emory stepped into the workshop and found a workbench clogged with birdhouses, along with another workbench peppered with tools. He picked up one of the birdhouses and turned it over in his hands. "So you made these, Chester?"

Chester nodded, dusting off the corner of the workbench as he watched Emory with a reluctant expression. Did he expect Emory to criticize his craftsmanship?

"They're really *gut*."

"Not really."

Walter lingered back by the door and smiled at his grandson. "They are *gut*, Chester. I've told you that many times, but you never seem to believe me."

"Do you sell them?" Emory picked up a birdhouse made out of cedar and turned it over in his hands.

"*Mei mamm* offered to sell them for me in her booth, but I told her no."

Emory tilted his head. "Why not?"

Chester shrugged and walked over to join Emory at the table. "Because they're not *gut* enough." He pointed to one. "Look how those angles don't match. It's obvious I'm an amateur. Why would you buy this birdhouse when you can get a perfect one at the hardware store where I work?"

"Nothing in this world is perfect." Emory picked up another one that was stained dark walnut. "Look at this one. It's beautifully made." He pointed to the angles on the roof. "They look like they match up." Then he pointed to the cedar one. "But they both have character. And I promise you the birds won't measure the angles before they go into the birdhouse out of the rain."

To Emory's surprise, Chester laughed at his lame joke.

Emory smiled. "Who taught you how to build them?" He looked over at Walter, who still smiled by the door. "Was it you, Walter?"

Walter shook his head. "Tell him, Chester."

The young man's smile dissolved. *"Mei dat."* He picked up a birdhouse and handed it to Emory. "We made this one together a few weeks before he died. *Mei mamm* wants me to hang it in her garden, but I like looking at it when I'm working out here."

Emory's chest constricted as he touched the birdhouse. "It's nice."

Chester was silent.

Emory scanned the workshop, taking in the birdhouses and the tools strewn about, and suddenly an idea took shape in his mind. He turned toward Chester. "Remember when you told me you don't like working in the hardware store?"

"*Ya*, I do."

"Do you like working with wood more than working at the hardware store?"

Chester snorted. "*Ya*, a lot more."

"How would you like to come work for me?"

Chester's mouth opened and no words escaped for a moment. "You want me to build sheds with you?"

"*Ya*, I would. What do you think about that?"

"I-I have no experience."

"Sure you do." Emory held up one of the birdhouses. "This right here tells me that you know how to measure, cut, and build something with wood. That counts as experience."

Chester looked over at his grandfather.

Walter held his hands up as he smiled. "Don't look at me, Chester. I've already said you can choose your career. If you want to build sheds, then you should try it."

Chester turned back to Emory. "Let me think about it and talk to *mei mamm*."

"That's a *gut* plan." Emory set the birdhouse on the workbench and then shook Chester's hand. "I look forward to your answer."

. . .

"Who taught you how to sew and quilt?" Leanna asked Maggie as they finished cleaning up the kitchen. While Leanna scrubbed dishes, *Mamm* dried them and stowed them, and Maggie swept the floor.

"*Mei mamm* introduced me to a sewing machine, but *mei mammi* was the one who really taught me how to quilt." Maggie emptied the contents from the dustpan into the bin.

"Leanna's *mammi* quilts too," *Mamm* said as she set the last pot into the cabinet. "You should show her the Tumbling Blocks quilt *Mammi* made for your *dat*."

Leanna snapped her fingers. "That's a *gut* idea." She beckoned for Maggie to follow her into the family room, which included two recliners, a sofa, two end tables, a coffee table, and two propane lamps.

They walked over to *Dat*'s recliner, where the beautiful primary colors Tumbling Blocks quilt was neatly folded over the back of the chair.

"*Mammi* made this for *mei dat* for Christmas probably twenty years ago, and he still uses it all the time. *Mei mamm* had to fix it more than once."

"Wow." Maggie ran her fingers over the stitches. "It's gorgeous."

"It is, isn't it?" Leanna smiled at her. "Would you like to meet *mei mammi* and see more of her quilts?"

"Does she live close by?"

"*Ya*. She lives in the *daadihaus* just across the way."

"Oh. Then that would be nice."

Leanna, *Mamm*, and Maggie walked down the short rock pathway to the small, one-story, two-bedroom house where Leanna's paternal grandparents lived. Above them, the sky was still bright blue and dotted with a few white, puffy clouds.

Mammi's small garden next to the house was filled with colorful summer flowers that seemed to smile and wave as a warm breeze blew past them.

Leanna climbed the porch steps and knocked on the front door.

The door opened, and *Mammi* smiled out at her. "Leanna! Rachelle! What a nice surprise." She looked past Leanna and grinned. "Why, hello there! Who's this lovely *maedel*?"

"*Mammi*, this is *mei freind* Maggie Speicher. She likes to quilt, and she wanted to meet you."

"How nice to meet you, Maggie." *Mammi* reached out and shook Maggie's hand. "Please come in. Just ignore the snoring coming from the bedroom. My husband decided he needed a nap after supper. And then he wonders why he can't sleep when it's time to go to bed."

Maggie giggled, and Leanna shared a grin with *Mamm*.

Oh, how Leanna adored her grandmother! Her white hair and wrinkles gave away her age, but her wrinkles outlined the same warm blue eyes she'd given Leanna's father. Although she was petite like Leanna and walked with a slight limp because of her painful knee, she still managed to keep up with her grandchildren and her great-grandchildren—even Karrie and Kaylin.

Mammi also was in tune to her grandchildren's lives. She enjoyed hearing stories of Leanna's and Bethany's adventures at the marketplace and also how Salina's and Christiana's little ones were doing.

And, best of all, she was never short on good advice. Leanna prayed she'd keep *Mammi* by her side for many more years.

"Why don't we go to my sewing room? That's where I keep most of my quilts." *Mammi* made a sweeping gesture, inviting them to come with her through the small family room and kitchen to the little bedroom located at the back of the house.

Leanna and *Mamm* followed Maggie and *Mammi* into the little room, which included two small tables with two sewing machines, two chairs, and a larger table clogged with material, spools of thread, and other supplies.

"I don't do much quilting now since my eyes aren't what they used to be." *Mammi* sat down in one of the chairs. "Also, I have terrible arthritis in my hands. It's awful to get old, Maggie." She clucked her tongue. "I don't recommend it."

Maggie giggled again, and warmth filled Leanna's chest.

Mammi laughed and then pointed to the pile of quilts. "Those are some I've made. I'm planning to give them to my great-grandchildren this Christmas."

Maggie walked over to the table and touched the top quilt. "This is *schee*." She held up the Log Cabin design bursting with deep purples and blues. "I love it. The stitching is so careful and small."

"*Danki.*"

Maggie studied the quilt and then looked over at *Mamm*. "Have you made a lot of Log Cabin quilts?"

Mamm nodded as she sat down in the empty chair. "I've made a few, but Erma is a much better quilter than I am." She nodded over at *Mammi*.

"Oh no." *Mammi* waved off the compliment. "You're just being nice, Rachelle."

Maggie turned back to the stack of quilts and touched another one. "This one is just breathtaking. Tell me about it, please."

Leanna sat on the edge of one of the sewing tables as Maggie and *Mammi* continued to discuss the quilts. She smiled and hoped that Chester and Emory were having just as much fun in the barn.

Later *Mammi* invited Maggie, *Mamm*, and Leanna to join her for cookies and lemonade on her front porch.

"I would love to see one of your quilts someday," *Mammi* told Maggie as they sat beside each other in rocking chairs.

Leanna picked up a peanut butter cookie from the table beside her, then kicked her feet beneath her on the porch swing. "Maggie also makes pillows, dolls, and other pretty things."

"Is that so?" *Mammi* turned toward Maggie, who nodded. "Well, I'd love to see those too."

"Maybe Maggie can bring one of her crafts to show us the next time she comes to see us," said *Mamm*.

"Oh, I would love that," *Mammi* said as she lifted her glass of lemonade. "I made a few dolls when Leanna and her cousins were younger, but I seemed to do a better job at making quilts."

Leanna shook her head. "Well, I still have the doll you made me. I love it, *Mammi*. Salina, Bethany, and Christiana still have theirs too."

"What did your dolls look like, *Mammi*?" Maggie asked, and then she blushed. "Is it okay if I call you *Mammi*?"

Mammi placed her wrinkled hand on Maggie's. "Of course it is, *mei liewe*."

Leanna's heart turned over in her chest. How she loved seeing Maggie bond with her grandmother! She wondered if Chester and Emory were getting along, too, both together and with her *dat*. If so, could Emory and Maggie become permanent fixtures in her life?

She sipped more lemonade as she imagined what that would be like. Perhaps as time passed, he and Maggie would want to spend more time with Leanna and her family. The idea sent a little thrill racing through her veins.

She took another bite of the cookie and peered out toward the row of her father's barns just as *Dat*, Chester, and Emory stepped out of Chester's workshop. *Dat* looked over toward *Mammi*'s house, and then pointed. *Mamm* waved, and he returned the gesture as the three men started toward them.

Mamm stood. "I'll go get three more glasses of lemonade."

"Do you need help?" Leanna offered.

"No, no. You sit with your guests."

"Hello, there," sang *Mammi* when the men reached the porch. "Who's this young man?"

"This is *mei dat*," Maggie said.

"I'm Emory." He reached his hand out to *Mammi*.

"Nice to meet you. I'm Erma, Walter's *mamm*." *Mammi* shook his hand, then gave Leanna a sideways glance before looking back at him. "We've had a nice time discussing quilting with your lovely *dochder*. Please join us for some lemonade and *kichlin*."

"*Danki*." Emory looked over at Leanna. "May I join you?"

"*Ya*, of course." Leanna scooted over on the porch swing.

Emory sank down beside her, and she flinched when his leg rubbed against hers. "Your *dat* and Chester have given me an excellent tour."

Mamm returned with three glasses of lemonade and another plateful of cookies. She handed a glass to each of the men and then took a seat in a rocker beside *Dat* while Chester leaned back against the railing in front of him. He and *Dat* fell into a conversation about the farm while the women picked up where they'd left off.

Emory took a long drink of lemonade and then swiped a cookie from the plate. He turned toward Leanna on the swing. "It looks like Maggie's having a *gut* time."

"*Ya*, she is. She really took to *Mammi*."

Then Emory leaned close to Leanna and lowered his voice. "I offered Chester a job."

"What?" Leanna sucked in a breath, trying to ignore the way his voice close to her ear sent a thrill through her.

"He showed me his wood shop, and I was so impressed by his birdhouses. He told me he'd rather be a carpenter than work at the hardware store. I actually have an opening at my shop, and I need another carpenter."

Leanna angled her body toward him as surprise continued to waft over her. "Are you serious?"

He grinned. "Why wouldn't I be? He's worried he doesn't have enough experience, but he already knows how to work with wood. *Mei bruder*, Lee, and I can teach him the rest."

"Emory, I . . ." She shook her head as happiness filtered through her. "I don't even know what to say."

"Well, now you need to convince him to say yes. He said he'd think about it and talk to you." He looked over toward Chester again. "I know he's unhappy at the hardware store. He said his *dat* taught him how to make the birdhouses, so maybe woodworking can be a way for him to keep his *dat* in his heart. The same seems to be true with Maggie and her sewing. Maybe working as a carpenter can help Chester cope with his grief."

Leanna nodded as hope ignited in her chest, and she quelled the urge to hug him. "*Danki*, Emory."

"*Gern gschehne*. I just hope he takes the job." He nodded out toward the barns. "I love it out here."

"What's going on out here?" *Daadi* appeared in the doorway with a wide smile. "Oh, we have guests." Although he sported thinning white hair and wrinkles, *Daadi*'s bright, intelligent blue eyes and quick wit made him seem much younger.

"Get out here, Sylvan," *Mammi* ordered, and everyone laughed. "I told you you were missing out by taking your *gegisch* after-supper naps!"

Leanna appreciated how *Daadi* and *Mammi* continued to tease and enjoy each other.

Dat stood and gestured at his rocking chair. "Come out here and join us, *Dat*. Meet our new *freinden*, Emory and Maggie."

He turned to Emory as *Daadi* stepped out onto the porch. "This is *mei dat*, Sylvan."

"So nice to meet you." Emory leaned over and shook his hand.

"I'll get you a glass of lemonade," *Mamm* said.

Soon *Daadi* was drinking lemonade, eating cookies, and joking with the rest of them. Emory laughed as he talked with her parents and grandparents. Maggie and Chester also smiled when they joined in as well.

The evening seemed to come to a close too soon as the sun began to set, lighting up the sky in an explosion of bright orange and yellow. Disappointment filled Leanna when Emory stood and faced her.

"It's getting late, so I suppose we should get going. It's been such a pleasure meeting you all." Emory shook her father's hand and then moved down the line to her mother and grandparents. "*Danki* for having us."

"We enjoyed it too," *Dat* said, and *Mamm* and her grandparents agreed.

Emory turned to Leanna. "Would you please walk us to the buggy?"

"Of course," she said, her cheeks warming beneath his gaze as they strode across the field.

Emory had stowed his horse in the barn earlier during his tour of the farm. He hitched up the horse while Maggie hurried into Leanna's house to retrieve her pie plate.

After his horse was ready, Emory turned to face her. "*Danki* for inviting us over. I really had a great time."

"I did too."

He held out his hand, and when she shook it, heat danced up her arm.

"Talk to Chester about the job," he said.

"I will."

Maggie appeared behind her. "*Danki* for having us. I had fun."

"I did too," Leanna told her. "And *danki* for bringing the pie. Be safe going home."

Once Emory and Maggie's horse and buggy had disappeared from the driveway, Leanna headed into the house and found her mother sitting at the kitchen table.

"That went well," *Mamm* said.

"You don't even know the half of it." Leanna sat down across from her. "Emory offered Chester a job because he saw his talent with his birdhouses. I can't believe it."

Mamm gave her a knowing smile. "Emory is a *gut* man, and it's obvious he cares about you and Chester. The Lord has blessed you with his friendship."

"I know."

"I can't wait to see what the Lord has in store for Emory and you."

Leanna's hands trembled as she nodded.

CHAPTER 11

"D id you have a nice time?" Emory asked Maggie as he guided the horse onto Old Philadelphia Pike in Bird-in-Hand.

"I did." Maggie's smile was bright in the light of his lantern in the buggy. "Leanna's *mammi* is so talented. I loved seeing her quilts. And she was so funny! Her sewing room was full of quilts and fabric. Rachelle was sweet too. She and *Mammi* said she'd like for me to bring some of my crafts over to show them."

Emory couldn't help but smile as he watched the excitement dance over Maggie's face. This was just what she'd needed!

Maggie wasn't the only one who had enjoyed herself. He had enjoyed seeing Leanna, who seemed different tonight. She'd looked even prettier than usual, and she'd seemed more relaxed around him. More than once he was certain he'd seen her blush, and she had looked adorable. He longed to sit next to her on the porch swing all evening so that they could have more time to talk. Perhaps they would have more time together in the future.

"*Dat?*"

"*Ya*, Maggie?" Emory looked over at his *dochder*, who was staring at him.

"Did you hear what I said?"

"No." He gave a little laugh. "I was lost in my thoughts."

Maggie frowned. "Are you okay?"

"Of course I am. Now, what did you ask me?"

"Did you enjoy your time with Chester?"

"I did. I found out he likes to work with wood, so I offered him a job."

"Why would you do that?"

"We need the help at the shop, and I think it would be *gut* for Chester since he's unhappy working at the hardware store."

Maggie's expression became incredulous. "Did you offer him a job because you like Leanna?"

Emory was speechless for a moment. "No. I offered him a job because I like Chester and need the help. And by the way, I'm not planning to ask Leanna to be my girlfriend. So you can breathe easy, Maggie."

Maggie was silent for a moment, and he could almost hear her churning thoughts.

"I feel called to help Chester," Emory explained. "He lost his *dat* like you lost your *mamm*."

She nodded. "I understand."

Emory felt the tension in his shoulders relax as they continued down Old Philadelphia Pike and he recalled his conversation with Chester. He looked forward to hearing Chester's response to his job offer.

And more than that, he looked forward to seeing Leanna again.

. . .

Leanna hummed to herself as she headed down the stairs the following morning. She slowed her steps when she heard her father and son talking at the breakfast table.

"I think I want to take it," Chester said. "I thought about it and prayed about it last night, and I feel like it's a *gut* choice."

"That sounds like a great decision," *Dat* responded.

"I agree," *Mamm* said.

"*Gude mariye*," Leanna sang as she stepped into the kitchen and took her usual seat across from Chester. The table was cluttered with platters of pancakes, bacon, and home fries, along with a carafe of coffee. She looked at her mother. "Everything smells *appeditlich*. I'm sorry I overslept. I meant to get down here earlier, but I forgot to set my alarm."

Mamm shrugged. "It's no problem."

Leanna bowed her head for a silent prayer and then reached for the pancakes. She divided a look between her son and father. "What were you all talking about when I came downstairs?"

"Emory offered me a job last night," Chester said as he lifted his mug of coffee.

"Is that so?" Leanna hoped her shock sounded convincing. "What did he say?"

Chester's expression brightened. "He said my work with the birdhouses was enough experience to get started at his shed business."

"That is *wunderbaar*!" Leanna peered at her mother. "Don't you think so, *Mamm*?"

Mamm beamed with pride. "I do!"

"Emory told me to think about it." Chester looked at *Dat*. "But I want to take the job."

"It would be a great opportunity." *Dat* refilled his coffee cup as he spoke. "You've already figured out that you don't like farming, and you're not a fan of retail. Building the birdhouses brings you joy, so the Lord could be opening this door for you."

Leanna smeared butter onto her pancakes and then dripped syrup over the top. "I agree." She bit her lip, longing to say more but not wanting to overwhelm Chester.

Chester looked down at his half-eaten stack of pancakes, which had been smothered in butter and syrup, the way he enjoyed them most. "I'll make a final decision by the end of today."

Leanna's heart leapt. "I'm proud of you, Chester. I bet Emory would be a fantastic mentor and boss."

Mamm gazed over at Leanna and gave her a warm smile that seemed to hold a hidden meaning.

"You'll have to give notice at your job at the hardware store," *Dat* said.

"I know." Chester nodded.

Dat smiled. "I think this will be *gut*."

Leanna nodded. "I do too."

. . .

"You're awfully chipper today. I guess you had a nice supper last night at Leanna's *haus*," Justin commented as Emory whistled on his way to put his lunch box into the propane refrigerator in the shop's break room.

The small room at the back of the building included a counter with a sink, a small table with four chairs, cabinets, a refrigerator, and a doorway that led to the bathroom.

"I did have a nice time." Emory set the lunch box on the top shelf of the refrigerator and then smiled at Justin. "We had a delicious supper and then spent time with Leanna's parents and grandparents." He leaned on one of the chairs.

"Interesting." Justin rubbed his dark brown beard that had

just recently started boasting a shimmering of gray hairs. "Sounds like you and Leanna are getting to know each other."

"We are, and I'm enjoying getting to know her family too. Chester likes woodworking, so I offered him a job here."

Justin's dark eyebrows careened toward his hairline. "What kind of woodworking does he do?"

"He likes to build birdhouses."

"He builds birdhouses?" His younger brother's brow furrowed. "That's it?"

"*Ya*. He has real potential."

"Potential? You mean he doesn't have experience."

Emory crossed his arms over his chest. "He doesn't like his job at the hardware store, and he obviously has some basic skills. We're supposed to help others in our community, right? So why not give him a chance?"

Justin's eyes narrowed as he pointed a finger at Emory. "Is this about helping Chester, or is this just a way for you to get to Leanna?"

"Hold on." Emory held his hands up. "This is about Chester. Leanna has had problems with him, and I want to help them. I know what it's like to feel lost while raising a child alone."

Justin pursed his lips. "Just remember this is our livelihood that *Dat* built for us, and we need to protect it."

"I know that, and I respect this business and the opportunity it has given us to take care of our families. *Dat* gave us a chance. I want to do the same for Chester. I'll train him."

Justin shook his head. "I would love to see you settle down and find a *mamm* for Maggie, but don't use Chester to get there."

Emory's jaw clenched as his temper flared. "I'm offended you would even suggest I'd use someone's child to get a *fraa*.

And besides, I don't even know if Chester will take the job." He marched past Justin into the shop, his gut tied in a knot as he contemplated his brother's words.

"*Gude mariye*, *Onkel* Emory!" Lee grinned as he looked over from a shed he was hammering. His smile faded and he stood up straight. "*Was iss letz?*"

"Nothing." Emory scrubbed his hand down his beard and then took a deep breath, despite the anger still simmering under his skin. "Do you need any help over there?"

"Sure."

As Emory walked over to his nephew, he tried to take charge of his reaction toward his brother. Did Justin have a point? Perhaps offering a job to someone who didn't have shed-building experience was a bad business decision.

Still, Emory couldn't let go of the idea that he was supposed to help Chester and Leanna. In fact, he could feel it to the depth of his bones, as if the Lord himself had put the thought in his mind.

And he refused to second-guess it.

. . .

Leanna hummed as she stepped into her booth later that morning and set her purse and tote bag on the counter. The delicious aroma of Bethany's donuts and coffee permeated Leanna's booth and made her stomach gurgle with delight.

When she heard a chorus of meows, she turned as Lily and Daisy scampered in to greet her.

"*Gude mariye!* Did Bethany feed you?"

The cats meowed again as they rubbed on her legs.

"I guess not, huh? Or are you fibbing?" When the cats

meowed again, Leanna chuckled. "Well, I think I have some treats back here."

She found a bag of cat treats and gave each of them two. The cats ate them and then trotted off toward the used book booth to continue making their morning rounds in search of food.

Leanna shook her head and then began straightening the jars of jams and jellies on her shelves.

"So? How did last night go?"

Leanna turned toward the familiar voice. "*Gude mariye*, Bethany! We have some time before the market opens. Why don't we grab a cup of *kaffi* and talk?"

"Perfect."

Leanna followed Bethany into her booth and read the coffee specials on the blackboard. "Oh, you made my favorite today! Cookies and cream. I'll take a cup of cookies and cream and a vanilla donut with sprinkles."

"Coming right up." Bethany retrieved the coffee and donut and handed them to Leanna.

After Leanna paid, she picked up a handful of creamers and sweetener packets and took a seat at one of the empty tables. Leanna relished these quiet moments before the market opened when she could talk with her cousin in private, when they could catch up on each other's news without interruption. She missed the days when Salina and Christiana were with them too.

Bethany gripped her cup of coffee. "Tell me everything."

"We had a great visit!" Leanna shared how they ate supper and then the men went out to the barn while the women visited with *Mammi*. "Maggie likes crafts, so I thought she'd enjoy seeing *Mammi*'s quilts."

"Oh, I bet *Mammi* loved having visitors." Bethany took a sip of her coffee.

"She did." Leanna couldn't stop her grin. "But the best part was that Emory offered Chester a job."

"What?"

"Emory saw the birdhouses Chester makes and then offered him a job at his shed business. Sounds like Chester is going to take the job. He said he would decide by the end of today."

Leanna broke her donut into pieces. "Chester told me that making birdhouses helps him feel closer to Marlin, so maybe working as a carpenter would help him work through his grief and make him feel better. This job offer feels like a real blessing, and I'm praying Chester will take it." She took a bite and savored the warm, cakey donut.

"Isn't it amazing how God works in our lives? Emory seems like a *wunderbaar* man."

Leanna nodded. She couldn't wait to see him again, but then a twinge of worry started at the base of her neck. What if she was getting too close to Emory? She wasn't looking for a relationship, and getting too close to him would only run her the risk of winding up with a broken heart. Plus, Chester had made it clear that he didn't want her to date, and her relationship with him was fragile enough without adding a man into her life.

Bethany suddenly sat up straight, and her trademark smile evaporated as she looked at something over Leanna's shoulder.

"*Gude mariye*," Sara Ann sang as she sashayed into the Coffee Corner.

"Hi, Sara Ann," Bethany said, her words flat.

Leanna lifted her hand in a limp wave. "Hi."

Her mind clicked through all of the problems Sara Ann

had caused for Bethany and Micah when they were first getting to know each other. She had wedged between them by trying to date him herself, and even worse, she had spread gossip about Micah that caused him to be shunned. While Leanna believed it was the Amish way to forgive, she would never trust Sara Ann or forget how much pain she'd caused her cousin.

Sara Ann approached their table. "Did I see Emory Speicher here again yesterday?"

Leanna felt her back go ramrod straight. "You did."

"How interesting." Sara Ann's pretty gray eyes homed in on Leanna. "Are you dating him?"

"No. We're just acquaintances."

"Huh. His *fraa*, Sheryl, was just lovely. She was tall, taller than I am. And she had beautiful blond hair and dark eyes. She was such a talented quilter. Almost as *gut* as I am." Sara Ann tittered. "Such a shame what happened to her. A real tragedy. She and Emory always seemed so in love when I saw them together."

Leanna looked at Bethany, whose eyes had narrowed.

"Did you want a cup of *kuffi*, Sara Ann?" Bethany hopped down from her stool and started toward the counter.

Sara Ann followed her. "*Ya*, please. I'll take a cup of cookies and cream and a chocolate-covered donut."

Bethany served up Sara Ann's coffee and donut and then took her money. Leanna stayed put on her stool, holding her breath as Sara Ann made her way to the condiment stand and added creamer before grabbing a lid.

"You two have *gut* sales today," Sara Ann called as she exited the booth.

Bethany climbed up on the stool again and glowered. "I know

it's unchristian to say, but I would love to see her close up her booth and stay out of our lives. Her behavior has proven her intentions are never *gut*."

"I wholeheartedly agree." Leanna lifted her cup in a toast, and Bethany touched her cup against it.

CHAPTER 12

H ow was your day?" *Mamm* asked Leanna later that evening.
    "*Gut.*" Leanna set her tote bag and purse on the counter and began to wash her hands in the sink. "The booth stayed busy." She nodded over to where *Mamm* pulled a pan of baked chicken from the oven. "The kitchen smells wonderful."

"*Danki.*"

Leanna pulled a pile of dishes from the cabinet and utensils from the drawer and began setting the table while *Mamm* moved the chicken from the pan to a platter. "How was your day?"

Mamm smiled. "Nice and busy, which is how I like it. I got quite a few chores done here. You know, the usual—sewing, cleaning, and cooking."

Leanna crossed to the counter and picked up a basket of rolls and a bowl of green beans and set them on the table beside the chicken while *Mamm* set out glasses and then retrieved a pitcher of water.

The meal was served and ready when *Dat* and Chester walked into the kitchen.

Leanna's heart warmed when she spotted a smile on Chester's face. "Chester. It looks like you had a *gut* day."

Chester smiled at her as he washed his hands. "I did."

Dat kissed *Mamm*'s cheek on his way to the sink. "Everything looks *appeditlich*, Rachelle."

"*Danki*, Walter." *Mamm* made a sweeping gesture toward the table. "We're ready for supper."

After the men had washed and dried their hands, they all sat down to eat. They bowed their heads in silent prayer and began to fill their plates with the delicious meal.

"I've made a decision," Chester announced as he slipped a chicken breast onto his plate.

"Oh?" *Mamm* asked.

Leanna sucked in a deep breath. "What did you decide?"

Chester sat up straighter. "I'm going to take the job working for Emory."

"That's *wunderbaar!*" *Dat* clapped his hands.

Leanna and her mother shared a smile. "I'm so *froh* to hear this." She touched Chester's shoulder. "Did you speak to your boss?"

"I did." Chester added a pile of green beans to his plate. "He said he has enough staff to cover my hours, which means today was my last day at the store. He also wished me well in my new career."

Dat smiled. "I had a feeling Henry would understand."

"I'll go tell Emory tomorrow." Chester's smile seemed to falter. "I just hope I can live up to his expectations."

Mamm patted his hand. "I'm certain you will. He sees potential in you."

"Your *Mammi* is right. You will do great." Leanna smiled at him and silently thanked God for Emory's vote of confidence in her *sohn*.

• • •

The next morning Emory set his hammer down on his work-bench when he heard the bell in the front office ring. He turned toward where Justin and Lee worked on a nearby shed. "I'll go see who it is."

Emory stepped out into the front office and found Chester examining a poster featuring all of their sheds. "Chester. How are you doing this fine Saturday morning?"

"Hi, Emory." Chester walked over to the counter. He appeared nervous, and Emory was almost certain he could detect the faint smell of cigarettes clinging to his clothes. "I've been thinking about your job offer."

"And?" Emory asked.

"And I'd like to accept it."

Emory rubbed his hands together. "That's just great. I'm so glad to hear it. When can you start?"

"As soon as Monday. My boss at the hardware store said he has enough staff to take over my shifts."

"That's fantastic!" Emory shook his hand. "Why don't we discuss your salary and schedule?" He shared the salary and their hours of operation, which Chester agreed to. "Now, come out back so you can meet *mei bruder* and *bruderskind*."

Emory beckoned for Chester to follow him into the shop, where Justin and Lee were hunched over a shed floor, hammering it.

"Justin! Lee!" Emory called over the hammering, and it stopped. "Come meet Chester Speicher." His brother and nephew stood and crossed the shop. "Chester, this is *mei bruder*, Justin, and his *sohn*, Lee."

"So nice to meet you." Justin shook his hand. "We've heard quite a bit about you."

"Chester has decided to accept my offer and start working for us," Emory announced.

Lee grinned and divided a look between Emory and Justin. "Really?"

"*Ya*, that's right." Emory held his brother's gaze, expecting Justin to frown, but he held a pleasant expression. "He'll start on Monday."

"That's great!" Lee said. "Have you built sheds before?"

Chester looked nervous. "No, I haven't."

"I'm going to train him," Emory said.

Lee waved off Chester's worried look. "You don't need to fret. *Mei dat* and *Onkel* Emory are great teachers. You'll learn everything you need to know in no time."

"If you say so." Chester's stiff posture seemed to relax slightly.

"We'll see you Monday then," Justin said.

"Enjoy your weekend," Lee added.

Chester shook their hands again. "*Danki.*"

"I'm so glad you came to this decision," Emory said as he walked Chester back to the lobby. "We'll see you at eight on Monday?"

"I'll be here. *Danki*, Emory." Chester wrenched the door open.

"Tell your *mamm* hello for me."

Chester nodded. "I will." Then he headed back out into the morning sun.

Emory turned toward the counter and found his brother watching him from the doorway.

Justin frowned as he crossed his arms over his chest. "I hope you didn't just make a mistake."

"Have faith, Justin. I do." As Emory pushed past him toward the workshop, he once again had an overwhelming feeling that God had led him to hire Chester. And he was certain to the depth of his soul that it was not a mistake.

. . .

Leanna sat in a rocking chair on her parents' porch Sunday afternoon and sipped on iced tea. She peered out over her mother's garden and took in the colorful flowers smiling up at the hot afternoon July sun while birds sang in nearby trees.

Since it was an off-Sunday without a church service, her favorite cousins and their families, along with their parents and siblings, had gathered to spend the afternoon at Leanna's parents' house. She enjoyed these restful Sunday afternoons with her cousins after a busy few days at the marketplace.

While their mothers talked in the kitchen, the men gathered by the barn. And Leanna and her cousins rocked on the porch with *Mammi*.

"I heard Chester starts a new job tomorrow," *Mammi* said as she picked up a chocolate chip cookie from her plate sitting on the little table next to her rocker.

Christiana, who was rocking Angelie in her arms, turned toward Leanna. Kaylin and Karrie were napping in Leanna's parents' room. "A new job?"

"What?" Salina asked at the same time as her dark eyebrows rose.

"He took the job with Emory?" Bethany blurted out before clapping. "I'm so *froh* to hear this!"

Salina's brow furrowed as she exchanged a confused look with Christiana. "What are we missing out on here?"

"Hang on. I'll explain." Leanna held her hand up. "Emory offered Chester a job working at his shed business, and Chester accepted. He starts tomorrow."

Salina gasped as Christiana began asking questions.

"Is this the same Emory you met at the police station?" Christiana asked. "He has the *dochder* that's the same age as Chester, right?"

Mammi sat forward in her chair. "The police station? I thought Emory was that handsome man who came for supper."

"Came for supper?" Salina held her hand up. "Hold on! I think Christiana and I have missed a lot."

Leanna felt her cheeks heat as her cousins and grandmother looked at her. "*Mammi*, I did meet him at the police station." Then she explained how Chester and Maggie had gotten into trouble the night they had trespassed.

"Oh my," *Mammi* said. "Your *dat* didn't share that." Then she pressed her lips together. "Unless, of course, your *daadi* forgot to tell me. He's been known to do that."

Leanna and her cousins chuckled. Then Leanna turned to Salina and Christiana. "Emory came to see me at the market on Thursday, and I invited him and Maggie to come for supper. We had a lovely time." She explained how she took Maggie to meet *Mammi* while Chester showed Emory his workshop. And she told them how Emory asked him if he wanted to be a carpenter. "Chester talked to his boss on Friday and then met with Emory on Saturday. And he starts his new job tomorrow. I'm hoping this is what Chester needs to finally find what makes him *froh*. He needs something to ground him."

"Leanna," Salina started slowly. "This is amazing. You've finally found someone for you and Chester."

Christiana rocked and rubbed Angelie's back. "Exactly. Sounds like you and Emory are perfect for each other. He's giving Chester a new career, and I'm certain Maggie enjoyed spending time with you and *Mammi*."

Mammi's smile was wide. "I thought Emory was perfect for Leanna too."

"See?" Bethany chimed in. "I told you."

"If *Mammi* says it, then it's definitely true," Christiana added.

Leanna felt a sting of frustration. "I've told you before that we're just *freinden*. Why do you all have to jump to these conclusions? Isn't it possible for a man and a woman to just be *freinden*?"

"Leanna, what are you afraid of?" Christiana asked.

Although Christiana's question was simple, it stumped Leanna into blinking in response. "Why do you think I'm afraid?"

"Because it sounds like you won't even entertain the idea of dating him." Christiana shifted Angelie to her other shoulder, and the child only snored in response.

"I think I'm meant to be alone. I feel it in my heart."

Salina shifted in her rocker to face Leanna. "But what if Emory is the one you're supposed to be with, and you reject him?"

"After Marlin passed, I never expected to find love again." Leanna sipped her iced tea and then picked up an oatmeal raisin cookie.

Mammi shook a gnarled finger at Leanna. "All things are possible with the Lord."

"Exactly," Salina said.

"You need to listen to *Mammi*," Bethany chimed in.

Leanna sighed and looked out toward the barn where the men talked and laughed.

"Salina," *Mammi* began, "how are you feeling?"

"*Gut*, but tired."

While her cousins moved on to the subject of Salina's pregnancy, Leanna tried to imagine the Speichers as a part of her family—Emory spending time with the men while Maggie sat on the porch with Leanna, her cousins, and their little ones.

But that seemed so unlikely—a fantasy, a silly dream—when Leanna couldn't even imagine falling in love again after so long.

She believed that all things were possible with God, but would God grant an answer to a prayer Leanna hadn't even spoken?

. . .

The following morning, Emory stepped into the kitchen and found two bowls of oatmeal and blueberries and two cups of coffee sitting on the table.

"*Gude mariye*," he sang to Maggie as he pulled up a chair. "*Danki* for this *appeditlich* breakfast."

"*Gern gschehne*."

After a silent prayer, they dug into their food.

"So, Maggie," Emory began, "what's on your agenda today?"

She wiped her mouth with a napkin. "I was going to take care of the laundry, make a shopping list, do some cleaning, and continue preparing for hosting church at our *haus* on Sunday."

"I can help you with the chores for church. I don't expect you to do it all."

"What's on your agenda for today?"

Emory swallowed more oatmeal and then sipped his coffee. "Chester starts today."

Maggie stopped and her eyes widened. "He accepted the job?"

Emory nodded and then drank more coffee.

"Will we see Leanna again?"

Emory tilted his head, surprised by the question. "Do you want to?"

"She was nice." Maggie shrugged and seemed to avert her eyes by staring at her cup of coffee.

Emory scooped more oatmeal. "Why didn't you go to youth group yesterday?"

Maggie shrugged again and drank more coffee.

"It's *gut* to spend time with people your own age."

"We have so much to do this week," Maggie said. "I need to weed my garden and make sure the bathrooms are spotless. Not to mention, the men will be here with the benches later this week, so we have to make sure the barn is swept out."

Emory huffed a breath. Maggie was avoiding the subject of her lack of a social life again. "I will be here to help you this week, Maggie. You don't need to carry the load for me."

As Maggie continued to talk about chores, Emory tried to think of a way to get through to her. He wondered if perhaps she needed to hear it from another woman. And as the thought crossed his mind, he asked himself: Could Leanna be the one to help her get out of this rut? To see the value of youth and friendship and carefree time spent with friends? The idea settled over him as he finished breakfast and then headed to work.

CHAPTER 13

Emory arrived at work a few minutes early and found *Dat* in the office sifting through a stack of invoices. "*Gude mariye, Dat.*"

"How are you today?" *Dat* peered at him over his reading glasses.

"*Gut.*" Emory sank down into the chair in front of his father's desk. "You remember how you recommended we hire some help?"

"*Ya.*"

"I have a new employee starting today."

Dat's smile was wide. "Who is he?"

"He's the young man I met at the police station. Remember when Maggie was picked up for trespassing?"

"Of course I do."

Emory quickly explained how he had gotten to know Chester and his mother and about Chester's hobby birdhouses. "He loves to work with wood, and I feel like this job would help him cope with losing his *dat.*"

"That's *wunderbaar.*"

"You think so? Because Justin doesn't agree."

"Why not?"

Emory paused. "Justin thinks I'm making a mistake hiring

someone who has never built a shed, but I feel God leading me toward this decision. The *bu* has potential, and I feel it's more important to help someone right now than to worry about experience. We all had to learn."

Dat rubbed his graying beard and nodded. "I agree with you. If you think this young man is promising, then I trust you. Justin will come around when he sees Chester doing *gut* work."

"*Danki.*" Emory stood.

"I look forward to meeting him."

Emory nodded and then walked out to the front of the shop as Chester walked in holding a small cooler. "*Gude mariye!*"

"Hi, Emory." Chester raised his hand in a wave.

"How was your weekend?"

"*Gut.*"

Emory shook his hand. "Did you have a nice Sunday?"

"*Ya*, it was an off-Sunday, so our family came over to visit."

"It was our off-Sunday too. How's your *mamm*?"

Chester hesitated and then nodded. "She's fine."

"Great." Emory patted his shoulder. "Are you ready to get to work?"

"*Ya.*"

"Let me show you the break room, and then we'll go into the shop and get started." After Chester stowed his lunch in the refrigerator, Emory led him into the workshop and gave him a tour of the workbenches, explaining where the tools were located and where the job list could be found.

As Emory spoke, he noticed that Chester's expression began to relax.

"So," Emory said, "are you ready to learn how to build a shed?"

. . .

Leanna filled the last jar with apple cranberry jelly just as she heard footsteps on the basement stairs. *Dat* had built Leanna the second kitchen in the basement five years ago when her jam and jelly business had taken off.

She appreciated not only having a long counter and tables to spread out on when she worked but also having the second stove, sink, and refrigerator, and a wall of shelves to keep her stock organized. Although she had enough stock of the apple cranberry jelly to last about another month or two, Emory had been on her mind all day, inspiring her to make more of his favorite jelly.

"How's it going?" *Mamm* asked as she walked over to the counter.

"It's going well. I've finished making apple cranberry jelly and I'm going to start on strawberry jam next."

Mamm peered down at the jars. "Oh, it looks fantastic."

"Danki." Leanna sighed. "I can't stop thinking about Chester and praying he has a *gut* day. He just needs to find his way, and maybe a job he loves will help him do that."

"I'm certain that he will. He left here so excited this morning."

Leanna nodded. "I hope so."

"Why don't I help you with the strawberry jam?" *Mamm* rubbed her hands together.

Leanna gave her mother's shoulder a squeeze of gratitude. Then as she turned her attention back to the jelly, she sent up another prayer for Chester.

. . .

"Great job today," Emory told Chester as he walked him to the door later that evening. "You worked hard, and I appreciate your effort."

"*Danki* for showing me the ropes." Chester shook his hand. "I'll see you tomorrow."

"*Gut nacht.*" Emory waved as Chester headed outside.

"I think he's going to be a great employee," *Dat* said as he appeared behind the counter.

"I do too." Emory walked over to the counter and leaned on it. "He seems to be really interested in learning. I just hope someday he'll open up a bit more."

"What do you mean?"

"We had lunch together in the break room, and I felt like I was just babbling to him. He only nodded and gave me one-word answers when I asked him questions."

"He seems a little shy, but he'll get used to us."

Emory looked through the doorway, and his thoughts turned to his brother. Justin had been pleasant to Chester, but Emory could still detect the resentment in his brother's eyes. "Has Justin said anything to you about Chester?"

"No. Justin seemed fine all day."

Emory tapped the counter. "*Gut.* So far, so *gut.*"

• • •

Leanna and *Mamm* had supper sitting on the table when *Dat* and Chester came in later that evening. The delicious smells of turkey tenderloin, rice, and broccoli permeated the kitchen as Leanna set a pitcher of water in the center of the table.

"How was the new job?" Leanna asked Chester as he stood at the sink and washed his hands.

"*Gut*," he managed through a yawn.

"Do you like it more than the hardware store?"

He shrugged. "I guess so."

Leanna felt her lips press down into a frown as she peered over at her mother, who shook her head as if telling her not to give up hope.

"I'm glad you had a *gut* first day," *Dat* said as he took his turn washing his hands. "Jobs get easier the longer you do them."

Chester sank down into his usual spot across from Leanna and yawned again. "I hope so."

Leanna and her parents took their seats and bowed their heads in silent prayer before filling their plates with food.

"Tell us more about your first day, Chester," *Mamm* said, piling rice onto her plate.

Chester cut off a large piece of tenderloin. He had apparently worked up an appetite. "I got a tour of the shop, and then Emory started teaching me the basics of building a shed. We started with the floor. We're going to move on to the walls tomorrow."

"Emory trained you?" Leanna asked.

Chester nodded as he chewed.

"Is he a *gut* teacher?"

"He didn't make me feel stupid when I asked questions."

Leanna's heart swelled. She had gotten the impression that Emory was patient and kind—exactly the kind of mentor Chester needed. She had only known him for a short time, but Emory was already blessing her family left and right.

She stilled at the thought. Was Emory what *Chester* needed? Or did *she* need someone like Emory in her life too? Suddenly *Mammi*'s words and her cousins' urgings came back to her. Could Emory be more than a *freind*?

"Tell me more about your day," *Dat* said. "What are the dimensions of this shed you're building?"

As *Dat* and Chester talked on about the shed, Leanna lost herself in thoughts of Emory. Her feelings for him were morphing, and she would have been hard-pressed to deny it.

• • •

"We've all worked hard this week," Emory announced Friday morning as he stood in the middle of the workshop. "We finished two sheds, and they're on their way to the new owners. We're working great as a team. As a result, I think we deserve a break."

He looked around at Justin, Lee, and Chester, who all blinked at him with anticipation. Then Emory clapped his hands together. "So let's go to the Coffee Corner in the Bird-in-Hand marketplace for some *appeditlich kaffi* and donuts."

Lee grinned. "That sounds great, *Onkel* Emory."

Justin shrugged. "A break and a snack sounds *gut* to me. Let's clean up and then head out there."

While Justin and Lee headed toward the breakroom to wash their hands, Chester lingered behind, his expression unreadable. Was it confusion? Irritation? Suspicion?

Emory walked over toward where Chester stood by a large toolbox. "Do you want to go?"

"Sure. I just need to wash up," Chester said, moving past Emory toward the break room.

Emory rubbed at his beard-covered jaw.

After a short buggy ride, the men walked through the market to the Coffee Corner, where a line had already formed.

Emory peeked over toward the Jam and Jelly Nook. He

spotted Leanna talking to a young *English* woman with a golden blond ponytail and purple glasses. Leanna smiled as the woman spoke, and she looked pretty today clad in a dark green dress and a black apron.

"Blueberry, French toast, and coconut?" Justin read the coffee specials listed on the blackboard aloud and then looked over at Emory. "How do I choose?"

Emory nodded at him. "I've told you, the *kaffi* here is spectacular."

"And the donuts look just as *gut*." Lee rubbed his hands together. "I'm going to have a French toast *kaffi* and a cinnamon donut."

"That sounds *gut* to me too," his *dat* agreed.

Emory looked at Chester, who still wore the same unreadable frown. "How about you, Chester?" He pulled his wallet from his pocket. "My treat."

"I'll have the same." Chester's voice was flat.

"All right."

"*Gude mariye*," Bethany sang when they finally made it to the counter. "So nice to see you, Emory and Chester."

"*Gude mariye*," Emory echoed before introducing his brother and nephew. He placed their order and paid, then Bethany began handing the men their donuts and coffee.

Lee took a drink and grinned. "Wow. This is fantastic."

"How do you come up with your *kaffi* flavors?" Justin asked.

Bethany leaned on the counter. "I like to experiment with flavoring I find at a store."

"Which one is your favorite?" Lee asked.

Bethany shrugged. "I really don't have a favorite, but my husband's is peppermint mocha."

Emory peered over his shoulder toward the Jam and Jelly

Nook and saw Leanna stocking shelves. Then he looked at Justin. "I'm going to go say hello to Leanna."

"All right," Justin said. "We'll grab a table."

Emory picked up his coffee, wrapped his donut in the wax paper Bethany had provided, and headed toward the booth. He was grateful when he found it empty of customers. He walked over to where Leanna added another jar of strawberry jam to the shelf.

"Hi, Leanna."

Leanna pivoted toward him, and a wide smile lit up her pretty face. "Emory. What a nice surprise. What are you doing here?"

"I decided we needed a treat after working so hard all week." He held up his cup and donut and then nodded toward the Coffee Corner. "Chester, Lee, and Justin are over there. They're chatting with Bethany."

She peered over toward Bethany's booth, where the men sat around one of the high-top tables. Then she looked back at Emory. "*Danki* for giving Chester a chance."

He set his cup of coffee and donut on a shelf beside him. "*Gern gschehne.* He's doing well. He's learned a lot this week. Does he like it?"

"I think so." Leanna gave a little laugh. "He comes home exhausted every night."

He cringed. "I'm sorry to wear him out."

"No, it's *gut* for him, and he seems satisfied with his work. I heard him talking about it to *mei dat*, and it made me really *froh*."

Warmth curled in his chest, and his lips turned up again. "I'm thrilled to hear you're *froh*."

"How's Maggie doing?"

"Fine. We're hosting church on Sunday, so she has a list of chores a mile long. Of course, she thinks it's all her job, and I keep telling her I'll help when I get home. I'm taking tomorrow off to get everything ready."

"Preparing for church is a lot of work."

"It is." He pointed to the strawberry jam on the shelf behind her. "By the way, I'd love to try a jar of orange marmalade."

"Oh." She picked up one from a nearby shelf and handed it to him. "Do you need any others? I made strawberry jam and apple cranberry jelly this week."

He smiled. "You made my favorite?"

"I did." Was she blushing? "I can get you one of each."

"I'll just take the orange marmalade and another jar of strawberry." He read the label—Marlin's Strawberry Jam. And then he pulled his wallet out of his pocket.

"I can't take any money from you."

"Please take it." He held out a few bills. "You can't make a profit if you give your jam away for free. Just like I can't make a living if I give away my sheds."

She shook her head. "It's not the same. This is a gift for all you're doing for Chester."

"Fine." He shoved the bills back into his wallet and then slipped it into his pocket. "I appreciate it, Leanna."

She reached behind the counter for a little shopping bag, then slipped the jars into it. "You'll have to tell me what you think of it." Then Leanna looked past him and smiled. "Hello, *mei liewe*."

Emory gazed over his shoulder at Chester, who watched them with narrowed eyes. "Hey, Chester." He picked up his coffee and took a sip.

"How's your day going?" Leanna asked him.

"*Gut.*" Chester glanced at Emory. "Justin said we need to go since we have a lot of work to do today."

"Right. Would you please tell him I'll be there in a minute?"

Chester pursed his lips. "Sure," he said, turning to leave.

"Have a *gut* day, Chester," she called as he walked away.

Disappointment zipped through Emory as he took in Leanna's deflated expression. "It was *gut* seeing you. Have a *gut* day, and *danki* for the jam."

He slipped his donut into the bag with the jam and then turned to go.

"Emory." She took a step forward and touched his hand. "*Danki* for coming to see me today."

Heat rushed to the spot where her skin touched his, and the contact sent a warm glow through his body. "Of course. I'll see you soon."

And he hoped that was true.

CHAPTER 14

Emory could barely contain his smile as he weaved past a group of young Amish women pushing strollers and made his way toward the marketplace exit. He stepped outside into the humid July morning and stopped when he heard someone call his name. He spun and nearly walked into Chester, who stood glowering at him.

"Chester!" Emory took a step back from him. "I'm sorry. I didn't see you there."

"Why did you really want to come to the market this morning?"

Emory felt his eyebrows shoot up. "What do you mean?"

"Tell me the truth." Chester took a step toward him. "Did we only come here so that you could see *mei mamm*?"

Emory took in Chester's hard expression for a moment. Was *this* the source of the boy's irritation? That Emory might have romantic feelings for Leanna? Guilt pummeled Emory because he hadn't intended for Leanna to be anything more than a *friend* to him. At the same time, he couldn't deny the heat he'd just felt when she'd touched his hand. Something seemed to be developing between them.

But he couldn't risk ruining Chester's trust or his friendship.

Emory held up his cup. "I wanted a *gut* cup of *kaffi*, and your cousin serves the best. And we all deserved it since we worked hard this week. I'm staying home tomorrow to prepare for church at *mei haus* on Sunday, so this was the best day to do it. That was my thinking when I made this plan."

Chester's expression remained unconvinced. "*Mei mamm* is doing fine on her own. In fact, I heard her talking to our cousins last Sunday, and she said she's not looking for a relationship. She's not interested in dating. So I think it would be best if you two were just *freinden*."

"I understand and agree. I do consider her a *gut freind*." Emory smiled even as disappointment curled through him. He would never want to upset Chester or hurt his feelings.

Chester's warning had been clear. Now Emory had to figure out what to do with the spark of attraction for Leanna that had begun to set fire in his heart.

. . .

Emory stood by the barn Sunday morning, smiling and shaking hands with the men in the congregation as they arrived for the service. He tried his best not to grimace, even though every muscle in his body seemed to ache and exhaustion threatened to overtake him at any moment.

The house was as perfect as it could be in preparation for today. Maggie had scrubbed it from top to bottom, and her garden had no trace of weeds as the colorful flowers smiled and greeted the women making their way into the kitchen to gather before the service.

Emory leaned forward for a look into the barn, and his back and the knots in his shoulders responded with a painful twinge. He had spent all morning yesterday sweeping the inside, and he was grateful Justin and Lee had closed down the shop early to come help him set up the benches. Now he had to find the strength to keep smiling all day long.

Amid the line of congregation members walking toward the house and barns, he spotted Justin, Lee, and Natalie standing by an unfamiliar woman who looked to be in her midthirties. With blond hair and a bright smile, she laughed at something Natalie said. Together the women made their way toward the kitchen to visit with the other women in the congregation.

"*Gude mariye*," Justin said, walking over to Emory.

Emory grasped his brother's hand. "Thanks again for your help yesterday."

"*Gern gschehne.* You always help us when we host church, so I'm *froh* to help you." Justin pointed toward Natalie and the other woman walking toward the house. "Natalie convinced her *freind* to come to church with us today. She's anxious to meet you."

"What do you mean?" The muscles in Emory's jaw flexed.

"That's Madelyne. She's thirty-five and has never been married." He leaned in closer and lowered his voice. "She's still young enough to give you more *kinner.* Maybe you can have a *sohn.*"

Emory pushed him away. "Oh, come on. Quit pressuring me."

Justin's brow furrowed. "Why are you so opposed to dating again? We all agree that Maggie needs a *mamm*, and you need a *fraa* to help you."

Emory opened his mouth to protest just as a group of men approached them. He fastened a bright smile on his face and held out his hand. "*Gude mariye. Wie geht's?*"

Emory masked his irritation with his brother and sister-in-law and continued greeting the men until it was time to file into the barn for the service at nine. As he took a seat beside his brother in the married men's section and picked up his hymnal, Emory tried to focus on the Lord and prepare for worship.

But he couldn't stop dreading the introduction Natalie was about to foist upon him. How bold she was to bring her friend to church to meet him!

Maybe Natalie wouldn't make a big deal about introducing him to Madelyne, but trepidation filled him anyway. He knew he could count on Natalie to do just that.

. . .

Leanna walked into the Glicks' kitchen when the service ended and smiled and nodded at the other women preparing to carry trays of food into the barn for the men, who ate during the first shift of the noon meal. She had enjoyed the service this morning, sitting with her favorite cousins in the married women's section of the congregation.

While she treasured her Sundays, today she found thoughts of Emory lingering in the back of her mind. She hoped the service went well at his home. She kept wondering if he and Maggie had gotten their chores done yesterday and managed to have a restful night.

And she also kept contemplating how she had boldly touched his hand before he left her booth on Friday. She'd surprised herself when the impulse had seemed so natural.

Had she imagined the heat of that small touch? Or had he felt it too?

He had told her that he'd see her soon, something he wouldn't have said if she had behaved too forwardly. Her thoughts and feelings continued to scramble, and a strange wave of excitement skittered through her.

"Leanna, would you please take *kaffi* into the barn?" Marian Glick asked as she pointed toward the percolator.

"Of course." Leanna filled a coffee carafe and headed toward the door to return to the barn and fill cups.

She pushed open the back door and walked down the steps. The hot afternoon sun kissed her cheeks. She looked toward the barn and spotted *Mammi* hobbling along toward the house.

"Leanna!" *Mammi* waved. "I was looking for you."

Leanna quickened her pace to meet her. "You were?"

"*Ya.*" *Mammi* motioned for them to step away from the parade of women carrying trays of food into the barn. "I wanted to see how Chester's first week at the new job went."

"I think it he enjoyed it, and I'm so very grateful."

"*Gut.*" *Mammi* smiled. "Have you seen Emory again?"

Leanna couldn't stop her cheeks from heating, and she bit her lower lip. "*Ya.* He came to see me at the market on Friday."

"And?" *Mammi*'s blue eyes seemed to sparkle with mischief in the afternoon sunlight.

"And it was nice. He's so easy to talk to. I hope to see him again."

Mammi squeezed her hand. "The best relationships start out as friendships."

"I know." *But it feels like it's too good to be true.* She pointed the carafe toward the barn. "I'd better start filling cups before the *kaffi* gets cold."

Mammi nodded, and then Leanna made her way into the barn, where the men had already converted the benches into tables and were ready for their lunch.

As Leanna began working her way down the table filling cups, she once again thought of Emory. She said a silent prayer that he was enjoying his Sunday with his congregation and family and that God might see to it that their paths crossed again.

. . .

Emory stood by the barn as the youth in the congregation began dispersing to hitch up their horses and buggies to head out for the afternoon. He looked up on the porch and spotted Maggie sitting with his mother.

"Maggie," he called as he hurried over to the porch. "You should go with the youth today."

Maggie pulled at a loose thread on her apron and shook her head. "I don't think so."

Emory directed a pleading look at his mother.

"Your *dat* is right," *Mamm* said. "You should go."

Thank you, Mamm*!*

"You think so?" Maggie divided a look between them.

"I do," *Mamm* said.

Maggie stood up, and Emory tried to hide his grin as she made her way down the porch stairs to where he stood. Behind her, *Mamm* gave Emory a thumbs-up.

As Maggie approached him, apprehension filled her pretty face. "I think I should stay home. After all, I have to make supper for you."

Emory huffed out a breath. "Maggie . . ."

"No really." She held her hands up. "It's my job to make you supper."

He shook his head. "It's not, and I keep telling you that." He took her hand. "I can handle it. And it would make me very *froh* to see you go and have fun with your *freinden*."

"But *Mamm*—"

"Your *mamm* would want you to have fun." He nodded toward the young folks who were climbing into buggies and leaving. "Go." He spotted her friend Alea and pointed. "Catch up with Alea and try to enjoy yourself. Forget about your chores for the afternoon."

Maggie bit her lower lip and looked out toward her peers. Then she nodded. "Okay, if you say so."

"Great." Emory blew out a breath of relief. "I'll see you tonight."

Maggie hurried out toward her friends, and Emory grinned. *Please God, let her have fun and be safe!*

"Emory!"

He turned at the sound of Natalie's voice to see her and her friend walking toward him. Though he groaned inwardly, he tried his best to keep a neutral expression.

"I have someone I'd like you to meet." Natalie gestured between them. "Emory, this is *mei freind* Madelyne Swarey. And Madelyne, this is my brother-in-law, Emory."

"Nice to meet you." Emory held out his hand, and Madelyne shook it. When their hands met, he felt nothing—no spark, no heat. The contrast to the touch from Leanna's hand was a stark one.

"You too. I've heard a lot about you." Madelyne's smile was pretty, as were her green eyes.

"Oh no," Emory joked as he turned to Natalie. "I hope it wasn't only the bad stuff."

Natalie snorted. "If that were true, Madelyne wouldn't have come today."

Madelyne gave a little laugh. "I'm sure there aren't any bad things to say about you."

Emory folded his arms over his chest. "I have a feeling *mei bruder* wouldn't agree with that."

"Well, my siblings would certainly have plenty of interesting things to say about me too." Madelyne laughed again.

Natalie gave Emory a pointed look. "Madelyne helps take care of her nieces and nephews. She's *wunderbaar* with *kinner.*"

Emory held back an eye roll. He was not in the mood for this today. Frankly, he wouldn't be in the mood for Natalie pushing him toward romance on any day.

He gazed out over the driveway as a long line of horses and buggies began their trek down the road toward their homes. Then he looked back at Madelyne and wondered if she would leave soon too. Surely, Natalie didn't expect Emory to spend the afternoon keeping her company.

"I invited Madelyne to spend the afternoon with us," Natalie announced as if reading Emory's thoughts.

"Wunderbaar." Emory pointed toward the back door. "Why don't we go inside, and I'll put on some *kaffi.*"

"That sounds perfect," Natalie said.

Emory climbed the back porch and headed into the house, where the women had already finished cleaning up after the meal. He put on the percolator while Natalie pulled out a container of cookies Maggie had baked during the week.

Soon his parents, Natalie, Justin, and Madelyne were seated at the table. Emory handed each of them a mug of coffee.

Emory took a seat beside Madelyne, and she gave him a shy smile. He smiled halfheartedly in return, then poured creamer into his mug.

"Emory, I am so *froh* that Maggie went to youth group today," Natalie began. "I was telling Madelyne about how you've struggled with encouraging Maggie to spend time with *freinden* her age."

Emory pressed his lips together at his sister-in-law's words. What other private information had she shared about Maggie?

Natalie seemed to sense his frustration, for her eyes widened for a moment and then went back to normal. "Madelyne has some great ideas for ways to bring Maggie out of her shell."

"I do," Madelyne said, her voice soft and sweet. "I have a niece who is very shy, and I've been working with her to help her make more *freinden* at school. It seems to be working. I can tell you how I did it if you'd like."

Emory rubbed a spot on his neck as he considered his answer. While he appreciated Madelyne's concern, he didn't know her and wasn't ready to trust her with his worries about his precious daughter. On the other hand, he didn't want to embarrass himself or his family by responding rudely.

"Maybe some other time," he said, working to keep his tone gentle.

"Okay." Madelyne's smile was bright despite his dismissal. "Natalie told me Maggie likes to sew and quilt. I do too."

"That's nice," Emory said.

"What does your *dat* do, Madelyne?" *Dat* asked her.

"He's a carpenter. He builds furniture, such as bedroom suites, china cabinets, and dining room sets. He owns the business with a few of *mei bruders* and *onkels*."

Mamm's expression perked up. "How many siblings do you have?"

"Three *bruders* and four *schweschdere*." Madelyne picked up a cookie and took a bite.

"Really?" *Mamm* asked. "You must have quite a few *bruderskinner.*"

"I do. More than a dozen."

Mamm continued to pepper Madelyne with questions about her family. While Emory knew he should participate in the conversation, he was lost in his own thoughts. He worked to keep an interested expression on his face as he drank his coffee and nibbled on a cookie.

Lately, his thoughts wandered all too often toward Leanna. She seemed to already have embedded herself into his mind and now his heart, making it impossible for him to even consider this friend of Natalie's as a romantic prospect.

. . .

Later that afternoon, Emory heated a cheesy taco casserole Maggie had prepared the day before, and then served it for supper. The conversation continued on as Madelyne, Natalie, and *Mamm* talked sewing while Justin, *Dat*, and Emory discussed work.

After supper they enjoyed one of Maggie's peach cobblers and more coffee. When the sky had begun changing in the west, Emory's parents stood up.

"Well, it's getting late," *Dat* said. "We should head home."

"*Ya*, it is after seven," Justin agreed.

Madelyne pointed to the sink, where she had helped the women stack their dirty dishes. "Do you need help with the dishes?"

"Oh, no. *Danki*." Emory waved her off. "I can handle it." He held his breath, hoping Justin wouldn't volunteer him to take Madelyne home. What on earth would they talk about during their ride to her house? She seemed sweet and friendly, but he couldn't envision her becoming anything more than an acquaintance.

"Okay." Madelyne smiled, seeming satisfied with that. She lingered behind while his parents, brother, and Natalie padded outside through the mudroom. "I really enjoyed meeting you today."

"*Ya*. And you as well."

"I thought maybe we should get together again sometime since we have so much in common."

We do? "Sure." He started toward the door, and she followed him.

"What if I came over one night this week and brought supper for you and Maggie?"

Emory wasn't sure what he was feeling, but he panicked and agreed. "*Ya*," he said, only half listening as they walked down the porch to where his mother and Natalie waited for *Dat* and Justin to bring their horses and buggies.

"*Wunderbaar.*" Her pretty face lit up again. "I look forward to it."

His mother gave him a satisfied expression, but he ignored it. He was grateful when Justin and *Dat* arrived with the buggies and the women climbed in.

He waved as they disappeared down the lane, and he released a deep breath. He opened the door to his house, strode with heavy feet through the living room, then dropped onto the sofa. He had survived the day. Now he was ready to rest.

CHAPTER 15

"Tell me all about your new job, Chester," *Daadi* said as he sat across from Chester at Leanna's parents' table while the family ate supper Tuesday night.

Leanna shared a smile with *Mammi* as Chester took a bite of pot roast and wiped his mouth with a napkin.

"I like it. It's not as easy as I thought it would be. In fact, it's really challenging."

"What do you mean?" *Mammi* asked.

Chester shrugged and fixed his gaze down at his plate. "*Mei dat* was *gut* at woodworking, and I thought maybe the skills would come to me naturally. But it turns out I need to work hard at this. I just hope Emory doesn't regret hiring me."

"*Ach, mei liewe.*" Leanna's chest clutched at the frown on his face. "I doubt Emory would regret hiring you. Didn't you say you like working for him?"

Chester met her gaze. "I do. He's kind and patient, and I'm learning a lot every day."

"There you go! He obviously likes you if he's taking his time with you," *Mamm* chimed in.

Chester pressed his lips together. "I worry I'm letting him down, though. I'm not *gut* enough. What if he decides he should have hired a more experienced carpenter?" His low self-esteem nearly crushed Leanna's heart.

"Chester, look at me." She leaned over and placed a hand on his arm. "He hired you because he saw potential in you. Do you think my first jars of jelly came out perfectly?"

Chester gave her a half shrug.

"Were they perfect, *Mamm? Dat?*" Leanna grinned at her parents. "How were those first jars of jelly?"

Dat chuckled and shook his head. "I'll just say that they were quite sweet."

"Quite sweet is right!" *Mamm* cackled, and Leanna's grandparents joined in.

Leanna let out a relieved breath when Chester smiled too.

"I do remember that, *Mamm.*" Chester snorted. "I told you it was *gut* because I didn't want to hurt your feelings."

"I thought so!" Leanna wagged a teasing finger at him as they all laughed. Oh, how she loved to hear her son laugh again!

"So, Chester," *Daadi* began, "are you planning to join the baptism class next year with your *freinden*?"

When Chester paused for a moment, Leanna held her breath once again.

"I-I don't know," he stammered.

"What do you mean?" Leanna asked, her voice trembling.

"I'm just not sure." His gaze dropped to the half-eaten supper on his plate.

"Are your *freinden* going to join the class?" *Dat* asked.

"We haven't talked about it."

Leanna turned to *Mammi*, who gave her an encouraging smile. Then Leanna closed her eyes for a moment and sent up a silent prayer: *Please God, help Chester decide to be baptized and keep the Amish ways. Don't let his heart stray. He's all I have left.*

The remaining minutes of dinnertime were quiet. After everyone's plates were clean, they shared pieces of the chocolate pie *Mammi* had made earlier in the day. Then the men headed outside to sit on the porch while the women cleaned up the kitchen.

"Don't worry about Chester, Leanna," *Mammi* said as she washed a serving platter.

Leanna looked over from wiping down the table. "What do you mean, *Mammi*?"

"I could tell you were upset when he said he might not join the baptism class, but I'm certain he will."

"I agree with you." *Mamm* gave *Mammi* a knowing smile and then set the stack of clean dishes in the cabinet.

Leanna walked over to the counter. "I hoped that finding a job he enjoys would cure his unpredictable moods." She pointed to where he had sat at the table. "Yet he's still so down on himself. He sounds like a person who is very unhappy with this life." Her words nearly stole her breath. "Why do you both believe he'll be baptized and stay in the community?"

Mammi reached over and patted Leanna's forearm. "Because you are a *gut mamm*. He loves you, and you love him." She gestured toward *Mamm*. "He knows his whole family cares for him. He's young, but he'll realize this is where he belongs." She pointed to the floor. "This community is his home."

"God is *gut*," *Mamm* said.

"Exactly. Have faith. God knows what Chester needs and will find a way to lead him there." Then *Mammi* gave Leanna's hand a squeeze.

Leanna prayed her grandmother was right.

. . .

"You're doing a great job," Emory told Chester Wednesday morning as they worked together to build the walls for a small shed. "You're really getting the hang of this."

"Am I?"

Emory could see the self-doubt in Chester's hesitant expression. "*Ya*. I even think we'll have this one ready well before Saturday's delivery." He peered across the shop to where Justin and Lee worked on another small building. "We're keeping up with them, aren't we?"

Chester looked over at them and shrugged. "If you say so."

"I know so." Emory pointed to the wall they were building. "And if we don't waste time, we can finish even more before lunch."

They worked in silence for several moments, then Chester stopped hammering and turned toward Emory.

"*Mei dat* built fences."

"Your *mamm* told me." Emory swiped his hand across his sweaty brow.

"He was planning to open his own business before he died. *Mamm* once told me that he and his *freind* had found a shop, and they even had a name ready. They just needed to get money, and they were each planning to ask family members for a loan."

Emory rested his hammer on the workbench behind him.

"I remember the day he told me about building fences. It was the day we built that birdhouse I showed you." Chester looked down and fingered a piece of wood. "He said we would work together when I got older and he'd make me a business partner."

Emory's breath seized at the grief in the young man's brown eyes. "Oh, Chester."

Chester leaned against the wall they were building. "I feel closer to him when I'm working with wood."

"That makes sense." Emory patted his shoulder. "What do you say we finish this wall and then have lunch?"

Chester's expression relaxed. "Sounds *gut* to me."

"So, what else do you remember about your *dat*?" Emory asked, retrieving his hammer.

"He was tall like you and Justin," Chester said.

"You're almost my height."

Chester grinned. "*Ya*, and I'm hoping I'll be taller than you."

Emory chuckled. "You probably will be. I didn't stop growing until I was almost twenty. What else?"

"He was funny. Always cracking jokes. One time he had *mei mamm* laughing so hard at something that she wound up crying. At least that's what she told me."

Emory smiled as Chester continued sharing memories of his father. And for the first time since they'd met, he saw the young man opening up.

Maybe, just maybe, Chester would consider him a friend and a confidant. Maybe he already did.

· · ·

The following evening Leanna walked out into Chester's workshop and found him sitting at his long workbench, staining a birdhouse. She breathed in the familiar, pungent smell of the stain as she sat on a bench beside him.

The stench of cigarettes also filled her nostrils, and she spotted his cellular phone half hidden beneath some papers on the workbench. She considered asking him when he planned to give up cigarettes and his cell phone, but she decided against it. Right now she wanted to bridge the gap between them, not widen it.

"That birdhouse is lovely," she said.

"Danki." He smiled at the birdhouse and then over at her. "Did you need my help with something?"

"No." She leaned on the workbench. "I just wanted to check on you." She pointed to the birdhouse. "I like that color. What is it called?"

"Honey oak."

"It's perfect."

He pursed his lips and raised an eyebrow. "So if you don't need anything, is there something you wanted to discuss?"

"I just wanted to talk to you alone to see if you still liked the job. Are you glad you quit the hardware store?"

He nodded. "I am." He looked down at the birdhouse again. "Emory and I have been talking a lot this week."

Curiosity nearly overwhelmed her. "About what?"

"Things." He returned to staining the birdhouse. *"Dat."*

"Your *dat*?"

He kept working as if to avoid eye contact. *"Ya.* I told him about how *Dat* planned to open his own fence business and had said I'd work there with him."

Leanna felt a familiar clutching at her chest as Chester shared more stories that he'd told Emory. But then the clutching released slightly when it dawned on her that Chester must have opened up to Emory. God was using Emory to answer her prayers!

Her lips turned up as happy tears stung her eyes.

"Mamm?" He seemed worried. *"Was iss letz?"*

"Nothing." She sniffed and cleared her throat, then pointed

to the birdhouse he'd been working on. "Would you reconsider selling birdhouses at the marketplace?"

He glanced down at the birdhouse and then back at her. "I still don't see how you'd have room for them in your booth. Your shelves are full, and you need the room since your sales are so *gut*."

"I can make room for them near the entrance. Maybe I could double up on the shelving for my jams and jellies." Then she snapped her fingers as another idea gripped her. "You could build a little display for them, and we could set it right near the entrance."

Chester tapped his chin. "Maybe."

Leanna's heart leapt with joy as she folded her hands. Had Chester finally found some confidence in his talents?

He glanced at the birdhouses that lined his other shelves. "I would have to stain all of them." He hesitated. "But I'll think about it. Okay?"

"Sure." She stood. "I'm going back inside. Don't stay out here too late."

"I won't."

As Leanna walked toward the house, she looked up at a beautiful sunset sending bright bursts of orange and yellow across the sky. "*Danki*, God, for bringing Emory into our lives. Please keep guiding me toward the right words to be the *mamm* that Chester needs."

CHAPTER 16

Emory's shoulders, legs, and feet ached as he walked into the barn to stow his horse Friday night. He breathed in the warm, humid air mixed with the smell of animals as he led his horse to the stall.

He'd spent all day working beside Chester to finish a large shed that would be picked up tomorrow by their delivery service. By the time they'd finished, Emory had felt as if he'd hammered for a week. But the shed was done, and it was one of the best he'd made this month.

He smiled. Chester had come so far in only a week. He seemed more confident and comfortable in his skin. And, best of all, Chester seemed happier than the day he'd met him. Had Leanna noticed the change in him too? Warmth swirled in his chest as he thought of Leanna. He hadn't seen her in several days, and he missed her.

Emory shook his head. Why would he miss someone he hardly knew? He had to be losing his mind.

He stepped out of the barn and looked toward the house, and the delicious aroma of burgers on the charcoal grill filled his senses. His eyes lit up when he spotted Maggie standing by the grill.

Maggie had surprised him with a special supper after a long and hard week. He had always appreciated how thoughtful

Maggie was. She'd definitely inherited many of her mother's qualities.

As Emory started toward the grill, another woman stepped out of the house. At first Emory couldn't see her face, but she was taller than Maggie and thin with blond hair under her prayer covering. He could tell it wasn't Maggie's friend Alea, who was around Maggie's height and had dark hair.

The woman walked over to the grill and said something to Maggie, who smiled. Then the woman turned toward Emory and waved.

Madelyne Swarey.

Emory slowed his steps for a moment as surprise settled over him. And then he remembered—Madelyne had offered to bring supper over one night this week, and he had agreed. How could he have forgotten!

"Dat!" Maggie turned toward him and waved. "Madelyne and I have a special supper ready for you." She pointed to the grill. "Hamburgers and potato salad that Madelyne brought, along with potato chips and baked beans. And Madelyne and I also made a lemon *kuche* earlier."

"Sounds *appeditlich*." Emory hoped his shock wasn't evident on his face as he joined them near the grill. He tipped his hat to Madelyne. "Nice to see you."

She grimaced in response, and he was sure he hadn't hidden his surprise as well as he thought he had. "You weren't expecting me."

"Uh. Well." He gave a little laugh as he lifted his straw hat and pushed his hand through his hair. "No, I wasn't. I had forgotten that we were going to get together. It's my mistake."

"I'm so sorry," she said. "When we spoke on Sunday, I had mentioned coming over to make supper one night, and I thought we had agreed on tonight." She looked toward the barn. "Is your phone in there? I can call my driver and ask him to come and get me."

"No, no, no." Emory shook his head. "Don't be *gegisch*. It just slipped my mind. It's nice to have company. Right, Maggie?"

Maggie nodded. "It is. We've had a fun afternoon."

"Afternoon?" He divided a look between Maggie and Madelyne. What else had he missed?

"*Ya*. I checked the messages this morning, and Madelyne had left one last night saying that she was planning to come over. She asked what time she should come."

"I'm so sorry," he told Madelyne. "Sounds like I forgot to check the messages last night.

Madelyne shrugged. "It's no problem."

"*Ya*," Maggie agreed. "I called her back and told her to come anytime since I was caught up with my chores. We decided on hamburgers since I had planned to grill them for you tonight. We even had time to do some sewing before it was time to start supper."

When she grinned at Madelyne, Emory couldn't stop his own smile. Apparently Maggie and Madelyne had bonded today, which was a happy surprise. Still, he had been looking forward to relaxing tonight. Not to entertaining company after a long week at the shop.

"Oh no!" Madelyne scooted to the grill. "I need to check the burgers." She opened the grill, and the delicious smell made Emory's mouth water. She picked up a spatula and flipped each patty before she gave a satisfied nod, then began scooping them one by one into a large metal pan.

"What can I do?" Emory asked.

Maggie steered him toward the house. "Go in and wash up."

She pointed to his trousers. "And get changed. You're covered in sawdust and paint."

Emory glanced over at Madelyne and found her suppressing a smile. "Maggie takes care of me," he said.

"I can tell." Madelyne gave a little laugh.

"Go, please." Maggie waved toward the house. "We'll finish getting supper ready while you clean up."

Emory stepped into the house and found the table already set for three with baked beans, a bag of chips, potato salad, buns, and condiments sitting in the middle of the table.

Guilt and embarrassment rained down on him as he washed his hands at the sink. How had he forgotten Madelyne had planned to come over to make supper? He must have been too distracted with work this week to recall it.

He finished washing his hands and then hurried to his bedroom where he changed into a fresh pair of trousers and a gray shirt.

When he stepped out of his bedroom to walk back to the kitchen, he heard laughter erupt in the kitchen, and he quickened his steps toward the sound.

"What's so funny?" he asked as he entered the kitchen.

Maggie's cheeks were bright red as she pointed to the floor, where the burger had splattered. "I put some cheese on the burgers, and it melted because they're hot. But when I went to put this one on a bun, I dropped it on the floor, cheese side down."

He chuckled. "Did you make that one especially for me?"

"I did!" Maggie hooted as Madelyne joined in.

Emory shook his head. "My thoughtful *dochder*!" he teased.

Maggie cleaned up the burger and dropped it into the trash

while Madelyne filled their glasses with water. With the table set, they all sat down to eat.

After a silent prayer, they began to add condiments to the cheeseburgers, along with piling beans, potato salad, and chips on their plates. Soon they were eating, and silence filled the kitchen as Emory searched for something to discuss with Madelyne as she smiled across the table at him.

Madelyne patted the corners of her mouth with a napkin. "Maggie, you'll have to show your *dat* what we worked on in your sewing room."

"*Ya.*" Maggie's expression brightened even more. "Madelyne helped me finish a doll, and then we worked on one of my quilts."

"How nice." Emory nodded as he picked up his glass.

Madelyne smiled at Maggie. "Your *dochder* is very talented."

"*Danki,*" Emory said. "I agree."

"We had a lot of fun." Madelyne smiled at Maggie. "I learned from you too."

Maggie shook her head. "Surely not. You're a much better quilter than I am."

"You are an expert at making the dolls, though, and we know how much tourists love those dolls."

Maggie blushed and looked down at her plate, but she never stopped smiling. She looked at Madelyne shyly. "*Danki.* I guess we learned from each other today."

"*Ya,* that's right," Madelyne agreed.

Emory took a bite of potato salad and then stilled as he watched the interaction between Madelyne and Maggie. He hadn't seen Maggie warm up to someone as quickly as she had seemed to warm up to Madelyne.

For the first time since he'd lost Sheryl, he found himself

wondering if Natalie and Justin were right. Maggie *did* need a mother, and she was missing out on something important. Perhaps he should consider marrying again in order to give Maggie the female companionship she so desperately seemed to need and want.

The notion sent confusion and anxiety surging through his veins. Although Sheryl had been gone for six years, he had never seriously considered marrying again. Hadn't wanted to, really. But as he watched Maggie smile at Madelyne, he realized that perhaps he'd been selfish. Perhaps he'd been wrong to believe he was the only parent Maggie would ever need.

"Emory?"

He met Madelyne's concerned expression as he chewed and swallowed. "*Ya?*"

"*Was iss letz?*"

"Nothing." He shook his head.

She tilted her head and then pointed toward his plate. "Is the potato salad okay?"

"*Ya*. It's *appeditlich*."

Madelyne looked unconvinced. "You don't have to eat it if you don't want to. I know some people have strong preferences when it comes to potato salad."

"It's very *gut*." He turned to Maggie. "Everything is fantastic. I appreciate this meal."

Maggie grinned at Madelyne. "We had fun making it, right, Madelyne?"

"We did."

As Madelyne gazed back at Maggie, Emory felt his world shift into a new view. He hadn't taken his daughter's feelings into consideration for the past six years. Was he a terrible father?

Then again, would marrying a woman like Madelyne solve all of Maggie's problems—especially if she wasn't the woman Emory loved?

His head spun as he considered the question. He was grateful Madelyne and Maggie fell into a conversation about sewing while they finished their supper so he could ponder in peace.

After their savory supper, Madelyne brought the lemon cake to the table.

"It looks *wunderbaar*," he said as she cut into the cake.

"I'll get the *kaffi*," Maggie offered, standing and moving toward the percolator.

Madelyne peppered Emory with questions about work while they ate cake and drank coffee. When they finished, Emory went outside and cleaned the grill, and the women cleaned up the kitchen. As he scrubbed the grates with a steel brush, his mind continued to churn with questions and doubts.

He covered the clean grill, walked over to the porch, and peeked through the kitchen window. Maggie smiled as she wiped down the table and listened to something Madelyne said. The joy on her face was almost palpable.

Emory stepped back into the kitchen and stood at the doorway, trying to imagine having Madelyne as his wife. Would they be happy together?

Would he be able to fall in love with her?

"*Dat?*" Maggie asked. "Are you okay?"

"*Ya*," he said, shaking off his thoughts.

Maggie seemed to study him, but he ignored her questioning eyes and turned to Madelyne. "Would you like me to take you home?"

"Oh, no." She shook her head. "I didn't expect you to." She

looked up at the clock above the sink. "My driver should be here any minute now."

Maggie frowned. "Already? Today went by too quickly."

Madelyne gave her a sad smile. "I had a great time. Maybe we could do this again someday." She looked at Emory, as if asking permission.

"Can we, *Dat*?" Maggie asked.

"Of course." Emory nodded, and they both smiled.

Madelyne continued to look at Emory. "Would you please walk me out? We can talk while we wait for my driver."

"Sure."

Madelyne slipped a few refrigerator jars into a tote bag and then pointed toward the counter. "I left the potato salad and cake for you."

"You can take them to your family if you'd like," Emory told her.

"Oh, no. You and Maggie enjoy them." Madelyne walked over to Maggie. "I'll see you soon."

To Emory's surprise, Maggie hugged her. *"Gut nacht."*

Madelyne shouldered her tote bag and then stepped past Emory through the mudroom and out to the porch. She stood by the railing and pointed toward Maggie's garden. "I told Maggie that her flowers are *schee*."

"Ya, they are." Emory leaned back against the railing beside her. "Madelyne, I'm so sorry for not remembering you were planning to come tonight. I'm so embarrassed."

"It's fine. I'm the one who should feel embarrassed." She touched her chest. "I had assumed we had plans, but I should have waited for you to confirm." She rested a hand on the railing. "I didn't mean to be so forward. I understand if you don't want to see me again."

Emory turned back toward the house and recalled how happy Maggie had seemed all evening. "It's obvious Maggie would enjoy spending more time with you."

Madelyne's eyes were hesitant. "And you?"

"I would like to get to know you better." But inside, confusion rained down on him. While he was grateful Maggie liked Madelyne, he still wasn't sure what he wanted. "Tonight was fun."

Her smile was bright. "It was."

Just then an engine rumbled up the driveway, and headlights bounced off the barn door as a red van came to a stop by the back porch.

She held her hand out to him, and he shook it. "I had a lovely day."

"*Danki* for the delicious meal and for spending time with Maggie."

"See you soon, Emory." She gave him a warm smile and then flitted down the porch steps toward the van.

Emory waved to the driver as Madelyne climbed into the back seat. Then the van reversed down the driveway and disappeared toward the road.

He gripped the porch railing and looked up at the sky, which was bathed in bright shades of orange, red, pink, and yellow as the sun began to set.

"Lord," he whispered, "I feel you trying to guide me, but I'm confused. For years I was comfortable with my decision to remain single while doing my best to raise Maggie alone. But now I'm doubting my decision and wondering if Justin and Natalie have been right all along. Are you telling me to date again? If so, did you send Madelyne into my life as a blessing for Maggie and me? Are you telling me to give her a chance?"

He scrubbed his hand down his face. "Please guide me, Lord. I'm listening for your word."

Emory stepped back into the kitchen and found Maggie setting the last dish in the cabinet. "It sounds like you had a *gut* day."

"The best!" Maggie set the dishcloth in the sink and then grabbed Emory's arm. "I have to show you this quilting trick Madelyne taught me. Also, I want you to see the doll we finished." She led him to the stairs and began jogging up them.

Emory followed Maggie into the sewing room, where she picked up a Log Cabin patterned quilt and brought it over to him. "That is gorgeous, Maggie. You did a great job." He ran his fingers over the intricate stitching.

"*Danki*, but Madelyne really helped. I'm so glad Natalie introduced Madelyne to us. She's so nice! We have so much in common, and I had more fun with her than with the *maed* in my youth group. They aren't as interested in sewing as I am. Not even Alea is."

As she carried on about Madelyne, Emory felt as if the room were closing in on him. He needed someone to talk to about his confusing feelings about his failings as a father. He needed someone he could trust.

He needed to talk to Leanna.

CHAPTER 17

S unday afternoon Leanna moved the rocking chair back and forth on *Mammi*'s porch and listened to Christiana share a sweet story about Kaylin. The early August air was hot and humid and smelled of flowers, animals, and moist earth as the sunshine smiled down from the azure sky above them.

"Before I could stop her," Christiana continued, "Kaylin had grabbed the broom and tried to drag it across the kitchen. I was so stunned that I couldn't move for a moment. And she was so proud of herself for trying to help me that I didn't want to burst her bubble."

"You need to get her one of those brooms for *kinner*," Salina said. "I saw one at the grocery store just the other day."

"That's a *gut* idea," Bethany agreed.

"She's going to be your little helper," *Mammi* chimed in.

Leanna smiled over at her cousins. How she enjoyed the off-Sunday without the church service when they could visit and catch up after the week.

Bethany had suggested that they sit on *Mammi*'s porch today, and after Christiana and Salina had put their daughters in their travel play yards for naps in Leanna's parents' bedroom, they had headed over to *Mammi*'s to drink lemonade and eat cookies. Their mothers were visiting in Leanna's kitchen and said they would be happy to watch out for the girls.

"Leanna, are you expecting more company?" Salina asked.

"I don't think so. Everyone is already here." Leanna looked over as a horse and buggy stopped by the barn. "Who's that?"

Bethany sucked in a breath as a man climbed out of the driver's seat. "Is that Emory?"

"It is." Leanna's heart trilled as Emory waved toward the group of Leanna's male relatives.

"*That's* Emory?" Salina asked.

"Wow," Christiana said under her breath.

"Well, I'll say what you two are thinking," *Mammi* announced. "He *is* handsome."

Her cousins chuckled.

Leanna stood, worry threading through her. Was he okay? Had something happened to Maggie?

"Excuse me." She scurried down the porch steps toward Emory as her father walked over to him. "Emory!"

Emory turned toward her and smiled. Then he raised his hand in a wave. "Leanna. *Wie geht's?*"

Dat stuck his hand out, and Emory shook it. "Emory. So nice to see you again."

"You too, Walter."

"*Danki* for giving Chester the job," said *Dat*. "He really seems to enjoy it."

"The pleasure is all mine. He's a great help."

Dat looked at Leanna and then back at Emory. "I'll let you two visit. I'm *froh* you came to see us today."

"*Danki*, Walter." Emory turned toward Leanna. "How have you been?"

She studied his eyes, which somehow seemed bluer today. "Well enough. And you? Is everything okay?"

"*Ya*, of course. Why?"

"I'm just surprised to see you here."

His smile faded. "I'm sorry. I should have called first, but Maggie surprised me and went to the youth gathering again for the second week in a row. I wanted to come see you, and today seemed like the perfect opportunity."

Her heart swelled at his words. "I'm glad you came. And it's great to hear that Maggie is socializing again." She peeked back over her shoulder and found her cousins smiling at her. She felt her cheeks heat as she looked at Emory. "Would you like to meet Salina and Christiana?"

"I'd love to. I don't expect Maggie home before late tonight, so I have some time." He pointed toward the barn. "Let me just put my horse in your barn first."

After Emory took care of his horse, they walked together to the porch, and Leanna longed for her cousins to stop grinning at her. She was certain her cheeks might burst into flames.

"Emory," she said, "this is Salina."

"Hi." Salina gave him a wave.

"And this is Christiana." Leanna pointed to her redheaded cousin.

"It's very nice to meet you. We've heard a lot about you," Christiana said.

"I hope it was all *gut*," Emory joked.

"Oh, it was," Bethany chimed in as she waved at him.

Emory shook *Mammi*'s hand. "How are you today?"

"Fine. What brings you out here today?" *Mammi* asked.

"*Mei dochder* made plans for the afternoon, so I thought I'd pay Leanna a visit." Emory smiled at her, and her heart did a funny little dance.

Leanna saw meaningful looks pass between her three cousins—looks she hoped Emory wouldn't notice. "Emory, would you like to have lemonade and *kichlin* with us? Or would you like to spend some time with the men?"

Emory looked out toward the barn and then back at Leanna. "I suppose I should get acquainted with the men, and then maybe we can talk later?"

"Perfect."

Emory nodded at the women, and he and Leanna walked across the way to the barn, where the men stood and talked. "Everyone, this is *mei freind* Emory. Emory, this is Jeff, Christiana's husband, and Will, Salina's husband. And this is Micah. He's married to Bethany."

"Emory!" Micah stuck his hand out. "Nice to meet you."

Leanna smiled as Emory and Micah fell into an easy conversation. Then she backed away and walked the short path to her grandmother's porch and her rocking chair.

"So, Leanna," Christiana began, swiveling to face her. "It's obvious Emory cares for you. Has he asked you to be his girlfriend yet?"

"You took the words out of my mouth," Salina declared.

"Nothing has changed since the last time we talked." Leanna looked out toward the barn, where Emory seemed to be enjoying himself, and her heart warmed once again.

"I think he's going to ask you to date him," Salina said.

"She's right," *Mammi* chimed in. "He seems to care for you, and he's a *gut* man."

"*Ya, Mammi.* He is a *gut* man." Leanna picked up a cookie and continued to watch as Jeff and Will joined Emory's conversation with Micah.

She cherished the sight of Emory making himself at home with her family. Before she knew it, she was imagining Emory as a permanent part of her life.

But it felt like a dream—a fantasy—something that was out of her reach. Perhaps she was wasting her emotions even thinking about it.

Leanna brushed off the thought and turned to Salina. "How are you feeling these days?"

Salina rubbed her protruding abdomen, which seemed to have grown quite a bit since she saw her last week. "Achy and tired, really. But I felt that way right before Karrie was born."

"It's hard to believe you will soon be a family of four," *Mammi* sang.

Leanna settled back on the rocking chair as her cousins and *Mammi* talked on about Salina's new baby. She looked back over to the men, where Emory and Jeff seemed to be sharing a good laugh. Her heart gave another kick. For the first time since she'd lost Marlin, she found herself longing for a man like Emory in her life.

Could God possibly have someone like him in her future? At the thought, excitement bubbled up in her like water in a spring.

. . .

Later that evening, Leanna sat on her parents' porch, rocking on a chair beside Emory while the cicadas sang the daylight into the night. She felt her body relax as she recalled her day of rest. Around suppertime, her cousins and their families had all headed back home. Mustering all of her confidence, Leanna had invited Emory to stay for supper and had been delighted when he'd agreed. He had talked and laughed with her and her parents while they enjoyed the chicken and rice casserole and then cherry pie Leanna had prepared yesterday.

Now she couldn't seem to wipe the smile off her face as she enjoyed Emory's company.

"I get the feeling Chester enjoys his youth group."

Leanna turned toward Emory's warm smile. "He does."

"So, you've never had any trouble getting him to go to youth group gatherings?"

"No, he was anxious to join the youth group with his *freinden*."

Emory sipped his mug of coffee and rested his right ankle on his left knee. "I used to wonder if Maggie would have been more social if she'd had an older or younger sibling." Then he glanced over at Leanna again. "But maybe it's just her personality if Chester didn't have any problems joining his youth group."

Leanna gripped her mug. "I used to wonder if Chester would have been happier if we'd had another *kind* too."

"Did you want more *kinner*?"

She looked up into his warm blue eyes and her pulse ratcheted up. "I did. Since I was an only *kind*, I always dreamt of a large family."

"Sheryl did too."

"Marlin was an only *kind* too. We wanted six *kinner*."

He gave a chuckle. "Six?"

"*Ya*, that sounds *wunderbaar*."

"You think so?" He tilted his head, his expression seeming curious.

"I do." She nodded. "It just wasn't in God's plans for us."

"Us either. But I would have enjoyed a few more *kinner*." He shrugged. "Even six."

He smirked, and she laughed. Oh, she enjoyed their easy conversations.

His smile faded. "Can you imagine how tough it would have been to have six *kinner* after losing our spouses?"

She blew out a huff of breath. "That would have been even more devastating. Of course, the older ones would care for the younger ones, but I can't even imagine burdening my parents with helping care for me and six *kinner*."

"You would've had to remarry right away."

She scowled. "As if I could find a man who'd want to take on me *and* six *kinner*!"

Emory's expression became thoughtful as he rubbed his beard and looked out toward the barn. "I think I told you *mei bruder* and his *fraa* are determined to marry me off."

"You've mentioned that."

"Well, Natalie, his *fraa*, has a *freind* she's been pressing me to meet, and she brought this *freind* to church last week." He set his mug on the table between their chairs.

A dart of nerves shot through her stomach. "Did she?"

He nodded. "Her name is Madelyne, and she's never been married. She's thirty-five. Natalie insists Madelyne is *gut* with *kinner* since she's helping take care of her *bruderskinner*."

"Oh?" She hoped her voice sounded calm despite her sudden anxiety.

"Well, she showed up for supper Friday night. I had forgotten that she'd offered to bring supper over." He shook his head. "It was my fault—a misunderstanding. Anyway, she was there cooking with Maggie when I got home. They had spent the afternoon sewing and baking together. Then she stayed for supper and dessert."

She worked to keep her expression pleasant despite the jealousy taking hold of her. "It sounds like you had a *gut* time."

Emory shrugged. "She's *gut* with Maggie, and it's clear Maggie likes her."

Leanna thought she might be sick, but she swallowed back

the bile rising in her throat. She had no hold over this man and had no right to feel possessive of him.

She tried to imagine what Madelyne looked like. Surely, she was perfect—tall, slim, funny, beautiful. She closed her eyes and bit back a sob.

"Maggie took to her so quickly, and I actually found myself wondering if Justin and Natalie are right . . . Maybe I should have remarried for Maggie's sake after I lost Sheryl. If I had, maybe she wouldn't feel like she always has to take care of me. She would have more *freinden* and be enjoying her youth."

Silence fell between them as Leanna's vision went blurry. The unspoken care she'd begun to feel for Emory began crashing down, crushing the happiness that had filled her earlier in the day. She worked to calm her pulse and cleared her throat.

"Do you like Madelyne?" She hoped her voice sounded calmer than she felt.

He shrugged again.

More silence stretched between them, and the cicadas' song seemed to become louder.

Emory twisted his body toward her. "You sure are quiet. Is something on your mind?" Her eyes met his—so full of tenderness that they took her breath away.

Leanna rubbed her arm and searched for something to say. "Not really."

He leaned his head back on the chair and looked over at her again, and she felt itchy under his intense stare. "What's your biggest fear?"

"Losing Chester," she responded without hesitation. "He admitted the other night that he's not sure if he'll be baptized. I'm praying he'll stay in the community and not leave."

"Really?" He seemed surprised by this. "I can't see him

leaving. He's going to be a solid Amish man. Just give him time."

She smiled, hoping he was right. "What's your biggest fear?"

"For Maggie to not come out of her shell and to spend her life alone. I want her to have a family and a *froh* life."

He was such a good father. He looked up toward the stars, and Leanna took in his handsome profile—his chiseled cheeks, long nose, pink lips, and thick dark hair—and she longed to have a man like him in her life. Could God possibly have him in his plan for her?

Emory turned toward her. "I should probably get going. It's getting late." He stood and picked up his mug.

"I'll take care of that." She reached for his mug, and when their hands touched, she felt the familiar heat skitter up her arm. She held back a gasp, then placed the mug on the table beside hers.

He pointed toward the door. "Would you please thank your parents on my behalf? For supper and for their company?"

"Of course."

They each picked up a flashlight from the porch and walked out to the barn, where he retrieved his horse and then hitched up the buggy.

"I'm so glad you came to visit today," she said.

"I am too. *Danki* for allowing me to spend the afternoon and evening with you." He reached out to shake her hand, and when they touched, Leanna's skin hummed once again. He lingered there a moment longer as he looked into her eyes. "Take care, Leanna," he said, finally releasing her fingers from his grasp.

She tried to swallow, but she felt as if she had a throat full of sand. "You too. Be safe going home."

Head still spinning, she headed back toward the porch while he climbed into the buggy. She looked out toward the road as he departed, and as his taillights disappeared from her sight, she felt a tug in her chest.

Behind her the storm door opened and clicked shut, then *Mamm* stepped out onto the porch. "He was here a long time. He obviously cares for you."

Leanna shook her head and hugged her arms to her waist. "He's met someone else."

Mamm gave her a knowing smile. "If he met someone else, then why did he spend the day with you?"

Leanna could not answer the question, so she ignored it. Then she moved toward the house. "I'm going to bed, *Mamm*."

As she made her way up to her bedroom, Leanna resolved to put romantic thoughts of Emory out of her mind. Since she couldn't stop him from falling in love with someone else, she would cherish his friendship for as long as she could.

And she hoped that would be for a long, long time.

CHAPTER 18

Emory couldn't stop smiling on his way home from Leanna's house. He'd relished every moment of the day, but sitting on the porch with Leanna had been the highlight of his entire week.

She was so beautiful that he could watch her for hours, memorizing the depth of her deep brown eyes, her gorgeous bright smile, her sweet laugh, her long neck, her high cheekbones, her button nose, and her pink lips.

And talking to Leanna had been so comfortable that he felt as if he'd known her for years instead of only a month. Even the silent moments felt easy. He'd opened up to her and shared his private feelings, and Leanna had listened and responded without criticism. Talking to her felt natural, and he didn't have to search for something to say like he did when he spent time with Madelyne.

And yet he wondered if Leanna had held back some of her feelings. She'd seemed to go quiet at times, and he longed to find a way to encourage her to open up to him more. Perhaps in time Leanna would share all of her thoughts and burdens with him as he got to know her better.

He felt a flutter deep in his veins at the idea of a deepening friendship. Would he ever have the chance to be more than a friend to her? To date her, even?

Then he recalled what Chester had said to him last week when they visited the marketplace. Chester specifically said Leanna wasn't looking for someone to date. Was that true? Or had Chester just said it to discourage Emory from pursuing his mother?

And where did Madelyne fit into all of this? It was obvious that Maggie liked her, and Emory had to take her feelings into consideration. Maggie's happiness was important too—if not more important than his.

Emory blew out a frustrated sigh as his emotions continued to jumble within him. While his heart craved Leanna, his mind told him to get to know Madelyne better.

As he guided the horse into his driveway, he spotted a lantern glowing in the kitchen. A black feeling settled in his gut when he realized Maggie must have come home early. Had she not had a good time? How long had she been home alone?

He did a mental head slap. He should have left her a note before he went to Leanna's house.

After stowing his horse and buggy, he stepped into the kitchen, where she sat at the table and fixed him with a look.

"Where have you been?" she snapped, standing up and marching over to where he stood in the doorway.

"Whoa." Emory held his hands up. "I was out visiting."

She wagged a finger at him as her eyes sparkled with tears. "I was worried sick about you. I searched the *haus* and then walked to *Mammi*'s *haus* and *Onkel* Justin's *haus* looking for you. When you weren't there, I started to get really upset. I had visions of you in an accident. I thought I lost you like—like—" Her eyes spilled over, and she covered her face with her hands.

"*Ach, mei liewe.* I'm so sorry." Emory clucked his tongue and pulled her into a hug. How could he have been so careless? "I should have left you a note, but I thought you'd be out late with your youth group. Why did you come home early?"

She sniffed and looked up at him. "We went swimming. Then we went back to Rhoda's *haus* to play games, and I was tired. Tomorrow is my laundry day, so I need to get up early to get started on my Monday chores. I told Alea I wanted to come home, and Johnny brought me."

He looked down at her blue eyes and sighed. "You don't need to worry so much about chores. You could have stayed later and slept in a little tomorrow."

"But your breakfast—"

"Maggie," he interrupted. "It's not your—"

"I know," she cut in and held her hand up. "It's not my job to take care of you, but I like doing it. It makes me feel closer to *Mamm* when I'm doing the chores she always did. I think she'd be proud of me for doing them."

More guilt loomed over him. "I'm sorry for upsetting you, Maggie. It never occurred to me that you might come home early and then worry about me." Then he pressed his lips together. "But Maggie, you need to remember that I'm your *dat*. I'm an adult. If I decide I want to go visiting, then I will. I should I have left you a note, but it's not your place to lecture me or look after me. *I'm* supposed to look after *you*."

"I know. I'm sorry. I'm just glad you're okay." She sniffed and dabbed the back of her hand under her eyes. "Where did you go?"

"I went visiting."

"Madelyne?" He shook his head, and her eyes narrowed with suspicion. "Then who?"

"Leanna."

Maggie's brow furrowed. "Why would you go to see Leanna? We had such a *gut* time with Madelyne on Friday."

Emory rubbed his chin. "Well, we've become *freinden*, and I hadn't talked to her in more than a week." *And I missed her.*

Maggie's eyes rounded. "You must like her." She shook her head. "I don't want or need a new *mamm*. We're fine, so don't feel like you need to date and get married just because *Aenti* Natalie says you do."

He held his hands up. "You don't need to worry, because I don't think Leanna likes me that way."

"But you like *her* that way."

Emory sighed. "Maggie Anne, it's late. I need to get some rest before another busy week starts tomorrow." He gave her shoulder a squeeze in an effort to calm her. "You have nothing to worry about. I'm not dating anyone."

"Okay."

"Please get some sleep." He touched her face and smiled. "I'm *froh* you went to the youth group gathering tonight. Did you have fun?"

She nodded. "I did."

"*Gut.*"

She hugged him. "*Gut nacht, Dat.*"

"*Gut nacht.* I'm sorry for worrying you." He closed his eyes and savored the hug.

She carried the lantern up the stairs toward her room, and he used his flashlight to walk into his room on the first floor. With a sigh, he sank down onto the corner of his double bed, which creaked under his weight. He began to unbutton his shirt as a prayer formed on his lips.

"Lord," he whispered, "please guide my heart. I feel myself falling for Leanna, but I wonder if you're leading me to

Madelyne for Maggie's sake. Am I imagining all of these feelings? Do I truly belong alone? Lead me, Lord. I'm confused
and lost."

He gazed behind him to the side of the bed where Sheryl
had once slept, and he wished more than ever that he could
talk to her.

"Sheryl, I wish I could talk to you right now—but if I could,
then I wouldn't be in this predicament. I don't know what to
do. I feel like I'm stuck at a crossroads, and no matter which
road I choose, it will be the wrong one. Would you approve of
my dating again? And if so, who would you choose as the best
stepmother for Maggie?"

He cupped his hand to his forehead. "Maybe I am losing my
mind. What makes me think either of them would even want
to marry me? And why would my late *fraa* want to be the one
to choose? I must need sleep."

After changing into his nightclothes, Emory climbed into
bed as thoughts of Leanna hijacked his brain once again. As
he waited for sleep to find him, he found himself wondering if
Leanna ever thought of him too.

. . .

Two and a half weeks later, Emory retrieved his lunch box from
the refrigerator in the break room and then sat down at the
table. Justin and Lee had eaten earlier since they were at a stopping point with their projects while Emory and Chester had
chosen to work a little longer in order to finish what they had
started.

He looked toward the doorway as Chester walked in and
crossed to the sink to wash his hands. Emory spotted a cell

phone sticking out of his back pocket and noted the acrid stench of cigarette smoke floating toward him. Chester had not been able to hide his afternoon smoke breaks, but Emory hadn't felt the need to say something until that moment.

"How long have you smoked, Chester?" Emory asked. He picked up half of his turkey sandwich and took a bite.

Chester turned toward him, his expression seeming surprised. "About six months."

"What inspired you to start?"

"*Mei freinden* smoke." Chester moved to the refrigerator and retrieved his lunch box.

"So, you smoke to fit in?"

Chester shrugged and then sat down across from him. After bowing his head in a silent prayer, he pulled out his lunch—a roast beef sandwich, a small bag of chips, a bottle of water, and an apple.

"Cigarettes are expensive, though. Wouldn't you rather spend your money on other things? Or even save it?"

Chester kept his eyes focused on his lunch as he chewed a bite of sandwich.

"Cell phones are expensive too—and unnecessary unless you have a business that requires it. That's another waste of money. But cigarettes are bad for you on top of the price."

Then Chester looked up and met Emory's gaze. "Did you ever smoke when you were a teenager?"

"I tried it once." Emory took a sip of water from his bottle.

"You did?"

"*Ya.* I didn't like how the smoke felt in my lungs, so I never did it again." Emory grinned. "Does that surprise you?"

"I just imagined you to be the person who always followed the rules."

Emory snorted. "I was young once, too, and I got into plenty of trouble."

"Doing what?" Chester looked fascinated as he crunched down on some chips. He held the bag out to Emory, and he took one.

"Danki." As Emory chewed, he tried to think back on what ruckus he and his friends had caused. "Well, one time we went camping and one of my buddies pulled a boat behind his buggy. When we tried to put the boat in the water, the horse got spooked, and the boat, buggy, and horse all wound up in the lake. The horse was fine, of course, but we were laughing so hard that we got thrown out of the campground for being too 'rowdy.'" He made air quotes with his fingers.

Chester laughed. "That's hilarious!"

Emory grinned. "Another time I got into trouble for racing buggies with a buddy. We were certain the road was abandoned until the police showed up."

"No way!" Chester leaned forward. "Did you get into trouble?"

"We only got a warning from the police, but our parents weren't very *froh*. Kind of like when you and Maggie got caught a few weeks back."

Chester shook his head and ate another bite of sandwich.

"You really shouldn't smoke, though. It's not *gut* for you. Haven't you read the warnings on the packages?"

Chester frowned.

"Think of it this way. You could use that money to buy more supplies for your birdhouses."

Chester nodded and cast his eyes downward. *"Mei mamm* wants me to sell my birdhouses at the market. She says she'll make room in her booth."

"*Wunderbaar!* Are you going to do it?"

"Maybe." Chester spun his bottle of water around in his hands. "I don't know."

"Why not?"

"I'm not sure anyone would really buy them. They aren't that well made."

"Sure they are." Emory took another chip. "Why would you say they aren't?"

"I still have so much to learn. Remember how I messed up that one wall yesterday on the shed?"

"But you've learned so much since you started here. And we all have more to learn." Emory pointed to his chest. "I still learn something every day. I become a better carpenter with each shed I build." He fixed his gaze on Chester. "God gave you a talent. You're a *gut* carpenter, and your birdhouses are unique. You should sell them if you want to."

Chester ate another bite of sandwich.

"What would you do with the money if you sold them?"

"Help *mei mamm.*"

Emory felt his eyebrows raise. "Really?"

"*Ya.*" Chester nodded. "She's always worked hard to take *gut* care of me since *mei dat* died. I want to do something to help her for once."

Emory smiled at the boy. "That's a very grown-up plan."

They ate in silence for several moments.

"When were you baptized?" Chester asked as he lifted his water bottle again.

"I was around your age."

"How did you know you were ready?"

"I knew in here." Emory tapped his chest. "Also, *mei freinden* and I joined the baptism class together. We all felt it was time to grow up and become members of the church." He took the last bite of his sandwich.

"Did you ever feel like you weren't sure you belonged in the community?"

Emory stopped chewing as he recalled his conversation with Leanna when he'd visited her at home. Leanna had mentioned that Chester wasn't sure about joining the church, and losing Chester was her biggest fear. He needed to choose his words carefully and not accidentally give her son the wrong advice. The last thing Emory ever wanted was to hurt Leanna.

"Forget I said anything," Chester added quickly. "I didn't mean it. I was speaking hypothetically."

"No, it's okay. It's a *gut* question, and you can talk to me."

Chester picked at the edge of the table. "Sometimes I'm not sure if I should be Amish."

"Why not?" Emory worked to keep his tone gentle despite his concern.

"I don't know. I just . . . I wonder if I fit in."

"Why wouldn't you fit in?"

"I don't know. All of *mei freinden* have two parents. They all have fathers."

Emory tilted his head and lifted his water bottle. "Why would that make you not fit in? Maggie doesn't have a *mamm*."

"I can't explain it." Chester scrubbed his hands down his face and then glowered. "I guess it makes me doubt my faith when I don't understand why God had to take *mei dat*. What did *mei mamm* and I do to deserve losing him? Why did God have to take him away?"

Emory set his bottle down on the table. So this was the true reason for Chester's moods, behavior, and self-doubt. He was still trying to wade through his grief. "I know how you feel."

"You do?" Chester lifted an eyebrow.

"Well, Maggie and I still struggle with our grief too. We all wonder why bad things happen, even if we know we won't receive the answers on this side of heaven. But I've also learned over the years that God's will is what it is; and no matter how angry we get at some of the things that happen to us, God loves us all the time and blesses us even when we think he's forgotten us. He shows us his love when we're not even watching."

"What do you mean?"

Emory gestured between them. "New friendships. God puts people in our lives when we need them the most."

Chester ate another chip as he seemed to consider that. "I never thought about it that way."

"God's love is everywhere, even when we don't see it. You may not have a *dat*, but you have a *mamm* who loves you and works hard for you. And you have grandparents and great-grandparents who love you and take care of you—not to mention your cousins. Of course you will always miss your *daed*, but you have your *mamm*'s support and the rest of your family's support. You should embrace them and appreciate them."

Chester nodded slowly as if he was letting the words sink in. "That's a great way to think about it."

"You deserve to be a community member as much as I do. Of course you fit in. And your family would be crushed if you decided to leave."

Chester looked down at his empty bag of chips. "You're right."

"Just think about it before you make a decision you might regret, okay? Your *mamm* loves you. It's obvious. Don't break her heart. She's doing the best she can without your *dat*, and you're proof that she's doing a great job."

Chester met his gaze and nodded. "She is doing her best."

Emory looked at the clock on the wall. "*Ach!* We'd better get back to work before Justin comes looking for us."

As Emory cleaned up the table, he looked over at Chester and hoped he'd used the right words with this heartbroken, grieving young man.

CHAPTER 19

E mory," Justin called from the doorway that led to the front of the store later that afternoon. "You have a visitor."

"Who is it?" Emory swiped the back of his hand across his sweaty brow and then took a long, cold drink of water from his bottle.

"It's Madelyne."

Emory hesitated and took another drink as Justin walked over to him. The familiar confusion that had plagued him for the past few weeks settled over him, and a muscle in his neck tensed. He wasn't in the mood to deal with this today. "Would you please tell her we're busy and I'll call her later?"

"How can you dismiss her?" Justin asked him. "She came to see you, and she brought you a gift." He lowered his voice and pointed at Emory. "You should give her a chance instead of spending the rest of your life alone."

Emory peered over to Chester, who stood nearby and watched him with a suspicious expression, causing more guilt and confusion to batter his insides. He turned back to his brother. "Fine. I'll talk to her."

After wiping his hands on a shop rag, Emory made his way to the front of the shop where Madelyne stood holding a pie plate. She looked pretty in a pale green dress under her black apron.

When she spotted him, her face lit up. *"Wie geht's?"*

"Hi, Madelyne, I'm well," he said, stepping around the counter. He nodded toward her pie plate. "What have you got there?"

She handed it to him. "It's a strawberry pie. I thought you might need something sweet."

"Danki." He lifted the delicious-looking pie to his nose. "Wow, it smells amazing."

She grinned. "I hope you enjoy it. So, how have you been? We haven't spoken in almost three weeks."

He set the pie on the counter behind him. "Well, we've been working long hours to try to keep up with the flood of orders we suddenly received."

"Oh, that's *gut* news then. What a blessing to be busy."

"Ya, but it's exhausting."

"It sounds like you need a *gut* supper then." Her eyes widened and her cheeks flamed pink. "Oh, I don't mean that Maggie doesn't make you a *gut* supper. I only meant that I would enjoy making you another supper."

He smiled weakly at this sweet and eager woman. Perhaps he should take his brother's advice and give her a chance. "I know what you mean, and . . . that would be nice."

Madelyne brightened. "Really?"

He nodded.

"Okay then. Why don't I look at my calendar and give you a call?"

"That sounds perfect." He jammed his thumb toward the shop. "Anyway, I really need to get back to work. *Danki* for coming by. And for the pie."

"Gern gschehne. Talk to you soon."

He held up his hand in a wave and she headed out the door, the bell jingling as she disappeared into the parking lot.

"You're making a *gut* choice."

Emory spun to where his brother stood in the doorway. "You think so?" He hated the doubt in his voice.

"I do." Justin walked over to the counter and rested his elbows on it. "Madelyne told Natalie how well your supper went. She went on and on about how she bonded with Maggie. Isn't that what matters most?"

Emory nodded. But he still needed to convince his heart.

. . .

Later that evening, after washing and drying his hands at the kitchen sink, Chester appeared in front of Leanna and took the platter of fried chicken from her hands. "Let me help you with that, *Mamm*."

Leanna shared a surprised look with her mother. "Sounds like you had a *gut* day today."

"I did." He carried four glasses to the table and filled them with water.

Leanna stood by the counter and watched him, feeling as if she'd stepped back in time to when Chester was younger and always eager to help her. She considered pinching herself to make sure she wasn't dreaming.

Leanna's mother elbowed her in the side and grinned, then placed a bowl of creamed corn on the table. Leanna laughed to herself and set the egg noodles on the table just as *Dat* walked in.

"I didn't see you come home, Chester," *Dat* said. "How was your day?"

"*Gut*. Yours?"

"Great." *Dat* sat down and they all followed suit.

After a silent prayer, they began filling their plates.

"I have an announcement," Chester began as he dropped a small pile of noodles onto his plate. He looked over at Leanna. "I've decided to sell my birdhouses at the market."

"Really?" Leanna's voice squeaked as her parents gasped.

Chester nodded. "If the offer is still open."

"Of course it is." Leanna clapped her hands. "I'm so excited. This will be *wunderbaar*. How soon?"

"How about tomorrow? We can load up the birdhouses in my buggy tonight, and then I'll take you to the market early to set up. I can leave a message for Emory to tell him that I'll be just a few minutes late to work."

He placed two chicken thighs on his plate. "I was thinking I could even start taking you to the marketplace on the days you work in order to save you money paying a driver. I know you come home earlier than I do, but it would at least save you money in the mornings."

Leanna held her glass suspended in the air as she fixed her gaze on her son. It had been months since he had offered to do something for her that would save her money, and she had no idea what to say.

"Great idea, Chester," *Dat* chimed in. "How thoughtful of you."

Mamm nodded. "*Ya*, very thoughtful."

"*Danki*," Leanna said. "I love the idea."

After supper, Leanna helped clean up the kitchen and then went out to the workshop, where Chester was putting birdhouses into boxes.

"May I help?" she asked.

"*Ya*." He pointed to an empty box. "Why don't you pick out

four more birdhouses and put them in that box?" He pointed to a small shelf. "I just built that little shelf for a display. It's simple but functional, and I can fit ten birdhouses on it. Do you think it will work in your booth?"

"It's perfect. You're so talented."

"Not really." He shrugged. "I just threw it together."

Soon they had the birdhouses packed and ready to be loaded in the buggy in the morning. Then they walked back toward the house together. When they reached the porch, she turned toward him.

"I'm so proud of you," Leanna said. She reached up and touched his shoulder. "You're becoming a *wunderbaar* carpenter. Your *dat* would be proud of you too."

Chester swallowed and looked down at the toes of his boots before meeting her gaze again. "*Mamm*, I'm sorry for all of the headaches I've caused you lately."

"What do you mean?"

"I'm sorry for getting into trouble the night I trespassed with Danny. And I'm sorry for my attitude lately. I'm going to do better, starting now. I hope you can forgive me."

Leanna stood up on her tiptoes and hugged him around his neck, trying to ignore the faint smell of cigarettes that clung to his hair and clothes. "You're always forgiven, *mei liewe. Ich liebe dich.*"

"I love you too, *Mamm*." He gave her a squeeze and then released her.

As they walked up the steps, Leanna thought she might burst from joy. Emory was making a difference in Chester's life, and she couldn't wait to thank him.

· · ·

Leanna stood back from the display of birdhouses in her booth and smiled the following morning. "You couldn't have done a better job, Chester."

The shelf Chester had built fit perfectly at the entrance to her booth, and the beautiful birdhouses added character to her display of jams and jellies.

"You think so?" Chester rubbed his chin. "You don't think the booth is too cluttered?"

"Not at all." She rested her hand on his shoulder. "Did you decide on a price? Do you want to charge the same amount for all of them? Or do you want to charge more for the larger ones?"

"It's up to you."

"Why should it be up to me? You paid for the supplies, and you took the time to make the birdhouses."

He shook his head. "I want you to keep the money."

"What?"

"I told you last night that I want to start doing more for you. I'm sixteen now. You've struggled to take care of me ever since *Dat* died. It's time for me to start helping out." He gestured toward the display of birdhouses. "This is only the beginning. I'm going to start doing more."

Leanna shook her head as tears burned her eyes. "I didn't do it on my own. Your grandparents helped me."

"I know you started this booth as a way to make money to take care of me. Let me help take care of us now."

"Okay. *Danki.* But I still want your opinion on the prices."

They agreed on a price, and then she wrote out the labels while he affixed them to the birdhouses. They were pricing the last birdhouse when Lily and Daisy sauntered into the booth, meowing as they rubbed against Chester's shins.

"Hi there." He looked over at Leanna. "May I give them some snacks?"

"Of course."

Chester called the cats over to the counter, where he filled two bowls with food and treats.

Bethany stepped into the booth to examine the display of birdhouses. She held two cups of coffee in her hands, and the delicious aroma of chocolate mocha filled Leanna's senses. "These birdhouses are fantastic, Chester!"

"*Danki*," Chester called from where he stood with the cats.

Leanna grinned. "I'm so thrilled he finally decided to sell them!"

Bethany held out the two cups. "Would you two like some *kaffi*? I added creamer and sweetener already."

"*Ya. Danki.*" Leanna took the cup and then pulled her wallet out of her pocket.

Bethany waved off the money. "It's on me today."

Chester took the other cup and thanked her.

They chatted for a few minutes before the morning rush, then Bethany looked out past the entrance to the booth. Her smile drooped, and Leanna was almost certain she also heard her groan.

Soon Leanna saw what Bethany had already seen. Sara Ann was making her way toward the Jam and Jelly Nook.

"Oh, what do we have here?" Sara Ann asked as she flounced over to them. "Birdhouses!" She touched a few of them and then looked at Chester. "Did you make these?"

He nodded and then sipped more coffee. Leanna had warned him more than once not to say too much to Sara Ann, and she was grateful he had listened.

"Very nice," Sara Ann said.

"*Danki*," he muttered.

Sara Ann looked around the booth and then over at Leanna, who braced herself for one of Sara Ann's passive-aggressive barbs. "You'll have to get a new sign now."

"Why?"

"Well, this is the Jam and Jelly Nook. Birdhouses really don't go with the theme. You might confuse the customers." Then Sara Ann tittered, and the sound reminded Leanna of nails on a chalkboard.

"Thanks for the suggestion," Leanna managed to say through gritted teeth.

Sara Ann then looked at Chester. "But they *are* nice."

Chester nodded at her before she turned to leave.

"Make *gut* sales today," Sara Ann sang over her shoulder as she sauntered toward the next booth.

"Oh, she's so infuriating," Leanna grumbled.

"One of these days she will get her due," Bethany whispered. "And I hope I'm there to see it."

"Well, I need to head to work before Emory thinks I'm not coming in," Chester announced. "See you later, *Mamm*. And thank you for the *kaffi*, Bethany."

"Have a *gut* day," Bethany said.

"See you tonight," Leanna told him. Once he was out of earshot, she turned to Bethany. "I've seen such a difference in him since he started working for Emory. Last night he told me that he was sorry for being so difficult lately, and he said he wants to do more for me, such as let me keep the money from the birdhouse sales."

Bethany's blue eyes widened. "Wow. What a blessing!"

"I believe God is using Emory to get through to Chester, and I'm so grateful." Leanna reached down and touched one of the birdhouses as her thoughts turned to Emory. Oh, how she missed him! It had been too long since they'd spoken. She'd longed for him to come and visit her, but he hadn't.

"You care about Emory, don't you?"

Leanna nodded. "I do, but I haven't seen him since he came to *mei haus* that Sunday a few weeks ago."

"Maybe he's the one God has chosen for you."

"I don't think so."

"Why not?"

"Because I'm not sure he's interested in dating me. If he were, then he would have come to see me again."

"Maybe he just needs some encouragement. Could you pay the visit this time? Remind him that he enjoys your company?" Bethany winked.

Leanna smiled at her cousin. "Maybe I will."

CHAPTER 20

"Could we stop by your work on our way to the market-place?" Leanna asked Chester the following Friday. "I'd like to talk to Emory."

"Why?" Chester asked, keeping his eyes on the road as he guided the horse down Old Philadelphia Pike.

She held up two jars of jelly she'd picked out for him—apple cranberry and apricot. "I just wanted to give him something to thank him for being so *gut* to you."

Chester looked at the jars of jelly, and his face went slack. Then he turned his eyes back to the road.

Her stomach tightened with apprehension. "What does that look mean?"

"Nothing," Chester muttered.

"Chester," she began. "Please tell me."

He halted the horse at a red light and then turned toward her, his expression seeming sad. "*Mamm*, I don't know how to tell you this."

"Tell me what?"

He hesitated, and her stomach tied itself into a knot.

"Please, Chester, just say it."

"Emory is seeing a woman named Madelyne. She stopped by the shop last week and brought him a pie. I heard Justin saying something about giving her a chance."

She suddenly felt heavy and hollowed out, but she forced a smile to her lips. "Oh. I see." She shrugged. "I-I just wanted to thank him for being such a great boss and *freind* to you."

Not wanting her son to see the hurt in her eyes, she faced the windshield and stared out at the passing traffic. Her heart sank as she recalled the wonderful evening she and Emory had spent talking on her parents' porch. Since that day, she'd hoped he had felt a connection to her, but apparently that feeling was one-sided. They were only friends. That was all.

For the first time since Marlin died, she had finally felt something for another man—and now that man cared for someone else. All of her worries had come true. Emory had chosen Madelyne, which meant Leanna would lose Emory's friendship too.

Somehow she had to pick herself up and move on. Losing Emory's friendship was nothing compared to losing Marlin years ago.

And yet she felt the hurt.

Chester guided the horse into the parking lot and tied it up to a hitching post. She spotted the small stable at the back of the lot where Chester, Justin, and Emory kept their horses during the day while they worked.

Leanna climbed out of the buggy and then ambled into the shop with Chester. She tried to steel herself as she followed Chester into the office, where Emory sat at the desk. Chester waved at Emory and then continued past the office to the workshop.

His handsome face lit up. "Leanna. *Wie geht's?*" He stood and walked over to her.

"I'm well, *danki*." She held out the two jars of jelly. "I wanted to give you these and thank you for being so great to Chester."

"*Danki*, but it's been my pleasure to work with him." He reached out for the jars, and she was careful not to allow their hands to brush. The last thing she needed was another flush, another pang of longing.

He examined the jars, and his mouth hitched up into a warm smile. "Apple cranberry and apricot. *Danki* so much."

"*Gern gschehne*. I see such a difference in him since he came to work here. He finally agreed to sell his birdhouses at the marketplace. We set up a display last week, and he's already sold two."

"That's fantastic news, but I really can't take any credit."

"You deserve more than you know. You're a blessing to us." The words slipped out of her mouth without warning, and she inwardly cringed, wishing she could take them back.

Emory's smile faded and his expression became intense. Her breath paused in her lungs as they eyed each other, and she was certain she felt something pass between them. Why did she keep feeling this way when she knew he had chosen Madelyne over her?

Leanna took a step back away from him and cleared her throat. "Well, *danki* again. Chester was going to drop me off at work, but I can walk."

"Leanna. Wait."

She spun toward him.

"You and Chester should come for supper."

She blinked at him. "You sure?"

"*Ya*. Come tonight. Maggie and I haven't seen you in a while. It will be fun."

Leanna didn't quite know what to say. Finally she nodded in agreement.

"Great. I live over in Gordonville." He wrote down the

address on a slip of paper, and when he handed it to her, she grabbed it, trying her best to avoid his touch.

"I know where this is. Marlin and I used to live close by."

"Great. How does six sound?"

"Perfect. I . . . well, I guess we'll see you tonight," she said.

With her hands trembling, Leanna headed out of the office.

. . .

Emory's heartbeat skittered as Leanna padded toward the workshop to say good-bye to Chester. He'd missed her during the past few weeks, and it had been an answer to prayer when she appeared at the shop this morning.

When she said yes to dinner, his soul took flight. Not only had he missed her during the past few weeks, but he felt as if it would help Maggie to spend time with her. Maggie had skipped the last two youth group gatherings and seemed to be reverting into her shell.

If he were completely honest, he needed time with Leanna as much as Maggie did. He longed for the feeling he had when they were together. He hoped they could sit on the porch and talk for a while if they found a moment alone.

But first he had to let Maggie know that they would have two guests for supper. He dialed the number for their phone shanty and prayed she was outside and would hear the ring. After several rings, the phone picked up.

"Hello?"

"Hi, Maggie. I wanted to let you know I invited two *freinden* to join us for supper tonight. Can you cook a little extra for them?"

She hesitated for a beat. "Who did you invite?"

"Leanna and Chester." He bit his lower lip, hoping the news wouldn't upset her.

"Okay. I can make spaghetti and meatballs since I had that ground beef defrosted."

"Perfect. I told Leanna to come at six." Emory smiled as relief filtered through him. "*Danki*, Maggie. I'll see you after work."

"Bye, *Dat*," she said before the line went dead.

"Who was that?"

Emory nearly jumped out of his skin as he swiveled toward the doorway, where Justin stood, watching him. "I didn't hear you sneak up on me." He pressed his hand to his chest. "I had to call Maggie."

"Is everything okay?"

"*Ya*, I needed to tell her that I invited Leanna and Chester to join us for supper."

Justin's brow furrowed. "I thought you were seeing Madelyne now. How would she feel if she knew you invited another woman for supper?"

"I'm not dating Madelyne. I'm *freinden* with her *and* Leanna. And I think you need to worry about your own life instead of always obsessing about mine."

"You have no idea the trouble you might be causing," said Justin. "Look, I just want to see you and Maggie *froh*. I would hate for you to wind up hurt because you led Madelyne on. Just be careful." Then he shook his head, turned around, and walked toward the shop.

. . .

After telling Chester she was leaving, Leanna strode the few blocks from the shed shop to the marketplace. Once inside, she found Bethany in the Coffee Corner. She purchased a cup of coffee and a donut before they sat at a table together.

"Let me get this straight," Bethany began. "Chester told you that Emory is seeing Madelyne, but then Emory invited you both for supper tonight?"

"*Ya.*" Leanna shook her head as she stared down at her chocolate donut. "It doesn't make much sense. How would his girlfriend feel if she knew he was inviting me over for supper?"

"Maybe they're not really dating."

"Or maybe he wants to still be *freinden* with me."

"Well, no matter what, he's still not married to her." Bethany grinned and held up her cup of vanilla coffee. "That means you still have a chance."

Leanna sighed. While she wanted to hold on to hope, she didn't want to set herself up for disappointment. And also, she didn't want to behave like Sara Ann. After all, Sara Ann had tried to come between Bethany and Micah when they were getting to know each other. She'd nearly thrown herself at Micah, even though she knew Bethany cared for him.

After finishing her breakfast with Bethany, Leanna hurried over to her booth and began setting up for the day.

"Leanna?"

She turned as Kent Dobson, the marketplace manager, stood in her booth. He had a nice smile, and lately she noticed that he often wore horn-rimmed glasses. She guessed he was in his early fifties since his hair was more gray than brown.

"Hi, Kent. How are you?"

"I'm fine." He pointed toward the display of birdhouses. "I like those."

"Thanks. My son made them."

"He's very talented." He ran his finger over one of them. "I wanted to tell you that the candle shop next door to your booth is closing next week."

"Why?"

"Shauna is moving to New Jersey with her family. Her husband got transferred."

"That's a shame. I'll miss her."

"I will too." Kent pointed to the shelf of birdhouses. "Let me know if you want to expand. You'd have room for more birdhouses or more jams and jellies. I'll give you first dibs since you've been here so long."

"Thank you." Leanna smiled as Kent left.

She let the idea settle over her. Perhaps telling Chester he could expand and sell more items would make him happy. And seeing her son happy would help distract her from the feelings for Emory she knew she needed to control.

. . .

Leanna's stomach tightened as Chester guided the horse up a rock driveway that led to a large, two-story, brick farmhouse with a sweeping, wraparound porch dotted with rockers and a porch swing.

"Wow. This place is huge." Chester's reaction mirrored Leanna's unspoken thoughts. He halted the horse by the back porch.

Leanna gripped the pie she'd purchased in the marketplace and then climbed out of the buggy. She looked over toward the large, red barn just as Emory stepped outside into the evening sunlight and waved. Her knees wobbled at the sight of him.

He looked even more handsome than usual, dressed in a crisp gray shirt with his bright smile and gorgeous eyes sparkling in the late-afternoon light. She felt a longing take hold of her. Why had she allowed herself to fall for a man who could never be hers?

She chided herself for the thought, then balanced the pie in one hand as she waved the other. "Hi, Emory!"

"Hi there." Emory smiled at Chester. "Chester, you can put your horse in my barn."

"*Danki*," Chester said as he began unhitching his horse.

Emory walked over to her. "How was your day?"

"*Gut*." She held up the pie. "I picked up a chocolate cream pie at the Bake Stand in the marketplace."

"*Danki!*" He took the pie from her and then leaned in and lowered his voice. "But I'll remember it's not as *gut* as Christiana's, right?" His lips twitched.

She laughed. "You remember I told you that her Bake Shop was better?"

"Of course I do. I remember everything you've told me."

She studied his eyes as heat rushed to her cheeks. Why did this man have such a deep effect on her? She turned toward the house to untangle herself from his stare. "Your *haus* is just gorgeous, Emory."

"*Danki*. I built it for Sheryl, so she picked out the layout. It's much too big for just Maggie and me. I'm sure I'll get lost in it when she's moved on." He chuckled.

"The *haus* Marlin and I rented was only a few miles from here off Queen Road. We must have just missed the border of our two church districts."

"We were so close and didn't even know it. I wonder how many times we passed each other on the road and didn't even realize it."

"*Ya*, I wonder too."

They looked at each other for a beat, and she felt as if his eyes were pulling her in. She needed something to tear her away before she opened her heart to him.

She cleared her throat. "*Ya*, well, Marlin always wanted to build or buy a *haus* for us, but we couldn't afford it at the time," she began. "Of course, it all worked out. When I moved in with my parents, I was able to rejoin my old church district, which made me closer to my cousins. That was just what I needed, and, of course, Chester needed our family too. Marlin's parents passed away soon after we were married, so we've only had my family."

Her cheeks flamed when she realized she was babbling, but the understanding in his eyes sent another tremor through her.

"I can relate. Sheryl's parents live over in Lititz, so we don't see them as often as we'd like. Maggie is much closer to my family."

Just then Chester strode out of the barn, and Emory turned toward him.

"Let's go inside," Emory said. "Supper is probably ready. I hope you like spaghetti and meatballs."

Chester rubbed his flat abdomen. "One of my favorites."

"Mine too." Emory held the pie in one hand and clapped Chester on the shoulder with the other.

The camaraderie between them made Leanna's heart swell and also sent another flash of sadness through her. Not only had Leanna fallen for Emory but Chester was attached to him too.

And now Emory was dating someone else—which meant she'd be losing his precious friendship one day soon. She never should have agreed to come to supper tonight.

This had been a huge mistake.

CHAPTER 21

Leanna stepped into the house, and the delicious smells of meatballs and garlic bread swept over her. She scanned the large kitchen, taking in the beautiful oak cabinets and matching long oak table, which was already set for four. A bowl of salad, two bottles of dressing, and a container of parmesan cheese sat in the center of the table.

Maggie stood at the counter, dumping a colander of spaghetti into a large serving bowl. She peered over her shoulder and smiled. "Hi, Leanna."

"Hi, Maggie." Leanna stepped over to her. "How can I help you?"

"Could you please get the garlic bread out of the oven? There's a breadbasket on the counter there."

"Of course." Leanna washed her hands at the sink and then used two potholders to pull open the door to the propane-powered oven.

Emory moved to the counter and set down the pie. "Leanna brought us a chocolate cream pie."

"Ooh, my favorite." Maggie set the spaghetti on the table and then went back for the bowl of meatballs.

"I'll have to remember that." Leanna pulled out a pan of garlic bread and then used tongs to move the bread into the basket.

Then Maggie filled their drinking glasses with water from a pitcher while the men washed their hands at the sink.

Leanna set the breadbasket in the middle of the table and turned to Maggie. "Anything else I can do?"

"No, *danki*. We're all set." Maggie looked at her father. "Let's eat."

Leanna took a seat across from Emory and then looked around the table. She felt sadness coursing through her as she imagined this as her supper table every night, sitting with a blended family of four. Such a family she would never have.

Then it hit her. Maybe Emory had invited her over to tell her that he was seeing Madelyne and could no longer be her friend. A clammy feeling descended over her body, and her eyes stung with tears. *Oh no! Don't cry! Hold it together, Leanna!*

She pressed her lips together and tried to stop her soul from sinking. She bowed her head in silent prayer as the others did the same: Danki, *Lord, for this special supper with* freinden. *Please help me find a way to stop my heart from breaking apart every time I see Emory. I know he is in a relationship with someone else, but I can't imagine losing his friendship. Please make me strong enough to sustain the blow when he tells me we can no longer be* freinden.

Emory shifted in his seat, and Leanna looked up, pasting a smile on her face. She picked up her water glass. "Everything looks *appeditlich*, Maggie."

Chester nodded. "It does."

"*Danki*. I'm so glad you both could come tonight." Maggie smiled.

"Maggie," Chester began as everyone looked over at him, "I wanted to apologize for getting you into trouble that night we went out with Danny and Alea. I'm truly sorry."

Leanna sucked in a breath as she looked over at Emory, who smiled.

"I've already forgiven you." Maggie picked up the bread-basket and took a piece before passing it to Leanna.

"*Danki*," Chester said.

Soon their plates were full and they talked about work while they ate. Leanna laughed as Emory and Chester shared funny stories about their adventures at work and how Chester had struggled when he first started at the shed shop.

Maggie laughed along with them, then Leanna pulled her further into the conversation by asking about her sewing and quilting projects.

Once supper was over, Maggie served coffee and pieces of the chocolate cream pie Leanna had brought. Maggie and Chester talked about youth group and their mutual friends while they enjoyed their dessert.

"Oh, I am stuffed," Chester announced as he finished his slice. "You're a very gifted cook, Maggie."

"*Ya*, you are." Leanna stood and gathered up their plates. After placing a pile of utensils on top of the stack, she carried them to the counter.

Chester turned to Emory. "Would you please show me your shop that you told me about?"

"Of course." Emory pushed back his chair and stood.

Leanna returned to clear more of the table, and when her eyes met Emory's, he smiled at her.

"We'll be outside in the shop," he said.

Leanna turned to face Maggie, who stood at the sink, filling one side with soapy water. "After we finish the dishes, I'd love to see your sewing and quilting projects."

Maggie looked at her over her shoulder. "You would?"

"Of course." The women continued making small talk about recipes while they cleaned up the kitchen. Once the job was done, Leanna wiped her hands on a dishtowel and flashed a grin at Maggie. "Can we go see your sewing room now?"

Maggie gave her a shy smile. "Okay." She made a sweeping gesture for Leanna to follow her up the steep steps to the second floor. "It's upstairs along with my bedroom."

When Leanna reached the landing, she glimpsed down the hallway at the four doors. "Your *haus* is very spacious."

"You think so?" Maggie looked surprised.

"*Ya*, there are four bedrooms up here?"

"*Ya*, and *mei dat*'s is downstairs."

"It's bigger than most houses I've seen!"

Maggie smiled and shrugged. "It's all I've ever known. My parents were hoping to have many *kinner* when *mei dat* built it for *mei mamm*, but God had other plans." She pointed toward the first door on the right. "That's my room."

Leanna peeked in and found a single bed, two dressers, a cedar chest, and a desk in the large room. A beautiful pink and purple quilt featuring a large star in the middle flanked by roses covered the bed.

"Did you make that quilt?"

Maggie shook her head. "*Mei mammi* did."

"It's lovely."

They moved to the next door, and Maggie stepped inside. Leanna followed her and spotted the sewing machines and two worktables. Shelves around the perimeter of the room held colorful quilts, dolls, tote bags, purse covers, little travel packs, potholders, wall hangings, and pillows.

Leanna walked over to a faceless doll wearing a bright pink dress, black apron, and prayer covering. A male version of the doll sat beside it, wearing a shirt that matched the dress, along with a little straw hat and a beard. She turned the doll over in her hand and then looked up at Maggie, who watched with a hesitant expression.

"You made these, Maggie?"

Maggie nodded and pointed to the other dolls behind her. "I made all of them."

"They are adorable!" Leanna moved on to a pile of cosmetic bags created from material that showed a horse and buggy moving down the road past a farm. She picked up a matching purse. "And these?"

Maggie laughed. "*Ya*. I made all of them."

"Oh my goodness." Leanna then marveled over a shelf full of tote bags. "You have such talent!"

Maggie just smiled and hugged her arms to her waist.

Leanna stood in front of the table piled high with quilts last. She ran her fingers over the stitching of a gray and blue block pattern quilt, then shook her head and sighed. "I always wished I had *mei mammi*'s talent with quilts."

"I can teach you." Maggie sidled up beside her.

"That's a very generous offer, Maggie." Leanna touched Maggie's shoulder and once again felt disappointment swamp her. If only she could be the one Emory had chosen, then she would have the opportunity to get to know Maggie better and possibly even become her stepmother someday.

She faced Maggie as an idea filled her. "Have you ever considered selling your creations?"

Maggie shook her head. "No. I donate them to charity auctions. I also sometimes give them as gifts."

Leanna touched a Wedding Ring pattern quilt created in beautiful shades of green and blue as she envisioned the empty booth beside hers full of Maggie's creations and Chester's bird-houses. It was almost too good to imagine! But would Maggie even want to sell her quilts and crafts? And, more importantly, would Emory allow her to?

"Would you like to see my favorite quilt?" Maggie asked, snapping Leanna back to the present.

"Of course I would."

"*Mei mamm* gave it to me. It was the last one she ever made. I keep it in a special place so that nothing happens to it."

"I'd be honored to see it."

"I'll be right back." Maggie slipped out of the room.

Footsteps echoed in the stairwell as Leanna continued to examine the quilts. She ran her fingers over the stitching and imagined Maggie hard at work making the beautiful creations.

When Leanna felt as if someone was watching her, she turned and sucked in a breath at the sight of Emory leaning on the door frame. "Oof! I didn't hear you coming up the stairs!"

"Sorry, I didn't mean to frighten you." He stood up to his full height. "I came in to get a drink of water and thought I'd check on you and Maggie. What are you two up to?"

Leanna's mouth dried as she stared at him, speechless for a moment, words tossing around in her head. Why did his presence make her senses spin?

"Maggie has been showing me all her quilted creations, and I can't get over how talented she is." Her idea overtook her mind once again, and she crossed her arms over her waist, debating asking Emory his opinion.

"You look like you're dying to say something."

"Am I that transparent?"

He nodded. "To me you are."

Can you tell I care for you? She cleared her throat against sudden thickness. "There's a booth next to mine at the market that is going to be available next week. I was thinking maybe we could expand my booth and sell Maggie's quilts and crafts along with Chester's birdhouses there. The manager of the marketplace told me about it today. He said he wanted to offer it to me first."

Emory tilted his head and rubbed his beard, and Leanna longed to take back the suggestion. She'd been too bold. She opened her mouth to apologize just as the corners of his mouth lifted.

"I love the idea."

Leanna blew out the breath she'd been holding. "You do?"

"What idea?" Maggie appeared in the doorway behind him with a beautiful light pink and baby-blue quilt hanging over her arm.

Emory turned toward her and gave her a gentle smile. "Leanna just told me there's a booth coming available next to hers at the market, and you could sell your quilts and crafts there."

Maggie blinked, and her eyes widened as she divided a look between Emory and Leanna.

"You and I could run the booth together," Leanna said.

"But what about all of my chores?" Maggie began.

"The marketplace is only open Thursday through Saturday," said Leanna. "You'd still have time to do your chores. I do the bulk of my chores Monday through Wednesday."

Emory looked over at Leanna and smiled at her, looking grateful for her quick response.

"And you can keep all of your money. We'd open a savings account, and you could save it for your future," Emory added.

"I-I don't know." Maggie swallowed. "I'll have to think about it."

"That's fine." Leanna smiled at her.

"We'll talk about it later, but I bet Leanna will have to let the manager know soon if she wants the booth." Emory met Leanna's gaze and winked at her, sending another chill dancing up her spine.

Leanna ripped her attention away from him and pointed to the quilt in Maggie's arms. "Is that the quilt your *mamm* made for you?"

"*Ya.*" Maggie set it out on the free space on the table. "It's two linking hearts. She said one was mine and the other was hers."

"Oh, Maggie. It's so *schee.*"

"I wish I had her talent."

"You do, *mei liewe.*" Leanna touched her shoulder. "You truly do. I mean it."

"I'll leave you two ladies to your discussion." Emory's voice sounded raspy.

Leanna peered up at him, and she couldn't quite name the emotion on his face. Grief? Regret? Longing? Or maybe a combination of the three?

She smiled at him, and he returned the gesture before giving her a nod. Then he disappeared from the doorway before his heavy footfalls echoed in the stairwell once again.

If only he were as transparent to her as she seemed to be to him.

. . .

"I had a great time," Leanna told Emory as they stepped out onto the porch together later that evening.

"I did too," Emory said, regret welling up in him.

How had the evening flown by so quickly? He'd hoped to

spend time talking with her tonight, but he'd gotten so caught up with discussing carpentry projects with Chester in his shop that he'd lost track of time.

He'd only had a few minutes to visit with her in the sewing room, and when he'd seen her interact with Maggie, he felt that he should remove himself and allow them to continue to bond.

He'd been overwhelmed by their interaction—the way Maggie had opened up to her and how gently Leanna had spoken to her. The sight was so tender, he nearly got emotional right there in front of them.

Now she stood on his back porch looking out toward where Chester hitched up the horse and buggy, her face glowing in the light of the sunset above them. She wore a red dress that he had decided was his favorite on her because it brought out the warmth in her brown hair and beautiful brown eyes.

He tried to ignore his craving in the moment. Oh, how he wished he could spend the rest of the night next to her on the porch swing. Were such a thing permitted, he knew he could talk to her well into the night, or even until the sun began to rise in the morning.

"*Danki* for having us," she said. She turned toward the stairs.

Without thinking, he gently took hold of her hand and pulled her back to him. "Leanna, wait."

Her eyes wide, she gasped and pulled her hand back as if he'd bitten her.

"I'm sorry." He held his hands up. "I—please forgive me."

"No, no, it's okay." She looked up at him as if he'd lost his mind.

"I just wanted to thank you for inviting Maggie to sell her quilts and her other creations at the booth." He was careful to keep his voice low so Maggie didn't hear through the open windows behind them. "She stopped going to youth gatherings again. I've been racking my brain for a way for her to come out of her shell, and I think selling her quilts and crafts in a booth is the way to do it. It will force her to talk to people, and it will also boost her self-confidence when she sees how people appreciate her work."

Leanna smiled, though weakly. "I'll tell Kent I want the booth."

For another heartbeat, something magnetic pulled him to her. He longed to touch her hand again and then run his fingers over her cheeks.

But he resisted. She had pulled away from him just now—a gesture that had hurt him in its quickness. And Chester had warned him that she wasn't interested in dating. He had no business being so familiar with her. "I'll talk to Maggie, and then I'll be in touch."

Leanna gave him one more warm but weak smile. "Great. And again, *danki* for a lovely evening." She adjusted her prayer covering and turned to leave, rushing down the steps toward where Chester stood at the buggy.

He let go of a deep breath as the horse and buggy started down the driveway.

He heard Maggie step out onto the porch behind him. "They're gone?" she asked.

"*Ya.*" He nodded toward the swing. "Why don't you sit for a minute."

She sank down onto the swing, and he sat beside her.

"I think you should start selling all of those *schee* quilts and crafts you've made. It would be *gut* for you to get out of this *haus* some."

"Do you think *Mamm* would be proud if I did?"

He smiled and nodded. "*Ya*. Remember how she went to market to sell her quilts too?"

Maggie's expression brightened. "I'll do it then." Her smile faded slightly. "But I promise not to let my chores suffer."

"You can get them done on Mondays, Tuesdays, and Wednesdays like Leanna said she does. And I can do things around here, too, remember?"

"Okay."

He looped his arm around her, and she leaned her head on his shoulder. "I think you're going to love running the booth with Leanna." He looked up at the beautiful sunset. *Thank you, God, for bringing Leanna into our lives!*

"I like Leanna, but I don't want a new *mamm*."

Emory looked down at her and he felt a clutching in his heart. For the first time, he could imagine himself remarrying and starting a new life with a wonderful woman, but Maggie wasn't ready. Why would God bring Leanna into his life if it weren't the right time? But he had to consider his daughter's happiness too.

He cleared his throat past his disappointment. "I'm not dating her, Maggie. She's our *freind*."

As he pushed the swing into motion, he tried to imagine having Leanna in his life. Oh, how blessed he would be.

But he could only pray to be that blessed.

CHAPTER 22

Leanna slipped her cash into the battery-operated register in her booth Saturday morning. Then, humming to herself, she strolled around the booth and straightened her jars of jam and jelly before moving to the display of birdhouses.

"How much for one of those spectacular birdhouses?"

She stilled and then turned, surprised to find Emory standing at the entrance to the booth. "Emory. We don't open for another twenty minutes. How did you get in here?"

"I told the security guard I needed to get a message to you. I guess I look official since I'm Amish." He shrugged.

She laughed. "I guess so. What brings you here?"

"I spoke to Maggie after you and Chester left last night, and she agreed to open the booth."

"Oh!" Leanna clapped. "That is fantastic!"

"I know." He grinned. "I couldn't wait to come and tell you the news. I didn't want to lose the chance at getting the booth."

"Let's go talk to Kent now." She gestured for him to follow her, and they headed to the manager's office located at the back of the market, where they found Kent sitting at his desk.

Leanna knocked on the door frame. "Hi, Kent."

"Good morning, Leanna." Kent stood and shook her hand. "How may I help you?"

"Kent, this is my friend Emory Speicher," she said, and

Emory shook his hand. "Emory's daughter makes beautiful quilts and other handmade fabric crafts. I told Emory about your offer to allow me to rent the booth next door, and we would like to extend my booth and add in his daughter's crafts, along with more birdhouses."

Kent rubbed his hands together. "This will be great for the market!"

"When will the booth be available?" Emory asked.

"Since Tuesday is the last day of the month, Shauna has until Tuesday night to get everything out. That means you can move in on Wednesday."

Leanna turned toward Emory. "What do you think?"

"I don't see any problem with that," Emory said. "How much is the booth rent?"

Leanna pivoted toward Emory. "Oh, no, I was going to pay the rent."

"You shouldn't have to pay it if my daughter's quilts and crafts are going to fill the shelves."

"But this was my idea, and Chester will sell his birdhouses there as well."

Emory shook his head. "Maggie is going to make money off of your rental, so that wouldn't be fair."

"Wait." Leanna held up a pointer finger. "What if we split it?"

Emory considered this. "Fine."

Kent told them the monthly cost, and then Emory and Leanna signed the contract. Leanna tried to memorize his signature on the page and wondered if she'd ever have the chance to see his handwriting again. Would he ever send her a note or a birthday card? Maybe a Christmas card?

She did a mental head-slap. She was losing her mind!

"Thank you very much, Kent." Emory shook his hand again.

"I appreciate the business. I think your daughter will find this marketplace is very busy and profitable."

"Thanks, Kent," Leanna said before they walked back toward her booth. "I can't wait to get started." She stopped outside the candle booth and waved at Shauna as she placed jar candles into a box. The delicious smell of her candles filled the air around them. "This is the booth."

Emory rubbed his chin. "It's large. We can definitely make this work."

"Do you think you can come up with some fixtures or stands to hang the quilts?"

"Oh *ya*. I kept all of Sheryl's stands from when she used to sell her quilts. I also have some shelving units Maggie can use for the other crafts. I'll clean them up and get them ready."

"Sheryl used to sell quilts?" Leanna asked as they stepped into her booth.

"*Ya*, and she made a *gut* living at it too. That's actually what helped convince Maggie to say yes." Emory sat on a stool by the counter. "She was worried about her chores. And then she asked if Sheryl would be proud if she sold the quilts. I think she had forgotten that her *mamm* used to do the very same thing." He snapped his fingers. "And that's what sold her on the booth."

Leanna leaned on the counter beside him. "What a sweet *maedel*. She truly worries about what Sheryl would think."

He lifted his straw hat and pushed his hand through his thick, dark hair. "As much as I try to tell her that Sheryl would be proud, she still worries." He looked over toward the birdhouses. "I really like seeing those birdhouses here."

"I do too." Leanna took in his profile. "I feel like I have you to thank for that and for a lot of the changes in Chester. Actually, for all of the changes in Chester. He's been more agreeable and thoughtful of late. He actually apologized to me for getting into trouble the night we met. And I was surprised when he apologized to Maggie too. Anyway . . . *danki*, Emory."

"*Gern gschehne*, but God deserves the thanks. All I've done is talk to Chester. He started opening up to me a few weeks ago, and I've mostly just listened." He motioned around the booth. "I'm sure I'll be thanking you, too, very shortly."

She heard the whoosh of the market's front doors, and then a multitude of voices announced the arrival of customers. "Sounds like the market is open." Disappointment rained down on her. Their time together was over.

"Then I'd better get going." Emory hopped off the stool. "I'll talk to my driver about loading everything up Wednesday morning and then bringing it all over here, hopefully before noon. Justin won't mind if I take Wednesday off. How does that sound?"

"Like the perfect plan."

"Great." He held his hand out to her and she shook it, enjoying the warmth of his skin. "I look forward to seeing you Wednesday."

"Take care, Emory." She walked him to the booth entrance and watched him disappear into the sea of customers.

"Leanna!" Bethany called from her counter. "Come here! Quick!"

Leanna scurried over.

"What was that about?" Bethany motioned to where customers were strolling into her booth. "Tell me quickly before my line starts."

Leanna explained the plan to rent the booth next door. "Emory thinks having Maggie work in the booth will help build her confidence."

"What a *wunderbaar* idea." Bethany's smile became almost sly. "And if Emory trusts you to help Maggie, then he truly cares for you."

"I believe he does, but not in a romantic way." The words tasted bitter on Leanna's lips, but she believed it was the truth.

"We'll have to see about that." Bethany looked at the line forming. "Anyway, I need to go. We'll talk later. Make lots of sales!"

"You too." Leanna ambled back to her booth.

As she greeted her customers, Leanna's gaze fell on the booth next door that would soon be filled with colorful crafts handmade by the young people in her life.

Next week she and Emory would begin a new chapter in their friendship, and she couldn't wait.

. . .

Excitement filled Emory as he stepped out of the stable at the back of the parking lot at the shop. How he enjoyed seeing Leanna first thing in the morning. If only every day could be like this!

He shook his head and tried to clear that thought from his mind as he made his way into the shop. There he found Justin, Lee, and Chester already working on their next shed.

"Oh, look who decided to show up this morning," Justin quipped as he lifted a bottle of water to his mouth. "We were just wondering if you'd overslept or decided to stay home."

"I had to make a stop on the way to work." Emory crossed the shop to join them. "I had to go to the marketplace on Maggie's behalf."

Justin looked confused. "The marketplace?"

"Why?" Chester asked at the same time.

Lee sat back on his heels. "You were at the marketplace and didn't bring us *kaffi*?"

"I'm sorry, Lee. I didn't think of *kaffi*." *Because I was too distracted by Leanna's* schee *smile!* "Leanna has the opportunity to expand her booth, and she invited Maggie to sell her quilts and crafts there." Emory pointed to Chester. "Along with your birdhouses, which look fantastic there, by the way."

Chester smiled. "Thanks."

"Maggie agreed with the plan, and I wanted to stop by to tell Leanna before she lost her chance at getting the booth. We've seen how busy that marketplace is." Emory focused on his brother. "Would you mind if I took Wednesday off to move Maggie's things to the booth and help set it up?"

"I don't mind at all." Justin shrugged. "Business has slowed a little, and I can call *Dat* if we need an extra pair of hands."

"I was thinking the same thing. We know *Dat* loves to help, even though he keeps saying he's retiring."

"Could I help at the marketplace too?" Chester offered, dividing a look between Justin and Emory.

Justin nodded. "It's fine with me."

"Great. It's settled." Emory scanned the shop. "Did I miss much?"

"Not really." Lee chuckled, stood, and turned to Chester. "Help me fetch some more nails?"

Chester followed Lee out of the shop toward the supply room at the back of the building.

Emory sidled up to his brother once Lee and Chester were gone from the shop. "I want to explain why this is important to me. Maggie stopped going to youth group again, and I'm anxious to find a way to help her get more confidence. I think having her work at the marketplace will not only help her self-esteem but make her get comfortable talking to people. I believe this is an opportunity that God is giving Maggie to grow." *And God is using Leanna to help her!*

"Whatever Maggie needs, Emory. Lee and I will make do while you and Chester set up the booth." Justin patted his brother's shoulder.

"Danki." Emory cracked his knuckles. "Now—put me to work."

. . .

Sunday afternoon Emory and Maggie stepped into Emory's parents' kitchen, and the aroma of coffee and cookies teased him. Since it was an off-Sunday without a service, they planned to visit with family all day.

"Hello," Emory called as he smiled at his parents, Justin, and Natalie. He felt his smile slip when he found Madelyne sitting at the table beside his sister-in-law. "Hi, Madelyne. What a nice surprise."

Her cheeks blushed bright pink. "Hi, Emory. I hope it's okay that I'm here. Natalie invited me."

"Of course it is. It's great to see you."

Justin pointed to the counter where a baking dish sat. "She brought a peach cobbler."

"Even better. How have you been?" Emory grinned as he crossed the room and sat down beside her.

She looked pretty in a mint-green dress that made her eyes seem an even brighter shade of green, along with a black apron.

"Gut," Madelyne pointed to Maggie, who had sunk down

into an empty chair beside her grandfather. "I heard Maggie has some exciting news."

"*Ya*," *Mamm* chimed in. "Tell us, Maggie."

Maggie's smile was bright. "I'm opening a booth at the marketplace to sell my quilts and other crafts. I'm so excited."

"That's *wunderbaar*!" *Dat* exclaimed.

Natalie clapped. "Oh, I can't wait to come and see it."

"When are you opening it?" *Mamm* set a plate of peanut butter cookies and the cobbler on the table while Natalie carried over mugs.

Madelyne stood and crossed to the percolator.

"Wednesday. I spent most of yesterday figuring out what crafts I want to sell. I've divided them up in boxes by category. Tomorrow I'll get back to sewing."

"How will you display what you've made?" Madelyne asked as she filled mugs with coffee.

"I saved Sheryl's quilt stands," said Emory, "and I have some shelves I don't use anymore." He looked over at Maggie. "I can always build something if you need it, though."

Maggie beamed, and Emory's heart swelled at the happiness in his daughter's face. He hoped to see that look of joy more often.

"I'm sure you will sell out of your crafts. They are so unique and well made." Madelyne sat down beside Emory, and when her leg brushed his, she blushed once again.

"You're very kind. I'm having some trouble pricing them, though." Maggie pursed her lips. "How do I know how much someone will pay?"

"I can help you with that. I have a price list from when I used to sell my crafts at marketplaces," *Mamm* said.

"I do too," Madelyne said. "I remember."

"Could I look at your price list, *Mammi*?"

"Sure."

"Now?" Maggie pushed her chair back.

Mamm looked over at Madelyne and Natalie and then shrugged. "Why not? We can bring our *kaffi* and peach cobbler up to the sewing room. I have enough chairs in there for us."

Maggie picked up her mug of coffee and a cookie before following her grandmother, Natalie, and Madelyne up the stairs toward the sewing room.

"Justin told me about her booth at the marketplace," *Dat* said once the women were gone. "I think it's a great idea."

Emory cut himself a piece of peach cobbler. "I'm hoping it will help her overcome her shyness."

"*Ya*, and how about you, Em?" Justin asked.

"What do you mean?" Emory took a bite.

"When are you going to stop beating around the bush with Madelyne and ask her out?"

Emory swallowed and peered at his brother. "Now I see why Natalie invited Madelyne. So that you two could pressure me to ask her out."

"Well?" Justin gave him a palms-up. "You're not getting any younger, and neither is she. Make a move before you miss your chance with her. It's obvious you like each other, and she and Maggie get along. Before you know it, Maggie will be dating, married, and then gone. Do you really want to live in that big *haus* alone?"

Emory fixed his brother with a glare. "I've told you to butt out of my life. I'm a grown man, and I don't need you and your *fraa* trying to be my matchmakers."

Justin crossed his arms over his chest as a smirk overtook

his face. "I'm right, and you know it. Talk to Madelyne today. Ask her out."

Emory looked at his father, who nodded.

"He's right, Emory. Madelyne is a lovely *maedel*. She wouldn't be here if she weren't ready for you to take this friendship to the next level."

Emory nodded, but a question twisted through his mind—how could he be sure he was ready? And how could he be sure Madelyne was the one if Leanna filled his thoughts?

But if Leanna wasn't interested in him and Madelyne was, perhaps his family was right and he needed to jump at the chance at dating Madelyne before he wound up alone.

CHAPTER 23

Later that afternoon, Emory sat on a rocker on his mother's porch between Madelyne and Justin while Natalie talked on about how quickly the summer had flown by.

"How can Wednesday be September already? Wasn't it just June first?" she insisted.

"The years go by faster the older you get," *Mamm* said. "Wait until you're my age."

"That's coming quicker than we want to admit," Justin quipped, and everyone laughed.

Emory stared off toward the colorful flowers in his mother's garden. The last blooms of summer were also approaching the end of their season. He hadn't considered that maybe he was also running out of time to find a partner for the next season of his life. Was there truth in his brother's words?

"Emory?"

"*Ya?*" He turned toward Madelyne, who smiled at him.

"Are you okay?"

He smiled, and her expression warmed. "*Ya*, I am. Would you like to go for a stroll?"

She nodded with such vigor that the ties to her prayer covering bounced off her slight shoulders. "*Ya*, I would."

"Great." Emory stood, and his family looked up at him from their rocking chairs. Natalie winked at Emory, and he hoped

Madelyne hadn't seen the gesture. When he looked at Maggie, her brow crumpled in a worried frown—another problem to deal with later.

For now, he was going to give Madelyne a chance, and this was the only way to get her alone so they could talk.

Emory gestured for Madelyne to go down the porch steps first, and then they walked together down the stone path that led to his father's small pasture. Above them, gray, fluffy clouds dotted the azure sky, and the smell of rain overtook his senses.

"It's lovely here," Madelyne said as they padded toward the white, split rail fence.

"I agree. How far away do you live?"

She pointed toward the road. "Only a few miles down that way."

"Near Natalie's parents, right?"

"That's right. Natalie and I went to school together."

She stopped and rested her hands on the top rail of the fence and looked out toward where his father's horses stood.

"I didn't mean to intrude today. I told Natalie I didn't feel comfortable coming when it was family time, but she insisted." She looked over at him and her expression seemed earnest. "She's determined to see us together."

"I appreciate your honesty."

She laughed. "Natalie is not very subtle. She never has been."

"That is a true statement." He felt his body relax for the first time since he'd met Madelyne. It was as if the ice had finally been broken between them.

"I like you, Emory, but I'd like to get to know you better before dating you."

More relief flooded him. "I feel the same way."

"*Gut*. Then let's see where this goes." She tilted her head. "But I want us to be honest with each other. No secrets and no games. We're too old for games."

"That is refreshing to hear. So, we're *freinden* who are getting to know each other and don't have time for games. That is a deal." He held his hand out.

She shook his hand, then held on to it. "I look forward to getting to know you better."

"I do too." As he peered into her green eyes, he smiled. Madelyne seemed like a pleasant woman, but as they held hands, he didn't feel anything.

In the back of his mind, he found himself longing for Leanna instead.

. . .

"How was your afternoon walk?" *Mamm* asked Emory as he stood on the back porch with her, *Dat*, and Maggie.

The sweet smell of summer rain engulfed his senses as drops had begun falling, beating a light cadence on the porch roof above them. Madelyne had left with Justin and Natalie a few minutes ago after they had all eaten supper together.

Emory smiled. "It was fine."

"Are you dating her?" Maggie's voice creaked as her eyes scrutinized him.

"No," he said, careful to keep his voice calm. "We are just getting to know each other. That's all."

She looked unconvinced.

"Neither of us wants to rush into a relationship, so please don't worry, Maggie. We're not dating, and I'm not getting married. Nothing is going to change." He rested his hand on her shoulder and gave it a little squeeze.

Mamm and *Dat* exchanged a look, and Emory chose to ignore it.

"We should really get going," Emory said. "I think this rain is going to get worse."

"We're glad you came." *Mamm* gave him a quick hug.

"Danki." Emory shook his father's hand. "And I'll see you at the shop sometime this week." Then Emory raced out into the light rain to the barn to retrieve his horse. He quickly hitched up the buggy and then guided the horse to the porch, where Maggie hugged her grandparents before hopping in.

Soon they were making their way through the rain toward their house. "Are you going to price your crafts tomorrow?" he asked, guiding the horse slowly down the lane.

"Ya! I'm going to use *Mammi*'s price list. I think I'll start with the dolls and then work on the quilts."

Emory smiled as Maggie talked on about the prices and the work she had to do to prepare for the booth. He settled back into the seat and felt himself relax. It had been a good day. He had not only enjoyed seeing his family but had also enjoyed getting to know Madelyne a little better.

Still, he felt confusion clouding over his heart. As much as he had relished his time with Madelyne in the afternoon, his thoughts had turned time and time again to Leanna.

. . .

"Gude mariye!"

Leanna stepped out of the empty booth beside hers at the marketplace and then darted over to where Emory, Chester, and Maggie walked toward her carrying boxes filled with Maggie's crafts. "Oh my goodness. Let me help you."

She reached for the box Maggie held, but Maggie shook her head. "I got it."

Emory moved inside the booth and looked around. "Shauna left some of the shelves?"

"*Ya.* When I spoke to her Saturday, she said she didn't need them anymore. She sold off what stock she could and left me the shelves."

"How nice!" Emory said. "Those will be wonderful to display everyone's items."

Leanna gave a little smile before she turned toward the shelves to the far side of the booth. "These shelves are what separate my booth from this one. We can just move them and expand." Then she pointed toward the opening. "We could even block this opening and make it one big booth." She pointed toward the shelves. "Don't you think we should move them over here and make it so that there's only one entrance and exit?"

She looked at Maggie. "That way we can share the register. We can keep track of which sales are yours and which are mine and Chester's."

Emory nodded. "I think it's a great idea."

"Why don't we get the rest of the boxes and then worry about how to arrange it?" Chester said before heading back toward the marketplace exit.

Emory grinned. "He's getting awfully bossy like his *mamm.*"

Leanna gave a dramatic gasp, then swatted at his arm playfully.

They spent the next forty-five minutes unloading Emory's driver's pickup truck. While Leanna and Maggie carried the lighter boxes of crafts and quilts, Emory, Chester, and Emory's driver, Miles, brought in the heavier items, shelves, and quilt stands.

Once everything was unloaded, Emory and Chester rearranged the shelves and quilt stands, and Leanna and Maggie started organizing the crafts by category. When Leanna heard a meow, she turned as Daisy and Lily scampered into the booth and began investigating the scene.

"Who is this?" Maggie asked as Lily rubbed up against her shin and blinked up at her.

"That's Lily." Then Leanna pointed at Daisy. "And this is her *mamm*, Daisy. They live here, and we all feed them."

"Oh, how fun!" Maggie rubbed Lily's back. "I look forward to getting to know you, Lily."

While Maggie scratched the cats behind their ears, Leanna crossed to a nearby shelf displaying Maggie's dolls. She picked up a doll and examined it. The faceless fabric doll wore a pink dress, a white apron, and a prayer covering.

"Maggie, I can't wait for the customers to see what you've made." She turned the dainty doll over in her hand and looked at the handwritten price.

"Do you think my prices are fair?" Maggie asked.

"I do."

"I got a price list from *mei mammi* on Sunday when we visited at my grandparents' *haus*. Did you know *mei mammi* used to sell crafts too? Anyway, Madelyne was there, and she told me that she sells her crafts and quilts for similar prices."

Leanna stilled at the mention of Madelyne's name. She felt her smile flatten, but she kept her eyes focused on the doll. "I'm certain customers would love to have a doll as *schee* as this, so they will be *froh* to pay what you're asking."

Leanna snuck a peek at Emory as he and Chester moved another shelf. Her heart sank as she imagined Emory and Madelyne sitting down to a family dinner on Sunday at his parents' house. Once again, she envisioned a beautiful Amish woman laughing at Emory's jokes and blending in perfectly with Emory's family. The image knotted her insides.

Disappointment, heartbreak, and envy stung Leanna like a swarm of hornets. Then guilt swamped her. Who was she to decide who Emory should love? He was her friend, and he deserved to be happy, even if he chose to find happiness with another woman. Even if she was left feeling lonely in his wake.

. . .

"I think it looks perfect," Maggie said when they finally finished preparing the booth later that afternoon.

They had taken a short lunch break to eat sandwiches and cookies that Leanna and Maggie had brought, and then they continued to work until the shelves and quilt stands were ready. After the booth was arranged, they carried the empty boxes and trash out to the dumpster.

Emory rested his hand on Chester's shoulder. "We make a great team."

Chester beamed as he looked up at Emory, and a sharp, painful ache cut through Leanna's heart. What a wonderful stepfather Emory would make!

Leanna cringed. Emory had chosen Madelyne, and she needed to find a way to accept that.

Maggie strode over to a display of Chester's birdhouses and touched them. "These are fantastic."

"*Danki.*" Chester pointed toward all of Maggie's crafts. "But they pale in comparison to your talent."

Maggie blushed. "Thanks."

"I do foresee one problem though." Emory tapped his chin.

Leanna spun toward him. "What do you mean?"

"Well, it's not the Jam and Jelly Nook anymore." Emory made a sweeping gesture around the booth. "Is it?"

Leanna frowned as she recalled Sara Ann's comment. "I don't think it matters."

"I do." Emory reached into a nearby box and held up a wooden sign. "That's why I made this last night." He handed it to Leanna.

Leanna sucked in a breath as she took in the beautiful wooden sign that said *The Jam and Jelly Nook and Quilt and Gift Stand*. She ran her fingers over it and then gazed up at his hesitant smile. "Emory. This is gorgeous."

Maggie grinned. "I told you she'd like it, *Dat.*"

"It's perfect," Chester agreed.

Emory shrugged. "I'm not really great at engraving, but I did my best."

"How thoughtful of you." She bit back the urge to hug him, and instead turned her attention to her original sign, hanging over the booth entrance. "Would you please hang it for me?"

Emory took the sign and reached up to remove the original one and replace it with the new sign. Thankfully the slots for the hooks aligned perfectly.

"And now," Emory announced in a loud voice, "the new and improved Jam and Jelly Nook and Quilt and Gift Stand!" He made a sweeping gesture toward the booth entrance.

Leanna, Chester, and Maggie clapped and cheered.

"It's time to celebrate." Emory rubbed his hands together. "Who likes pizza?"

"I do," Chester said.

Maggie grinned. "You know I do, *Dat*."

"Leanna?" Emory's expression was hopeful. "Do you like pizza?"

"Who doesn't like pizza?"

"Great. I'll call my driver, and we can all go out and grab some supper."

"We can take my horse and buggy since I came straight from the shop," Chester said.

Emory grinned. "Okay then. Let's go get some food."

CHAPTER 24

Tell that fishing story about you and *Onkel* Justin, *Dat*," Maggie said through a laugh.

"Which one?" Emory asked with a grin.

For the past hour, Emory, Leanna, Chester, and Maggie had enjoyed two pepperoni pizzas in Emory's favorite pizzeria while sharing stories and laughing. And Emory had cherished every minute of it as he watched Leanna chuckle, her beautiful milk-chocolate eyes sparkling.

Maggie snorted. "The one where you had to climb the tree."

"Why would you have to climb a tree while you're fishing?" Leanna's brow furrowed.

"This has to be *gut*," Chester said.

Emory wiped his hands with a paper napkin. "Oh *ya*. So one time when we were teenagers, Justin and I went fishing at the pond near our *haus*. He always liked to do the dramatic cast, so he'd swing his arm back and then release it." Emory held his arm up as if to show them.

"This is so *gut*!" Maggie giggled.

"So, Justin released it, and the pole is stuck behind him. Then he looked around, trying to figure out where the line went. I started laughing, and he couldn't figure out why. Then I pointed to the tree behind him. He'd hooked a branch on the tree!" Emory started chuckling. "He realized what had happened and fell on the ground from laughing. I had to climb the tree and try to find his hook. It wasn't as easy as it sounds since I was laughing so hard I almost fell out of the tree."

Chester wiped his eyes. "That is hilarious."

Maggie held her hand up. "What about the time you went camping and the tent collapsed?"

"*Ya*, if you go camping with *mei bruder*, don't let him pitch the tent." Emory took a deep breath and wiped his eyes. "We went camping with our youth group, and I had to share a tent with him, of course. He said he could put the tent up without my help. Well, a windstorm came through, and the tent collapsed around us. He hadn't tied it down enough, and we nearly blew away!"

Leanna covered her mouth with her hand as she chortled. Oh, how he loved that sound! "You and your *bruder* have had some adventures," she said.

"We have." Emory picked up another piece of pizza. "And I never let him forget the *gegisch* things he's done."

Leanna smiled. "I'm sure of that."

Emory scanned the square table and suddenly felt his chest warm at the idea of having meals like this more often—of having Leanna and Chester as a permanent part of his family.

A longing began at his heart and branched out through his veins. He studied Leanna's beautiful face, and she gave him a shy smile.

"You okay?" she asked.

"*Ya*." He cleared his throat against a sudden thickness and set the piece of pizza on his plate. "I might have eaten too much pizza."

She pointed to the piece. "*Mei mammi* would say your eyes are bigger than your stomach."

He laughed. "I like that statement."

"What about ice cream?" Maggie asked. "We always have ice cream after pizza."

Emory guffawed at her. "You have room for ice cream?"

"Ice cream fills in the cracks," Chester said, and everyone laughed.

"Okay." Emory pointed toward the counter. "Why don't you two order some ice cream?" He glanced at Leanna. "Do you want some?"

"No, *danki*." She pulled her wallet from her small black purse. "Chester, let me give you some money."

"No, I got it." Emory pulled out his wallet.

Chester shook his head. "I'll pay for the ice cream. I insist. Would you like any, Emory?"

"No, *danki*." Emory smiled. He watched Maggie and Chester walk toward the counter. Then he turned toward Leanna, who watched them with a strange expression.

"Everything okay?" he asked.

"*Ya*, I'm just astounded Chester offered to pay for ice cream. He's never done that before." She pointed at Emory. "That's because of you."

He shook his head and felt his cheeks heat. "No, that can't be."

"It is. You've had such a great influence on him, and I'm so grateful." She hesitated for a moment. "I keep thanking God for bringing you and Maggie into our lives."

Emory thought his jaw might hit the table. For a moment he was speechless, stunned by her admission.

"I'm sorry." She looked down at her empty plate. "That was too bold. Please forgive me."

"No, no, no." He reached for her hand but then pulled his back. "I actually feel the same way about you and Chester. I can't thank you enough for what you're doing for Maggie. I've never seen her as excited about anything as I have about this booth, and I owe that all to you. Your friendship has changed our lives."

"I appreciate that." She smiled and a lock of her brown hair drifted down from under her prayer *kapp*.

Without thinking, he reached over and pushed the lock of hair behind her ear. She looked up at him, and her eyes widened as her mouth opened. And then the overwhelming urge to kiss her gripped him. His breath stalled in his lungs as blood began to stampede through his veins. The air around them felt charged—as if it would explode if he were to strike a match. Time froze.

"I got your favorite—cookies and cream with chocolate sprinkles." Maggie's announcement brought him crashing to earth.

Emory snapped to attention in his chair and turned toward where Maggie and Chester stood holding their ice cream cones.

"Really?" Emory's voice sounded strained.

Maggie held her cone out toward him. "Do you want some?"

"No, *danki*."

Chester licked his cone. "I got chocolate peanut butter."

Leanna gathered up their used plates and napkins and dropped them into a nearby trash can. "*Danki* for supper, Emory."

"*Gern gschehne*." Emory stood. "I'll need to ask to use their phone to call my driver."

"You can use mine." Chester pulled his cell phone out of his back pocket, unlocked the screen, and handed it to Emory.

Leanna gave a loud, dramatic sigh, frowning and shaking

her head at Chester, who seemed to avoid his mother's disapproval by looking down at his ice cream cone.

"That's okay. I'll use the restaurant's phone," Emory said before walking up to the counter and asking the clerk. He dialed the number for his driver on the pizzeria's cordless phone. After a few rings, Miles answered, and Emory asked him to pick up him and Maggie at the pizza parlor. Then he walked back over to where Leanna sat. He glanced out the front windows of the restaurant and spotted Chester and Maggie sitting together on a bench while talking and eating their ice cream.

"Miles will be here in a few minutes," he told Leanna.

"Great." Leanna fiddled with the straw in her cup of Diet Coke.

He watched her face, trying to comprehend her sheepish expression. Did she feel the invisible thread that seemed to always pull him to her? Did she also sense his overwhelming urge to kiss her? Did she want to kiss him too?

Or had he imagined all of it?

"I had a great time today," he said and then held his breath. *Please tell me how you feel, Leanna. Do you care for me too?*

"I did too." She sat up straight. "It's always a special day when you get to spend it with *freinden*."

And there was his answer. She still only considered him a *freind*. Anything he saw between them was a figment of his hopeful imagination.

Disappointment and sadness nearly crushed Emory's chest, but he kept his demeanor neutral. The last thing he wanted was for Leanna to know she was able to break his heart.

"*Ya*, that's true." He pushed back his chair and stood. "It won't take Miles long to get here. Maybe we should wait outside."

They strode outside together and found Maggie and Chester

still sitting on a bench finishing their ice cream cones and talking about mutual friends.

Chester ate the last of his cone and then wiped his hands with a napkin. "*Danki* for supper, Emory. It was great. I want to hear more of your camping stories tomorrow."

Emory chuckled. "I'll have to think of a few more to share."

Maggie walked over to Leanna and bit into her cone before swallowing it. "I don't think I'm going to sleep tonight."

"Why not?" Leanna asked.

"I'm so *naerfich* about tomorrow."

Leanna gave Maggie a sweet smile and then touched her shoulder. "Don't be nervous. We are going to have so much fun tomorrow, and the customers are going to love your crafts. I have a feeling you're going to have empty shelves in a week or two. Trust me."

Emory's heart melted at the tender expressions he saw shared between Maggie and Leanna.

If only Leanna wanted more . . .

He resisted the thought. Leanna was his friend, his very special friend, and he thanked God for her. He just had to find a way to be satisfied with only having her friendship and not having her heart as well.

Just then, headlights bathed the parking lot with bright yellow light as Miles steered his burgundy, king-cab pickup truck into a nearby parking space.

"Well, there's our ride." Emory shook Chester's hand. "I'll see you at work tomorrow."

Chester nodded. "Bright and early."

"Sleep well, Maggie," Leanna instructed his daughter.

Maggie took a step forward and pulled Leanna in for a hug. "*Danki*, Leanna."

Leanna clucked her tongue and held on to Maggie. "I'm just thrilled you want to share my booth."

Confusion, appreciation, and longing overwhelmed Emory. The Lord had brought this incredible woman into his life and then placed her just out of reach. *Why, Lord, why?*

Maggie stepped away from Leanna. "See you tomorrow." She waved and then climbed into the backseat of the king cab.

"*Danki* again, Emory." Leanna smiled up at him. "We worked hard today. I hope you have a restful night."

He nodded, struggling to recover himself. "You too." He tried to clear his throat past the sudden knot of emotion. "*Gut nacht.*"

Leanna gave him a warm smile and then strode toward the back of the parking lot, where Chester stood by his horse and buggy.

Then Emory climbed into the passenger seat of the truck and found Maggie telling Miles all about her booth, her voice full of excitement.

"All of my crafts are arranged by categories. So, I have the dolls in one section, the wall hangings in another, and then purses in another. The quilts are sort of spread throughout since they take up so much space."

"That's quite an endeavor, Maggie." Miles peeked at her in the rearview mirror. "Do you use a machine to quilt most things, or do you stitch more by hand?"

Emory was grateful Maggie filled their short ride with a conversation with Miles. While she spoke, he gazed out the windshield at the dark pastures, rolling hills, and farmhouses. He couldn't stop recalling how it had felt to sit beside Leanna and touch her face.

And that all-consuming need to kiss her! How long had it been since he'd been so drawn to a woman?

He scrubbed his hand down his beard and tried to redirect his thoughts toward work. After all, he'd taken the day off, and he would have to work extra hard tomorrow to catch up. He tried to concentrate on the shed he had been working on yesterday, but once again, Leanna's beautiful face overtook his mind. And the way she'd hugged Maggie. He hadn't seen Maggie bond with anyone outside of his family since—well, never. Leanna was special. So very special.

Miles nosed the truck into his driveway and put it in park.

"Thank you for your help today," Emory told Miles as he paid him. After telling him good night, he climbed out of the truck and walked into the house with Maggie.

"I'm going to shower," Maggie called as she hurried up the steps.

Emory sauntered into his room and dropped down onto the corner of his bed. He stared out the open window toward the dark pasture and sighed.

"Lord, please guide my confused heart. Leanna, the woman I care for, doesn't care for me romantically. But Madelyne, the woman whom I believe does care for me, is someone whom I see as a *freind*. My family is pressuring me to give Madelyne a chance, but I feel my heart resisting her. Is it truly possible for friendship to grow into love? I've heard it's true, but I'm not convinced."

He sighed and flopped back onto his bed. "Perhaps I'm making this more difficult than it has to be. Maybe if I just let go and let you guide me, I will find the answer. I know I'm stubborn. At least Sheryl always said I was."

He smiled as he thought of Sheryl. "Lord, thank you for the short time I had with Sheryl. I'll always miss her and cherish her. And help me through this bewildering season. I can't make it without you."

Emory rolled onto his side. "Sheryl," he whispered. "If only you could see Maggie now. You'd be so proud of her setting up her booth at the market. If only you could see the *schee* creations she's made that will bless her customers abundantly. She reminds me so much of you with her talent and her beauty. If only you were here with us. I miss you, *mei liewe*."

He stood up and forced his legs to carry him toward the downstairs bathroom. Perhaps a hot shower would wash away his burdens and bring him some clarity. He could only hope.

And if not, then he would keep praying. For only God could heal him and help him see the path.

CHAPTER 25

Maggie stepped into the booth the following morning, a hesitant smile on her face. She set her tote bag behind the counter and greeted Leanna, who was straightening jars of jelly and smiled at her.

"Did you sleep well last night, Maggie?"

"*Ya.*" Maggie grinned. "When we got home, I took a shower and then passed out in bed. I think I was tired from our hard work yesterday, even though I was *naerfich* for today."

"I knew you'd sleep."

Maggie smoothed her hands down her powder-blue dress and black apron. "Do I look okay?"

"Maggie, you look *schee.* That blue makes your beautiful eyes look even bluer." Leanna gestured around the booth. "The customers are going to go crazy for your crafts. There's no need to be *naerfich.*" She pointed toward the Coffee Corner. "Let's go get some *kaffi* and see Bethany before the marketplace opens for the day."

Leanna led Maggie into the booth, where Bethany was busy putting a tray of strawberry glazed donuts on a shelf. The delicious aromas of flavored coffee and donuts made Leanna's stomach gurgle.

"*Gude mariye,*" Leanna announced. "Bethany, this is Maggie. And Maggie, this is Bethany, one of my favorite cousins."

Bethany's lips quirked into a grin. "You mean your favorite cousin." She turned her attention to Maggie and gave her one of her trademark smiles that reminded Leanna of sunshine. "I'm so excited to meet you, Maggie. I've heard quite a bit about you."

"*Danki.*" Maggie shook her hand. "I've heard so much about your *kaffi* and donuts." She pointed toward the blackboard, which displayed the day's specials. "I'd love to try a cup of peanut butter cup flavored *kaffi* and a chocolate glazed donut."

"Coming right up!" Bethany looked at Leanna. "And for you?"

"I'll have the same."

Bethany quickly retrieved their orders, and Maggie pulled a change purse out of her apron pocket.

"No, no." Bethany shook her head. "It's on the *haus* today. This is your welcome to the marketplace gift."

Maggie smiled. "*Danki.*"

"You're more than welcome." Then Bethany turned to Leanna. "But I'll take your money."

"Of course you will," Leanna deadpanned, and they all laughed.

Bethany handed Leanna her change. "Let me get myself a cup, and I'll meet you at a table."

After adding creamer and sweetener to their coffee at the condiment station, Leanna and Maggie took a seat at one of the high-top tables.

Maggie sipped her cup of coffee and grinned. "This is fantastic."

"*Danki,*" Bethany said as she sat beside Maggie. "I'm always the first one here since I have to start making the donuts so early. I stopped in your booth, and the way you've set it up looks so impressive. Maggie, your quilts and crafts are spectacular. The customers here will be thrilled to buy what you've made."

Leanna lifted her cup and took a sip. "That's what I keep telling her."

"And I love the new sign. The name is so cute." Bethany pointed toward their booth.

"*Mei dat* made the sign," Maggie said. "He wanted to surprise Leanna with it."

Leanna stilled at the admission. "I was very surprised. It was so thoughtful."

"Do you quilt?" Maggie asked Bethany.

Bethany gave a little laugh. "Not really. I can make clothes for my husband and me, but I never learned to quilt. I was always astounded by how talented our *mammi* is, but I didn't inherit her skills."

"Oh, you could learn," Maggie insisted.

As Maggie and Bethany talked on about quilting, Leanna took a bite of her donut and recalled how perfect yesterday had been. She'd stayed awake in bed last night, tossing and turning for what felt like hours as she analyzed the entire day. How attentive Emory had been while they worked in the booth. How much thought and care seemed to have gone into the sign he made. How funny and open he'd been during supper, sharing stories and laughing with them.

And how tender he'd been when he'd touched her face. Her heart had pounded so hard that she was almost certain he could hear it. His touch had sent her senses swirling like a cyclone. For a moment, she was almost certain there had been a deep connection between them, something only two people in love would feel.

But then reality had crashed around her, reminding her that

Emory's heart belonged to another, and she was certain she had imagined the connection. Her cruel heart had played a trick on her, sending sadness and loneliness circling through her, stealing her joy.

"Don't you agree, Leanna?"

"What?" Leanna looked up and found Maggie and Bethany staring at her. "I'm sorry. I was lost in thought."

"You okay?" Bethany's bright blue eyes seemed to assess her.

"*Ya*, of course. What did you ask?" Leanna sipped more coffee and then took another bite of her donut.

Bethany raised a blond eyebrow with suspicion.

"Bethany thinks I'll have a busy first day since it's still warm out and the tourists are still in Amish Country." Maggie seemed oblivious to Leanna's inner turmoil.

"Oh yeah. It stays busy here until about Thanksgiving," Leanna said.

Maggie turned toward Bethany. "Yesterday Leanna mentioned that you have two other cousins who used to have booths here. Why did they close them?"

"They both got married and had *bopplin*." Bethany's smile dimmed slightly. "We miss them, though. We used to have lunch together every day."

"Will we have lunch together?" Maggie asked, gesturing around the table.

Bethany smiled. "Of course."

"Great. So, tell me about your cousins' booths."

Maggie listened with eyes wide as Leanna and Bethany shared stories of Salina's Farm Stand and Christiana's Bake Shop. Before long, they had finished their breakfast, and it was nearly time for the market to open.

After they disposed of their empty coffee cups and napkins,

Leanna and Maggie said good-bye to Bethany and hurried back
to their booth.

"I like Bethany," Maggie said as she strode over to the counter. "She's sweet."

"She is sweet and she likes you too." Leanna touched Maggie's
shoulder. Oh, how she enjoyed getting to know this young
woman, who seemed to fit in so well with her family. If only . . .

The whooshing of the front doors opening and then voices
bouncing off the walls interrupted her thoughts.

The marketplace was open for business!

"Are you ready?" Leanna asked Maggie.

Maggie stood up straighter and grinned. "*Ya*, I am."

"*Gut*, because it's time." Leanna rubbed her hands together
and turned her attention toward the customers making their
way to their booth.

. . .

"What a great day I had!" Maggie gushed as she tallied up her
daily sales. She stuck a pencil behind her ear and studied the
notebook in front of her. "I can't believe I sold a quilt, two sets
of dolls, two purses, and four potholders."

Leanna counted out the total she and Maggie had figured,
then zipped up a money bag with Maggie's share of the booth's
earnings. "I'm not surprised in the least. I knew your quilts and
crafts would sell!" Then Leanna handed her the money.

"*Danki*, Leanna."

"You earned it!" Leanna separated out her sales and Chester's
from their change and then closed the cash register. She
planned to offer Chester his money from the birdhouses, even
if he refused it.

Maggie sat on a stool beside her and got a faraway look in her lovely blue eyes. "I keep thinking about *mei mamm* and the quilts she sold. If only I could ask her which of her quilts sold the best. I'd love her advice on what colors I should use the most and what she thinks of the ones I have here for sale."

Leanna blinked, wondering how best to respond. Of course the poor dear was missing her mother's approval on a day like this!

"Well," Leanna began, working to keep her tone light, "I have no doubt in my mind that your *mamm* would be bursting with happiness today if she could see you following in her footsteps." She paused. "As for the business questions, you could always ask Madelyne for advice. Didn't you say she sold quilts?"

"*Ya.*" Maggie ran her finger over the edge of the counter. "I could, but it's not the same as talking to *mei mamm*."

"I understand."

Maggie's expression brightened. "I had so much fun today. I really enjoyed working with you in the booth. And I loved having lunch with Bethany."

"I had fun too." Leanna looked around the booth. "We can finish straightening in the morning." She reached for her tote bag and lunch bag from under the counter and then dropped the money bags inside of the tote bag. When she turned, Bethany and Micah appeared at the booth entrance.

"Micah, this is Maggie Speicher, Leanna's *freind*," said Bethany. "Maggie, this is my husband."

"So nice to meet you." Micah shook her hand. "Is Emory Speicher your *dat*?"

"*Ya*, he is."

"I know him." Micah gazed over at Leanna and jammed his thumb toward the exit. "Are you two heading out?"

"We are." Leanna and Maggie followed them toward the back entrance.

"How were your sales the rest of the day, Maggie?" Bethany asked.

Maggie gushed about her first day of work as they exited the market together. When they stepped out into evening sunlight, Leanna looked across the parking lot toward where Chester stood by his horse and buggy, talking and laughing with Emory. Her heartbeat thumped at the sight of Emory.

Leanna and Maggie said good-bye to Bethany and Micah before walking over to Chester and Emory.

"I didn't expect to see you today," Leanna told Chester. "I thought you had to stay late to finish up a project."

Emory's smile was nearly as bright as the sun. "We got it done, so we thought we'd surprise you. Chester called and canceled your ride home." He turned his focus to Maggie. "I want to hear all about your first day."

The two families said their good-byes for the evening, then climbed into their respective buggies. Emory tipped his hat toward Leanna as she settled in the seat beside her son. Then Chester guided the horse out of the lot and toward the road.

She looked out and waved as they passed Emory's buggy, and her heart gave a little tug.

If only things could be different between them.

If only . . .

CHAPTER 26

*G*ude mariye!"

Leanna turned and blew out an excited breath when she found Christiana and Salina standing at her booth entrance the next morning.

"Oh my goodness! What a nice surprise!" She turned toward Maggie, who was standing by the counter looking confused. "Maggie, these are my two cousins Bethany and I were telling you about yesterday. Meet Christiana and Salina."

"Hi." Maggie waved.

"This is Maggie," Leanna said.

"It's so great to meet you." Christiana crossed the booth and shook Maggie's hand, then turned to Leanna. "*Mammi* told us about your new booth yesterday when we went to visit. Apparently your *mamm* told *Mammi* all about it after you set it up on Wednesday. We left the *kinner* with *mei mamm* and tried to get here before the market opened so we had time to visit. I'm so glad that the security guard remembered us and let us in."

"I love the sign." Salina pointed toward the entrance, her other hand resting on her protruding belly. "Oh my goodness." She ambled over to a rose-colored Wedding Ring pattern quilt. "Maggie, you made this?"

Maggie nodded.

"Look at these dolls!" Christiana perused another shelf. "And purses! Everything is just lovely."

Maggie smiled at Leanna.

"I bet you've made a lot of sales," Christiana said.

"She did great her first day, and it's only going to get better and better."

Maggie bit her lip and looked embarrassed by the attention.

Leanna gestured toward the Coffee Corner. "Do you have time for *kaffi*?"

"Of course," Christiana said. "We can't stop by without seeing Bethany."

"Oh, we'd never hear the end of it," Salina said, and they laughed.

They made their way into the Coffee Corner, where Bethany was excited to see them. After ordering coffee and donuts, they took a seat at a table, squeezing in a fifth chair for Maggie.

"Oh, this feels like old times," Bethany gushed. "It's great to have you all here."

"I know," Christiana said.

Salina nodded. "It's been too long."

"How are you feeling, Salina?" Leanna asked after taking a sip of her vanilla roast.

"Ready to have this *boppli*." Salina rubbed her belly as she frowned. "I feel like I've been pregnant for two years."

Christiana snorted as Bethany looked down at her cup of coffee.

Leanna's heart squeezed for Bethany. Oh, she hoped the Lord would bless Bethany and Micah with a baby soon!

"It's coming quickly, though," Christiana said. "You could

have this *boppli* any day now. You're at thirty-eight weeks, and Karrie was a week early."

"The sooner the better." Salina smiled and then sipped her decaf coffee.

"Gude mariye."

Leanna craned her neck over her shoulder as Sara Ann waltzed into the booth, and she pressed her lips into a frown. Everyone stiffened at the sight of the market's most infamous gossip.

"Hi, Sara Ann." Leanna tried her best to sound bright, but she sounded as phony as she felt.

"Oh my goodness! Why, it's a cousin reunion here!" Sara Ann sashayed over to their table. "Christiana, you look fantastic."

"You too." Christiana lifted her cup and took a sip.

"And Salina." Sara Ann gave a wry smile. "You look like you're about to pop."

Salina smirked and then tossed a piece of her chocolate donut into her mouth.

Then Sara Ann turned toward Maggie, and Leanna suddenly felt protective of her young friend. She longed to grab Maggie's hand and whisk her off to the booth, away from Sara Ann's big, gossipy mouth.

"Who's this?" Sara Ann's voice was saccharine.

"I'm Maggie."

"Hi. I'm Sara Ann King, but you can call me simply Sara Ann." She laughed as she shook Maggie's hand.

"It's nice to meet you."

Sara Ann seemed to study her, and Leanna's jaw clenched. *Oh no.*

"What's your last name, Maggie?"

Maggie shifted on her seat. "Speicher."

"Speicher?" Sara Ann hesitated and then snapped her fingers. "I *knew* I could place you! You're Sheryl and Emory Speicher's *dochder*."

Maggie's eyes widened. "You knew *mei mamm*?"

Bethany shot Leanna a worried looked.

Sara Ann's expression seemed self-satisfied. "I did. She was a talented quilter."

"Did you quilt with her?"

"I saw her often at quilt frolics."

Leanna gripped the side of the table and looked over at Bethany again, searching her mind for a way to change the subject—and fast.

"Maggie is a talented quilter too," Christiana's voice was bold. "You should see her quilts and other crafts. She's selling them in Leanna's booth."

"Is that so?" Sara Ann looked taken aback. "I had heard Leanna was selling quilts."

Leanna grimaced. *Oh no. Christiana should have kept her mouth shut.*

Sara Ann looked over at Leanna. "How interesting that we'll have two quilt stands here now."

"*Ya*, it is." Salina lifted her cup of coffee, and Leanna noticed her cousin covering a smile.

"Did you want *kaffi*, Sara Ann?" Bethany asked, sounding impatient.

"*Ya*, please." Sara Ann followed Bethany to the counter, where she bought a cup of dark roast and a cinnamon donut before returning to the table. "Well." She looked around the table. "You all have a nice day. And make great sales."

"You too," Bethany chirped as she hopped back up into her chair.

Leanna held her breath until Sara Ann was gone. Then she turned to Maggie and lowered her voice. "Steer clear of her."

Maggie blinked and gazed around the table, where Leanna's cousins all nodded. "If you say so, but why?"

"She's the marketplace gossip," Christiana explained. "We call her Simply Sara Ann because she's two-faced."

Salina tapped the table. "And she likes to cause problems and hurt people's feelings."

Bethany picked up her cup. "That's the truth."

"I can't believe she knew *mei mamm*," Maggie said.

"I wouldn't trust anything she says about your *mamm*." Leanna glanced over at Bethany. "Is it okay if I tell her what she did to you?" Bethany nodded and Leanna turned to Maggie again. "She's been known to be very hurtful. She tried to break up Bethany and Micah when they were dating."

Maggie gave a sharp inhale. "An Amish *maedel* did that?"

"*Ya*, she did." Bethany rested her elbow on the table and then her chin on her palm. "I'm grateful Micah realized who Sara Ann truly was."

"Oh please, Bethany!" Christiana guffawed. "Your husband could see right through her. He knew who the genuine *maedel* was, and it wasn't her."

Maggie nodded. "Okay. I'll be sure not to talk to her."

"You can talk to her, of course. Just . . . just be careful of what you say," Leanna said.

At Leanna's prompting, Christiana and Salina shared stories about their daughters while they finished drinking their coffee and eating their donuts. When the marketplace doors opened and the customers began coming in, Leanna, Maggie, and her cousins said good-bye to Bethany and walked back over to Leanna and Maggie's booth.

Salina looked around as customers began filing into the booth. "How did you manage to snatch up the space? The booths seem to go so quickly."

"Kent offered it to me." Leanna summarized how the idea came together. "When I saw Maggie's quilts and crafts, the idea came to me. Emory agreed, and we put the booth together Wednesday." She looked over toward where Maggie showed a traditional Log Cabin pattern quilt featuring blocks of different shades of tans and browns to a young *English* woman.

"Speaking of Emory . . ." Salina started.

Christiana gave a knowing smile. "Has he asked you out yet?"

Leanna sighed, and they both frowned. "We're *freinden*."

"Still?" Salina asked.

Leanna nodded. "Chester said he's dating someone else—someone his *bruder* is encouraging him to see. Her name is Madelyne." *And I'm sure she's beautiful and perfect.*

"*Ach*, I'm so sorry." Salina rubbed her arms.

Christiana scrunched her nose. "That doesn't make any sense. He seemed to care about you that Sunday he came to see you when we were all at *Mammi*'s. Why would he come to visit you and then date someone else? Wouldn't he have gone to see her instead?"

"Maybe he decided he prefers her to me."

"Nope. I don't believe it." Christiana shook her head.

Salina rubbed her belly. "Neither do I."

Leanna sighed and glanced around the counter where Maggie stood ringing up the woman with the quilt. "It looks like Maggie just sold her fourth quilt of the week."

"And I wonder how many Simply Sara Ann has sold," Salina quipped.

Leanna and Christiana turned toward Salina, who pressed a finger to her chin.

"Did I say that out loud?" Salina asked with feigned innocence.

"*Ya*, you did." Christiana grinned.

Leanna laughed. Oh, how she'd missed her cousins!

. . .

Sunday afternoon Emory stood by the Esh family's barn and looked on as Maggie talked to her friends after the church service.

Maggie had awoken with a bright smile on her face, excited to go to church to see her friends and tell them all about the booth. Warmth filled him as he watched Maggie speak animatedly, using her hands as she explained something to Alea and two other young women.

Mamm sidled up to Emory and pointed at Maggie. "I don't think I've ever seen her smile like that."

"I was just thinking the same thing."

"*Dat!*" Maggie jogged toward him. "May I go with Alea to play games at Annie Lantz's *haus*?"

"Of course you may. Have fun and be safe."

Maggie gave him a quick hug. "I will. *Ich liebe dich, Dat.*"

"I love you too," he whispered, his voice faltering.

Maggie looked at *Mamm*. "Bye, *Mammi*. Love you." Before *Mamm* could answer, she had rushed off toward her friends.

"Opening that booth for her was a brilliant idea, Emory." *Mamm* faced him. "She's a different *maedel*."

"I really can't take the credit for it. Leanna's the brilliant one. Now the booth is all Maggie talks about, and I owe it all to

Leanna. Maggie couldn't wait to get here this morning to tell her *freinden* about it. She even told me to hurry up when we were getting ready for church." He snickered.

"That's funny," *Mamm* said.

"What's funny?" Madelyne appeared behind him, looking curious.

Emory had invited Madelyne to join him for church today when she'd stopped by the shop to see him yesterday. She'd seemed surprised when he invited her, and he had even surprised himself. Yet it seemed to make sense to try to cultivate a relationship with Madelyne. After all, Leanna wasn't interested.

"Maggie couldn't wait to get here this morning to tell her *freinden* about the booth," *Mamm* explained.

Madelyne smiled. "She told me all about it earlier too. I'm so *froh* for her. She made great sales her first week."

"And she just went to youth group," *Mamm* chimed in. "It seems like everything is working out for you, Emory."

He could hear a hidden meaning in his mother's voice, and he did his best to gloss over it. Oh, how he hoped his family wouldn't start pressuring him to get married. He wasn't even officially dating Madelyne!

"Would you like to come back to my *haus* to visit?" Madelyne asked.

Emory stilled.

She blushed as if reading his concerned thoughts. "The *haus* isn't empty. My younger siblings are all at youth group, but my parents told me they were staying home today instead of visiting."

Emory looked out toward where Maggie climbed into a buggy with Alea and a few friends. He didn't want to spend this afternoon alone in his big house, and since he was able to visit with his parents often, he welcomed the opportunity to get to know Madelyne better.

It was time for him to take a chance and see what God had in store for his future.

He faced Madelyne and smiled. "That sounds nice. I'd love to meet your parents."

"Great." Madelyne turned toward his mother. "It was nice seeing you, Viola."

"You too, Madelyne. Take care." When Madelyne looked away, *Mamm* winked at Emory. "Go have fun."

As Emory led Madelyne to his buggy, he tried to imagine himself dating her, planning a future with her, and eventually marrying her.

While the idea sounded foreign, he realized he was ready to make a commitment. The problem was that he couldn't imagine making that kind of commitment with Madelyne. Although a relationship with Madelyne made sense, his heart still craved Leanna. When he closed his eyes, he imagined Leanna's smile, heard her laugh, and envisioned the way Maggie had hugged her the day they had set up the booth.

But here was Madelyne—longing to spend the afternoon visiting with him and patiently waiting for him to ask her to be his girlfriend.

Emory had to find a way to convince himself that Madelyne was the right woman for him. But how could Madelyne be the perfect woman for him when he couldn't stop Leanna from lingering in the back of his thoughts?

CHAPTER 27

Emory sat in the family room and read a devotional by the light of a lantern that evening. When the back door opened and closed, he stood and walked into the kitchen just as Maggie came in.

"How was it?" He leaned forward on the back of a kitchen chair.

"Fun!" She seemed to glow. "We played volleyball and Ping-Pong, and then we ate sub sandwiches and sang hymns. We had a great time." She touched her face. "My cheeks hurt from laughing."

Happiness and warmth curled through Emory. "I'm *froh* to hear that."

She crossed to the refrigerator and poured two glasses of water before handing him one. "How was your afternoon?" She sat down at the table, and he sat across from her.

"*Danki*. It was *gut*." He took a drink of water.

"What did you do?"

"I went with Madelyne and visited with her and her parents. Then I stayed for supper."

Maggie took a long drink of water and then nodded slowly as if contemplating something. "Are you dating her?" she finally asked.

"No." He ran his fingers through the condensation on the glass. "She's a nice woman, but we're not dating."

Maggie nodded and took another drink.

Emory cleared his throat and rested his elbows on the table. "But Maggie, how would you feel if I *did* date her?"

She swallowed. "I would find a way to accept it. But no one will ever replace *mei mamm*."

He smiled as he reached across the table and took her hands in his. "I agree with you."

Maggie smiled. "And I have a feeling she will say yes if you ask her to be your girlfriend."

"Why?"

She rolled her eyes as she grinned. "It's obvious that she cares about you, and she's just waiting for you to ask. What are her parents like?"

"They're very nice and friendly. We had a *gut* time."

"I'm glad you got out of the *haus*. You stay around here too much." She stood and carried their empty glasses to the sink.

Emory snorted. "You're one to talk about staying in the *haus* too much."

She laughed. "*Danki* for convincing me to open the booth and go to youth group. I'm so glad I did."

Emory stood and hugged her. "I am too."

"We'd better go to bed. You have work tomorrow, and I have to do laundry."

"*Gut nacht, mei liewe.*" He kissed her cheek.

"*Gut nacht, Dat.*"

Maggie hurried up the stairs, a flashlight guiding her way.

As Emory headed toward his bedroom, he smiled. Maggie was finally coming out of her shell. Now he just had to find the way out of his.

• • •

"How has your week been?" Maggie asked Leanna as she walked into the booth Thursday morning pulling a wagon full of boxes.

"*Gut.* Busy." Leanna set her tote bag and lunch box under the counter. "I did quite a few chores Monday and Tuesday and then made some jams and jellies yesterday. How about you?"

"The same. Chores Monday, Tuesday, and yesterday, but Sunday was fun." Maggie handed her tote bag and lunch box to Leanna, and she slipped them under the counter.

"What did you do on Sunday?"

"I went to youth group, and I told all of *mei freinden* about the booth. They were so excited for me. What did you do?"

"I went to church and then visited with my grandparents."

"*Wunderbaar.*" Maggie pulled the wagon to the back part of the booth. "Would you help me set out the quilts and crafts I brought?"

"Sure. But would you like to get *kaffi* and a donut first?"

"That's a great idea."

Leanna and Maggie went over to the Coffee Corner and sat at a high-top table with Bethany while they drank coffee, ate donuts, and discussed their week.

Then they headed back to the booth and began arranging the quilts and crafts Maggie had brought to restock her shelves and quilt stands.

"I think *mei dat* is going to ask Madelyne to be his girl-friend," Maggie said as she unfolded a Lone Star pattern quilt and slipped it over a stand.

Leanna's stomach dipped, a sick feeling sweeping through her as she stilled, the dolls she held frozen in place as if floating in front of her. She worked hard to calm her shaking hands.

Emory hasn't been dating Madelyne all of this time?

With her back to Leanna, Maggie continued on while straightening the quilt on the stand. "Madelyne came to our church service. Then while I was at youth group, he took her home and visited with her parents and had supper."

Leanna took a deep breath and forced her trembling hands to arrange the dolls on the shelf before she turned toward Maggie. "I thought he was already dating Madelyne."

"Who told you that?" Maggie's brow crinkled.

"Chester said Madelyne brought your *dat* a pie at work. He heard your *onkel* say something to your *dat* about giving Madelyne a chance."

Maggie shook her head. "He's not dating her yet, but he waited up for me Sunday night. And he asked me how I'd feel if he dated."

"What did you say?" Leanna held her breath.

"I told him I'd find a way to accept it, but no one will ever replace *mei mamm*." She ran her fingers over the quilt. "I've told *mei dat* for years that I didn't want him to date because I didn't want anything to change. But I've realized it was a selfish thing to say. *Mei dat* has been alone for a long time, and he deserves happiness. Hopefully someday I'll fall in love, get married, move out, and have a family of my own. And when I do, *mei dat* will be all alone. That's not fair to him."

Maggie moved to the wagon and pulled another quilt out of a box. "If *mei dat* wants to date Madelyne, then I need to support him. He's entitled to a *froh* life."

Leanna nodded as the coffee in her stomach began to curdle. "You're right, and that's very mature for you to say that.

And your *dat* knows no one will ever replace your *mamm*. Did he say when he's going to ask her out?"

"No, he didn't." Maggie turned her attention to hanging up the quilts on the stand.

Leanna tried to focus on adding the new dolls to the shelf. She had to be strong and keep her emotions in check. She prayed she could still be Emory's friend, even if he married Madelyne. But the idea of Emory marrying someone else sent a wave of nausea crashing over her.

"Do you think I could help you make jelly and jam sometime?"

Leanna spun toward Maggie, who smiled at her. "*Ya*, of course, Maggie! I'd love to show you how to can."

"*Wunderbaar.*"

Leanna smiled. Even if she lost Emory's friendship, she had a feeling that she'd always have Maggie's.

And she would cherish Maggie's friendship forever.

. . .

Leanna set the last dry dish in the cabinet later that evening just as *Mammi* hobbled quickly into the kitchen.

"I have news!" *Mammi* announced. "I just got the best phone call!"

Mamm spun. "What is it?"

"Salina had her *boppli*!"

"Oh my!" Leanna said. "What did she have?"

"A *bu*," *Mammi* said. "He was eight pounds, three ounces, and they named him William Junior. Salina and little William are doing great."

"I'm so glad to hear it. I know she was ready when I saw her last week." Leanna began filling the kettle with water. "Stay for tea, *Mammi*?"

Leanna enjoyed a cup of tea and oatmeal raisin cookies with her mother and grandmother while they talked about babies. Memories of when Chester was born overtook her mind and sent her emotions spiraling with a mixture of happiness and grief.

Later she took a shower and then climbed into bed. Propped up with a pillow, she tried to read a novel, but she found herself reading the same paragraph over and over again without retaining a single word. The lines seemed to dance on the page as if they were trying to get away from her.

Instead, she was overcome by thoughts of Salina and her new baby. While she was happy for her cousin, she couldn't stop her mind from clicking through memories of Chester's birth.

She recalled how happy Marlin was when Chester was born. The memory welled up like an undertow and dragged her down, down, down. How Marlin would rock Chester and whisper to him, telling him stories of his childhood. How he would laugh with Chester when they played blocks on the floor together. How he would insist upon getting up in the middle of the night to feed Chester so that Leanna could get some sleep, even though Marlin had to work the next day.

Marlin was such a good man, a solid, Christian man, who loved her and their son deeply. What would it have been like if she and Marlin had been blessed with more children? She was certain he would have been a supportive husband and doting father whether they'd had one more child or six more.

But Marlin was gone. He had been gone for seven years now.

And Leanna was alone.

All alone.

And the first man Leanna had cared about since Marlin had died had asked his daughter's permission to date another woman.

Tears stung Leanna's eyes as she recalled her earlier conversation with Maggie. "Why, God?" Leanna whispered. "Why would you lead me to Emory and then deny me a chance with him? What are you trying to teach me? I'm listening, but the pain is almost too much. I just don't understand."

Leanna flipped off her lantern and snuggled under her sheet and blanket as she hoped sleep would find her. She rolled over onto her side as more memories of Marlin settled over her. She could see his handsome face, his sandy blond hair, his baby-blue eyes. She could almost hear his deep voice, his loud, boisterous laugh.

Another wave of grief crashed over her and threatened to pull her under.

"Why did you have to leave me, Marlin?" she whispered as tears pricked her eyes. "It's been seven years, but it feels like I lost you yesterday. I need you now. Chester and I miss you. I thought I had my life together. I thought I might have even found someone else, but I was wrong. So wrong! I'm still just as lonely as I was the day you left. I'm a mess."

Then she dissolved into tears.

· · ·

Emory pored over a stack of invoices while he sat at the desk in his father's office at the shed shop on Saturday, one week later. When he heard the bell chime above the front door, he stood and padded out into the showroom. He smiled when he found Madelyne standing by the counter.

"Hi," he said.

"Hi. I was in the area and thought I'd stop by." Madelyne's smile was bright. "Have you had lunch?"

"Is it lunchtime?" He turned toward the clock on the wall and found it was eleven forty-five. "I guess it is lunchtime. No, I haven't eaten."

"Would you like to go to Zimmerman's Family Restaurant with me? It's the best buffet in town."

"Sure." Emory jammed his thumb toward the shop. "Let me just let Justin know."

"Okay."

Emory told Justin he was leaving, and then he and Madelyne walked down the street to the restaurant. They strode to the front of the building, where a sign with the name of the restaurant sat above a large picture window. He couldn't help but think of Leanna since her cousin Salina and her husband, Will, owned the restaurant.

Colorful potted flowers greeted them as they made their way up the steps next to a ramp. They headed inside to a counter, and a Mennonite woman with a name tag that said Danielle led them into the large dining room, where conversations buzzed as customers sat at the oak tables and chairs, the afternoon sunlight spilling in through large windows.

After Danielle led them to a table, they made their way to the buffet, and they filled their plates with salad, fried chicken, mashed potatoes, fresh rolls, and green beans.

They chatted about their week while they enjoyed the delicious food. After scrumptious pieces of chocolate cake for dessert, they headed back out into the parking lot toward the sidewalk.

Emory gazed across the street toward the marketplace, and

his thoughts turned to Maggie and Leanna. Were they having a good day?

"Do you have time to stop in and see Maggie?" Madelyne asked.

"I can spare a few minutes." Emory grinned. "Justin can't exactly fire me."

"That's a *gut* point." Madelyne laughed.

They waited until it was safe to cross the busy street and then weaved through the marketplace parking lot, which was clogged with cars, along with horses and buggies lining the hitching posts at the back of the lot.

Emory held open the door for Madelyne, and they stepped into the building, moving over the worn, creaky oak floors.

They moved past the candy booth and the Quilt Shop before rounding the counter. The delicious smells of Bethany's coffee floated over Emory as the sign he'd crafted welcomed them to the Jam and Jelly Nook and Quilt and Gift Stand.

"Here it is." Emory made a sweeping gesture toward the booth, which was already busy with customers examining the wares for sale. Leanna stood at the counter, talking to a woman, while Maggie was in the back of the booth, showing another woman a quilt.

From the entrance to the booth, Emory watched both Leanna and Maggie, his heart jumping up to his throat as he took in Leanna's beautiful face. He'd missed her.

Maggie peeked up from the quilt, and a smile broke out on her face when she saw him. She waved and then looked back at her customer.

"You can tell Maggie has worked so hard," Madelyne said. "Everything looks *schee*."

Emory smiled. "*Ya*, it does."

Leanna gave the woman her change and bag, and then she met his gaze. At first she smiled, but then her smile faded when she looked at Madelyne. Storm clouds seemed to gather across her face.

"Hi, Leanna," Emory said as he and Madelyne approached the counter. "This is Madelyne."

"It's nice to finally meet you," Leanna said.

Madelyne held her hand out. "You too. I've heard a lot about you."

Leanna gave Emory a sideways glance and then shook Madelyne's hand.

"*Dat!* Madelyne!" Having finished helping her customer, Maggie hurried over. "What are you two doing here?"

"We had lunch and decided to stop by," Madelyne explained. "I wanted to see your booth." She pointed toward the quilts. "Give me a quick tour?" She followed Maggie over to the quilts and crafts area.

Leanna fingered the edge of the counter, her expression hesitant. Although she wasn't cold, she seemed different— standoffish, nervous, on edge. So unlike the Leanna he knew. "Madelyne is *schee*."

Emory nodded. *So are you.* "How have you been?"

"Fine. You?"

"The same."

"Where did you go for lunch?"

"Zimmerman's Family Restaurant."

"My cousin Salina and her husband own that place."

"I know. Will told me."

"Right. I forgot you met him." She looked over her shoulder to where Maggie and Madelyne talked over a quilt, and something that looked like sadness flickered over her pretty face.

Then she pivoted toward him again. "Maggie and I have had a great day so far. She's so courteous and patient with the customers. You should be proud."

"I am."

They gazed at each other for a moment, and his lungs seized, his breath frozen in his chest.

Then a woman with white hair dressed in pink sneakers, a purple shirt, and orange shorts approached the counter. "Excuse me. Do you have any strawberry jam?"

Leanna smiled at the woman. "I do." Then she looked at Emory. "Take care."

"You too," he managed to say before Leanna led the woman over to the jam.

Emory turned and saw Maggie and Madelyne walking over to him.

"I have to help a customer," Maggie said. "But *danki* for stopping by. I'll see you tonight, *Dat.*"

Madelyne and Emory said good-bye to Maggie, and Emory snuck a look at Leanna before they left the booth.

"I'd better get back to work before Justin thinks we ran off," Emory told Madelyne as they headed out of the marketplace.

Madelyne made small talk about the beautiful mid-September weather as they strolled back to the shed shop.

"I had fun," she said when they walked into the showroom. "*Danki* for having lunch with me."

"*Danki* for inviting me."

"Let's do this again sometime." Madelyne hesitated as if expecting something, and then she took a step back. "Call me."

"I will." As he watched Madelyne go, his thoughts were stuck on Leanna and how different she seemed today.

Maybe she was having a bad day. Or maybe she was upset about something.

All he knew for sure was that he missed their closeness.

He blew out a sigh and shook his head. He needed to remove all thoughts of Leanna from his head and concentrate on Madelyne. She was the one who wanted to date him. She could possibly be the future God had chosen for him.

Now he just had to find a way to convince his heart. But that seemed an impossible task.

CHAPTER 28

Leanna sipped a mug of tea as she sat with her cousins at Salina's kitchen table Sunday afternoon.

"He's so handsome," Bethany said as she gazed down at baby William Junior in her arms.

Salina beamed at her infant. Although dark circles rimmed her pretty blue eyes, she looked radiant. "*Danki*. I can't believe he's finally here." She looked over her shoulder to where Karrie, Kaylin, and Angelie played with blocks near them.

She cupped her hand to her mouth to cover a yawn. "Will has been helping at night, which is a blessing. But you know how it is when they're first born. We'll hopefully get into a schedule at some point."

Leanna touched Will's little hand. "How's Karrie adjusting?"

"Well enough! I bet she'll be a *gut* helper someday." Salina smiled. "She's been carrying one of her dolls around and feeding it a bottle."

"Aww," Leanna, Christiana, and Bethany all responded.

"How is the booth going, Leanna?" Christiana asked as she picked up a macadamia nut cookie from a plate in the center of the table.

"Busy. Maggie's quilts and crafts are flying off the shelves. My business is picking up too. I think customers come in to see the quilts and add a few jars of jams and jellies to their baskets before they leave."

Salina picked up a chocolate chip cookie. "That's *gut*. I got the impression you and Maggie get along well."

"We do. She's a sweetheart."

"And how's Emory?" Christiana asked.

Leanna couldn't stop her frown as a queasy feeling spread through her.

Salina's eyes widened. "What happened?"

"Tell us what's going on," Christiana said, a worried look on her face.

"He's seeing someone, and I'm having a hard time with it. I met her yesterday, and she's just as perfect as I imagined her to be."

Salina scowled. "Perfect?"

"Leanna, you have to be kidding me." Christiana shook her head. "How could she be any better than you? You're sweet and lovely."

"And we already told you it's obvious he cares about you," Salina added.

Leanna sighed and looked down at her mug again. Her grief ran deep. "She's tall and slim. She has hair the color of sunshine and the most gorgeous green eyes that remind me of *mei dat*'s pastures in the summertime. She's stunning. I can see why he would pick her over me."

Salina groaned. "Stop it, Leanna."

"Salina is right," Christiana insisted. "If Emory can't see how wonderful you are, then it wasn't meant to be. Maybe he's not the one God has in mind for you. Maybe you haven't met your future husband yet."

Leanna held her hand up. "It's okay. I'm trying to convince

myself we're only meant to be *freinden*. Perhaps God brought Emory into my life so I could help Maggie through a hard time, and he could help Chester, which he already has. Maybe it wasn't about Emory and me at all. Maybe I'm supposed to be a blessing to Maggie. She has certainly been a blessing to me."

Bethany looked up at her again and shook her head. "I think that's only part of it. I think Emory cares for you, but something is holding him back."

"*Ya*, and that something is Madelyne," Leanna quipped. "But truly, I'm getting over my heartache. I'm just doing my best to not let my disappointment come between Maggie and me or between Chester and Emory. God will help me find peace."

Her cousins all exchanged sad expressions, and Leanna thought she might scream.

"We didn't come here to talk about my failed love life," Leanna said. "Today is about this handsome young man. Let's talk about William Junior."

Salina smiled. "He looks like his *dat*."

"I see you in him too," Bethany said.

As the conversation turned to baby William, Leanna tried to sit with her heartache. What was God trying to show her in this time?

She hoped someday she could forget her feelings for Emory Speicher. But she knew to the depth of her bones that it wouldn't be easy.

. . .

Leanna helped Maggie restock her quilts on Thursday two weeks later. "I can't believe you sold four quilts last week."

"I know," Maggie said. "I'm going to have to start quilting again. I'm almost out of stock at home."

"Isn't it a great feeling? When I run out of jelly, I get so excited to make more."

"*Ya*, but it's a lot of work! Still, I'm grateful it's work I like."

They set the last quilt on the stand and moved to the front of the booth as Sara Ann stepped in.

Dread pooled in Leanna's belly. "Hi, Sara Ann," she croaked.

"Hi." Sara Ann focused her gray eyes on Maggie. "I heard you two were selling a lot of quilts down here."

Maggie's eyes widened.

"*Ya*, we have been," Leanna said.

"I wanted to come see them for myself. Are you pricing them too low?" Sara Ann made a beeline back to the quilts and began studying them. "Hmm."

Maggie looked at Leanna, and Leanna held her hand up to tell her not to say anything.

"Well." Sara Ann looked over at Maggie and a wry smile spread across her pretty face. "They're *gut*, but maybe someday you'll be as *gut* as your *mamm*."

A small noise escaped Maggie's throat as her eyes filled with tears.

Something inside of Leanna snapped. She stood up straight and glared at Sara Ann.

"Do you consider yourself a Christian, Sara Ann?" Leanna's voice was louder than she'd meant it to be.

"Of course I do." Sara Ann's eyes widened with shock.

"Then why would you even *think* of hurting a young woman's feelings with thoughtless words like that?" Leanna pointed at Maggie as she wiped her eyes. "You're just jealous that

Maggie is selling quilts and you're not the only quilt seller here anymore."

Sara Ann opened her mouth and then closed it, reminding Leanna of a fish caught out of water.

"I've seen one of Sheryl's quilts, and Maggie's are just as *gut*, if not better. And yours are *gut* too. There's no reason why we can't have two quilt sellers here since you're both talented, and your quilts are unique in their own way." Leanna pointed toward the market entrance as her body vibrated with fury. "There's no sign on the door that says only one quilt booth can be in this marketplace, so stop acting like you own it. You don't. You pay rent just like I do."

Sara Ann's shoulders dipped.

"Stop picking on Maggie, Sara Ann," Leanna continued, her voice thick. "She's a lovely young *maedel*. She's sweeter and more genuine than you could ever hope to be, and maybe that's the reason why she's selling more quilts than you are. Maybe customers can see that Maggie is a truly kind person and not a gossip or a bully like you."

Sara Ann gasped.

"Oh, and by the way," Leanna continued, "stop interfering in others' lives, just as you did to Bethany and Micah. You caused a lot of trouble for Micah with your gossip! Go back to your booth and leave all of us alone."

Sara Ann blinked and then hurried out of the booth.

Maggie, still sniffling, gaped at Leanna.

"Just try to forget what she said, Maggie." Leanna huffed, then turned back to the nearest shelf, straightening the jars of jelly she had already straightened, her hands still trembling. She'd finally said the words she'd always wanted to say to Sara

Ann. Perhaps Sara Ann had listened and would change her ways, but Leanna doubted it.

"Leanna?"

She turned to face Maggie. "Are you okay?"

"*Ya. Danki.*"

Leanna smiled. "*Gern gschehne.* Now, let's sell more of your gorgeous quilts."

Maggie wiped away her last tear and grinned.

. . .

"How was your day?" Emory asked Maggie as they ate supper later that evening.

Madelyne smiled at Maggie from across the table.

"It was interesting," Maggie began as she cut up her pork chop. "There's this woman named Sara Ann King who has a quilt stand at the marketplace. She told me she knows you and she used to quilt with *Mamm.*"

A frown pressed down his lips. He recalled Sheryl once lamenting that Sara Ann was a bit of a gossip at their quilting frolics. "I know who she is."

"Leanna and her cousins warned me to stay away from her because she's the marketplace gossip. They also said Sara Ann tried to break up Bethany and her husband when they were dating."

"Really?" Madelyne asked with a surprised expression. "How terrible!"

Then Maggie retold the story of what Sara Ann had said about Maggie's skills and her mother's. Madelyne sucked in a breath, and Emory's blood boiled.

"She said that to you?" Emory's voice rose.

Maggie nodded and then she smiled. "But Leanna took care of it."

"How?" Madelyne asked.

Maggie animatedly described Leanna's defense of her. "She also told Sara Ann I probably sell more quilts because people can see I'm sweet and not a gossip or a bully." Then Maggie grinned. "Leanna finally kicked her out of the booth and told her to leave me alone. Sara Ann looked so stunned!"

"*Gut* for Leanna," Madelyne said.

Emory smiled as an overwhelming appreciation for Leanna welled up in him. "I'm so glad she did that."

"When I saw Sara Ann later in the day, she turned and hurried away from me. I was so relieved. Leanna is amazing."

Emory nodded. *Yes, yes she is!*

Madelyne and Maggie turned to discussing planting fall flowers in their gardens during the rest of supper and dessert, while Emory found himself reviewing the story about Leanna in his mind.

After the women had cleaned up the kitchen, Emory sat on the porch with Madelyne and looked out over his dark pasture. The aroma of a wood-burning fireplace drifted over him, and an early autumn chill in the air caused him to zip up his light jacket.

Madelyne shivered and hugged her wrap closer to her body. "The fall weather is here. Hard to believe it's October already."

He turned toward her. "Do you want to go back inside?"

"No, it's nice out here. Don't you like the night sky?" She pointed up at the stars twinkling above them. "It's so romantic."

He nodded as his thoughts turned back to Leanna. "I keep

thinking about how Leanna defended Maggie today. She's been so *gut* for her. Maggie has truly changed since she started running that booth. She's more confident and she's happier. Leanna has been such a blessing to her."

He looked over at Madelyne and found her staring at him. *"Was iss letz?"*

"Do you care for Leanna?"

Emory stilled and then nodded. *"Ya*, as a *freind."*

Madelyne looked at him, her expression telling him she was unconvinced.

"You don't have to worry. Leanna isn't looking for anyone to date."

"Are you looking for someone to date?"

Emory hesitated. He was looking for someone to date, but that someone was Leanna, not Madelyne.

He swallowed as reality crashed around him. Madelyne was the one who wanted him. She was also the one opening her heart to him and offering him a future. He needed to grab that future now while he could. She was kind, pretty, and sweet. And she was here now.

But how could he let go of Leanna when she was the one who had made such a difference in Maggie's life? Leanna was also the one who had stolen his heart.

When Madelyne's expression dimmed, he felt the urgency of the situation. He couldn't allow this opportunity to pass him by.

He forced his lips into a smile. *"Ya*, I do want to date, but I want to take it slow. It's been a long time for me, and it's a big adjustment for Maggie."

"I can respect that." Her expression became expectant. "Does that mean you might want to date me?"

He blinked, his heart insisting he say no. Leanna was the one he wanted! But Madelyne was offering her hand. She was a reasonable choice, a good option for both him and Maggie! Why couldn't his heart accept that truth?

"*Ya*," he said, his voice thin. "If your *dat* gives me permission. How does that sound?"

"That sounds perfect." She looked over at him, and her expression became intense, her green eyes glittering in the light of the lantern. "I care about you, Emory."

He swallowed, his heart screaming for him to reject her, but his mind pushed him forward toward a future with her. "I care about you too. Why don't we go see your *dat*?" He took her hands in his, and when their skin touched, he waited for a thrill or a spark to race up his arm, but he felt nothing.

Maybe it was too soon to feel something for her.

Or maybe he was expecting too much.

He plastered a smile on his face despite his doubts. "I'll get my horse and buggy ready," he said.

Dating Madelyne made good sense. Surely his heart would change toward her.

. . .

"So, it's official." Emory stood on Madelyne's parents' porch later that evening.

Emory had taken Madelyne home, and while she talked in the kitchen with her mother, Emory followed her father into the family room to speak to him alone.

Then Emory had asked him if he could have permission to date her, promising to be respectful to her. Her father had responded with a grin and a strong handshake, saying he was grateful Emory had asked. And just like that, Emory was officially dating Madelyne Swarey.

But instead of feeling the intense elation he'd felt when Sheryl's father had given him permission, he felt . . . apprehension. Where was the happiness?

Maybe it was different because he was older and he had a clearer view of dating and marriage. But still—shouldn't he be excited about a future with Madelyne? After all, she was beautiful, sweet, and kind. She was a wonderful match for Maggie.

But still something was missing.

"I knew he'd say yes. My parents like you very much." Madelyne stepped over to him and gave him a coy smile. "And I do too."

"Do you?" He chuckled.

"*Ya*, I do."

Emory cupped his hand to her cheek. "Well, I'm glad we have that in common." Then he bent down and brushed his lips over hers. He waited for the explosion of emotions he recalled when he kissed Sheryl.

But once again, he felt nothing.

Curious.

Would he ever feel those emotions again? Or was Sheryl the only woman who would warm his heart that way?

When he broke the kiss, Madelyne gazed up at him, her cheeks flushed and her eyes sparkling. "Be safe going home."

"I will. *Gut nacht*." He jogged down the porch steps with the beam of his flashlight guiding his way. Then he climbed into the buggy and guided the horse toward home.

As he drove, his mind swam with confusion and worry. He looked in the rearview mirror toward Madelyne's house, and a black feeling settled in the pit of his gut. He hoped he hadn't just made the biggest mistake of his life.

And if he had, he would only wind up hurting Madelyne, which was the last thing he wanted to do.

CHAPTER 29

L et me get this straight," Bethany said Friday morning while sitting at a table in the Coffee Corner. "You told off Sara Ann yesterday." Her blue eyes glimmered as she clucked her tongue at Leanna. "And you didn't tell me right away?"

Maggie beamed. "You should have heard it, Bethany." Then she summarized what Leanna had said to her.

"Did I really say all of that?" Leanna chuckled as she picked up her cup of caramel mocha. "I was so angry and shaking so hard that I don't remember it all."

"I'm so proud of you, Leanna." Bethany grinned. "Oh, if only I could have been a fly on the wall!"

"Sara Ann saw me yesterday and then turned and went the other way. I think she got the message loud and clear to leave me alone." Maggie touched Leanna's arm. "I can't thank you enough."

Leanna shook her head. "When she picked on you, something inside of me snapped. I was tired of Sara Ann hurting the people I care about."

Maggie's expression warmed.

"We have to tell Salina and Christiana when we see them again," Bethany said. "Oh, they will be stunned and delighted."

They each were quiet for a moment as they drank more coffee and enjoyed the morning stillness.

"*Mei dat* asked Madelyne to be his girlfriend last night. He told me on the way to the market this morning. She came for supper, and then they went to see her *dat*, and he asked for permission."

The floor below Leanna seemed to drop out. She kept her eyes focused on her half-eaten strawberry glazed donut, even though her appetite dissolved. She felt as if she'd been kicked so hard in the stomach that she couldn't breathe.

It was official. She had lost Emory, and Madelyne had won. She should be happy for him, but she couldn't lift her spirits enough to take part in his joy. The pain of her heart shattering into a million pieces was too much.

"How do you feel about it, Maggie?" Bethany's voice was calm, but it seemed to hold a thread of worry.

"I'm okay. I know I have to accept it, but . . ."

"But what?" Bethany asked.

"I don't think Madelyne is the one for him."

Leanna looked over at Maggie, who gave her an unreadable expression that piqued her curiosity.

"Well, it's almost opening time," Bethany said. "We'd better get our booths ready for another busy Friday."

Maggie hopped down from the stool and carried her empty cup and napkin to the trash can.

Bethany gently grabbed Leanna's arm. "Don't give up on him."

"But he picked Madelyne," Leanna whispered. "Wouldn't it be *schmaert* to accept that Madelyne won and move on?"

Bethany smiled. "With God all things are possible, Leanna. Don't ever forget that."

Leanna nodded, but doubt still whipped over her. Emory had made his choice. And that was the reality she needed to accept in order to try to mend her battered heart.

. . .

"How was your Sunday?" Emory asked Chester as they started working on their next shed project Monday morning.

"*Gut*. I had church and then youth group." Chester chose a nail and then began hammering the floorboards. He sat back on his heels and looked over at Emory. "Yours?"

"It was nice. We had church and then visited with family." Emory began hammering too. He glanced across the shop to where Justin and Lee were also working on a shed.

"I made a decision yesterday," said Chester.

Emory turned back toward him. "Oh *ya*?"

"I'm going to join the church."

"Really?" Emory knelt and put down his hammer, then clapped the boy on the shoulder. "That's fantastic news. How did it come about?"

"*Mei freinden* and I were discussing it at our youth gathering, and we want to join the church together. I know the baptism class won't start until the spring, but I'm ready to start making changes in my life now. I'm going to turn in my phone at the cell phone store at lunch today. *Mei freinden* are too. We're all making a commitment to get rid of our cell phones and stop smoking as a way to sort of wash away some of our worldly sins now. Then we'll join the baptism class in our district in the spring and be baptized together in the fall."

"I'm so *froh* to hear that. Does your *mamm* know?"

Chester shook his head. "I haven't told her yet."

"Well, I'm sure she'll be delighted to hear it." Emory tilted his head. "How is your *mamm*?"

"She's fine. She's been busy making jams and jellies for her booth. Apparently sales have been through the roof."

"That's what I hear." Emory turned his attention back to hammering as thoughts of Leanna hijacked his mind. He missed her and wished he could see her face when Chester told her the happy news.

"Are you dating Madelyne?"

Emory looked up at Chester. "*Ya.* Why?"

"I heard *mei mamm* say something to *mei mammi* about it. I was wondering if it was true."

"Well, it is." Emory longed to ask what else Leanna had said about him, but it was none of his business.

"How's it going?"

Emory almost chuckled. Why would a teenager want to hear about his love life? "It's going fine. *Danki.*"

"*Gut.*" Chester turned back to his hammering.

As Emory returned to the same task, he found himself wondering when he'd feel himself falling in love with Madelyne and if he ever would.

· · ·

"Hi, Leanna!" Maggie called as she descended the basement stairs later that afternoon.

"Maggie!" Leanna stepped away from the counter where she'd been filling jars with the strawberry jam she'd made. The basement was full of the sweet, rich aroma of the jam.

"Oh, it smells great down here!"

"*Danki.* I was so excited when *mei dat* said you'd called and wanted to come over to make jam with me."

"*Ya*, we've been talking about it, and today seemed like the perfect day since I'm caught up on my chores and I already have a casserole in the refrigerator for supper. I had Miles drop me off. I called *mei dat* at the shop, and he said he'd pick me up after work."

Maggie set her tote bag and sweater on the empty counter and then crossed the room to Leanna. "How can I help?"

"I already made some strawberry jam this morning, so I'm filling the jars now. Then we can seal them and add the labels after the jars have cooled." Leanna pointed to the labels on the counter. "I have a local printer create them for me."

Maggie picked one up and examined it. "Marlin's Strawberry Jam?"

"*Ya*, that was my husband's favorite. Grape is Chester's favorite, so that jelly is named after him."

"I love that. I'm embarrassed I never noticed."

"Not to worry." Leanna smiled as she filled another jar. "What's your favorite flavor?"

Maggie grinned. "Raspberry jam. What's yours?"

"Cherry jam."

"Yum!" Maggie washed her hands at the sink.

"Did you go to youth group yesterday?" Leanna asked while filling another jar.

"I did. I came home early since it rained last night, though. *Onkel* Justin, *Aenti* Natalie, and Madelyne were there. They had come over to visit and for supper."

Leanna's lips pursed at the mention of Madelyne's name, but she carried on with her task. "How's Madelyne?" She hoped she kept her boiling jealousy out of her tone.

"She's nice, but I don't think *mei dat* loves her." Maggie stood beside her and began filling a jar with the jam.

Leanna froze, and her throat dried. "How can you tell?"

"Just by the way he acts. He seems to be going through the motions, but . . . It just seems to me like something is missing."

Maggie looked over at her. "You know how couples tease each other and play around?"

Leanna tried to swallow against her dry throat as she nodded.

"They don't do that. They're not cold to each other, but there's no spark. I see the connection between *mei aenti* and *onkel*. They're always laughing at each other and holding hands when they think no one is looking. I haven't seen anything like that between *Dat* and Madelyne."

Leanna blinked, not knowing what to say or what to do with this information. Why would Emory want to date a woman that didn't warm his heart? Was he that desperate? And if so, then why wasn't Leanna good enough for him?

"How did you meet Marlin?"

Maggie's question pulled Leanna back to the present.

"I knew him my whole life. I had a crush on him from the time I was barely a teenager. We started dating after we were baptized."

"That's so romantic."

Leanna chuckled. "*Ya*, I guess so."

"What did he look like?"

"He was tall, like your *dat*, but he had sandy blond hair and bright blue eyes."

"Tell me more about him," Maggie said as they finished filling the jars.

Leanna reminisced about Marlin, and then they moved on to other subjects, such as Maggie's friends and their favorite books. Before long, the jam had all been ladled into jars and it was time to start on the raspberry recipe.

Leanna enjoyed Maggie's company as they worked, and she hoped they could share more days like this. The afternoon began flying by too quickly, and Leanna hoped it would never end.

. . .

Emory tied his horse to Leanna's father's fence and then climbed the back porch steps later that evening. He had followed Chester home, and while Chester disappeared into the barn to help his grandfather with their animals, Emory headed toward the house to retrieve Maggie.

He'd been pleasantly surprised when Maggie called to ask if she could go to Leanna's to make jam today. He was so grateful Maggie had decided to spend more time outside of the house and away from the chores.

The early October evening air was chilly, causing him to stick his hands in his pockets after knocking on the back door. He heard footfalls in the mudroom before the back door opened, revealing Rachelle.

"Hi, Emory," Rachelle said. "So nice to see you."

"You too."

"You must be here for Maggie. Come on in." Rachelle opened the door wide, and he followed her through the mudroom and into the kitchen. "They're downstairs with the canning stove. From the sounds of it, they're having fun. Go on down." She pointed toward the basement door.

Emory pushed open the door and laughter floated up from downstairs. He recognized both his daughter's and Leanna's voices, and he couldn't stop his grin. He began to descend the stairs, careful to keep his footsteps as quiet as possible.

Once he reached the middle of the stairs, he stopped and took in the scene in front of him. Leanna and Maggie laughed and talked as they filled jars with what looked like orange marmalade.

Emory gently lowered himself down on the step and continued to watch them, enjoying the sight in front of him. His daughter seemed completely at ease, as did Leanna, while they worked together.

"What happened after Marlin found out you had accidentally spilled bleach on his favorite blue shirt?" Maggie asked.

"He wasn't very happy, if that's what you're asking," Leanna quipped. "He said he'd do the laundry himself, and I told him to have a *gut* time while doing it."

Maggie hooted, throwing her head back. Then she turned and sucked in a breath as she looked toward the stairs. "*Dat!*"

Emory waved at her. "Hi."

"How long have you been sitting there?" Maggie slammed her hands onto her small hips.

Leanna spun to face him, her pretty chocolate eyes wide in surprise. She looked beautiful in a dark blue dress that complemented her dark hair. "I didn't hear you come down the stairs."

"I was enjoying the story about the bleached shirt. Did Marlin do the laundry for you after that?" he joked.

"No. Sadly, he didn't." Leanna gave an uneasy laugh as she wiped her hands down her black apron.

"It sounds like you two are having a *gut* time." Emory pulled himself up with the help of the banister.

"We are," Maggie said. "We made strawberry jam, raspberry jam, and orange marmalade. I've learned so much."

"That's *wunderbaar*." Emory came the rest of the way down the stairs. "Why don't I help you clean up?"

Leanna waved him off. "Oh, no. That's not necessary. I can handle it."

"I don't want to leave you with this mess." Maggie turned to Emory. "In fact, I don't want to leave at all."

Leanna's expression brightened. "Why don't you stay for supper?"

Maggie grinned. "Can we, *Dat*? Please?"

"Sure. That sounds nice." Emory smiled, but Leanna looked away as if avoiding his gaze.

Maggie began washing the pots and bowls they'd dirtied, and Emory grabbed a wet rag and wiped down the counters. Leanna took up the job of drying the dishes and stowing them in the cabinets.

"You have a nice setup down here," Emory commented as he wiped down a table where the jars sat.

"*Danki*," Leanna said over her shoulder. "*Mei dat* built me this kitchen when I opened the booth. This way I can keep all of my supplies down here and not get in the way upstairs."

They finished their cleaning in silence.

Leanna began putting the cooled jars into the cabinets. "Maggie, would you please go tell *mei mamm* that you and your *dat* are staying for supper?"

"Sure. I'll help her set the table."

"*Danki*." Leanna smiled at her and then turned back toward the cabinets.

Emory stood by the stairs and searched for something to say to her. How had he and Leanna gone from being close friends to almost strangers? What had changed between them? He missed their closeness so much that his heart ached.

"Would you like some jelly?" she suddenly asked.

"Oh. Sure." Emory sauntered over to her and reached in his pocket for his wallet.

Leanna frowned over at him. "You're not going to pay me, Emory. Your *dochder* just spent her afternoon helping me."

He smiled. "In that case, I'll take a strawberry."

"And a raspberry for Maggie." She handed him a jar of each. "How about a grape too? And an apple cranberry?"

"Sure. *Danki.*"

She pulled a small shopping bag out of a drawer, put the jars in it, and handed it to him. "Here you go. Enjoy."

He watched her. "How have you been?"

"Okay." Something unreadable flashed in her eyes. "How's Madelyne?" There was a sharp edge to her tone, despite her blank expression.

"She's fine."

"*Gut.*"

They stared at each other, and a coldness radiated off her in waves. Something had changed with her.

For the first time since he'd met Leanna, he felt a great chasm expanding between them. Had he forfeited their friendship somehow?

"Supper is ready!" Maggie called from upstairs.

"Let's go eat." Leanna moved past him and marched up the stairs.

CHAPTER 30

Emory shoveled another delicious spoonful of beef stew into his mouth while his *dochder* carried the conversation. Maggie had spent most of supper discussing how much fun she'd had with Leanna, while Rachelle peppered the chatter with questions about the booth.

Emory's chest warmed as he watched his daughter smile, but he also was struck by how Leanna had beamed at Maggie. He was mesmerized by the close relationship Maggie and Leanna had cultivated since opening the booth together.

Although Maggie and Madelyne seemed to have a nice friendship, this was different. There was a deeper closeness between Maggie and Leanna, and it had captured Emory's heart.

Emory turned from Leanna and felt someone watching him. He looked across the table to Chester. Emory smiled at him, but Chester looked away.

"So, Emory," Walter began, "I hear the shop is staying busy despite the cold weather."

"*Ya*, that's true. Spring and summer are our busiest times, but we have enough business to sustain us during the fall and winter."

"That's always *gut*," Walter said.

Emory looked over at Chester. "Have you told your *mamm* your decision yet?"

Chester bit his lip and shook his head.

"What's that?" Leanna divided a look between them.

Chester looked at Emory and then at Leanna. "I've decided to join the baptism class in the spring."

Leanna huffed out a breath. "Chester, that's great." She looked as if she might begin to cry. "When did you make this decision?"

"Yesterday. *Mei freinden* and I talked at youth group, and we're all going to join together."

Leanna touched her chest. "That makes me so *froh*."

"And that's not all you told me this morning," Emory prompted him.

Chester cleared his throat. "*Mei freinden* and I have also decided to make changes in our lives. We're giving up smoking and our cell phones. I turned in my phone at the cell phone store at lunchtime today, and I threw out the last of the cigarettes I'd bought."

Leanna bit her lower lip as tears glistened in her eyes. She looked across the table at Emory and gave him a half smile before nodding at him. That familiar stirring filled his chest as he nodded in return. Then he felt something unspoken pass between them before she broke the gaze and looked back at Chester.

"I'm really *froh* to hear this, Chester," she said. "I'm proud of you."

"I am too," Rachelle said as Walter nodded.

Emory ate another bite of stew and scanned the table. As the cheery conversation carried on, he found himself so grateful this family had welcomed him and his daughter.

. . .

Leanna sat on a rocking chair between Emory and *Dat* later that evening. She hugged her sweater against her body as an autumn breeze caused her to shiver.

She found herself still reeling from the news that Chester had decided not only to join the baptism class in the spring but to stop smoking and give up his cell phone too.

She couldn't believe it. It almost felt too good to be true, but her prayers had been answered. God was so very good!

Deep down, she knew she also had Emory to thank for this happy news. After all, he'd told Emory before he'd told Leanna or her parents. That was proof Chester trusted the man.

She glanced over at Emory as he talked to *Dat* about his early days at the shed shop. She took in his handsome profile; his warm, rich, deep voice; his broad shoulders; and his trim waist. She'd yearned for him all evening, memorizing the details of his face and the sound of his voice so that she could recall them later when he was gone. But such thoughts were indulgences, she knew. He was already lost to her. She forced herself to look out toward the dark outline of her father's three rows of red barns.

While hugging her sweater tighter against her waist, she recalled their strained discussion in the basement. He hadn't flinched when she'd asked him about Madelyne. Her heart sank even lower. What had she expected? Did she think he'd say they had broken up and he was there to ask *Dat*'s permission for her to date him?

Oh, but she still found herself dreaming of that day, even though she knew it would never come. He'd made his choice, and the choice hadn't been Leanna. A hollow ache swelled in her soul.

She rocked her chair back and forth and looked out toward her grandparents' house. She craved some time to talk to *Mammi* about all of her heartbreaking emotions. She needed to make time to go see her.

"Well, I guess we should get going." Emory stood and turned toward her parents and Maggie. "*Danki* so much for supper. It was very generous of you to invite us." He shook *Dat*'s hand and then *Mamm*'s.

"We're so glad you and Maggie could stay," *Dat* said, and *Mamm* nodded.

Then Emory turned to Chester. "I'll see you at work tomorrow."

"I'll be there," Chester said with a grin.

Emory swiveled around to Leanna. "*Danki* for spending the afternoon with Maggie. It's obvious she enjoyed herself and learned so much from you." He held up the bag of jars. "And I will enjoy the fruits of your labor." He grinned. "Get it? Fruits?"

Leanna couldn't stop her laugh. "You're so *gegisch*."

"Ah, there it is." He pointed at her face. "A smile."

She swallowed back a sudden rush of emotion. "Be safe going home." Her voice quivered.

"I will." He nodded and then held his hand out to her.

She hesitated and eyed him. As much she wanted to shake his hand, she feared the jolt of heat touching him would cause. She looked up into his eyes. At that moment, she was certain that she loved him, and that realization sent grief crashing through her.

"*Gut nacht*," she whispered before turning and rushing back into the house. She fled up the stairs and into her room as tears began to stream from her eyes.

"Help me Lord," she whispered as she crawled onto her bed.

"I'm in love with a man who loves someone else. Help me. Heal my broken heart."

She buried her face in her pillow and sobbed.

. . .

"Leanna!" Anthony Gingerich, Bethany's younger brother, burst into the Jam and Jelly Nook Friday morning. "*Mammi* is in the hospital."

"What happened?" Leanna stepped away from a group of customers as panic scraped up her throat.

"She fell walking out to her garden earlier this morning. Your *dat* called *mei dat*. He thinks she may have broken her leg or hip. She was going into shock by the time the EMTs showed up."

Tears stung Leanna's eyes. "*Ach* no! Poor *Mammi!*"

"What's going on?" Maggie appeared at her side, her eyes wide with concern.

"*Mei mammi* fell and is badly hurt. She's on her way to the hospital."

"Your *dat* rode to the hospital in the ambulance, and your *mamm* got a ride to the hospital with her driver," Anthony continued. "My parents are already on their way to the hospital too. Micah called his driver, and we came here to get you and Bethany." He beckoned her. "Micah is helping Bethany close up her booth now."

Leanna began wringing her hands as worry and fear raced through her.

"Go," Maggie said. "I'll run the booth."

"By yourself?" Leanna asked.

"*Ya.* I'll be fine. I can handle the customers, and I know how to close out the register. Just go. Call me later and let me know how she is."

"*Danki.*" Leanna gave her a hug and then grabbed her purse, lunch bag, and tote bag from under the counter.

"I'll be praying for your *mammi*," Maggie called.

Leanna waved at her and then caught up with Anthony, Micah, and Bethany before they rushed out to Micah's driver's van and climbed in.

. . .

Later that afternoon Leanna sat in the waiting area of the hospital with Christiana, Bethany, and Micah. Her heart continued to pound as she prayed for God to heal *Mammi*. She was certain her worry might eat her from the inside out.

"Not knowing how she's doing is killing me," Christiana said as she cupped her hand to her forehead. She had ridden to the hospital with her parents while her husband, Jeff, had stayed home with their daughters. "I want to call Jeff with an update, but there's nothing to tell him."

Leanna nodded. "I know what you mean. I'm sure Salina and Chester are worried, too, but we have nothing to share."

"Oh," Bethany announced. "There's your *dat*."

Dat hurried over to them, and when Leanna saw his pale expression, her stomach lurched.

No, no, no! Please God, no!

"She made it through surgery," he said, and Leanna and her cousins let out the breath they'd been holding.

"Praise God," Leanna said.

Bethany grabbed Micah's hand.

"How is she?" Christiana asked.

"It was a complicated surgery," *Dat* said. "She broke her hip and her leg. She also has bruised ribs. She had to have a rod put in her leg. Since she's in ICU now, we can't see her. When she leaves here, she'll need to go to a rehabilitation center to learn to walk again. She has a long road of recovery ahead of her, and with her age and other health issues . . . Anyway, she will need everyone's help."

Leanna sniffed as tears trickled from her eyes. "But she will be okay?"

"With God's help. We all have to pray." *Dat* gave her hand a squeeze.

"We're all praying, Walter," Micah told him.

"*Gut*," *Dat* said before he stood and walked over to join *Mamm* and Leanna's aunts and uncles.

Leanna closed her eyes and opened her heart to God.

Please, Lord, heal mei mammi. *I don't know how I'd make it without her love and guidance.*

. . .

Emory stepped into the kitchen later that evening and found Maggie carrying a casserole to the table. "Have you heard from Leanna?"

He'd spent all day worrying about Leanna and her family after Chester had told him that her grandmother had taken a terrible fall and wound up in surgery. Chester had gotten a ride to the hospital as soon as he heard the news. More than once, he'd considered calling his driver to take him to the hospital so that he could offer his support to the family.

But that would have been inappropriate. Emory wasn't a part of Leanna's family, after all.

"No, I haven't." Maggie sighed. "I've been so worried about her and *Mammi*."

Emory pushed his hand through his hair as he debated what to do. "I'm going to call her." He headed toward the door.

"Supper is ready. I made one of your favorites—cheesy chicken casserole. Why don't you eat first?" Maggie suggested.

Emory stopped at the door and then nodded. "*Ya*, of course."

After washing his hands at the sink, he sat down at the table and bowed his head in silent prayer, begging God to heal Leanna's grandmother and also grant Leanna and her family peace and comfort during this difficult time.

Then he scooped a mountain of casserole onto his plate.

"*Danki* for making my favorite," he told Maggie.

"*Gern gschehne.*"

"How was the booth?"

She groaned as she scooped casserole onto her plate. "Pure chaos. I missed Leanna so much, but I understand why she had to go. She wanted to close the booth down, but I told her I could handle it. We sold a lot today, and I had a line at one point. Still, I was able to keep my cool and take care of all of the customers."

Emory put his fork down as he studied his daughter.

"Why are you staring at me?" She looked down at her lap. "Do I have a big blob of cheese on my apron?"

"No." He pointed at her. "Two months ago, you wouldn't even go to youth group, let alone run a busy booth at the marketplace. But look at you now. You just handled an entire day of selling not only your quilts and crafts but also Leanna's jams and jellies and Chester's birdhouses. How does that feel?"

Maggie's smile was wide. "Amazing."

"It is truly amazing." *And I owe it all to Leanna.*

After supper, Emory headed out to the phone shanty and dialed the number to Leanna's father's farm. After several rings, the voice mail picked up, and Walter's voice filled Emory's ear.

"You have reached the Gingerich family. Please leave a message, and we will call you back. Have a blessed day."

Emory cleared his throat as the beep sounded. "This message is for Leanna. It's Emory. Chester told me about your *mammi*, and I'm worried sick about you and your family. Maggie is too. Please call us and let us know how your *mammi* is and how you are. Is there anything we can do for you? Please let us know, okay? We're thinking of you and praying. I hope to hear from you soon. Good-bye."

He hung up the phone and set out into the cool evening air. Then he looked up at the sky. "Lord, bless Leanna and her family and heal her grandmother. Please, Lord."

Then he walked back to the house and hoped she would call soon.

. . .

Leanna stepped into the phone shanty later that evening and set her lantern on the counter before dialing the number for the voice mail. She shook her head with wonder as she wrote down messages for her mother from friends calling to check on *Mammi*. It always astounded Leanna how fast news traveled in their community, and the messages of care and prayerfulness soothed her spirit.

When she came to the last message, she froze. Emory's deep voice sounded in her ear, and her heart lifted when she heard the concern in his tone. He sounded so worried and so eager to help her that it warmed her troubled heart.

She played it again and then she played it once more, enjoying the sound of his voice. Then she dialed his number and waited for the voice mail to pick up.

Maggie's voice sounded through the phone as she announced, "You have reached the Speicher family. Please leave us a message, and we will call you back. Thank you."

"Emory," she began, her voice quivering. "This is Leanna. *Danki* for your message and for your concern. It means more than you know. *Mei mammi* is not doing well, and we're all worried. She made it through a long surgery. She had to have a rod put in her leg, and she'll have a long road of recovery ahead of her. Right now she's in intensive care, and we can't see her, which is so difficult. I'm so worried about her."

She paused to sniff as tears welled up in her eyes. "When she gets out of ICU, she'll have to learn how to walk again. Right now my family needs me, so Maggie can run the booth tomorrow if she'd like, or we can close until next week. It's up to Maggie. Please tell her thank you for stepping in for me today. I'm sure she did a great job. I'll let you know how things are going once I find out more. *Danki* again for reaching out. Take care, Emory. *Gut nacht.*"

Leanna hung up the phone and then covered her face with her hands as her tears began to spill over. She cried for *Mammi* and she cried for her own broken heart.

She pulled a tissue out of her pocket and wiped her eyes and nose and then gathered up her mother's messages before walking back toward the house.

When she reached the porch, she looked up at the cloudy evening sky and thought of Marlin. She tried to open her heart to talk to him, but for the first time since she'd lost him, she couldn't. Instead, all she could think of was Emory and how much she wanted to talk to him instead.

Oh, how she missed Emory! She needed him by her side right now during this terrible time! But Emory wasn't hers to miss.

But what if there was a way he could be?

A seed of hope took root in her heart.

"Please, God," she whispered. "Heal *mei mammi*, and if it's your will, find a way to bring Emory back to me. I love him, and I need him in my life."

CHAPTER 31

I'd love to skip youth group and instead go see Leanna today," Maggie announced as she and Emory ate breakfast on Sunday morning.

"I would love to go, too, but I promised to see Madelyne today since we don't have services," Emory said before spooning more oatmeal into his mouth. "You could come with me if you'd like. We're supposed to meet at Justin's *haus*."

Maggie sprinkled more cinnamon on her bowl of oatmeal. "You could cancel on her, and we could go see Leanna and her family instead."

Disappointment tried to swallow him whole as he frowned and shook his head. "I can't."

He'd spent the past two days worrying about Leanna and her family after receiving her message. He could hear the tears in her voice, and they had nearly broken his heart.

Emory had hoped to get an update from Chester at work yesterday, but Chester had left a message saying he wasn't coming in and instead would spend the day at the hospital with his family.

He had prayed and prayed repeatedly for Leanna, her grandmother, and her family, but he longed to see Leanna in person. He wanted to sit with her and hold her hand while she shared the burdens of her heart.

"When are you going to admit to yourself that you love Leanna and not Madelyne?"

Emory's gaze darted to Maggie's. Had she just read his mind? "Excuse me?"

"It's obvious, *Dat*. You're more concerned about Leanna than about visiting with your girlfriend. I think you need to pay attention to your feelings."

He pressed his lips together. "I think you need to worry about your own affairs and stay out of mine."

Maggie's eyes widened, and he immediately felt guilty for his words.

"I'm sorry, Maggie." He sighed. "You're right that I have feelings for Leanna, and I've been struggling with it."

"Why are you struggling?

He sat up taller. "Because I know Madelyne cares for me. I don't want to hurt Madelyne, but I also care for Leanna. I'm confused."

"Have you told Leanna how you feel?"

"No, I haven't."

"If you care about Leanna, then you should tell her. She might surprise you and feel the same way."

He smiled. "*Danki*, but I can handle my own life. Don't worry about me, okay?"

Maggie shook her head. "That's not possible, *Dat*. I'll always worry about you."

Emory smiled. "And I'll always worry about you."

"I'll come with you to see Madelyne," she said.

"*Gut*."

They finished breakfast, and then he helped her clean up the kitchen.

When he looked up at the clock, his shoulders sagged with

the weight of his disappointment. It was time for him to go to his brother's house to see Madelyne. But at the back of his mind, he wondered if Maggie was right. Maybe he should pay attention to his feelings for Leanna. And maybe, just maybe, she could feel the same way he felt.

. . .

Leanna opened the back door later that evening and took a surprised step forward when she found Emory and Maggie standing on the back porch. She pushed the storm door open. "Hi. I wasn't expecting to see you."

"We wanted to check on you." Maggie held up a casserole dish. "I had an extra cheesy chicken casserole in the refrigerator, and I thought your family might like it."

"*Danki.* That's so thoughtful." Leanna took the casserole and then motioned for them to follow her inside. "Please come in out of the cold."

Emory and Maggie walked into the kitchen, where Leanna's mother sat at the table.

"Hi, Rachelle," Emory greeted her mother.

"*Wie geht's?*" Maggie asked as she sat down at the table. "And how's *Mammi*?"

Leanna set the casserole in the refrigerator and then leaned back against the kitchen counter. "She's in a regular hospital room now, and we were able to see her yesterday. She's in a lot of pain, but she seems determined to get better. She'll move to a rehabilitation center in a few days, and she'll be there at least a couple of months. She has to recover and then learn how to walk again."

"She has a long recovery ahead of her, but we're leaving it all in the hands of the Lord," *Mamm* said.

"We've been so worried," Maggie told *Mamm*. "*Mei dat* and I were anxious to come over and check on you all."

"*Danki*," *Mamm* said. "How was it running the booth on your own this week, Maggie?"

"It was really busy. We made a lot of sales. I have your money separated from mine, Leanna."

"I appreciate it more than you know. I promise I'll be back Thursday."

"You can take all the time you need," Maggie said. "I've got it."

Leanna smiled at Maggie. "*Danki.*"

Then Leanna looked over at Emory, and the concern in his eyes made the breath seize in her lungs. An overwhelming urge to talk to him gripped her, and she crossed the kitchen to him.

"Would you like to sit on the porch and catch up with me?"

"*Ya*, I would like that a lot."

Leanna reached for her heavy sweater before they stepped out to the porch. She sat down on the porch swing and looked up at him. He stood beside the swing, seemingly hesitant, watching her as if waiting for permission to sit. She patted the spot beside her, and he sank down.

She looked out toward the three rows of red barns and then pushed the swing into motion with the toe of her shoe.

"How are you, *mei freind*?" he asked.

Leanna cast her eyes down. She couldn't find the words.

"Leanna, please look at me."

She turned toward him, and the anguish in his expression almost tore her in two.

"I could hear the worry in your voice when I listened to your message. I've been worried sick about you. How are you really? Please tell me the truth." His eyes seemed to plead with her.

"I've been a mess." She peered down at her lap. "I haven't been this frightened since I lost Marlin. It all happened so fast, and she had complications with the surgery. And then she wound up in ICU, and we couldn't even see her. I thought for sure we were going to lose her, and she means so much to me. I wouldn't even know how to go on without her."

She sniffed and then her tears began to fall. She covered her face with her hands and cried.

The swing bounced as she felt Emory shift his weight. Then strong arms pulled her to him. She rested her cheek on his shoulder as he rubbed her back. She felt her body relax against his hard chest as she breathed in his familiar scent—hints of cedar mixed with soap and something that was distinctly Emory.

"She's going to be fine," Emory whispered into her ear, causing goosebumps to skip over her skin. "God keeps his eye on every sparrow and lily."

Leanna smiled into his shoulder as comfort settled over her. Emory was here. Emory was with her. This was what she'd needed. This was what she'd prayed for.

Thank you, God.

But the moment of peace was short-lived. Once she remembered she was in the arms of another woman's boyfriend, she pulled back from the embrace. Emory was with Madelyne . . . Was he not?

Leanna was just as bad as Simply Sara Ann!

She could sink into the ground under the weight of what she'd just done! A pang of guilt cut through her.

"Oh no." She sat up and scooted to the far end of the swing, the chain biting into her skin.

He looked confused as he gave her a palms-up. "What is it?"

"Are you still seeing Madelyne?"

He swallowed, and his Adam's apple bobbed. Then he nodded. "*Ya.*"

The word sent a shaft of ice through her heart.

"I'm sorry." She stood as humiliation took hold. "I never should have—"

"You didn't do anything wrong, Leanna. I'm the one who hugged you." He pointed at himself and then at her.

She folded her arms over her chest as if to shield her heart. "This was wrong. You should go."

"But, Leanna, I—"

"You've checked on me, and I'm fine. Now you should leave."

He stood, his handsome face clouding with a deep frown. "Leanna . . ." His voice had a pleading note to it.

"What would Madelyne say if she knew you were here right now? What would she say if she saw what we just did?" She nearly spat the words at him.

He sighed and hung his head, looking shattered, defeated.

"Besides, I'd rather be alone." She marched back into the kitchen, where Maggie and *Mamm* were still talking at the table. "Maggie, *danki* so much for coming and for bringing the casserole. We were at the hospital all day yesterday, and then I had a hard time sleeping last night, and . . . I'm just so tired. I think I need to go to bed now. I'll see you Thursday."

Leanna looked over at Emory as he stood in the doorway. His blue eyes were intense as he watched her. "*Danki* for coming, Emory. Take care of yourself."

"You too."

"Tell Madelyne I said hello."

He pressed his lips together. "Sure."

Leanna looked at her mother, who gave her a confused expression. "*Gut nacht, Mamm.*"

"*Gut nacht,*" *Mamm* echoed.

Then she hurried upstairs to her bedroom and sat down on her bed and opened her heart to God. A fresh crush of sadness battered her, and she yearned for God's comfort.

"Lord, please heal my heart and help me move on from a man I can't have."

. . .

"Did you and Leanna have a disagreement on the porch?" Maggie asked as Emory guided the horse toward home.

He kept his eyes on the road ahead while he gripped the reins with unnecessary force. "Why do you ask?"

"You weren't out there very long, and then when you came in, she looked upset. You looked angry or confused. Is everything okay?"

"*Ya*, it's fine. We talked." *And I held her while she cried. And I didn't want to let her go.* "She said she was tired. That's all. The whole family is dealing with a lot of stress right now."

Emory couldn't tell his daughter the truth. What would Maggie think if he admitted he had held Leanna in his arms?

Besides, it was inappropriate for him to even touch Leanna, but reaching for her had felt so natural and so right.

"It's a shame Walter and Chester were checking on the animals," said Maggie. "I really like Leanna and her family. They're so warm and friendly. They make me feel like I'm a part of their family, you know? Even Chester has become a *gut freind.*"

Emory nodded, but his mind continued to reel with confusion. He'd never once been tempted to cheat on Sheryl. He had never dreamt of it, and he'd never once had feelings for another woman while they were together.

Yet here he was dating Madelyne and thinking about Leanna. Even worse, he had *hugged* Leanna. He was a terrible person. A cheater. A liar. A sinner.

"You were so right that I needed to get out and meet people. I feel like a new person now that I'm going to youth group and spending time with *freinden*. Having the courage to run the booth alone for two days really showed me what I'm capable of doing." Maggie touched his arm. "Are you okay, *Dat*? You look like you're going to be sick."

"I'm fine." He gave her a sideways glance, and she released his arm. "I'm just tired."

When they arrived home, Maggie headed into the house while he stowed the horse in the barn. He walked outside and looked up at the sky, which was clogged with gray clouds as the scent of rain filled his nostrils.

He closed his eyes and took a deep breath as a cool mist of rain kissed his cheeks. He suddenly saw everything in a clearer view—everything he'd been denying and fighting—and he knew to the depth of his soul that Leanna was the one he loved.

And now he had to figure out what to do about it.

"God, I need your help. I've been so confused, and I've made a mess of everything," he said as the rain continued to pelt him, dripping off the brim of his straw hat and soaking through his black jacket.

"I thought I needed to have Madelyne in my life, and I thought you were leading me to her—but perhaps I've loved Leanna all along. I don't even know when I fell for her. She's the one I think of. She's the one I want to tell my secrets to. She's the one I want to hold in my arms. But I don't want to hurt Madelyne. And I also don't think Leanna loves me."

He took a deep breath as the rain began increasing, beating harder on his hat. "Lead me, Lord. Guide me. If I belong with Leanna, then show me the way to her heart. I can't do this without you."

Soaked, Emory walked back toward the house. Now he had to wait for the Lord's sign. He would work hard to keep his heart and mind open to hear it.

. . .

Wednesday afternoon Leanna walked into the hospital with her parents to visit *Mammi*. She carried a vase of flowers she had picked from *Mammi*'s garden earlier that day. She hoped the marigolds and orange mums would brighten her room and bring her some joy during this difficult time.

Leanna couldn't wait to see her. She hadn't visited her since Sunday, and she'd worried about her. She also was anxious to tell *Mammi* about Emory. She hoped she had the opportunity to speak with her alone and share the burdens that had been on her heart.

When they reached the hospital room, *Daadi* stepped out, and her parents immediately began asking him questions about *Mammi*'s recovery and transition to the rehabilitation center later that week. Leanna took that opportunity to sneak into the room and speak with her alone.

"*Mammi!*" Leanna exclaimed as she hurried into the room and dashed over to her bed. She was grateful *Mammi*'s roommate had been discharged a few days ago, giving her a private room.

Mammi was propped up in bed and smiled as Leanna approached her. Her skin was still ashen, and the dark circles rimming her eyes seemed darker. But her bright smile gave Leanna some hope that she'd make a full recovery.

"Oh, it's so *gut* to see you, Leanna." Her voice was gravelly. "Look at those *schee* flowers."

Leanna set the vase on the table beside *Mammi*'s bed. "I borrowed them from your garden. I thought you might enjoy them more here."

"Borrowed them." *Mammi* laughed, and Leanna enjoyed the sound.

Leanna pulled a chair over and sat beside her. "How are you?"

"The pain comes and goes. They say I may go to the rehabilitation center tomorrow. That sounds like it will be a lot of work." *Mammi* touched her wrinkled hand on Leanna's. "How are you, *mei liewe*?"

Leanna's lip quivered. "I've been worried sick about you."

"I won't be here forever."

"But what would I do without you?"

"You have your *mamm* and your precious cousins." Then *Mammi* grinned. "And what about that handsome *freind* of yours?"

"He's dating someone else."

"What? But it was so obvious you two are close. Why would he choose another *maedel*?"

Leanna shook her head. "He's dating a woman named Madelyne."

"I was certain he was in love with you when I saw him with you that day."

"I've been so confused." Then she shared how Emory and

Maggie came to visit her on Sunday and she wound up crying in his arms on the porch.

"You're the only one I'm telling this to because I'm so embarrassed and I feel like a sinner." Leanna looked down at the worn white tile floor. "But at the same time, it felt so right to be in his arms. Still, what we did betrayed Madelyne. I also feel like Marlin would be so disappointed in me."

Mammi clucked her tongue. "You have a right to be *froh*, and Marlin would want you to move on too."

"I just don't know how."

"Tell Emory how you feel about him." *Mammi* patted her hand again.

"How do I do that when he's with someone else?" Leanna groaned. "It's not fair that I've fallen in love with someone who doesn't want to be with me."

Mammi gave a knowing smile. "Does he really love Madelyne if he came to see you Sunday night and held you while you cried?"

Speechless, Leanna blinked at her.

"Have faith and follow your heart. God will lead you on the right path."

Leanna nodded as her parents walked into the room. Was *Mammi* right? Could Emory care for her? She wasn't sure, but if he did, she needed to find the courage to tell Emory how she felt about him.

CHAPTER 32

Sunday afternoon Emory guided his horse and buggy down the road from Justin's house to Madelyne's house.

Since Justin and his family had hosted church today, Emory had invited Madelyne, and they had stayed and visited with Emory's family during the afternoon.

"It's a *schee* day," he said as he gazed out the windshield at the bright cerulean, late October sky.

Autumn had descended upon Lancaster County, turning the air cold and transforming the leaves to brilliant shades of red, orange, and yellow. How he loved the fall!

"You haven't said much today," Madelyne suddenly said. "You were quiet even while we ate with your family. Is something on your mind?"

Emory gave her a sideways look. "Not really. It was a long week at work."

"How's Maggie?"

"She's fine. She had to run the booth by herself for a couple days. Did she tell you about that? I'm so proud of her. She's really matured and become so much more independent since she and Leanna opened that booth together. I'm so grateful for all Leanna has done for her."

When Madelyne remained silent, he looked over at her and

found her glaring at him. The coldness in her green eyes sent a chill through him.

"What?" he asked.

"Do you love Leanna?"

Emory swallowed against his dry throat. "Why would you ask me that?"

"Because you talk about her all the time."

"I do?"

Madelyne nodded as her eyes shimmered. "It was also obvious to me when I met Leanna that she cares for you too." She paused and took a trembling breath. "Tell me the truth, Emory. How do you feel about me?"

He halted the horse by the side of the road and angled his body toward her. "Madelyne, listen, I care for you. I really do."

"Do you love me?"

He stilled, unable to respond.

"Emory, do you love me?" She enunciated the words. "Tell me the truth and *only* the truth."

He frowned and shook his head. "I care for you, but no, I'm afraid I don't love you. I hoped my feelings for you would grow over time."

"I'm thirty-five years old, and I'm ready to get married and have a family." She sniffed and wiped at her eyes, but her expression clouded with a deep frown. "I don't have time to play games, and I told you that when we started seeing each other. If you don't love me and don't see yourself ever wanting to marry me, then I think we should break up. I don't have time to wait to see if you change your mind about me."

"Madelyne, I'm sorry."

She stared at her hands in resignation. "It's obvious you and Leanna are in love. I should have said something sooner, but I was hoping I was imagining it. I just wish you had been honest with me." She nodded toward the road ahead. "Please take me home."

They were silent for the remainder of the trip, and the only sound that filled the buggy was the spinning buggy wheels, the roar of the passing traffic, and Madelyne's occasional sniffs. He felt a hard pit in his stomach, coupled with a sharp sting of guilt.

Emory's thoughts spun as he considered Madelyne's words. She believed Leanna loved him.

Leanna loved him?

But how could he even think of Leanna when it was obvious he had hurt Madelyne so badly? He felt like a terrible person!

When they reached her family's two-story white house, Emory guided the horse into her driveway and then angled his body toward her.

"Madelyne, I'm sorry. I never meant to lead you on. I care about you. You're *schee*, sweet, and kind. You're *wunderbaar* to *mei dochder*. I really hoped for things to turn out well between us."

She glowered at him. "I want to find a man who loves me with his whole heart, not someone who thinks that one day he'll love me even though his heart is set on someone else."

"You deserve that, Madelyne." He reached for her hand, then pulled himself back. "I hope someday you can forgive me. I never meant to hurt you."

She pushed the door open and climbed out. "Good-bye, Emory. Please give Maggie my love."

Then she shut the buggy door and hurried through the cold toward the house.

· · ·

Later that evening, Emory sat at the kitchen table reading a book when Maggie came in from youth group.

"How was it?" he asked.

"*Gut.*" She sat down across from him. "How was your afternoon?"

"Eventful." He closed the book and then rubbed his beard. "Madelyne and I broke up."

Maggie nodded, looking not at all surprised. "Are you okay?"

He nodded. "*Ya.*"

"Is Madelyne okay?"

He grimaced. "Not so much. I think she believed we'd get married someday."

Maggie ran her fingers over the table and then tilted her head. "You know, *Dat*, you have a right to be *froh*. I'll support you if you fall in love and decide to get married again."

He smiled as relief filtered through him. "*Danki.* I appreciate that."

Now he had to find a way to tell Leanna how he felt.

And he prayed that she felt the same way he did.

. . .

Later that evening, Leanna washed the mugs she and her mother had used to have tea in the family room. She couldn't stop thinking about Emory and wondering what he was doing today. Had he spent the afternoon with Madelyne? Had he hugged her and kissed her?

She leaned her weary body against the counter and closed her eyes.

"Leanna?" *Mamm* sidled up to her. "You okay?"

Leanna stood up straight and spun to face her mother. "No,

Mamm. I don't think I am. I . . . Well, I'm in love with Emory, but he's dating Madelyne. When he came to see us last Sunday, I started talking about *Mammi* while we sat on the porch, and when I cried, he pulled me into his arms. I was so disgusted with myself, I told him that he needed to go home."

"So that's why you came rushing into the kitchen and said you wanted to go to bed."

"*Ya.*" Leanna leaned back against the counter. "I told *Mammi* about it, and she said I should tell him how I feel. That I should follow my heart and be honest with him."

"That's *gut* advice."

Leanna peered at her mother. "You think it's *gut* advice to tell a man who is dating someone else that I love him?" She snorted. "Don't you think I'll sound like a *dummkopp*?"

"Not if he loves you, too, and I think he does. The look on his face when you said good night to him last Sunday was almost painful to see. He looked like you'd ripped out his heart and stomped on it. He may be dating Madelyne, but nothing is written in stone." *Mamm* touched her shoulder. "They're not married, Leanna. Tell him before it's too late."

"But what if he doesn't love me?"

"And what if he does? You won't know until you talk to him."

Leanna nodded and then looked at the counter where a jar of jelly sat. Suddenly a plan began to form in her head.

She turned to her mother and smiled. "*Danki, Mamm.*"

· · ·

"I can't believe November is next week. Where has the month gone?" Bethany asked as she picked up her cup of dark chocolate roast and sipped it Thursday morning.

"I know," Leanna agreed as they sat in the Coffee Corner at their usual table before the marketplace opened. "I'm just relieved *Mammi* is doing well in the rehab center. I went to see her Monday and again yesterday. She looks like she's getting stronger every day."

"I'm so glad to hear that," Maggie said.

"How has your week been, Maggie?" Leanna asked before taking a sip of coffee.

"*Gut.*" Maggie looked over at Leanna. "*Mei dat* and Madelyne broke up on Sunday."

Leanna gave a sharp inhale as she drank her coffee, and then she started to cough. She set her cup down and coughed again and again as she tried to get ahold of herself. Her eyes watered and tears streamed down her face as she choked.

"Oh no!" Maggie rubbed her back. "Are you okay?"

"Leanna?" Bethany asked.

"I'm okay!" Leanna held her arm up and took a deep breath. "Whew. It went down the wrong way." She wiped her eyes and sniffed. Her mind spun with Maggie's news as she tried to gain her composure. She peeked at Bethany, who watched her with concern.

"Can you breathe?" Bethany asked.

Leanna cleared her throat. "*Ya*, I'm fine." She took another sip of coffee and debated asking Maggie for details about Emory and Madelyne, but she didn't want to appear too interested. Still, she couldn't stop the excitement roaring through her veins. She was grateful she had already started working on her plan to tell him how she felt.

"Is your *dat* okay after the breakup?" Bethany asked before shooting Leanna a look as if to tell her that she was excited by the news too.

"*Ya.*" Maggie shrugged. "He's fine."

"That's *gut* to hear." Bethany snuck Leanna a wink.

"Have you done any sewing or quilting this week?" Leanna asked.

"I have. I'll bring in some more dolls and purses tomorrow, but I'm still working on my quilts. Those take longer, of course."

After their cups were empty, Maggie gathered them up and carried them to the trash can, and then she hurried along toward their booth.

Bethany hopped down from her stool and grabbed Leanna's hand. "I need to tell you something."

"What?" Leanna asked.

"I took a test this morning," she whispered. "Turns out I'm pregnant."

Leanna pulled her in for a hug. "Oh my goodness! I'm so *froh* for you! Congratulations! Have you told anyone?"

"Only Micah." Bethany sniffed and wiped her eyes. "Micah was so happy, he was in tears this morning. We're not going to tell anyone else until I'm further along, just in case something happens. But I wanted you to know. You've always been so supportive."

"Of course. I'm so thrilled for you. I know you've been praying hard."

"And I'm excited for you. Emory is single now. Now is your chance."

Leanna's heart pounded. "I have a plan and almost have all of the pieces together. Once I do, I'm going to tell him how I feel."

Bethany hugged her. "I'm sure it will work out. I have faith."

"*Danki.*"

. . .

Emory took a deep breath and then walked over to Chester in the shed shop Saturday afternoon. He'd spent all day waiting for the perfect opportunity to talk to Chester about Leanna, and now he was running out of time. Since they normally closed up early on Saturdays, he needed to find the courage to talk to him before they climbed into their buggies and headed home.

"Hey, Chester. Could I speak to you for a moment?" He hoped he sounded more relaxed than he felt as his blood pounded through his veins.

Chester looked up from the workbench and nodded. "Sure."

"Let's walk outside."

Chester looked nervous as they walked toward the side door together. "Is everything okay?" he asked.

"*Ya*, it's fine. I just needed to discuss something personal with you."

They stepped out into the parking lot, and a wall of cold late October air hit them, making Emory shudder and regret not grabbing his coat.

"What's going on?" Chester asked.

Emory cleared his throat and then decided to just plow ahead. "You've told me that your *mamm* doesn't want to date, but I can't stop thinking about her. In fact, with your permission, I would like to date her. I also would ask your *daadi* for permission, of course. But I wanted to talk to you first. I won't ask your *daadi* if you say no."

Chester eyed him with suspicion as he crossed his arms over his chest. "What about Madelyne?"

"We broke up Sunday." Emory rubbed his bearded chin.

"The truth is that I've cared for your *mamm* for a long time, but I didn't think she was interested because you told me she wasn't looking for someone to date. Madelyne liked me, and I thought maybe we could have a future. But I couldn't make myself care about Madelyne when all I think about is your *mamm*."

Chester looked down at the asphalt and then up at Emory. "I think she cares about you."

"You do?" Emory's pulse skittered.

"I heard her talking to *mei mamm* about you, and from what I could gather, she cares about you a lot. I think you should talk to *mei daadi* soon."

Emory studied Chester. "Does that mean you'll give me your blessing?"

Chester smiled. "Of course I will. I'd love to see you and *mei mamm* together."

"*Danki*." Emory rubbed his hands together as excitement poured through him. "I'll come over tomorrow since it's an off-Sunday."

"I'll let my grandparents know in secret so they don't invite anyone over or plan to go anywhere."

"I appreciate it." Emory looked up at the cloudless sky as a thrill raced through him.

"I'm sorry I lied to you."

Emory's gaze snapped to Chester's. "Lied to me?"

"*Ya*." Chester nodded. "I told you *mei mamm* wasn't interested because I wasn't ready for her to date. I never should have done that. The truth is, I think she's cared for you since she met you, and I was scared of what that could mean for my life. I was out of line, and it wasn't my place to interfere."

Emory's eyes narrowed. "I've had feelings for her for a long time, too, but your lie kept me from telling her."

"I'm sorry." Chester looked down at the toes of his work boots. "I'll tell my grandparents that you're coming to see them. I'll make sure they convince her to stay home and wait for you without telling her that you're coming." Chester held his hand out to him. "Please forgive me?"

"Of course I forgive you." Emory shook Chester's hand, too excited and relieved to be upset with the boy. Now he had to talk to Maggie and set his plan into motion.

. . .

"What's on your mind, *Dat*?" Maggie asked Emory as they ate supper later that evening. "You've hardly said a word while I've babbled on and on about my day at the marketplace."

Emory swallowed a piece of baked chicken and then wiped his mouth with a paper napkin. "I wanted to talk to you about something, and I've been trying to figure out how to say it."

"Just spit it out, *Dat*."

He chuckled at his *dochder*, then took a sip of water. "Okay then! Truth is, I'm in love with Leanna and I want to ask her father's permission to date her. I talked to Chester today, and he gave me his blessing. Now I want to ask for yours."

"Yes! Yes! One hundred times, yes!" Maggie jumped out of her chair and wrapped her arms around Emory's neck as he laughed. "This is the best news."

"How would you feel if she agrees to marry me one day?" He held his breath and awaited her reaction.

Maggie continued to beam as bright as the afternoon summer sun. "I would love to have Leanna as my stepmom, and to be honest, I think *Mamm* would approve of her too."

"*Danki*, Maggie." Emory's eyes welled up with happy tears.

Her words were like a beautiful hymn to his ears, and his heart tripped over itself.

Maggie leaned over and kissed his cheek. "I told you that you have a right to be *froh*, and I think Leanna would make you so very happy. When are you going to ask her?"

"Tomorrow. I'm going to go to her *haus* since it's an off-Sunday in her district and in ours."

"That will be perfect."

He nodded and took Maggie's hand in his as hope surged in his heart. "I hope so."

CHAPTER 33

"Oh *gut*," *Mamm* said when Leanna walked into the kitchen Sunday midmorning. "I was hoping you'd put on your best dress today. You look so *schee* in red."

Leanna eyed her mother. Her parents and Chester had been acting strange ever since she got up this morning. Her mother kept looking out the window as if she were expecting company, and her father seemed twitchy. Chester had come inside from taking care of the animals and put on his best pair of trousers and his brown shirt.

If she didn't know any better, she would guess that a long-lost relative was coming to visit. But if that were true, then why hadn't they told Leanna?

"*Mamm*, what's going on?" Leanna asked.

"Nothing! Nothing!" *Mamm* flittered over to the sink and began filling it with water, even though the breakfast dishes were already clean.

"I'm going downstairs," Leanna called and then opened the basement door.

Mamm gasped. "You're not going to make jam, are you? On a Sunday?"

"No, I just wanted to sit for a while." Leanna sighed. She stepped onto the staircase and then closed the door before descending the stairs and sitting down at the table, where the four special jars of jelly sat. She pulled out a pretty basket with a purple bow and then set the four jars in it.

Her heart began to race as she picked up each jar and examined it. First she held the apple cranberry flavor and turned it over and read the label—Emory's Apple Cranberry Jelly. Then she lifted the jar of cherry jam and read—Leanna's Cherry Jam. Next she picked up the jar of grape and read—Chester's Grape Jelly. And lastly, she lifted the jar of raspberry jam and read—Maggie's Raspberry Jam.

She arranged the jars in the basket in that order and then held her breath. She'd planned to go by the shed shop tomorrow and present the basket to Emory, telling him that this was how she had imagined her family. She just hoped he would accept it and not hand the basket back to her. If he rejected her, she might never recover. The thought sat hard and cold over her heart.

Upstairs she heard a flurry of footsteps and then loud voices. It sounded as if the mystery company had finally arrived.

She bit her lip and considered going upstairs to investigate, but she needed some time alone to think and pray.

. . .

Emory stepped into Leanna's parents' kitchen, his heart hammering so fast he feared it might explode. He was grateful when he found her parents and Chester sitting at the table. "Hi."

"We've been expecting you." Rachelle's smile was wide, giving Emory the courage to continue.

"*Danki.*" Emory looked at Walter. "I wanted to speak to you all today about something very important to me."

Walter's expression was warm. "Go on."

Emory took another deep breath. "I never thought it would be possible for me to find love after losing Sheryl, but I'm in love with Leanna, and I'm anxious to start the rest of my life with her. I want your permission to ask her to date me and possibly even more if she'll agree."

He nodded at Chester. "Chester gave me his blessing yesterday." Then he touched Maggie's shoulder. "And Maggie gave me hers last night." He turned to Walter. "I wanted to talk to you, Walter." Then he turned toward Rachelle. "And you, Rachelle, before I tell Leanna how I feel."

Maggie sniffed and smiled while holding a pie plate.

"You have our blessing." Walter stood and shook Emory's hand. "Rachelle and I think the world of you and Maggie, and we'd be honored to have you in our family."

Rachelle nodded and sniffed. "That's the truth."

"*Danki.*" Emory blew out a sigh.

"Leanna is downstairs." Rachelle pointed to the basement stairs. "Go to her."

Emory walked over to the basement door and gripped the doorknob.

"Could we please put on *kaffi*?" Maggie asked. "I brought a lemon meringue pie."

"Of course," Rachelle said.

Emory wrenched the door open and started down the steps, his body vibrating with a mixture of excitement, fear, and worry.

The next moments would define the rest of his life. And he prayed God would guide his words.

. . .

Leanna sat up straight at the table when she heard heavy footsteps coming down the basement steps. She sucked in a breath when she spotted Emory, and she grabbed a dishtowel from behind her and tossed it over the basket as he descended the stairs and studied her.

He looked handsome dressed in dark trousers and a crisp dark blue shirt that made his gorgeous eyes shine.

Was he the visitor her mother had been expecting? But that wouldn't make any sense. Why would her parents know that Emory was coming to see her?

"Hi." He shifted his weight on his feet as if he were nervous. "Could we please talk?"

"Sure." She motioned to the chair beside her at the table. "Have a seat."

"Danki." He sank down on the chair and then paused and licked his lips. "Leanna, I thought I'd never find love again after Sheryl died. I was certain my heart was broken and irreparable. Whenever someone tried to set me up with a *freind* or an acquaintance, I felt like other people were trying to run my life. It only got worse when Maggie would cry and say she didn't want a new *mamm*."

Leanna nodded as a knot began to swell in her throat. "I understand."

"Then I started dating Madelyne because I thought I was ready to fall in love, but the problem was, I'd already fallen in love."

Leanna tried to swallow against the knot in her throat as her eyes burned with tears.

"I love you, Leanna." He took her hands in his, and his eyes seemed to plead with her as they sparkled in the light of the gas lamps humming above them. "I want to be with you. You're everything to me. You've become *mei* best *freind*. You're the one I want to tell my secrets to, to share my dreams with, to share my joys and my sorrows with, to grow old with."

She sniffed as tears began to stream down her face. Her heart clutched as he wiped a tear away with the tip of his finger.

"I love how you treat Maggie. I love how you brought her out of her shell and showed her how strong and confident she can be. I love how you defended her against Sara Ann and how you made Maggie learn to believe in herself." He paused to lift her hand to his lips and kiss it. "And I love you, Leanna. I love you with my whole heart. I've loved you for a long time, but it took me a while to realize it. And when I did, I was afraid you didn't care for me."

She sniffed and wiped her eyes and nose with a napkin.

"So, Leanna, I'm here to ask you if you would consider giving me a chance to show you just how much I love you." His voice caught, and then he cleared his throat roughly. "Could you ever see yourself dating me?"

She cleared her throat and then removed the dishtowel from the basket and pushed it toward him. "I made you this. I was going to bring it to you tomorrow." She pointed to the four jars. "This is how I've imagined my family for a long time, but I was afraid to tell you because I didn't think you ever wanted to be more than just *freinden* with me."

He picked up each of the jars and read the labels and then looked at her with wide eyes. "Leanna, this is beautiful. I-I had no idea you thought of me as more than just a *freind*. I thought you weren't interested in dating, and then when you sent me away last week, I was certain you hated me."

She shook her head. "Emory, I've been in love with you for a long time. I thought you'd chosen Madelyne over me, and it ripped me to pieces. I sent you away because I felt guilty for being in love with another woman's boyfriend."

"I'm so sorry for not telling you how I felt sooner." He ran his finger down her cheek and she leaned into his gentle touch.

Then he leaned down and brushed his lips against hers. Happiness blossomed in the pit of her belly, and she lost herself in his kiss as she melted against him.

When he broke the kiss, he took her hands in his again. "I want to be with you, and I would like our future to start as soon as possible. Chester and your parents have already given me their blessing. Would you marry me?"

"Yes." She nodded as her tears began anew. "Yes, I will marry you."

"I've never been happier in my life." He placed his hands on her cheeks, leaned down, and brushed his lips across hers once again, making her lose track of everything. She closed her eyes and savored the feeling of his lips against hers, and a shiver of wanting vibrated through her body.

When he broke the kiss, she stood and took his hand in hers. "Let's go tell my family. We need to celebrate."

. . .

Later that evening, Emory sat on the porch swing and held hands with Leanna. He smiled as he took a sip of hot cocoa and then gazed over at her.

She turned toward him and blushed. "You're doing it again."

"Doing what?"

"You're staring at me."

"I'm allowed to stare at my fiancée."

"I like the sound of that. Fiancée." She rested her head on his shoulder. "I'm so *froh*. I thought for sure when I brought that basket to you that you'd reject me."

He shifted in the swing and faced her, causing her to sit up. "Leanna, I can't resist you. I would never be capable of rejecting you."

She smiled at his tender words. "So, when should we get married?"

"How about right away? After all, second marriage ceremonies are small and private. We'll just have our bishops, parents, and *kinner* with us. Why not in a couple of weeks?"

"How about the second Thursday in December? That will give me a little over a month to make dresses for Maggie and me. And then maybe we can have desserts for our families later in the day. I know my cousins would be heartbroken if they couldn't celebrate with us."

Emory nodded. "*Mei bruder* and parents would be too."

"Okay then. It's settled. We're getting married in about six weeks."

"I can't wait." He kissed her again, this kiss lingering longer than the first two.

Warmth swept through his body, and he suddenly forgot that it was October. This was how true love was supposed to feel! Leanna was the woman God had chosen for him. He could feel it to the depth of his soul.

. . .

Leanna felt as if she were floating on a cloud! Earlier in the day she and Emory had been married by her bishop and his bishop in a ceremony in her parents' family room. The ceremony had been small and intimate with only her parents, Emory's parents, Chester, and Maggie there to witness.

Keeping with Amish tradition, Leanna had made her and Maggie matching red dresses to wear for the ceremony since Maggie was her attendant. Chester was Emory's attendant, and they both wore their traditional Sunday black and white suit.

After lunch, their families had joined them for a celebration at her parents' house, including a lot of laughter, along with casseroles, side dishes, flavored coffees, and trays of desserts her cousins had provided. She was so grateful to celebrate with her family, and she was thrilled when *Mammi* came with the help of a wheelchair. God was so good!

Leanna had given each of their guests a basket containing four jars—Emory's Apple Cranberry Jelly, Leanna's Cherry Jam, Chester's Grape Jelly, and Maggie's Raspberry Jam. She had had so much fun that she had lost track of time and hadn't even realized that it was almost midnight when her guests began leaving.

Now Leanna stood in Emory's kitchen, and her heart pounded. This was her home, her new home. She and Chester had moved most of their belongings over to Emory's house last night. Chester had chosen a spare bedroom upstairs across from Maggie's bedroom, and he and Maggie had headed up to bed earlier.

Emory stepped out into the kitchen, set a lantern on the counter, and eyed her with curiosity. "Leanna?"

"*Ya.*"

He leaned against the counter. "Are you thinking about how you need more space for your jams and jellies? I told you I'll add a kitchen for you in the basement in the spring."

"*Danki*, but that's not what I was thinking about." She smiled.

"What is it then? You seem a little . . . lost."

"No. Not lost." She shook her head. "I feel like I've been found."

He raised an eyebrow. "Sorry, but I'm not getting what you mean."

"I feel like I've been lost for the past eight years, just wandering around trying to find my way." She made a sweeping gesture around the kitchen. "But then God sent me you, and now I'm found. Now I'm finally home."

Emory made a little sound in his throat and his eyes misted as he held his hand out to her. "Come here, *fraa*."

She walked over to him, and he took her hand in his.

"You have made me the happiest man alive, Leanna Speicher."

"I like the sound of that."

"I do too." He held her hand, picked up the lantern, and steered her down the hallway.

When they stepped into the bedroom, he set the lantern on a nearby dresser and then turned toward her.

"*Ich liebe dich*," he whispered, and his husky voice made her skin hum with excitement.

"I love you too," she whispered.

Then he wrapped his arms around her waist, and Leanna's breath hitched in her lungs as his lips met hers. She looped her arms around his neck and pulled him down to her. He deepened the kiss, and it sent a fire burning through every cell in her body. She closed her eyes and savored the feel of his mouth against hers.

As she lost herself in her new husband's kiss, she felt her body relax. Her most fervent prayer had finally come true.

EPILOGUE

Six months later, on the first Thursday in June, Leanna sat at a high-top table in the Coffee Corner while drinking a cup of coffee and eating a donut with Bethany and Maggie.

"Gude mariye!" Emory called as he and Chester sauntered into the booth.

Leanna jumped down from where she sat and walked over to him. "What are you doing here?"

"That's a nice hello, isn't it, Chester?" Emory asked, his lips lifting in a teasing smile.

"I'm not getting in the middle of it." Chester chuckled as he walked over to the table. "Could I get some *kaffi* and a donut, Bethany?"

"Sure." Bethany gingerly climbed down from the stool and walked over to the counter, her belly protruding in front of her.

"I can't believe she's still working," Emory whispered in Leanna's ear.

"I know. She's insisting on working until she delivers, even though Micah wants her to rest."

"It sounds like stubbornness runs in your family," Emory teased.

"Remember it's *your* family now."

"Right." He gave a teasing grimace. "I keep trying to forget."

She swatted his arm, and he laughed.

"Emory," Bethany called. "Did you want *kaffi*?"

"*Ya*, please." He looked toward the blackboard where the specials were listed. "I'll take a cup of bananas foster and a chocolate glazed donut."

"Wait! Make that five more cups!"

Leanna turned as Salina, Will, Christiana, Jeff, and Micah all walked into the booth. Salina and Christiana both pushed double strollers with their children riding along, Salina's infant sitting in his seat.

"Oh my goodness!" Leanna exclaimed. "Was this planned?"

"Sort of," Salina said with a shrug. "Christiana and I were talking about how we wanted to have a reunion. It's been so long since we all met at the Coffee Corner."

Christiana nodded. "Our families have grown so much that we wanted to include everyone."

"Let's push some tables together." Jeff patted Micah's shoulder. "We can all sit together."

While Jeff and Micah began rearranging tables and chairs, Salina moved to the counter and gathered up cups of coffee, and Christiana picked up a tray of donuts, creamer, and packets of sweetener.

Leanna turned to Emory. "Did you know about this?"

"Maybe." He gave her a sheepish grin. "Micah called me at work yesterday. You mentioned to me recently that you missed your cousins, so I wanted to keep it a surprise."

"*Danki.*" She touched his chest.

"You know I'd do anything for you."

She threaded her fingers with his. "I love you."

"I love you too." He steered her over to the table, where they sat and enjoyed coffee and donuts with her cousins.

Leanna laughed and talked while silently thanking God for

her special cousins. How she loved her family! Daisy and Lily came in for a visit, and the children giggled as the cats rubbed up against the strollers, meowing their hellos.

When they were done eating, Leanna helped the women clean up the cups and napkins, and the men wiped down the tables before pushing them back to where they belonged.

Soon everyone was getting ready to leave. Leanna hugged Salina and Christiana before they left with their husbands and children.

Once they were gone, she took Emory's hand in hers again. "I need to talk to you alone." She looked over to where Maggie and Chester stood talking with Bethany and Micah by the counter in the Coffee Corner.

"Let's go to the booth." She squeezed his hand as they stepped out of the Coffee Corner and into the Jam and Jelly Nook and Quilt and Gift Stand, where she led him to the back of the booth. "Oh, I forgot to tell you Madelyne stopped in last week and introduced me to her fiancé. He seemed like a really nice man."

"I'm glad to hear it." Emory looked curious. "Is that what you wanted to tell me?"

"No." She bit her lower lip and then took a trembling breath. "I have news."

"What kind of news?"

"I took a test this morning after you left for the shop, and it was positive."

He eyed her, his brow furrowed. "A test." Then he sucked in a breath. "A test? *That* kind of test?" He pointed to her belly. "You're pregnant?"

She nodded. "Yes."

"Oh my goodness! Praise God!" He lifted her up and twirled her around as she laughed.

"Shh," she hissed through a giggle. "My age makes me higher risk, so I want to keep it quiet for a while."

"We'll do that. I'll go with you to all your appointments." He hugged her. "I've never been happier."

"I haven't either."

"*Danki* for making all of my dreams come true."

"I could thank you for the same."

He grinned before kissing her. She relaxed against him as she lost herself in the feel of his lips and the bliss bubbling through her veins.

As he pulled her close for a hug, she silently thanked God for bringing Emory and Maggie into her life, and she prayed that the next generation of cousins would be as close as the first.

ACKNOWLEDGMENTS

As always, I'm thankful for my loving family, including my mother, Lola Goebelbecker; my husband, Joe; and my sons, Zac and Matt. I'm blessed to have such an awesome and amazing family that puts up with me when I'm stressed out on a book deadline.

Thank you to my mother, who graciously read the draft of this book to check for typos. I'm sure you had some giggles due to my hilarious mistakes!

I'm also grateful to my special Amish friend who patiently answers my endless stream of questions.

Thank you to my wonderful church family at Morning Star Lutheran in Matthews, North Carolina, for your encouragement, prayers, love, and friendship. You all mean so much to my family and me.

Thank you to Zac Weikal and the fabulous members of my Bakery Bunch! I'm so thankful for your friendship and your excitement about my books. You all are amazing!

To my agent, Natasha Kern—I can't thank you enough for your guidance, advice, and friendship. You are a tremendous blessing in my life.

Thank you to my amazing editor, Jocelyn Bailey, for your friendship and guidance. I appreciate how you push me to dig deeper with each book and improve my writing. I've learned so much from you, and I look forward to our future projects together.

Special thanks to editor Becky Philpott for polishing the story and connecting the dots. I'm so grateful that we are working together again!

I'm grateful to each and every person at HarperCollins Christian Publishing who helped make this book a reality.

To my readers—thank you for choosing my novels. My books are a blessing in my life for many reasons, including the special friendships I've formed with my readers. Thank you for your email messages, Facebook notes, and letters.

Thank you most of all to God—for giving me the inspiration and the words to glorify you. I'm grateful and humbled you've chosen this path for me.

Discussion Questions

1. Leanna enjoys spending time with her three favorite cousins. Do you have a special family member with whom you like to spend your time? If so, who is that family member, and why are you close to him or her?

2. At the beginning of the story, Emory's family pressures him to date Madelyne. He gives in to the pressure and dates her, but as the story progresses, he realizes he loves Leanna. What do you think helped him realize he deserved happiness?

3. At the beginning of the story, Chester struggles with his place in the community and whether he wants to stay Amish. By the end of the story, he decides to give up some of his "sinful" ways and join the church. What do you think made him change his mind throughout the story?

4. Bethany struggles with fertility issues. Do you know anyone who has struggled with that? Can you relate to her?

5. Maggie is painfully shy and not comfortable spending time with her youth group at the beginning of the story. By the end of the story, she has confidence not only to spend time with her friends but also to run the booth at the marketplace. What do you think changed her during the book?

6. What role did the marketplace play in the cousins' relationship throughout the Amish Marketplace book series?

7. Leanna and her cousins consider Sara Ann King to be the marketplace's gossip. Leanna is so fed up with Sara Ann's actions that she tells her to leave everyone alone. Gossip, even in a community that is supposed to be Christlike, can hurt and lead to misunderstanding. Do we do this in our own church communities—judge and gossip about our fellow Christians without considering the consequences?

8. Which character can you identify with the most? Which character seemed to carry the most emotional stake in the story? Was it Leanna, Emory, or someone else?

9. Leanna is devastated when her grandmother is hurt in an accident. Think of a time when you felt lost and alone. Where did you find your strength? What Bible verses helped?

10. What did you know about the Amish before reading this book? What did you learn?

About the Author

Amy Clipston is the award-winning and bestselling author of the Kauffman Amish Bakery, Hearts of Lancaster Grand Hotel, Amish Heirloom, Amish Homestead, and Amish Marketplace series. Her novels have hit multiple bestseller lists including CBD, CBA, and ECPA. Amy holds a degree in communication from Virginia Wesleyan University and works full-time for the City of Charlotte, NC. Amy lives in North Carolina with her husband, two sons, and six spoiled rotten cats.

Visit her online at AmyClipston.com
Instagram: @amy_clipston
Facebook: @AmyClipstonBooks
Twitter: @AmyClipston
Bookbub: @AmyClipston

From the Publisher

GREAT BOOKS
ARE EVEN BETTER WHEN THEY'RE SHARED!

Help other readers find this one:

- Post a review at your favorite online bookseller

- Post a picture on a social media account and share why you enjoyed it

- Send a note to a friend who would also love it—or better yet, give them a copy

Thanks for reading!

Follow four cousins and their journeys
toward love and happiness while
working at the local market!

When a jilted romance novelist returns to the small beach town she once loved, she discovers not only inspiration but also a romance to call her own.

Coming May 2022

THOMAS NELSON
Since 1798

Bestselling author Amy Clipston transports readers to a picturesque lakeside town in this heartwarming contemporary romance.

Available in print, ebook, and audio